Legend

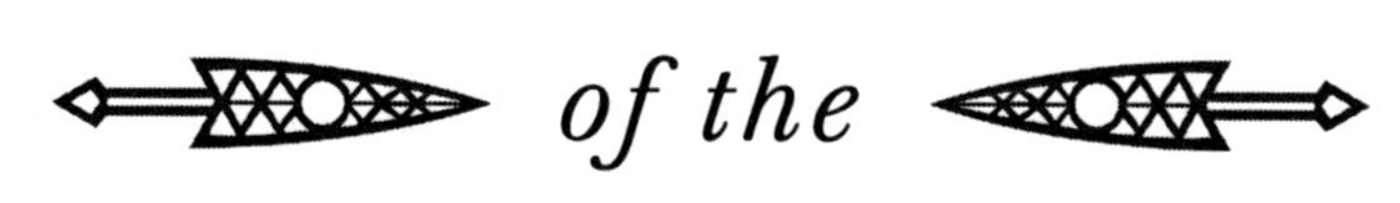

of the

Drunken Rancher

Jake Shelton

First Edition

PAGE PUBLISHING, INC.
New York, NY

First originally published by Page Publishing, Inc. 2015

ISBN 978-1-68213-039-1 (pbk)
ISBN 978-1-68213-040-7 (digital)

Printed in the United States of America

I would like to personally dedicate this book to my grandma.

You are truly missed, and we love you!

Eilene Elizabeth Ehr

October 10, 1930 - January 7, 2015

"Erin go braugh."

Chapter 1

Riding under the Influence

It was a hot, sticky day in the Teanaway Valley, and the ranch was bustling with life, branding the ruminates of spring cattle. Now, it was one of those days that just kept dragging on by the warmth of the sun, creating a sticky, sweltering heat. In fact, the clock in the break room grounded to a halt, and one could imagine that the heat was to blame, when actually, it was just some batteries that had lost their power. At any rate, a young rancher by the name of Barry was thirsty and decided to leave early due to the fact that his daily tasks were completed. On the rancher's way out, several of the men were bullshitting about the heat, so this thirsty rancher approached them to listen in on the conversation. After hearing their voiced concerns, Barry concluded that the men and himself should head over to the bar and quench their thirsty palates. All in agreement, the ranchers made their way off the ranch, riding on horses that carried the men's tired, thirsty bodies swiftly to the bar.

Within a reasonable time, everyone had reached the bar, which was peculiarly busy, primarily in light of the influx of tourists, enjoying everything the Upper County had to offer. From floating the river on inner tubes, fly-fishing, and camping, the mountainous region sported some of the most breathtaking views that this particular area had to offer. Anyhow, the men tied their horses off and entered the bar. Due to the swelling number of customers, one of the ranch hands placed the order, and they made their way to the back patio area then pulled up a chair. After a few minutes, the drinks were in front of the ranch hands, and they began to sip the heat of the day away. After hours of drinking passed, the day drew to a conclusion, and the bar that was once filled to occupancy was thinning to a handful of regulars, tourists, including the group of very intoxicated ranchers.

The bar had all but closed out, except for a regular who'd been sitting in the same spot, as for Barry and another rancher. When the ranch hands arrived earlier that afternoon, the gentleman tipped his hat and ordered a round for the ranch hands, so when Barry and Jasper came back in the bar, the old man graciously ordered another round. Now upon first glance, this older man looked like a remnant from past glories of the old West. The cowboy sported a black button-up long-sleeve dress shirt, firmly pressed wranglers with a shiny belt buckle that this old crow probably won at a rodeo. His boots were some highly polished V tips, and upon his head was a worn but still very presentable Stetson. So Barry graciously asked if anyone was sitting by him, and the cowboy told the young ranch hand no, so the boys grabbed the barstool and sat next to the kind man. After a brief pause, Barry ordered the man a beer, and they began striking up a conversation about ranch work; for this man knew more than anyone, the toils of running and operating a ranch. One thing you may not know about this gentleman is that he may appear to be a wealthy successful businessman, but this particular cowboy's life was anything but ordinary.

One thing you have to remember about this fellow is that his life has been nothing but an adventure, and most of the old man's journey took place here in the Upper Kititas County. The rancher started to ask about Barry and Jasper's adventures, so the ranch hands shared some stories, making the cowboy smile. Even though the evening was getting late, the ole cowboy and ranch hands ordered more drinks because when you live the life they choose, shutting down bars are part of the repertoire.

At about half an hour before closing, the rancher looked Barry in the eye and said, "You know, son, I believe that you're an outstanding young man who likes to tell stories. Well, do I have a humdinger for you!" With that being said, the cowboy polished off his beer and ordered another round for the boys. "Son, I'm going to tell you a story about a man who found discovered adventures within the borders of this very county," the rancher stated while taking a pull off of his longneck bottled beer. "This story is about his stupid friends that, till this day, believe that they're somehow smarter than this old rancher. Son, this story is about a son of a bitch by the name of Tom Wyatt."

The boys paused at first, and then started to laugh.

Barry looked the old man in the eyes and stated, "Sir, not to offend you, but we've heard everything that there is to know about Mister. Wyatt."

The old man then let out a laugh and stared Barry directly in the eye and replied, "Son, I used to know the Wyatts very well, and I'll bet you that you don't know the whole story."

Barry laughed and slapped his hand down on his knee and exclaimed, "Well, unless you're Tom Wyatt in the flesh, I don't even see how you could know every detail!"

"Son, it's going to be a pleasure telling this story," the old man replied while ordering another round of long necks.

* * *

Remember back in the days when we were kids and life was simple? Well, that definitely wasn't Tom, to some extent. Now, I know the title to the chapter isn't currently relevant, but this story after all is about a rancher's adventures that Tom and his buddies went through. Also, poor Tom was temporarily detained by the side of the road of his property sitting atop ole Trigger, and one perplexed officer scratching his head like a poker player that just lost his fortune. Now Tom knew for a fact that the deputy was a rookie, and the rancher had never seen him before in his forty-plus years riding down the dirt road from the bar, just a-mindin' the drunken fools' own business. To add to that, the deputy sprang out of the car, surprised that Tom's horse just pissed on him, while they was a-moseying by. I'll bring

Trigger in here and there because I'm sure that prick has peaked your curiosity; and how he gets his leg to lift like that, I will never know. He tends to be "complicated" as the young folk say.

Back to my original sentence: Tom did not have the traditional upbringing that most folks have nowadays. He was born Thomas Eugene Wyatt in a military hospital in San Diego in 1970. Tom's dad was a retired military man who served thirty years in the service before an RPG ruined his day; in a part of the world that still remains classified till this day. It took the man two years to only regain 80 percent of his full movement. So in a way, I guess an assault rifle was replaced with a wooden cane. Up till a few weeks ago, he finally set it down, thanks to Wiley, whom I will fill you in.

Tom's mother was a stay-at-home army wife who had the misfortune of dying when he was a young boy. It's okay because it took the lad many years to realize that she liked to spread eagle when several dozen of Dad's fellow soldiers returned home. That's beside the point because Tom's dad spent more time at the bar, as opposed to his wife's more than loving embrace. Anyhow, it was evident that Thomas was to spend some nonspecified amount of time with his grandparents—which scared the boy to death because he never really spent a whole lot of time with them. Honestly, if they were anything like his dad, Tom best just settle down into a pattern of loneliness and despair going to the bars, while drowning in his sorrows.

Tom was seven when this exchange had occurred, and it couldn't have happened at a more opportune time. No offense to you, bar patrons, but this seven-year-old's attention was mainly limited to a pool table, dartboard, jukebox, bathroom stalls filled with phone numbers and vulgar language etched into the walls. So on the day of Tom's sudden departure from his father, his granny Tildy and gramps Eugene came into the smoke-ridden honky-tonk, only to find Dallas passed out on the bar. Tom's heart sank at first but was replaced with hugs and some candy that Granny had picked up at a gas station. Seeing that Gramps couldn't wake dad up (who had been passed out for some three hours) left Tom hugging his father and leaving a note explaining as to where the child had vanished to, as tears streamed down his face.

Tom's dad, Dallas Wyatt, eventually came around from time to time to be the father that he couldn't be at the bar. As a matter of fact, Dallas quit drinking, found Jesus, and married a Southern gal named Lupita. No offense to you, Southerners, but she was from the Deep South—if you know what I mean—and makes a hell of a homemade tortilla among other foods indigenous to her homeland. When all of this came to fruition, ole Tom had been with his grandparents roughly about four years and was well adjusted on their ten-thousand-acre ranch, nestled in the heart of the Cascade Mountain range near to Cle Elum in the Teanaway. Lupita and Dallas wanted Tom (at one point)to come back home, but by that particular time in his life, it just wasn't an option because he was well adjusted and thriving. However, Tom would go spend time with Lue and Dad for the holidays. It was well worth the plane ticket and the added benefit that if there was three feet of snow on your property, wouldn't Florida look like the perfect destination holiday spot?

As for Grandpa, he was a military man (as well as Dallas), and a couple years back on Tom's many adventures on the ranch, Gene would always disappear into the tree line. As I recall, it was the summer of 1980, and Tom had nothing but free time on his hands. So like any eight-year-old boy (at that time) who spent all of his days between school and working on the ranch, he decided to follow his grandpa. Tom was certain that he had explored every inch of the property up until that point, but the boy followed his grandpa's tracks through an old trail pot marked with old undergrowth and dense vegetation. Let's just say that Tom was about to make a huge discovery that would change his life in ways yet to be explained.

After ascending several hundred feet up that trail, the forest opened up into a micro valley, and on the other side was a waterfall with a cave tucked away behind it; that was where gramps had disappeared. Concerned, as Tom was not, he continued to hide under a bush. After an hour of surveillance, his curiosity peaked when he heard muffled gunshots echoing from the cave. When all was said and done, Gramps emerged with a smile on his face and began meandering his way back down to the ranch. Intrigued, Tom made a beeline to the cave, and when he entered, his jaw dropped. It was like a museum for the military man at heart! Pictures (in frames, mind you) littered the walls of the cave with old war buddies, newspapers, or whatever else he could so elegantly cram within a reasonable space. That doesn't go without saying, the huge knife collection was also occupying those walls, as well as a tailored pick of pistols, rifles, and automatic machine guns spread across a table similar to a firing range.

With the fresh smell of gunpowder still floating in the air, Tom rushed to the table and grabbed the first pistol he could touch. The weapon of choice happened to be a German Luger. Looking past the table, Gene had three paper targets placed some twenty yards away, and the youngster noticed the pattern of holes that were all but visible. Tom could relate why his grandfather had such a smile on his face. All three targets had bullets in the torso region, and every bullet hole almost touched the other. Not bad for the old man who was in his late seventies at the time.

All of the sudden, a hand reached out for Tom's shoulder, scaring the young boy so that the Luger happened to discharge before the boy's brain could tell that little finger not to pull the trigger.

"Son," Gene stated with a serious look on his face. "May I ask how you managed to find my secret training facility?"

"I followed you here," young Tom stuttered. "I didn't mean to." He was carrying on helplessly, trying not to tick his grandpa off because when Gramps was angry—which wasn't often—no amount of curiosity could save him from the truth.

After explaining why he had followed his grandpa to the cave, fearing the worse, Gramps pulled a double-edged knife off the wall and said, "I'll trade you. It's pretty apparent that you're crap with a pistol—so let's start small!"

Relieved, Tom grabbed the knife. He could tell that it was an old one and inquired how Grandpa had received it. Gene told Tom that it was a special kind of blade that belonged to an associate who was a thirty commando, and if you know anything about that British unit, it is that they don't just give up such an efficient part of their armory, unless for good reason. Automatically, the curious boy wanted to learn more and told Gramps that he wanted to train to become a great military man like his dad, so Gene paused, then cracked a smile. "I will train you, but only under the promise that you'll never tell anyone, including Grandma, about this place." In agreement, they tucked the knife into its original sheath and headed back home with the deadly blade in Tom's hand. He still has the blade till this day and is the rancher's primary weapon of choice.

Now this rookie deputy obviously has taken his time—and his backup even longer,—because at this point, all Tom's horse, Trigger, wanted to do is go home and meet up with his date, and so did ole Tom.

"You mind asking me how much you've had to drink tonight, sir?" the deputy asked.

Tom replied, "Gee, uh, stopped keeping track after the first beer." Honestly, up to this point, Tom was wondering if the officer was going to ask Trig the same thing because the rancher's drunk horse would probably tell you if he could.

After ten minutes of blowing in some electronic doo-hickey and doing field sobriety tests, the officer's backup arrived. Remember, this is Kittitas county where people are few and far in between when you live out in the country. So I guess the same could be said about the local law enforcement. Anyhow, with the cuffs chaffing Tom's wrists, the deputy's half-assed backup smiles, and the asshole pops out of his patrol vehicle, pulling the rookie aside. After a few minutes of flailing arms and shouting from the youngster, the rookie took the cuffs off Tom as the officer tipped his hat to the rancher to wish the man a safe journey home; but the deputy struggled like he just crapped a condom out of his cornholio. The officer turned back into his rig with a perplexed look on his face, like he was trying to communicate with a rock then disappeared into the warm summer night—with a neigh from Trigger and a middle finger from Tom. Now, Trig and Tom have one more stepping stone left on their trip back to the ranch, in the form of a semi overweight, prematurely balding bill collector with a badge.

"Want me to follow you home, Tom?" he said.

The drunk rancher mumbled out, "Sheriff, I'm perfectly fine to ride."

"Tom, I know that you're okay, it's just the horse looks like he hit it hard at Wiley's tonight. How much did Trigger have to drink?" the sheriff asked curiously.

"Oh the usual. Like two pails full, I guess," Tom mumbled. "You off for the rest of the night, Larry?"

"Yes, I am, and I'm a little thirsty," the sheriff added as he petted Trigger's mane.

"Well, you could come over for a night cap," Tom invitingly asked. "Or did you go shakedown Jackie's Doughnuts again earlier today?"

With a stern gaze, the sheriff looked Tom humbly in his eyes and stated, "I may have a doughnut problem, but your horse is just a flat-out alcoholic like the rider!"

This was okay, however, because Tom laughed and agreed with the man. With that being said, ole Trigger's ears were started to sag and his tongue drooped out of his mouth like a teenager looking at titties in a *Playboy* magazine for the first time. Feeling his legs start to quiver, Tom dismounted almost falling on the ranchers behind but recovered quickly. With his feet firmly planted on the ground, Tom looked at the sheriff, and both were in general agreement that Trig's date had to be temporarily postponed. Glancing over at the drunken horse, the rancher reassured his trusty steed that everything would be okay and hopped in the sheriff's car.

"He knows the way back, right?" the sheriff asked while still parked on the side of the road.

"Come on, Larry. We're in my driveway. I think ole Trig will be just fine," Tom reiterated. "You want a brewsky, Larry?" he asked, pulling a cold one out of the rancher's portable horse cooler.

"No, but you can take a pull off of this." And the sheriff fetched a mason jar from his middle console, filled with one of Wiley's last batches of corn liquor.

With a keen eye, the rancher inspected the clear liquid, and Tom replied, "Wiley sure knows how to make some good hooch, don't you think?"

"A little too well, Tom," Larry stated, and before Tom could respond, the sheriff snatched the jar away from Tom's curious hands.

"Hop in the back seat, Tom. Let's make it look to Maddy like I'm actually going to do my job." Larry sarcastically said.

All of the sudden, Trigger decided to let out a fart smelling so bad that even with the windows rolled up, the men almost gagged from the stench emanating from the fowl horse's anal region. The sheriff, seeing Tom's poor horse in full-on pass-out mode, inquired if they needed to go back to the stable and grab the horse trailer and Betsy (Trigger's date) to coax the beast back. Tom implied that it wasn't necessary, but on the other hand, it would motivate his animal friend.

"God that's horrible, Tom!" Larry exclaimed as he passed the moonshine back to Tom. "Can you imagine where you would be sleeping if you stank as bad as that damn horse?"

"I can imagine that Maddy would have me sleeping in the stall with Trigger if I ripped one that smelly," Tom commented and passed the shine back to Larry.

So as it stands, we have a sheriff drinking shine (Tom as well) who is temporarily detained in the back seat of an police cruiser, and one drunk horse that was already asleep at the entrance of the rancher's two-mile long driveway.

Speaking of Maddy, the lucky woman is Tom's wife, and quite frankly, any woman that can tolerate the rancher's bullshit for some ten years now, personally deserves the title of saint! When they first met, Tom had hit a personal low in his life. Apparently, as invincible as his gramps was, ole Two Boots couldn't overcome cancer. However, Gene helped the rancher become the man that Tom is today, to some extent. Anyhow, whatever gutter Tom stumbled out of that day, the star-crossed lovers met. I would say it was fate, but Maddy was a temporary bartender who would have been an excellent stripper at Wiley's. Yet her moral fortitude forbade her from taking up such sinful behavior at the time. What can I say, everybody, is that there's just something about a Christian woman serving a fella drinks, and unbeknownst to her at the time, Tom was a terrible tipper.

Speaking of Wiley, I know you are curious about the man, so let me fill ya in on him. Wiley is one of those guys that when you see walking down the street, one tends to move out of the fella's way. There's just something about a scruffy unkempt version of an ex-Nam soldier having a conversation with himself. Wiley might be just one of the craziest men that Tom knows, yet he has always been a loyal friend and buddies with Dallas. In fact, the two men grew up in the Teanaway and went to boot camp together. Anyhow, the actual name of the bar was Wil-E Coyotes, and his name is Wiley. Catchy, huh? The reason why Maddy was a temporary bartender was due to the fact that Wiley's daughter, Jennie, got fed up with his bullshit about spaceships, lasers, and any involvement of certain government officials doing surveillance on him. She borrowed ten thousand dollars from Wiley's secret stash and disappeared to Mexico for three months. Oh yeah, I almost forgot to say that when she came back, she was sporting a significant baby bump. Wiley had gone on crazy for a bit, and he might be a loopy bastard yet accepted this change in the old boy's master plan and welcomed little Lupita Jr. with open arms. That's another story for another time concerning how the baby got her name, but as you can imagine, it's from Tom's side of the family.

Wiley's business practices might have always been shady and scrutinized by law enforcement, but Wiley is a good man who just made poor decisions, which will be explained in detail. One of the main contributing factors to Wiley's operation was that the man ran moonshine out of his bar. Also, Wiley had been accused several times of running a strip joint, but like I said, another story for another time.

All Tom remembered about that day he met Maddy was that he stumbled in through the door to only be invited by a beautiful blonde smile. Tom sat down at the bar in his usual spot, and she asked what the rancher wanted to drink, while the cowboy sat on the barstool enjoying his new view. Smiling even more than the mere seconds that had just passed since Tom saw that beautiful face, he immediately began to freeze and ordered a ginger ale. With a worried look on Maddy's face, she told the rancher about Wiley's beer or whiskey policy while asking Tom to move to another chair. Just to be funny, Tom asked for a beer and interrogated the young vixen why he hadn't been carded. Remember, this was the first time he met her, and women that are sober can only handle mere minutes with Tom's sarcastic bullshit—at least till they get smart, ditching the drunk rancher to go somewhere else. Even Jennie can only put up with so much BS before she had Tom doing chores. That's right! The man works for beer, and that fine little Philly was still hangin' with yours truly. Now, both eyes were locked together like opposite magnets, drawing the polarity of their loins, closer by their looks, so Tom slammed his ID down on the table, smiling into Maddy's pretty blue eyes.

"You from around here?" she asked, inspecting the ID closely.

"Oh, usually from four to close every day, darling," Tom humbly retorted, while smiling and trying to pierce those magnetic eyes staring back into his.

"Please tell me you're a permanent fixture around here, and that Jennie is in a ditch somewhere in Cancun?" the rancher drunkenly mumbled.

In reply, Maddy punched Tom in the shoulder (which stung like a bitch), and she said, "Probably not. The Mexican mob would sell her into sex slavery before they would off her, and I didn't know you were that particular Tom that's named on the chair."

More intrigued than ever, Tom asked her which star she fell from and if she wanted to take a ride on his mustang. I know that might not be the best pickup line, but Trigger was a 'stang. Let's just say that a pen and phone number etched into Tom's hands sealed any doubt he once had about how to get into the blonde's pants. After eight hours of talking to Maddy and watching her constant smile fixed to Tom, he helped her close up, grabbed Maddy's belongings—along with some beer—and introduced the fine young vixen to a very young Trigger at the time.

The rest of the night was spent rolling around with Maddy in the stable and hearing the sound of the cows mooing along with Trigger neighing. It almost sounded like he was laughing at them from time to time. Believe it or not, Trigger was a smart-ass horse, even back in those days.

The next morning, Tom awoke to the piercing of Granny's broom poking him in the back, telling the both of them that breakfast was ready. The tone in her voice asking Maddy if she was vegan made the two young lovers roll over with laughter. Granny was very old-fashioned and very much shocked by the escapades of today's younger generation.

As she parted, Tildy stated, "I left two towels for y'all up in the shower. Wash up before you eat." With that being said, Granny departed. Tom just didn't realize at the time that it would be a shower for two!

Coming inside the house, Maddy and Tom strolled by the kitchen, which was filled with the aroma of bacon, hash browns, and eggs sizzling. Tom escorted Maddy through the living room by which she was quite taken. Tom's grandpa spent thirty years of his life building the house, which started off as a log cabin only to evolve into an eight-thousand-square-foot beast. Maddy was really impressed with old photos of her date scattered through the hallway, commenting on how he got so dang ugly. Anyhow, Tom quickly shooed her along into the shower, and any memory from this point should best be left unpublished.

Anyhow, back to the present. Larry and Tom casually strolled up to the house. Noticing a couple vehicles, the boys figured they were Maddy's friends, so Larry flashed his lights and blared his siren as they pulled up the drive. Surprised by all the ruckus, the house guests curiously came out, only to find the sheriff removing an inebriated rancher from the back of the cruiser. An unsurprised Maddy reassured her guests that the two of them were just stirring up a ruckus. Unfazed, after a hug and kiss on the cheek for Larry, she approached Tom with the traditional stinging punch to the shoulder.

"Are you too out causing trouble tonight, darling?" Maddy asked Larry while Tom rubbed his shoulder.

"No, Maddy. Just found this piece of shit and his drunk horse in your driveway!"

"Trigger's drunk again? Isn't there animal AA or something for him, dear?" Maddy asked and, Larry laughed.

"Well, I don't want to speak for my horse," Tom added. "So I am not responsible for the decisions of a faithful horse that likes to drink a little beer and piss on sheriffs, as well as their vehicles!"

"Dang it, Tom," Maddy exclaimed. "Did he pee on you in the car again, Larry?"

"No, ma'am. It was one of my new rookies. When I pulled up to the scene, the only thing that could be done was not to crack a smile and send my deputy back to the station for a shower and some paperwork."

Relieved, Maddy asked about Wiley's whereabouts, and Tom told her that the man is on a crazy again, but the old coot was safe. In fact, Wiley was laying up in his cabin to stay away from computers and what-have-you. The thing to remember about Wiley is that when he is on a "crazy" as we call it, he makes Tom money; and the rancher's crazy friend is a moonshining genius when the UFOs come down from the atmosphere. All Tom knew is that they might not live in the Appalachian mountains, but they grow corn and tobacco, just like the South, which interprets to money for the rancher.

Moonshining might be as illegal as it is in, say Kentucky, yet Wiley and Tom don't have to deal with the Alcohol Bureau Control or whatever it's called. So Larry and Tom greeted the guests, which Maddy befriends those "goody two-shoes" church types—which the rancher likes to keep the conversation short, fearing the talk that tends to be put in poor Tom's ear, from Maddy's religious brethren about his drinking and carrying on. To avoid a religious confrontation, Tom told Maddy about their plight with Trig and that they'd better be getting him back to the ranch before the church goers try to save Tom's soul.

Anyhow, Larry and Tom hopped into the ranch truck, secured the horse trailer and headed down the driveway. They showed up to the spot where the two left Trigger only to find it mysteriously vacant. After hearing those noises behind a tree of snorting, and neighing, the men realized what had happened to Tom's lost partner. Trigger's date got out of her stall and was relieving some of the pressure that had built up in Tom's horse earlier that evening. Seeing that there was no breaking up Trigger's courtship, the sheriff and Tom looked at each other laughing then eased back in the truck, heading back to the party.

To readily avoid the religious function, Larry and Tom unhitched the trailer, while disappearing into the stable, where ironically the office is located. It was Tom's late grandpa's staging arena. From conducting important business deals, to chewing out the workers if they were drinking on the job, or generally doing things they shouldn't, it was a place of peace and calm for the old man. Even when Gene retired and handed the reigns over to Tom, he never really left. In fact, till Two Boots got too sick to get out of bed fighting his cancer, Gene stayed right by the young man's side doing what he always did so well. Let's just say that it was an easy job running the ranch till he stopped coming over. Even up till his death, he still told Tom what to do and how to handle affairs. After Gene passed away, he put a couple of close ranch hands in charge till young Tom was ready to handle the business. I admit, Tom may have not conducted business like Gramps did, yet he remembered Gene's advice and did the best that the rancher could.

Looking at the tons of photos littering the walls, Larry asked for a beer and reminisced about ol' Two Boots, as ranchers of years passed named him, due to the fact that he once rode a bull with nothing on but his boots. Tom then passed a cold one over to Larry, and he sipped it quickly due to the heat of the summer night.

"So what's on the agenda for tomorrow?" Larry asked, and Tom paused briefly while wincing.

"Well, I have twenty grand in cash from the bar to give to Wiley, and he isn't coming into the Coyotes anytime soon," Tom replied. "I'm going to head over to his place tomorrow and grab some more booze. Wanna go?"

"Sure, Tom. I'm gonna head home and hang out with the family. See you bright and early like around one in the afternoon," Larry sarcastically implied.

"Head on home, asshole," Tom replied. "I'll see ya at 2:00 p.m."

With Larry gone for the rest of the night, Tom sat in his chair with feet kicked up on the desk. The ole boy figured if he drank a few more beers and watched some TV that the guests would be gone by the time the rancher wanted to go to bed. Tom turned on the news, watching all the despair mixed with negativity that comes out of this day and age, when all of the sudden, his ears were diverted from the news to an ungodly sound outside. Tom sprang to his feet and left the office only to witness what his ears had heard. It was Trigger and his ole lady rockin' the stable. Tom figured that Trig got his date for the evening, so why couldn't he! Sure enough, the guests were gone, the kids were fast asleep, and his approaching nuptials with Maddy had finally arrived.

In the morning, the sound of the rooster singing his annoying song awoke the two sleeping lovers. Tom threw a boot out of the window only to see the roosters crowing come to an abrupt end with the displacement of feathers floating into the breeze. Maddy punched Tom square in the shoulder absconding the rancher for hurting the alarm.

"Maddy, the damn rooster is fine," Tom replied and sat up stretching and yawning himself back to life.

"Tom, I'm going to head into town today and go shopping," Maddy stated. "Do you need anything, sweety?"

"Well, the beer supplies are getting kinda low," Tom replied. "You mind topping off the tank, sugar?"

"Sure, honey," Maddy replied. "Until my return, I'm guessin' that you're gonna stroll on over to Wiley's for a beer in the meantime?"

"Well, I was thinking about riding Trigger over to the bar for a few," Tom implied, smiling into Maddy's baby blue eyes.

Maddy then gave a look of concern and said, "Trigger should really cut back on the beer, don't ya think?"

"Yeah, I suppose Trigger does," the rancher replied. "It's just that ever since the mustang got the taste for it, he's never been happier."

"Well, you and the ranch hands shouldn't have been partying in the stalls that one time," Maddy continued.

"Believe me, Maddy, if some ranch hands learned to finish their beers and not leave them on the stall post, ole Trig wouldn't have ever been tempted," Tom replied.

The story came out to be just that. A couple years back, ole Tom landed a huge beef contract with a certain fast food establishment that left him, and the men celebrating well into that night. Apparently, some half-drank beers were left on a post by Trigger's stall, and the horse knocked over the beers, only to find out that what the 'stang was sipping on the ground became the best thing he ever tasted. The next morning when the party had waned, so Tom took Trigger on a ride through the property, and his trusty steed seemed rather sluggish. Every time Tom cracked open a beer, however, the horse's demeanor changed from a slow donkey trot, to an Arabian run with every crack of the beer. It wasn't too long until Tom figured out Trigger's plight and began giving the horse beer, which in essence, made the steed perform better relieving any additional pressures to deliver Wiley's goods to the general public.

After the two fully awoke with showers and breakfast, Maddy made her way into town, which left Tom to his own devices. The rancher threw on his boots and Stetson then meandered his way out to the ranch office. The Windy River Ranch has always been a fast-paced business, always eclipsed by the hard work the ranch hands contribute to the operation on a daily basis. At least till Tom hit the stalls to pull Trigger out and noticed something very peculiar, which came in the form of utter silence. The rancher poked his head outside to the cattle stalls and noticed the cows were eating hay then heard a commotion from the break room. Curious, Tom walked over to the break room and opened the door, only to smell smoke billow outside into the hallway while the men drank and played poker.

"You mind telling me what's going on in here?" Tom asked in a stern ambiguous tone.

"Hey, boss," Rufalo (the main ranch hand) exclaimed while sipping down his beer. "We saved a seat for ya, boss! Sit down and take a load off."

Tom graciously accepted the request and took a seat while one of the other ranchers grabbed an ice-cold beer, passing it to the cowboy's general direction. "Looks like you boys wanna lose some cash today," Tom stated while drinking his beer and throwing some money down on the table. Felipe, one of the other ranchers, tossed Tom some cards, and the rancher picked them up, eyeballing them curiously with a look of disappointment.

"Boss, we're playing some good ole-fashioned Texas Hold 'Em with jokers wild," Felipe stated, so Tom shook his head and placed his bet.

As the chips mounted, Felipe laid down three cards, which were two aces and a king. Tom, peeking at his two lonely cards, noticed the jokers staring back at his face, so when the bet came back around, the rancher increased his bet, forcing the other men to follow suit. Felipe then laid down the fourth card, landing an ace, which Rufalo and a couple other men increased their bets, making the rotation again to Tom, who doubled up on his current bet. Felipe then got arrogant and went all in forcing all of the men to fold, accept for ole Tom.

"Come on, boss! Let's see how much money I can make off of you," Felipe exclaimed, leaving Tom laughing inside.

"All right, Felipe, here's my cash," Tom stated and pulled all of his chips into the pot, making the ranch hand arrogantly smile. With that, Felipe laid down two kings, then Tom laid down his jokers, pairing the four of a kind as the disappointed ranch hand flipped the last card over, only to be another ace.

"Damnit, Tom, that's six aces,, the pissed off rancher exclaimed as Tom pulled all of his winnings over to his general direction.

"Well, Felipe, most find it not good to play jokers in this particular game," Tom stated as he cracked open another beer.

This was about the time when Larry came strolling in with a grin on his face, so he pulled up a chair and glared happily at Tom.

"What happened, Larry?" Tom stated. "Did Laurie decide to give you some tail last night?"

"Well, yeah, but that's beside the point," Larry interjected. "Laurie and I are heading out to Hawaii at the end of the month, so it'll be nice to get away from work!"

"Hey, that's great, Larry!" Tom exclaimed while sipping his beer. "I wonder how you're gonna feel when Laurie has you slip into a G-string when she wants to hit the beach?"

"You're so fucking hysterical, Tom, that I don't even know how to dignify your statement with a response," Larry replied, cracking open another beer.

"Well, Larry, we married types are a rare breed with all of these domestic partnerships and such," Tom responded while taking a swig off of his beer.

"So are we headed out to Wiley's today to go for a visit?" Larry asked while scowling at Tom.

"As much as I'd like to sit and take everybody's cash, I think it's best Larry and I head out," Tom exclaimed, taking his winnings from the table.

As they departed, Larry looked at Tom with an almost look of distain. Wiley has been holed up on his property for most of the summer setting booby traps and such, so the boys knew that they were getting ready to walk into a humdinger of a time. Before long, Tom backed the horse trailer up to Trigger as Larry saddled up Betsy and with a cooler loaded down with beer, the two rode out of the Windy River Ranch, anticipating a more or less easy ride to Wiley's, in the heat of the midmorning summer day.

Chapter 2

CHECK YOUR NUT SACK

The thing to remember about Wiley when paying him a visit up in his cabin with a shitload of cash and moonshine supplies is to tread lightly. I remember one time when some former clients wanted to see the operation in which Wiley flipped out. You see, no one comes up here unless it's Tom, Larry, or Jennie—and they make no exceptions for anyone else. Even Maddy doesn't know the location because plausible deniability is best, in some instances. As for Wiley, he was an ex-military man who lost it in the service. He enrolled in a military program that had originally experimented on soldiers with a drug known as LSD back in the sixties. If you can imagine, the drug opened up his mind to an extent that it never really closed from the first dose. The only other problem is overtime, LSD can lead to severe mental illness. Wiley was given over one hundred doses over a stretch of six months, and that was the nail in his mental coffin. Due to the army's negligence of its experiments, they offered the man a huge settlement after his discharge, which enabled Wiley to reopen his father's bar and purchase the thousand acres of wilderness that the crazy ole coot is currently hiding in.

Wiley also loved explosives and high-end military hardware that would scare away a battalion of soldiers—if they got past the booby traps pot marking the perimeter of his property and driveway. Now

Tom, being familiar with the property, as well as Larry, proceeded very carefully because they knew that ole Wiley liked to throw in an unexpected surprise here and there. To say the least, Wiley's driveway is over two miles long till you reach his cabin, and if you're not cautious, the journey might as well be a day's trek. On their trip up to Wiley's, there is a bridge that intersects a stream that runs through his property, and Larry noticed something very particular: the wood on the deck of the bridge appeared to be replaced with new pieces. Now to the untrained eye, the regular Joe would chock it up to old rotting wood that was changed out, but Larry and Tom knew better. Hopping off of Trigger, Tom approached the bridge and carefully looked for ground wires or sensors because the last thing the rancher needed was to trip a mine with the county sheriff by his side. Seeing that it was clear to walk, Tom inspected the bottom of the bridge and started to look at the cross members underneath and noticed the reasons for the new wood.

"Looks like Wiley has booby trapped the bridge with C-4, Larry," Tom snickered while looking for any additional traps.

Larry hopped off Trigger's ole lady and took a look see for himself. "Looks like he has two bricks on this side, two in the middle, and I'm guessing two at the end," Larry said. "Hell, Tom, if this bridge blew and we were on it, we might as well kiss our asses good-bye."

The rancher then told Larry that they wouldn't have to worry about are asses getting blown off, as opposed to their "nut sacks," I believe was Tom's response.

"So who's going first?" Tom asked while Larry shook his head, telling the rancher not to be a smartass and that crossing the creek would be a more viable option. Tom agreed because anyone who knows Wiley realizes that the man hates water. Even to this point, Wiley won't shower. As long as the lasers that the government are hitting him, it ensured the both of them a booby trap–free creek.

So the boys mounted their horses and cautiously began the creek-crossing. Since it was going to be a bumpy ride, Larry and Tom removed the trailer that was hooked up to Trig. Now, in the late summer, the creek is really low, but the exposed rock in the creekbed makes for uneven footing during the crossing. From side to side, the whole creek was roughly twenty yards, and the current stream is about ten yards of that length. The two men cautiously crossed smoothly with Trigger prancing over the rocks with ease and Larry in a quick pace, second only to Tom's step. Up ahead in the distance, the boys suddenly heard a loud boom and expected the worse.

"We should get up there quickly, Larry," Tom exclaimed. "We all know what happened the last time Wiley blew up shit!"

"That's right!" Larry exclaimed suddenly. "He almost burned down his own bar and Jennie eighty-sixed him for a whole month, if I do remember that night correctly."

Picking up their speed from a relaxed walk to a fast trot, they accelerated cutting through the stream and dense vegetation that zig-zag through Wiley's property. Taking the fastest route, the men were at a full bore trot, hoping that no surprises would trip them up. The men arrived at Wiley's house within minutes of the bridge and heard the noise of a wolf howling in the distance, but then they realized that it was Wiley was on a crazy kick.

Now, Wiley isn't the type of person to expect someone to show up, and he knows when people are there, whether it be Tom or the police. That goes without saying, what with the hundreds of surveillance cameras polka-dotting the perimeter of the driveway. To that extent, Tom hopped off of Trigger and walked in his normal inebriated glide, cautiously entering through the back door. Wiley had been outside for some time now and even turned off their current ways to communicate back and forth—that is, walkie-talkies or shortwave radio. Telephones were not an option because Wiley believed that the government could easily pick up on their conversations. So naturally, Tom entered first into Wiley's kitchen and grabbed a beer out of the crazy ole coot's surprisingly clean fridge. Peeking out of his kitchen window, the rancher could see Wiley sitting Indian style around a freshly burnt crater.

"Oh screw it," Tom mumbled and opened the door, flickered the porch light on and off, and sat out on the steps, which caught ole you-know-who's attention.

"Hey, asshole!" Tom shouted. "What in the hell are you doing out here, you crazy ole goat?"

His curiosity peaked, Wiley sprang up from his seated position and excitedly strolled over to the porch. He approached, and apart from his normal unshowered and untrimmed appearance, Wiley reeked like he just fought Pepe Le Pue.

Wiley began with "Hi, Tom! Whatcha doin here? I'm killing skunks! Those fuckers keep eating my crops! Did you bring sugar, Tom? Were ready to harvest soon, and what about the rolling papers for tobacco?"

See what I mean about nuts? The man has no filter, and for a good reason. Tom answered all the crazy questions the best he could and they were all in general agreement that Wiley had killed the skunk since he was marked with little bits of flesh and blood that obviously wasn't his.

"Wiley, how long has it been since you've taken your medicine?" the rancher asked while keeping a modest distance.

"Tom, I can't take that shit right now. I'm on the verge of a breakthrough! I mean, that I've figured out a way to bypass the lasers that the government keeps hitting me with! They can take their reversed engineered extraterrestrial technology and shove it up their asses," Wiley snickered.

"Fair enough, Wiley" Tom added. "Hey, how's the new batch of moonshine going?"

"You're gonna love this batch, Tom," Wiley added, smiling in a sinister way. "Oh by the way, Tom, what is that piece of shit, pawn of the government doing on my property?" referring to Larry.

"Remember, Wiley," Tom gently reassured. "Larry has been with us since for some time now and is our legal eyes and ears of this operation. Remember who got you out trouble when you almost burned down the Coyote?"

"Oh crap, that's right," Wiley added then changed the subject quickly. "Hey, you guys want to check out this batch of beer I made?"

The three men made their way to Wiley's old stable, which was converted into a lab. As they came closer, the smell of skunk was unbearable. The rancher inquired as to Wiley's current skunk problem, and the stinky man said that it was just the one from tonight. Yet this particular smell, however, was different. It didn't have the reek of rotting skunk flesh; in fact, it almost smelled like beer that had been in a bottle too long. They all entered the barn, and the smell grew to an almost unbearable stench. Tom asked Wiley if a family of skunks burrowed under his barn. Wiley looked at Tom, while grabbing his head from laser pain, smirked, and carried on. Wiley guided them through a maze of stills into a smaller room filled with case after case of beer, and the scent had grown so strong that Larry and Tom realized it was the beer.

Covering his nose, Tom stated, “You know, Wiley, if you’re planning on selling this slop, you might as well just give it to me and I’ll drink your losses, but I don’t know if the beer can even be ingested!”

Wiley cracked open a cold one and passed it Tom’s way. He then smelled it like most concerned drinkers and took a swig. When the liquid hit his mouth, it was confusing at first because the skunky smell was replaced by an aroma that I don’t think could readily be explained. It was like a hoppy rose flavor with cotton candy undertones attacking every sense of the rancher’s mouth. Surprisingly, it was the best bottle of beer that the confused rancher enjoyed in quite some time. After slamming the beer, Larry tried one, who was equally impressed. After three more rounds, things started to feel a little off kilter.

“You guys shouldn’t drink too many of those,” Wiley said, laughing while moving around the boys like he knew something was wrong.

“How did you make this heavenly bottle of beer?” Larry inferred, and Wiley escorted them out of the room with a huge smile on his face.

“You boys are gonna get hungry after a bit,” Wiley said and disappeared into the house, returning with a bag of Funyuns. You know, the onion ring snack. “Follow me, boys,” Wiley said, and they began to walk out to the tree line, wondering what ingredients the crazy goat put in the bubbly concoction.

It was just a little after four as the three made their trek to Wiley’s secret location. The men walked by the usual stuff one would on a stroll by in a mountain farmhouse. Like chickens pecking for bugs, cows chewing on hay, and an original German Panzer tank, which is one of the main problems that will be addressed in the book. All of the sudden, Tom had an uncontrollable thirst; then as he looked at the scenery, it was somehow brightened and more interesting than normal. Wiley was rambling on to Larry how he scored some shells for the panzer, and each word that flowed out of his mouth became slower then lower, making the rancher laugh. As Wiley was talking off Larry’s ear, the ole sheriff would look Tom’s way and act like he was hanging himself then shooting himself with an imaginary gun that kept jamming, when he'd pull the trigger. Usually, it would get a normal smile out of the rancher, but today was different. Tom was grinning from ear to ear, and Larry's dumb ass was making him break out into an uncontrollable laughter, and Tom wasn't quite sure why.

So leave it up to Wiley to make this amazing beer that had the cowboy ripped off his ass. And to think Larry and Tom were only there to drop off ole Wiley some ingredients and to get some shine. Arriving at Wiley's secret location, in the thick of the forest, they were awestruck, and all Larry could do was say "holy shit" with a huge look of disbelief on his face. Let's just say Wiley had about one thousand "skunky" plants growing on his property.

Curious, Tom asked, "Wiley, why is there so much marijuana growing on your land?"

And without a pause, he shrugged his shoulders and informed Larry and Tom that the two men just drank some. Now, Wiley was standing there, Funyuns in hand, shaking the bag, then Larry proceeded to rip it out of Wiley's digits then popped open the bag, eating the chips like a bulimic model, making Tom laugh even more.

"Wiley," Larry mumbled. "I'm so pissed at you right now, but this bag of Funyuns tastes so good!"

Perplexed himself, Tom looked at the plants gently swaying in the breeze and felt the speed of life slow down to a sluggish crawl. Feeling flushed, the rancher then proceeded to strip down to his tidy whites and hopped in the creek, splashing water around like a toddler playing in a pool. Laughing hysterically, Wiley and Larry follow suit, and Wiley wasn't high; he was only adding to the insatiable roars of laughter echoing from the stream. Their laughter was suddenly broken by the voice of a woman standing by the bank, taking pictures with her phone and laughing along with the stoners swimming in the creek. It was Jennie and a very shocked Lupita Jr.

"LJ, cover your eyes," Jennie told her daughter while watching the view in front of her little virgin eyes and asked Wiley about all the ruckus.

In response, Wiley told Jennie about the beer. Shaking her head, she disappeared with LJ, asking them to get dressed and come into the house for some dinner. After a short time, the boys were cooled off and sat by the creek bed, sitting in their undies. Wiley laughed and told Larry and Tom that he thought that they should have a cigarette. Like a fool, Tom was the first to flick the lighter. Now I admit, in this climate of tree huggers and health nuts, Tom likes to indulge in a good smoke here and there. Tom just didn't realize that the cigarette was similar to Wiley's beer.

Now I thought that smoking weed was a discourse best left to the scientists and hippies that want to disconnect from society; and if it's any consolation, disconnecting wasn't so bad to the rancher and Larry. Lying down now, with the sunshine penetrating Tom's body with warmth, he heard the sweetest song emanating from Wiley's house. Apparently, Jennie followed suit and turned the immortal Beatles classic, "I get by with a little help from my friends."

Feeling hungry, Tom asked Larry to pass the Funyuns, and the sheriff handed the rancher a fresh empty bag, which was returned to Larry over his head. After some time of reminiscing about the past and present, they decided to put on their clothes and retreated to the house where the smell of the barbecue, penetrated the hungry men's nostrils with the sweet smell of pork ribs frying on the cooker. Excited, Tom reached for his clothes and motioned the boys that it was time for a non-Wiley beer and some grub.

So everybody started to put their clothes on, which was an interesting adventure when stoned. From Wiley trying to put on Larry's pants to Tom putting his boots on the wrong feet, the men eventually figured it out. All of the sudden, when Wiley was pulling up his camouflage army shorts, he fell to the ground, shaking his legs like crazy, screaming, "Holy shit! I just got bit by a rattler on my fucking nut sack!"

Now Larry and Tom were by his side, shocked and panicked, ripping off Wiley's shorts and inspecting the damage to his bitten member.

"Looks like the C-4 isn't apart of Wiley's worries today, Tom," Larry exclaimed while laughing yet holding a serious posture.

"So who's sucking out the poison?" Tom urgently inquired, looking at the county sheriff who already started to cringe by the thought.

Hearing the panic in Wiley's voice, Jennie and LJ came running out at a full sprint only to find Wiley naked, immediately covering LJ's eyes twice. Jennie turned LJ around and rushed to her dad's side, inspecting the bite mark.

"Wow, Dad, that's gonna get infected if we don't get some antivenom and antibiotics immediately," Jennie stated while Wiley painfully responded by telling her to go to his med station, which—if anyone knows Wiley—is because he doesn't do doctors, even if he has been shot in the chest and thrown off a four-story building. Instead, the nutty goat preferred to do any medical stuff by himself, or Jennie, if she's available.

Confused by the melee of Wiley's screams, Jennie rushed back to the house and ran into a room that was converted to a medical bay, filled with all sorts of medicine and instruments. Now Larry was struggling 'cause he knew that he must do something immediately to keep the poison from spreading any further, while Tom sat back, reassuring Wiley that everything was going to be fine. Now in the midst of the panic, little LJ, back turned, peeked an eye open only to see the culprit who bit ole Wiley in his manhood slithering nearby. As all this was happening, Jennie rushed back with the medicine. Now for you readers who can imagine, we have Wiley on the ground crying, Larry sucking out any venom he can, Jennie sticking Wiley with medicine—and LJ holding a baby, nonpoisonous bull snake, shouting to everybody, excited about her new find. If you can imagine, all of their jaws dropped, especially Larry's.

After the following events had transpired, Larry and Tom managed to carry Wiley back to the house, sitting him down in his rocking chair on the porch. Jennie passed a cold beer over to Wiley, demanding him to put the bottle on the infected area, so the snake-bitten old man followed suit. Now Larry was also sitting on the porch, moonshine in hand, swallowing the liquid and gargling like he just finished brushing his teeth. Larry passed the shine Tom's way, to which the rancher obliged, and then to Jennie, who sat there with a relieved smile on her face. By this time, dinner was almost completed; and Larry, traumatized by the incident, drank more moonshine and started to relax, numbing his mind from Wiley's drama. After a couple more passes of the jar, the timer on the stove buzzed, so Jennie went back into the kitchen with LJ to get the sides and plates ready, setting everything out outside on the table.

"You know, Larry," Wiley said thankfully, "I just wanted to say thank you for doing what you did for me."

In response, Larry told Wiley to shut up, as Tom turned his head fighting back the laughter and tears. After a few moments, Jennie brought the meat plate out to the patio and harvested the pork off of the barbecue. Let's just say that suppertime couldn't have happened at a more opportune time because all three of the men's stomachs were rumbling by this point and needed some nourishment.

With the food on the table, everybody dug in. Jennie is a very traditional cook, and the spread ranged from barbecued pork to fresh slices of watermelon she picked up on her way out to Wiley's. Sitting there watching everybody eat, even after the snake crisis, Tom looked at everyone and smiled. Even after a painful and somewhat traumatic experience (in Larry's case), to have such good friends surrounding the rancher was like a warm blanket on a cold winter's night, surrounding the group with happiness.

Little LJ was playing with her new snake, and Wiley was constantly rearranging his silverware; even though he ate with his hands the whole time. Larry, at one point, avoided getting kissed from Wiley, while the crazy ole goat jokingly pointed down at the snake-bitten idiot's nut sack.

After dinner, Jennie made a fire, and they all congregated around the warmth of the radiating blaze. With moonshine in one hand and pipe tobacco in the other, the boys began to drink and talk about their moonshine operation and how to incorporate the new devices that Wiley has created; that is, the weed beer.

Looking at Larry and Tom, Wiley said, "Guys, by the way, I owe two million dollars for the tank. My associates in Mexico are starting to lose their patience and want to collect on their tank. I feel really bad because I paid half at first—now with added interest (which might I say is outrageous) has doubled within a month, and I think they wanted a payment like three weeks ago."

Larry and Tom both looked at each other in total surprise. Almost in tandem, the two men stared at Wiley and shook their heads. Tom already knew that Larry was pissed, so he looked at the sheriff and said, "Hell, Larry, what do you think?"

"Can't you just return the damn thing, Wiley?" Larry asked while scratching his head.

"Well, I don't think there is a towing company around here capable of hauling a Panzer back to the Mexican mob," Jennie replied.

Also, Larry and the boys didn't want to draw too much attention to the operation, so it was agreed that they were on high alert till the financiers eventually showed up to potentially collect on the debt. You see, the crew runs a very lucrative operation that's beneficial to the sheriff of the Upper County. In fact, the only reason Larry ever agreed to such nonsense was due to his daughter Evelyn, who desperately needed money to cover important medical bills, and Tom wanted to help the sheriff any way he could. Tom always had a saying for the underworld ons and goings for keeping public officials quiet, yet Larry was a different case. The two have been friends since birth, quite literally. In fact, they were born in the same military hospital.

Dallas was fighting in Vietnam at the time but was on leave and thrilled when Tina's water broke. As for Wiley, the man took his ex-wife down to San Diego for vacation, and sure enough, both lifelong friends reunited in a collision course that would change the spatial fabric of the Upper Kittitas County.

"Wiley, you're such a goddamn idiot!" Larry exclaimed. "I'm trying to get cash for my daughter's heart transplant, and you're making deals with people that can threaten that, you damn fool!"

"I know, Larry, and I'm not trying to wreck this for us," Wiley abruptly said. "It's just the government has been hitting me with these lasers and their planning on invading my land!"

With those words, Larry rose with a scowl, said his good-byes, and hopped on Betsy, riding back to the ranch. Tom let him go because for one, Larry was a grown man who needed to cool off. Second, when Larry gets pissed off, the sheriff can be a tad bit overbearing. Larry respects Wiley because of their father's friendship, yet Tom wouldn't put it past ole Larry to get fed up, arrest Wiley for his own good, and back out of the operation. Larry's kind of the chick on the proverbial rag, so I guess that's intimidating enough, but that's not the point.

"Damn it, Wiley. You sure know how to piss people off," Tom stated. "I don't think you realize the shit storm that's going to come our way if you don't make right with your Southern friends. Also, we all know that that kind of unneeded attention from your financiers shouldn't be made public in the Upper County."

Wiley just shrugged his shoulders and sat there, silently watching the embers flicker in the fire. Sensing Wiley's shy, about to cry coming on, Tom smiled and grabbed his friends shoulder. "So how long has the government been hitting ya with those lasers?"

"Well, shoot, Tom. Just before you guys showed up, but since you've been here, there hasn't been one single laser, I guess," Wiley responded. "When people are around, there usually isn't anything. Just when I'm alone."

With that being said, Tom thought it best that Wiley needed to be around people a little more because the crazy fool only has so much time on this earth, and Tom realized that his friend shouldn't be alone. Anyhow, Jennie and Tom reassured Wiley that just as long as they were around, the lasers would stop hitting him. After a few drinks, Tom decided to call it a night. Trigger was fast asleep, but drunk Tom woke him up, hopped on the tired steed, and they made their way back to the Windy River Ranch. Loaded down with a haul of moonshine, amongst other illegal things at that particular moment.

It was a quiet ride home, and the rancher had decided to stop at the Wyatt cemetery—as the family calls it—to see his gramps. Two Boots always had an obsession with death, and Tom could only imagine it was due in part to Gene's service in the military. Years before his passing, Gene had built a tomb for the family to honor those that pioneered the lands where the old man spent all of his life. As a matter of fact, his great grandparents, mother, father, and brother are buried there. The rancher actually had their bodies exhumed and moved to the tomb because he thought that family should stick together, even in death.

Tom arrived at the tomb late in the night, hopped off Trigger, and approached the crypt taking a couple beers out of the cooler then cracked them both open. The tomb was in reasonably good shape for a monument that had been around for some twenty years now, but it was covered with vegetation in places and natural erosion that gave the cemetery a ghostly appearance. Tom took the other beer and saluted him while pouring Gene's beer on the ground while a single tear started to stream down his face. The rancher wondered if Gene knew the trouble that his grandson was in right now, and if Tom's prayers would reach his grandfather in the silence of the warm night. Tom remembered back to a time when Gene ran the ranch and saw the prosperity that Two Boots had by selling a ton of cattle, at least till the eighties. The economical signs of selling cattle started falling slowly in those days, but now with President Carson and a recession later, the ranch is in the hole with two hundred and fifty thousand dollars. Tom always considered government relief, but Gene taught his grandson how to be proud and to stand his ground no matter the strife or tribulation. So Tom did the only thing he knew how and called up Wiley, and I'm slowly paying off the debt. The moonshine business has been profitable for the ranch, and in two more years, Tom should be able to cut out the middle man and start a meat processing facility myself.

In the midst of all of this financial stress, the rancher dropped on his knees and prayed. Tom has not been one for such things but felt that Gene was closer to him more than the tomb the old man currently resides in. When Tom opened his eyes, an eagle was perched on top of the tomb, and it was unusual because the rancher never heard the majestic bird land. Now staring eye-to-eye, the bald eagle moved in a little closer but was cautious enough to not be touched by the cowboy. Staring in wonder, Tom slowly put out his hand to touch the predator, but the eagle fluttered his wings, and the bird flew off into the still night.

With a smile of amazement, Tom took that as an omen from his grandpa because Gene loved eagles, and Tom still has a memorabilia of those beautiful flying creatures back at the house. Satisfied with his prayer, Tom hopped back on Trigger, cracked open a cold longneck, and headed home. Unfortunately, they didn't make it very far. Trigger was slowing down considerably while swaying back and forth on both sides of the road. Tom had his tired mustang park the trailer in a grassy field where the rancher unhooked the four- wheeled contraption and commenced to lie down. Tom pulled a blanket and pillow out of the satchel then snuggled up to his sleeping horse. Closing Tom's tired eyes, the rancher drifted to sleep, dreaming of eagles, snakes, and tanks.

The next morning, Tom was awakened by the hot breath of Trigger snorting down on the cowboy's face. It was round about six o'clock in the morning and the sound of the birds chirping with the stream flowing gently in the background was soothing to Tom. The rancher sprang to his feet and wrapped up his blanket, placing it on the back of Trigger. After everything was secure, Tom hopped up on the steed and began his trek back to the ranch. Along the way, the two passed the eagle that the rancher spotted the night earlier and was amazed by the size of the salmon that said predatory bird recently fished out of the Teanaway River.

"It's amazing to think what those birds can lift out of a lake, eh, Trigger," Tom exclaimed, and the horse turned toward Tom, neighing away. "Well, boy, I think we'd better rush back home and grab a bite to eat." With that being said, Tom whipped the reigns and the two sped for the sanctuary of the Windy River Ranch.

Upon their return, the rancher spotted several cattle that broke out through a fence nearby, rummaging on the grasses that dotted the driveway, so Tom hopped off of Trigger with a rope and began containing the cattle. Tom raised the lasso and swung it in an urgent matter, roping a nearby calf that was beginning to wander off away from its mother. Safely secured, Tom picked up the helpless cow and placed the youngster on the back of Trigger which automatically raised the mother's attention, forgetting the lush grass that she was eating.

"Trigger, let's see how fast that bitch can run," the rancher exclaimed as he kicked Trig's side, springing the mustang into a more excited pace, sprinting down the road with a pissed off momma cow following behind, which raised the attention of the other cattle that were normally confused at first. Yet in all of the commotion, the beasts being startled by the mom's cries, began to run behind Tom, so the rancher decreased his speed to a safe ten miles per hour, so the cattle could keep up. After about thirty minutes of driving, Tom and Trigger had finally reached a reserve pen near the ranch and hopped off Trigger to open the gate while the momma cried and nestled the poor calf still on the mustang's rear. With the gate now open, Tom led Trigger and the rest of the cow flock into the gate and closed it, bringing the animals to a slow halt.

When Tom and Trigger exited the gate, the two made their way back to the ranch. Confused, Tom wondered how the cattle got out of their pen, and while he was reflecting on this, the rancher heard a commotion of people screaming and fighting. Tom kicked Trigger into high speed, and within minutes, the ole rancher knew why. Tom witnessed his lovely wife pulling hair, as well as the bitch-slapping, of someone who resembled Maddy's crazy sister. Now before we continue with the story, let me fill you in on good ole Fiona. Let's just say that the woman is a nonmedicated schizophrenic waste of life who unfortunately has kids that Tom or Maddy never get to see. As a family, the Wyatts have dealt with Fiona's constant river of bull-shit since Tom originally shook her hand. Fiona is on welfare and a life-sucking predator that will lay with any man. It doesn't matter the age or sexually transmitted disease, Fiona has spread for anything resembling a woody or that smelled like money. Hell, Fiona tried to pull a fast one on Tom one time, yet the ole boy knew better, and Maddy always watched Fiona like a hawk when the bitch was around because Maddy couldn't trust her own sister either.

So here are these two ladies having it out, and Tom swiftly hopped off Trigger, separating the women as Fiona cussed up a storm. Fiona then shouted, "Maddy, you're a fucking bitch! My kids need things, and you have the money!"

"Fiona, I get it if you need help, but I'm not going to give you five thousand dollars, just because your kids need diapers!" Maddy exclaimed. Fiona then backed off when she saw the rancher approach her with a pissed off look in ole Tom's eye.

"Fiona, I'll be damned if Maddy or myself is going to give you five thousand dollars," Tom stated. "Lemme guess, Fiona, I know that you're not on drugs of any kind, so I'm guessing this cash is for your loser boyfriend's diaper habit?"

"Fuck you, Tom!" Fiona shouted. "Andy is a good man and takes care of my kids! How could you say that?"

"Oh gee, I don't know, Fiona," Tom replied. "Maybe it's the countless calls from him needing money, or the time you butt-dialed me, and I might have heard a conversation involving you in several illegal incidents! Don't try to come around here and hit us up for cash anymore," Tom continued. "If you need diapers or groceries, Maddy will run you down to the store. Hell, she can even buy some toys for your kids. But don't ever come around here again and ask for money. God knows you're too lazy to get a goddamn job!" Then Tom looked Fiona squarely in the eyes with that intimidating rancher look he sports to drive home the point.

Fiona then replied, "No, I don't need diapers, groceries, or toys! I need that money or I'll never let you too see your nieces ever again!"

Tom shook his head and walked briskly to the office. After a few moments, the rancher returned and had in his possession a recorder that was hooked up to the office phone. Tom absolutely loved this particular recording device because when he does business over the phone, he likes to not only keep people honest but tends to dabble in harmless blackmail from time to time. Tom then began to roll the tape, which happened to be a conversation between Fiona and the goodie-two-shoes boyfriend, boasting how the duo beat up several people and robbed them of their personal belongings. Fiona then freaked out and told Tom to shut off the recorder, which Tom obliged while looking at Maddy, flashing a smile.

"Fiona, you know that I haven't had anything to do with you for years now, so I'm going to keep this simple," Tom stated calmly. "If you threaten us with your bullshit one more time, I'm going to invite Larry over here for a drink, and the man's gonna have a listen!" Tom then placed the device into his pocket. This was just about the point when just Larry happened to showed up, throwing Fiona off guard even more. Larry exited his patrol car and smiled at Fiona while putting on his sunglasses like uptight sheriffs do.

"Hey, Fiona! How are you and the kids?" Larry asked while wrapping his arms close to his chest.

Fiona shied away and replied, "Hello. Larry! The kids and I are doing very well!"

"Good to hear, Fiona," Larry responded. "Hey, Tom, can we go out into the office? I need a drink!"

Tom replied in earnest, and the boys walked away. Tom then gave a backward glance toward Fiona, jiggling his pocket, as the rancher walked away. The two men made their way to the office and both pulled up a chair. As Tom unscrewed the cap off of the moonshine; the rancher took a good pull and passed the jar over to Larry, who in return took an even larger swig.

"So I'm guessing Fiona's trying to swindle Maddy outta more cash," Larry asked as he took a second deep drink of shine.

"Well, she's trying, but I put an end to her bullshit pretty quick," Tom replied while smiling sardonically.

Larry then lowered his head then drew silent. Tom knew something wasn't right and offered Larry another drink, but the sheriff shied away.

"It's your daughter, isn't it?" Tom asked while holding his hand to an abrupt chin, resting it calmly.

"Yeah, Tom. She hasn't been doing too well lately," Larry replied. "You know, the insurance company states that her heart condition was spurred on by some bullshit excuse that the car wreck somehow created her issue. So the prick insurance agent tells me that her condition isn't their problem but mine!" Larry then raised the jar of moonshine and exclaimed, "This drink is for that fucking prick who wants to deny my ten-year-old child the means to live a longer life!"

Tom, seeing the worry and tears well up in the sheriff's eyes, responded, "I hope the piece of shit can sleep at night knowing the lives that he changes."

"The bad thing is that the idiot works in Ellensburg and gets to go home every night and watch his kids grow up healthy," Larry stated.

"You wanna treat him like a doughnut and shake him down?" Tom asked, and Larry laughed hysterically.

"Yeah, Tom. If it was that easy, the prick would have disappeared years ago," Larry replied. "I hate to ask, Tom, but I need like two grand for an upcoming appointment tomorrow so she can be seen."

"Larry, say no more," the rancher exclaimed, and Tom pulled out a wad of cash from the safe. "You just help us keep up appearances for Wiley, then the ole coot and myself will help you out any way we can."

"Oh I know, Tom, and I appreciate it," Larry answered while pulling a beer out of the fridge. "You know, this year's been uncommonly hot. You know what they say about the heat?"

Tom looked Larry in the eyes and replied in a calm tone, "Yeah, I believe the hotter the summer, the greater the problems. Hell, Larry, problems are what I handle best. That's why I conceded the election to you in the first place."

What Tom was talking about was the sheriff's election between Larry and current sheriff, Brock Walters. Larry has been the sheriff of the Upper County for some ten years now, but during that pivotal election, Tom decided last minute to throw his hat into the election. The only reason was due in part to impressing Maddy at the time, who the two had been dating only recently. Personally, the Upper County needed a change in power. Aside from the fact that ole Brock was in the early stages of senility, that old coot was damn near seventy years old and was sheriff for over thirty years. Yet the voters felt that the Upper County needed a fresh face. So Larry tossed in his chips and took the gamble. However, just because you hear citizens' opinions on the streets doesn't necessarily mean that the election would be cut and dry. In fact, the day Larry announced his candidacy, ole Brock had his sergeant's desk moved outside. The only problem was that in mid-February, the sheriff's heart softened (after a week) and put a space heater under Larry's desk.

When the day of the debate finally arrived, Larry couldn't handle Brock's constant mistreatment anymore, so the candidate went to seek council from Tom. After several drinks, the rancher managed to smooth out Larry's rough edges and offered to take his friend to the debate, to support his friend. The two found their way to the town hall in a car driven by Maddy—if you can imagine—and the best friends fell out drunk with a sheriff looking sternly into his sergeant's eyes. I believe the comment made by the Walters at the time was, "This is going to be a lot easier than I thought!"

Inside, Maddy was pouring coffee down Larry's throat when the drunken officer told Tom that he was going to concede the candidacy, but the cowboy felt sorry for his friend and told the drunkard to get past the debate before he made that announcement. Larry agreed and took his place at the podium, with Sheriff Walters standing by the sergeant, laughing. You see, the sheriff was very proud of his title and had spent a long time building his position, which involved, at times, making shady deals with criminals to help his financial prosperity. Little did Larry know that a bomb was about to drop.

With the room now full to capacity, the host began with all of the proper introductions and then asked, "Are these the only two candidates seeking election as sheriff of the Upper County, or does someone wish to step forth to contest?"

Now, Tom, being fully three sheets to the wind, looked Maddy in the eye and smiled. He then stood and announced his candidacy. For those of you who don't know, Tom's grandpa was sheriff once upon a time, and the county had never experienced such prosperity. Even the citizens with complaints were being treated fairly, as well as those involved in traffic stops. So when Tom stood, the room exploded into cheering and clapping, which did not go well with Sheriff Walters.

The guest commentator told Tom to take his place, so the rancher sat by Larry, and the debate was well on its way. At first, the host asked the candidates to talk about their experiences and how they can make the position better. Sheriff Walters took the podium first and talked about his years as sheriff and how the next term would be more prosperous for the citizens, as well as the sheriff's department. After the sheriff's statement, Larry then spoke to the voters and praised the sheriff for his service but talked about change. The change being one of a new era for prosperity and creating a safe county so more people could move there to experience and live in a truly safe place.

After Larry was done with his speech, Tom then took the podium amidst more clapping and cheering. Tom, not knowing what to say, told the audience that none of the candidates should be lucky enough to hold the office, yet at the same time that the office needed a man with true grit. The rancher told the audience that he could not hold a candle to his grandfather, yet Two Boots gave Tom the tools and training to tackle the position since he was a young boy. After Tom's speech, the crowd rose to their feet and applauded the rancher as he tipped his hat to the sheriff.

Anyhow, the debate went on without a hitch, and after a couple months, the day of the election dawned. After a long day of shaking hands, the voting had begun. So Tom and Maddy went over to Larry's camp to watch the results. After an hour, it was apparent that Sheriff Walters and Larry did not hold the votes, so Tom was elected. Larry shook hands with the new sheriff, and some supporters wanted Tom to speak, so the rancher took the podium. The only thing the people didn't realize was that Tom was going to drop a bombshell.

Tom then thanked everybody for their hard work and praised all of the supporters who wrangled the rancher into office, but Tom then smiled at Larry and conceded the office. Automatically, mouths dropped and eyes opened all for good reason. Since Walters finished third, he couldn't get his seat back; but Larry, on the other hand, smiled back at Tom and accepted Tom's concession. I do believe the rancher said this, "I would like to apologize for conceding the office of sheriff. You see, my grandfather also saw something in Larry too, and that was the reason my friend became an officer. He's caring yet strict and not the kind of person to back out of any situation that should come his way. In fact, if it wasn't for my grandpa, I'm sure that many of you would feel less safe or not be here at all if it wasn't for

Larry's due diligence in handling your affairs. I think someday that this position will be a good fit for me, but let's all reflect on Larry and his service to us in the days to come."

The room then temporarily paused in silence then burst out in cheer and celebration for Larry. In Tom's heart, the man could have snatched the title easily from Larry and Sheriff Walters, but in the end, he found it more feasible to see a friend follow his dreams. So the election secured Larry's spot; in fact, he secured four more elections due to the hard work that Larry and the Upper County sheriff's department had anguished so hard to secure for the people of Kittitas County.

Back in Tom's office, the old buddies had a couple more drinks and reflected on past adventures. Larry then soon departed, and Tom kicked his feet up on his desk and turned on the television, when all of the sudden, Wiley crackled in on a walkie-talkie sitting nearby Tom.

"Hey, Tom, you there? Over," Wiley asked.

Tom responded, "Yes, I am Wiley. How's the nut sack doing?"

"Very funny, Tom, but it's really fucking sore right now," Wiley replied while itching his underparts. "Hey, anyhow, I have a brand-new batch ready for transport, and the Yellow Jackets should be here in a few days to collect. You up for a run?"

"Hey, anything to help you out, asshole," Tom replied while taking another pull off of his jar of shine. "Let's just hope this goes smoothly this time, Wiley, 'cause after the last incident, Larry was ready to drag the both of us in!"

"No worries, Tom," Wiley cracked in. "Just get your ass down here tomorrow and let's get this going, copy?"

"Copy that, Wiley," Tom replied and set the walkie-talkie down while the news played on the TV.

Another run, Tom thought as he cracked open a longneck and took a swig. Thinking to himself, the rancher had a feeling that tomorrow as going to be a very long day, and with the Yellow Jackets driving closer to the Teanaway Valley, the rancher thought it best to get plenty of rest because the bikers would keep Tom's interests peaked. So the cowboy exited the office and headed to the house to hang out with Maddy and the kids, in anticipation for the coming dawn.

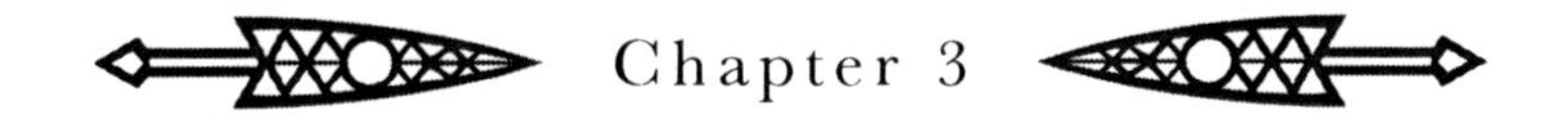

Chapter 3

The Yellow Jackets Swarm

After Tom watched some television, the rancher left the office and noticed something very peculiar, which came in the form of his dad's pickup truck parked in the driveway. Tom saw Dallas and Larry shaking hands and approached the two old friends. Now Larry and Dallas have had quite a history together; in fact, they would have never met had it not been for the rancher's grandfather. Dallas was a part of the first U.S. troops to invade Vietnam, and Larry's father was a private in the same company. The seventh Calvary airborne was deployed to Vietnam, and the men were not mentally prepared for what they were about to witness; which could have been a potential massacre, if not for the quick thinking of their leaders. As a matter of fact, Dallas's do or die attitude helped rally the troops during that three day battle. Anyhow, Tom approached Dallas, who was leaning on one of the pen rails they used to break in colts and shook his father's hand. Tom also noticed his oldest boy Tom Jr. swaying and thrashing around in the pen, which put a smile on the rancher's face, remembering a time when the rancher was young, doing more or less the same thing.

Not falling off once, TJ exhausted the colt, and Dallas hopped in grabbing the reigns, petting the tired steed.

"Geez, Tom, the oldest is really doing a great job working the pen, don't you think?" Dallas asked with a smile on his face.

Tom grinned, looking Dallas in the eyes and replied, "Well, Dad, he gets a lot of it from me, I guess!"

Dallas then asked where his son was last night, and Tom explained in great detail, getting a smile in the form of a spit- take trying not to say what really occurred out in Wiley's creek.

"Sounds like Wiley hasn't changed a bit," Dallas said and pushed for more information about when he was going to get to see Wiley again. In the midst of crazy Wiley, Tom informed Dallas that his friend was, as of current, mentally detained. Tom then proceeded over to TJ and gave him a high five for breaking the colt in. After the praises of breaking the young horse on TJ's first attempt, Lupita came out from the house and looked at Tom's oldest boy with that warm gentle smile and gave TJ a hug.

The story about Lupita is like the boy that sees a puppy for the first time and falls completely in love. Lue, as Tom calls her, is a six-foot-tall beauty—or how does one say, *muy caliente*! For all you youngsters, I best describe her as Shakira, the only exception being that Lue cannot only sing, but can also cook. Lupita has always been there for Tom growing up. From homework to bedtime, on his visits to Florida, Tom was witness to her guiding light, only with an ample rack—and not much has changed in the years that he has known her. I'm not quite sure how she maintains her looks, whether it be diet, exercise, or plastic surgery. Tom just hoped that when Maddy climbs up there in age that she can take care of herself like Lue.

"You know, Tom," Lue said, "I just made some fresh flour tortillas hot off of the pan." And like a child racing to the Christmas tree to open that first present, Tom vanished into the kitchen. Maddy was preparing some homemade salsa, and when Lupita comes over, she feels the need to upstage Tom's Mexi-mommy. Don't get me wrong. Maddy is an excellent chef in all aspects, but she has yet to imitate Lue's flour tortillas. During the week, Maddy's menu is very appetizing, except for tofu night, which the boys and Tom usually snack well before.

Maddy looked Tom in the eyes, glimmering in the sultry light of early evening and asked her husband, "What in the hell happened out at Wiley's?"

Larry, of course, sat in a bar chair, pouring a flask into a fresh cup of coffee that Maddy just prepared, grinning away.

"Oh, a bull snake bit Wiley in the nuts. Other than that, nothing outta the ordinary," Tom replied.

But before the rancher could pause, Maddy added, "So how many beers did you have over at Wiley's?"

With that glare of a trapped animal and the cool look of a poker player on a hot street, Tom looked over in Larry's general direction and asked, "Did you tell Maddy that you had to suck out the poison?"

With that being said, Larry casually rose, walking past Tom, gently slapping his back and strolled outside, smiling. With a curious smile wider than the sun, Maddy held Tom tight, eyes locked into the rancher's, and reassured Tom that it wasn't his fault that the beer was tainted.

"You know, I have over twenty cases of that tainted beer in the horse trailer," Tom stated, but Maddy doesn't partake in such things and laughed.

"Just keep to the unleaded beer for now on." And then Maddy added, "Is Wiley going to sell it in the bar?"

Tom replied, "Wiley has some biker buddies riding up from Oregon tomorrow to pick up some shine, and the buzz beer too. I imagine they will take some of the beer as well." Now the bikers are a different story, which will be explained further how the boys had business with them, but now it was time for a fresh tortilla. After Tom's snack, the full bellied rancher headed outside, and Larry hopped into his patrol car, so Tom followed after him.

"You gonna actually do some work today?" Tom asked with a sarcastic smile, and Larry replied, "I have to head into the office for a bit and then the wife has a get-together tonight for her church group. Gotta keep up appearances, you know?"

"Fair enough," Tom replied, and Larry tipped his hat to the house guests disappearing down the driveway.

After Larry left, Tom told Maddy that he was getting thirsty, which means in the Wyatt language that Tom was going to the bar. So Maddy gave the rancher a hug and a sock on the shoulder, telling the ole boy to be home before breakfast. Tom received her punch well and rounded up Trigger who was getting thirsty too. Tom signaled his horse to back into the trailer, which the horse did with ease. This is the point where Dallas strolled over, checking the bit and saddle, then asked Tom, "You still running booze for Wiley?" With a stern look in his eye.

"Well, not by choice, but he pays me generously for my time, and I drink all that's within an arm's reach," the rancher replied.

"Son, you're a grown man and it's not my place to dictate, but there's better things in life than runnin' shine for a crazy old goat like Wiley," Dallas reiterated.

Now the thing that Dallas didn't know was how much the booze running has saved the ranch. The economy has been exceptionally unkind to cattle ranchers this past decade, and selling cattle just isn't enough to pay the bills. Surprisingly, running booze has been equally profitable under the watchful eyes of Sheriff Larry Baxter, even though Wiley pays him to look the other way. A lot of people call it corruption, which isn't right by any means, but when you have a kid who needs a heart transplant, even sheriffs tend to step out of bounds to protect their own. Anyhow, Tom gave his dad a hug, hopped on Trig, and made their way over to the bar.

About halfway there, trotting in the summer heat, having a cold one, Tom spotted that infamous rookie deputy who was saturated with Trigger's urine the other night, sitting on the side of the road looking right back at the rancher through his driver-side mirror, thinking to himself, "Oh shit! Here we go again." Obviously seeing Trig, the rookie hopped out of his cruiser, and he approached the two while Tom petted Trigger, informing the horse to avoid a pit stop on the deputy and his vehicle.

"Mr. Wyatt, I just wanted to apologize for the other night. I didn't realize you were the Wyatt ranch boss." He then shook Tom's hand in earnest. "You're a legend around here, and I'm truly sorry about the other night."

"Son," Tom said, looking the deputy squarely in the eye. "I'm sorry what ole Trig did to ya the other night, and for that, I apologize," the rancher stated, tipping his hat back in kindness.

"I hear you and the sheriff took down the Bryant boys over in Robinson Canyon. Is it true that you and Larry went over the same night that they raided Wiley's and shook 'em down," the deputy asked, looking curious than ever.

In reply, Tom explained that Wiley was vengeful over the killing of his horse and bolted off of the property to go exact his revenge, but the thing that the deputy didn't know was that Jerry and his boys stole a batch of fresh moonshine from Wiley, and the guys were just coming to collect what had been taken from them. In fact, the story took place around the time that Maddy was pregnant and due with Tom's second oldest kid, so the boys knew that they had to act quickly when the Bryants broke into Wiley's still, making away with the moonshine. A gunfight had naturally ensued, being that Wiley was at home during the time of the incident. Since the neighbors living down the road at the time heard the gunshots in the wee hours of the morning, they called the sheriff's office, forcing Larry to drag Tom away from the bar, speeding frantically out to Wiley's.

Fearing the operation had been lost, the two men pulled into Wiley's amidst the several sheriff vehicles that had already arrived on scene, and Wiley was sitting next to his dead horse that had been shot by the Bryant boys. Larry interrupted one of the deputies that was questioning a disgruntled Wiley and pulled the crazy coot aside. Wiley told both Larry and Tom that his lips were sealed about the moonshine, but the Bryant boys had raided his stash, making away in their pick-up truck. When Wiley heard the commotion, he grabbed his M-16 and rushed outside, only to be greeted with gunfire, so he dived under the porch, returning fire. The Bryants, nonetheless, responded by shooting Wiley's horse and sped away. Hearing Wiley's account in disbelief, the three men piled into Larry's cruiser and left Wiley's in a cloud of dust bound for Robinson Canyon.

Larry, being acquainted with the Bryants on several occasions, figured that the men would hide the moonshine in a stash spot in the Canyon, near the Bryant's home. Now getting out to the stash spot would be all fine and dandy if it weren't for the fact that a good part of Robinson Canyon was owned by the Bryants. Let's just say that driving in would clearly be a dead giveaway to the boys' location, and the Bryants would just take the moonshine and disappear. So it was decided that the men would park and hike the three miles into the Bryant's land and fetch their shine.

In the cover of night, the boys parked on the side of an access road and loaded up on ammunition, as well as whiskey, to keep warm during the cool, brisk night. About an hour into their journey, the men noticed lights and some voices echoing in the distance, so they crept over for a listen. There were three men talking about the raid at Wiley's and that Leo Bryant, the oldest son, had accidentally shot the horse upon their departure, which infuriated Wiley even more. Tom kept Wiley's emotions contained in the meantime, and the men decided to make their way to the stash spot to retrieve the moonshine, with only one problem: How do they haul it away?

The boys then made their move after the Bryants had disappeared and crept around the property to the stash spot, which was only a breath away. When they arrived, Wiley heard an owl peep that was perched on top of the rickety old shack that was currently used to stash the shine. Larry told Wiley to stay put and keep an eye out for the Bryants, so Wiley agreed to lay low while carefully remaining hidden in the brush. Larry and Tom then carefully made their way to the shed stepping lightly, as not to disturb any branches that might give away the men's position. When they reached the door, Larry motioned Tom to draw his firearm and hold steady as the sheriff slowly opened the door.

Inside the shed, the men's hard work sat there ripe for the picking, until a noise behind the shed forced the men to take cover. A very drunk Arnie Bryant returned with a roll of toilet paper, complaining about not having an outhouse to conduct his business and opened a fresh jar of shine, sipping it wholly. Before the fool could react, the barrel end of Larry's pistol was pointed squarely at the back of ole Arnie's head, forcing the drunk idiot to lower his firearm and the jar of moonshine.

"You know, Arnie, what they say about a man's booze?" Larry asked while holding his gun confidently and snatched the shine.

"No shit! Dad didn't think you assholes would be here so quickly!" Arnie exclaimed.

Tom then came out of the darkness with his firearm pointed at Arnie. "You're lucky Larry and I are pointing our weapons at you and not Wiley right now," Tom asserted while looking Arnie deeply into the fool's eyes.

"Shit, Tom, Leo feels bad about shooting Wiley's horse," Arnie replied, who was now ordered to his knees, shaking uncontrollably over his current detainment.

All of the sudden, car lights in the distance frightened the boys, and Arnie called out to the vehicle to come and shoot up the men, but before he could blurt out another word, Larry's pistol whipped Arnie into an abrupt state of unconsciousness, forcing the boys to take cover yet again in the dark. The vehicle had arrived seconds later, and three men poured out of the truck. Seeing the current state of Arnie, the assailants drew their weapons and frantically looked around, to only see the calm still dark encircling them. Jerry motioned for Benny to have a look around while Leo and he check on Arnie, so Benny took off into the darkness, firearm at the ready. Jerry then approached Arnie and propped the boy up, inspecting the wound behind the fool's head.

"Damn, Leo, it looks like your brother got drunk again and hit the back of his head with a rock, I'd imagine," Jerry stated while inspecting his son's wound.

"I told that idiot to not drink the profits," Leo replied but then noticed footprints on the ground that seemed rather suspicious. Drawing his weapon, Leo began surveilling the area when a voice shouted out in the distance. It was Benny walking a very pissed off Wiley at gunpoint back to the shed.

"Well, look who we have here," Jerry said, laughing, and took a pull off of the jar of shine that Larry had dropped. "Wiley Holloway! Jeez, man, I was expecting you to pay me a visit, just didn't realize it would be so soon, and without company!"

"You jacked my booze, asshole, and your dipshit son shot my prize horse," Wiley counteracted, not being able to contain his emotions any further.

Leo then appeared out of the darkness empty-handed and approached Wiley. "Damn, brother! I am so sorry I shot your horse!" Leo exclaimed. "Man, you just came out of nowhere and scared the living piss outta us, Wiley!" Leo then put his hand on Wiley's shoulder, consoling him, but the crazy coot deflected the hand in defiance.

"So you mind telling us where Larry and Tom are so we can conclude our business?" Jerry asked, now starting to get riled up over Wiley's presence.

Before Wiley could offer up an answer, both Jerry and Leo had found themselves in a similar position as Arnie. Larry and Tom were now partially visible, yet their guns were drawn at both men, ordering the Bryants to lie facedown on the ground.

"Aw shit!" Jerry exclaimed. "I guess you boys are here to collect on the booze we just stole from you, I'd imagine?"

"Well, Jerry, you know what they say about grabbing a bull by the horns," Larry replied while smiling with contempt. "Gee, got a tipoff that you shot a horse, now I'm on your property following up—and look what we found here! Shoot, this much illegal moonshine will run a man nowadays ten years in the slammer. What do you think, Tom?"

"Yeah, Larry, I figure you're about right," Tom replied while smirking at Leo. "Well, Larry, I'd imagine you should radio ahead for backup now so we can go home!"

"Okay, Larry, you got us," Jerry stated. "Just take the moonshine and go. My god's honest word that we'll stay out of your business if we can let this one slide."

But Larry stood back and shook his head.

"You see, Jerry, there's this little word called *competition,* and you know what they say about that," Larry responded, laughing. "You see, when the competition is fierce, you have to eliminate it, and I believe you're the competitors!"

"Okay, Larry, point made," Jerry interrupted. "I've got twenty thousand dollars stashed away, and you can have it! Hell, we'll even load up the shine and drive it back for ya if you prefer."

Larry and Tom then huddled together and began whispering about the offer ole Jerry laid on the table. After a few moments, Larry returned and told Jerry that they had a deal. It was agreed that the Bryants would load the shine and cough up their peace offering to satisfy Wiley's dead horse. After about an hour, the Bryant boys had loaded up the shine, and they made their way to pick up the cash. Now Jerry Bryant might look as redneck as ever but was a smart man and never dealt with the banks, so he buried or hid his cash. Larry was very well aware of this fact and cuffed all the men, only to follow the Bryants to the cash stash spot.

After a short time, the men had finally arrived, and ole Jerry began to dig for the money. When he struck pay dirt, Jerry pulled out an old mason jar, only the contents were loaded down with the twenty thousand. As promised, Jerry coughed up the cash, with much disgust, and Larry radioed for Tom to drive ahead with the Bryant truck loaded with their missing shine. When Tom's headlights had appeared, Larry placed the men in the back and had Wiley sit up front, so there were no accidental misfires while the Bryants were being detained. The way back down to the valley floor was uneventful, and the boys were soon at Larry's patrol car. Little did they know that one of the Lower County deputies had spotted Larry's vehicle parked alongside the road earlier, so when the boys appeared, so did a brilliant barrage of police lights, shouting, and drawn weapons.

Anyhow, back to the present. After Tom had given a proper response to the deputy's question, Tom looked the young man in the eyes and smiled. "You know, son," Tom asserted, "the assholes had it coming, and the rest of you boys were spread throughout the county that Labor Day Saturday. I was just trying to do my part. I just didn't realize that the entire Lower County was going to show up with their party lights on!" Tom exclaimed, flashing a stern smile the deputy's way.

"You guys really got lucky finding all of that illegal moonshine," the officer continued. "You guys musta scored twenty gallons of that crap, yet the ATF came in and seized it from Larry after all, eh?"

Tom agreed with the deputy but laughed inside because the other tidbit that the officer didn't know was that the ATF agent was some dumb college kid the boys hired to reclaim their booze. That's a different story for a different time, though.

"Why hasn't the sheriff deputized you yet?" Deputy Thompson asked.

"Deputy," Tom replied while looking the officer sternly in the eyes, "we'd never git nothin' done, son! Hell, I'd have to move my office down to the Coyotes to git any work done."

The next question the deputy sheriff asked was concerning Tom's horse and urinating on him. The rancher reassured the boy that he was safe, so Deputy Thompson pulled out an apple from his lunch pail, placed it flatly in his hands, and moved it to Trigger's mouth; Trig, in reply, moved his head away.

"Try this," the rancher said and tossed the deputy a beer. "Mr. Wyatt, I'm much obliged, but I can't drink on the job," the deputy said, shrugging his shoulders.

"It's not for you, dipshit!" Tom replied. "It's for the goddamn horse." So the officer then cracked open the bottle, seeing the horse's head turn much more eagerly toward the beer. "Do I pour it in his mouth?" Deputy Thompson asked, and Tom told him to place the longneck in Trigger's mouth. So Thompson did as requested, curiously.

Taking the bottle, Trig popped his head up, chugging the beer down into an empty brown container. Now the deputy is amazed by the sudden affection of the rancher's horse, nestling his head on the officer's hand and neighing restlessly. The officer gave Tom a handshake laughingly, telling Tom how Trigger was one awesome horse, and hopped into his car, smiling. Moving along, Trig lifted his leg at the officer, neighing in a rare laugh, and proceeded down the road, horse trailer loaded down with illegal booze.

The day was beautiful, filled with the smell of fresh pine trees in the air and the late summer flowers, penetrating every sense of Tom's nose. Riding along, he heard the chirping of birds flying by and the gentle calm of the woods that was suddenly extinguished by some music blaring in the distance, in the form of an old Van Halen tune. When one hears classic rock on a stroll, they know that their close to Wil-E Coyotes.

Pulling up to the parking lot, Tom noticed fifteen Harley Davidson motorcycles lined up in a tidy line in the front and motioned Trigger to go in the back to unload. Approaching the back, the rancher spotted an old familiar friend rummaging through the garbage can. Chester, the brown bear, turned her head. Trigger paused cautiously yet dug his front heels in the ground, neighing, hot breath swirling in the air. The thing about Chester is that she's a bit of a fixture at the bar. She was an abandoned cub; in fact the mom probably got shot that same day. So Jennie started to feed her and never stopped. If you know anything about wild animals, it is that they feed like a tame one—only difference is that they're still wild and will attack without provocation. Now Chester gives out a warning growl, and in return, so Tom grabbed the apple that the deputy gave him and tossed it well into the tree line. That must have peaked Chester's curiosity because she bumbled away like a dog fetching a treat.

With Chester out of our hairs, Tom unhitched the trailer from Trigger, gave him a beer, and entered through the VIP entrance or the back door. Entering Wiley's, Tom smelled the aroma of tobacco floating through the air. Passing through the kitchen, he gave his salutations to Rob the cook then walked into the bar. Now if you can imagine a Washington state honky-tonk, this one resembled a hunter/stripper joint filled with animal heads of past kills, pictures of friends, customers of both past and present, also two stripper poles concocted on two adjoining small stages. Let me just say that strippers don't need much room to strut their stuff.

In fact, Wiley's definition of a stripper is just a customer who can go on the pole anytime and dance, clothes or none. However, as popularity grew, and the same women kept coming back, Wiley found it quite ingenious to let the nondancers offer tips to who may dance, giving the bar its infamous position. So we can see anyone from hot college girls to overweight patrons looking to take a picture. For situations where the women were not as attractive as the others, the customers watching enacted the "thumbs up, thumbs down" policy. So the catchphrase to Las Vegas very well applies to the bar as well because Wiley tries to make their stay as enjoyable and memorable as possible. Speaking of patrons, our favorite bikers had arrived and were hurdled up in a corner patiently, awaiting the first cute inebriated woman to come strolling in, looking to showcase her talents.

Jennie was busy, racing drinks over to the thirsty bikers, and everything was fine until one of the assholes decided to squeeze her butt cheek—which was immediately followed by a slap to the face then an aggressive tone of the perpetrator standing with a pissed, surprised look. Jennie motioned Tom to disperse the crowd, and she pulled away from the dipshit, only to get a hand on her turned-away shoulder, evolving to an arm around her neck.

"I wouldn't piss Jennie off," Tom stated and was met by all of the bumble heads standing up, laughing at the rancher, holding a baseball bat paused to strike.

From the jeering and foul language, Tom was beginning to sense that these idiots wanted to fight. So the rancher motioned over to Rob about the current issue afoot, and in response, the cook pulled out the AK-47 stashed away below the kitchen window.

"You should let the woman go before she hurts ya," Tom expressed. All of the sudden, the idiot holding Jennie pulled a knife, sticking the blade near her neck and demanded that the cook drop the gun. However, before he could say anything else, Jennie grabbed the knife and elbowed him in the nose, breaking it, with blood streaming down the prospect's face.

"Fucking idiots," Jennie stated aggressively and walked back to the bar, with Rob standing by Tom's side. Finally, they had an equal footing with the bikers, and Tom suggested a beer for each of them (on the house, of course) and explained the ingredients in the brew, only to get some angrily relaxed bikers, except for the hurt prospect that Tom and the biker president intentionally set up.

"You think we put on a good show for the tourists?" one biker jokingly asked.

"I think we put on a better show for your prospect." Then Tom added, "You mind telling me why you assholes are late"?

The president of the club laughed and rushed toward the rancher with a handshake. The club pres then apologized for his prospects actions and explained the reason for their tardiness. Tom approached the man who got elbowed, bar towel in hand, and applied it to his freshly broken nose. Suggesting he could go to a doctor, the prospect refused such a notion. Jennie took a look the nose, and she noticed that it was broken, so the gal retrieved an ice pack for the prospects hurt pride.

"Don't I get some pain medicine?" the biker asked, but instead of some strong morphine which was stashed away in the back of Wiley's office, Jennie tossed him the ice pack and a complimentary jar of shine.

"This one's on the house, asshole," she jested, smiling satisfied, looking at the prospect with a stern gaze that only a bartender could give a customer, and the biker took the alcohol with no further resentment. With the Yellow Jackets at bay and the tourists rested, Rob removed the assault rifle and disappeared back into the kitchen. Tom made his way back to the booze that was just delivered and grabbed a cooler packed full of Wiley's buzz beer, setting the bikers up accordingly.

The time was about five in the afternoon, and more people began to stream in, thirsty from the toils of their day, and so did the college girls who recently moved back to Ellensburg to start their education, looking to party and make an extra buck. Wiley's reasoning is that you should love the work that you perform—so being a waitress, bartender, or even a patron, should be no different; thus allowing the employees to literally drink on the job. He actually has a little campground setup that originally started with a few campers and rundown RVs, but Wiley pieced them together for the employees, which evolved to a site where the customers can park and camp, if they so desire. Wiley coined the phrase, "If the spouse is a bitchin', get your tent a pitchin'." He always had great ideas to meet the patrons' needs because when you show up to the Coyotes, you're gonna get drunk, or worse. So why not give the customers the benefit of the doubt? Larry also loved the RV park because it keeps the calls down so the sheriff's office can concentrate on other facets of law enforcement, as well as keeping attention off the bar.

Now with everything beginning to settle down to the normal chaos on a Sunday of a three-day weekend, the bikers ordered more beer (which was ten bucks a bottle but worth every penny). The brew began to take its desired effect, with laughing and taunting the younger women to take a ride on the pole; to which a hottie replied by going up to the stage, while a biker put change into the jukebox picking Van Halen's classic "Beautiful Girl."

The Yellow Jackets might have a bad reputation, but at least they have great taste in music. After a decent performance from the beginner, the whole audience cheered, giving the young vixen a thumbs-up, increasing her confidence with about twenty-five dollars in her panties. Now this enterprise that our three main characters had going on with the Yellow Jackets has been very fruitful, but they were wild and reckless, making the ole boys business together rather complicated. The president of the club, Terror, is named appropriately because if you cross him, that's one thing; but if double cross him, he will bring nothing but terror.

Speaking of which, their friendship started about four years ago. Terror was traveling to Wenatchee from California when he found himself on the side of the road with a flat tire. Seeing the man in the cruel summer heat, Tom happened to pass by the distraught biker and offered his services. Seeing that the man was a patched biker, Tom talked to Terror about where he needed to go. The rancher offered up his place to stay for the night, but Terror was in a rush. Little did Terror know that the rancher would loan him one of the sheriff's bikes that the current officer did not need because the deputy was in the station, preoccupied with a new secretary. So Tom did what every good man would do and called up Larry. After explaining the biker's plight, Larry protested at first but made an exception due to the fact that the biker's father only had hours to live. So Larry ended up escorting Terror to Wenatchee, and Tom heard that they reached their destination in forty minutes. Larry tends to exaggerate from time to time, but timing was everything, and that officer trying to get secretary tail was hated by yours truly.

Officer Morrison (or Moron, as Tom calls him) is one of those bad apples that was at the time, running in that year's sheriffs election. I'll explain his asshole demeanor later.

So the next day came around and the two men return, emergency lights flashing, pulling up to Tom's ranch. By that time, Tom's ranch hands had repaired Terror's tire, and he was awestruck by the kindness that Larry and Tom both showed him. Thus, a firm handshake had sealed a new friendship, and a new connection that would help facilitate their shine-running enterprise. They have been in business for some time now, and the Yellow Jackets have been great associates, yet Larry and Tom didn't realize at the time how the bikers kept drawing attention to the facets of the business. From dodging Officer Moran's bullshit, to an incident a year back where the Jackets were being investigated for running cocaine and weapons, they all came to a general agreement to turn the Yellow Jackets from that of a shoot 'em up, drug-dealing lifestyle to a more adventurous venture.

Anyhow, the prospect didn't know what Terror had planned for him, but nonetheless, the bikers and Tom's crew put on a good show for the tourists in the bar. A Midwestern gal and her hubby took some good selfies with the crew and the gang, even after they shit themselves. The bar has always been a spot for screwing with people, and pissed off prospects are not the only ones off limits—especially the regulars. Hell, there's this one patron that comes in for a drink every day, and he appreciates the attention Wiley's gives the poor fool, even if it's the little things like shaking up the patron's beer.

With everything settling down to its busy normal pace, Tom helped Jennie bar back and Rob was a flutter, cooking for the customers. After the craziness of the night simmered down to a dead crawl, Tom sat there at the bar in his normal drunken posture, doing impressions of Wiley and Larry during the snake encounter, making Terror and his crew laugh hysterically. After tallying up the till, Jennie gave the rancher the "it's time to pick up LJ" sign and departed. Rob and the bikers soon followed suit, retiring to the campground, while the empty bar echoed the jukebox, playing Tesla's "Love Song." Tom Wyatt might be a country man, but it doesn't necessarily mean that he has to listen to country. It was his grandpa's staple, and after Gene's passing, it was too hard to listen to the memories of Waylon Jennings, Johnny Cash, and Pam Tillis; so Tom fell back to listening to the classic rock music from his dad's bar so long ago.

Just when Tom was going to lock the door, a stranger walked into the Coyote wearing a nice suit and looked very tired. The rancher motioned for the man to sit at the bar, and he plopped down looking like the ole boy had just escaped from a church meeting. Don't get me wrong, Tom is not a racist by any means. But the man looked like he was an equatorial Southerner and looked like he needed a beer, so Tom obliged.

"What's your name, stranger?" Tom asked, looking at him chug down the bottle.

"Juan, and thank you for the beer," he said, shaking Tom's hand and weathering off the long day he had before showing up to the bar.

"So what brings you to Wil-E Coyotes?" Tom asked with curiosity while fetching another beer for the thirsty traveler.

"Well, I'm looking for the owner. I've come a long way from Mexico and heard that Wiley Holloway has a bar up here," Juan said cautiously.

"That's a long way to come up to a redneck tittie bar, and I believe Wiley's on a little vacation right now," Tom replied, trying not to give too much away for Wiley's sake.

"Do you know when he will be back, *hombre*?" Juan remarked.

"Well, Juan, honestly, he's been gone for a couple of months. He tends to go off on some jaunt here and there and eventually comes back, but if you need to talk to a co-owner, I can help," the rancher replied.

"Good," Juan said. "Then maybe you can help me find a piece of equipment, Mister Wiley is behind on…" he said, staring seriously now into Tom's unfazed eyes.

"Oh yeah, what kind of equipment?" the rancher asked curiously.

"A German panzer tank," the traveler replied, moving his hands nervously now.

"Wish I knew about that. I never really had Wiley pegged as a World War II collector," Tom said with a cheesy grin. "I can't even say that I've been to his property either, or I would take you up there and you can haul it back down to Tijuana in your vehicle. Or do you have something bigger?"

Realizing that Juan didn't have the temper to put up with Tom's bullshit, he flashed his 9mm handgun safely tucked away in the gangster's holster. The surprised rancher relented and took a step back because he only had his trusty thirty commando knife. How does the old saying go? "Don't bring a knife to a gunfight, you'll lose every time"? Now seeing that the tone had changed, Juan looked at Tom in that overpriced suit waiting for the inebriated rancher to say one more thing to piss the tired traveler off so the man could use his piece. He then grabbed Tom by the shoulders with both hands and laughed in an arrogant, hysterical tone.

"You are funny, my friend," Juan stated. "By the way, you never told me what your name was."

"Tom," the rancher replied, smiling, hoping not to give away his last name.

"You know," Juan stated, "There is a *vaquero* in your county that's a legend by the name of a Tom Wyatt, and also I hear this legend is friends with Wiley. Also, this is Wiley's bar and you're the only one in here closing whose named is Tom. Is it just me, or is that a coincidence?" Juan exclaimed, looking at the rancher more seriously.

"Yeah, I know the asshole, so what's it to you?" Tom bracingly replied, only to be met with a direct punch to the face. Falling to the floor, Tom landed on his back hard, almost knocking the wind out of the rancher's lungs, while staring down the barrel of Juan's 9mm. The only thing Tom could remember the rest of that night was the asshole wishing the drunk fool a good night and a pistol whip to the head as Tom faded fast asleep in a shroud of instant black.

As Terror was taking a drunken piss on the side of the bar, he heard the commotion playing inside. Not being sober enough to logically call out to his crew, he rushed inside the bar and pulled his pistol on Juan, then in turn, the thug pointed his gun at an unconscious Tom's head.

"Drop your gun now, *senor*, or you'll be mopping this man up off the floor," Juan demanded, and little be it for Terror to put a good friend's life in jeopardy.

Slowly, the biker lowered his gun to the ground and kicked it over to Juan. The thug then ordered Terror to drag the rancher outside to the parking lot and did so with no resistance. Grabbing another buzz beer, Juan followed Terror outside but was starting to feel a little stoned from drinking the beer and began to stutter his step. Outside, the two hostages were at the mercy of the vicious gangster and in his inebriated state, finished his beer, then cracked open another drinking it quickly.

"I think you picked a bad time to come interfering in Senor Wyatt's business," Juan remarked.

"Hey, I'm cool, brother," Terror replied. "I just heard a ruckus and went to see if everything was okay."

Seeing that Juan was succumbing to the buzz beer, Terror offered to go inside for another one, but Juan didn't trust him. The gangster promised to kill Terror where he sat if the biker moved an inch, so Juan proceeded into the bar slowly. When he was out of sight, a drunken Terror bolted for the campground, but while he was running, he tripped over a tree root poking out of the ground and fell, instantly knocking himself out cold. Well, I suppose things could be worse for our hero and his biker buddy because Juan did succumb to that beer and passed out on the bar.

Chapter 4

The Hidden Spaniard

It's kind of a weird feeling when you're drunk and get pistol-whipped. It happened so fast; and you don't feel the initial shock, only the fading of thought as your brain shuts down to help the head heal. When one finally wakes up, whether it's been for minutes or hours, the unbearable headache is all you can think about. Even more so when a Mexican mafia member is sitting in front of you, waving a gun in your face, and talking on his cell phone in Spanish to whomever it is that he answers too.

Anyhow, there Tom lay regaining his consciousness, with his hands tied from the back, his pounding head bleeding, and wondered when Larry was going to come by and shoot this prick.

Then it occurred to the rancher that Larry was, more than likely, in his bed banging the missus, probably with his walkie-talkie off. The tone in Juan's voice talking on the phone and flailing his arms up in the air, cursing in some Spanish/English tone, only made Tom's poor head feel worse. After the thug's phone conversation, he untied the rancher, still pointing his gun behind Tom's back, directing the cowboy to go to the back of the bar. So Tom followed suit. The two men headed out into the cool still night while Tom's head hurt from the hit to the cranium that the prick gave him. Nonetheless, the Spanish thug ordered Tom into the back of the bar while he could only wish that help would come from the commotion that was about to ensue.

"How's your head, *vaquero*?" Juan mumbled, starting to realize that the bottle of beer that Tom initially gave him was taking its desired effect. Juan then lost his balance and fell to the ground but recovered quickly, not taking his weapon off the rancher. Tom noticed Juan's once-aggressive demeanor change to one of a long lost friend, looking to chat. Still flailing his piece next to Tom (but less sporadically and more mellow than ever), he asked, "Senor Wyatt, I truly apologize to you for all of this, but I have a business to maintain and this is nothing personal."

"That's okay, Juan," Tom responded. "I'm being taken hostage by a prick in a classy suit, so this is a piece of cake!"

Juan looked Tom in the face, almost reassuringly and said, "You know, senor, I'm not the type of man to kill and do such horrible things. In fact, I think we might be able to help each other out. That was my father on the phone that I was talking to, and we had a big argument. Let's just say that I want out of my father's dealings, so maybe we can strike an agreement!" Juan then grabbed a fat stack of cash out of the inner lining of his jacket and offered Tom not only that, but offered the rancher four more of the same denomination. All Tom could think at that particular moment was that he was tempted, surely. Wanted it, absolutely. Going to do it, possibly—if the stoned thug was just going to give it away.

"You know, Juan," Tom reiterated, "I might just be mistaken, but are you bribing me?"

"Everybody has a price," Juan jested. "Even you, Senor Wyatt. And for the life of your friend, this is what I offer to you in return!"

Seeing that this was going nowhere, in one of Juan's drunken/stoned spins of the handgun, Tom easily secured the weapon and pointed it at Juan's head. He stood up at a safe shooting distance so that the thug couldn't retake his firearm. Tom instructed Juan to get up, but the fool was reluctant at first—up until the rancher offered him a tour of Wiley's farm (and a beer). With that being said, Juan rose, and Tom holstered his weapon and grabbed the thirty commando knife hiding it under his arm.

"You know, Juan, everybody has a price...even me, but I'm not about to sacrifice my integrity for an asshole in an expensive suit. I'm about respect and giving respect when it is earned. If Wiley owes you for a tank, then he will pay it back. Yet at the same time, I believe in a firm handshake, and when a deal is made, Wiley needs to follow it up honorably. So do you wanna earn my respect, or do we need to get on with killing each other?" Tom humbly asked.

"What do you want from me?" Juan replied. "It's just that I've never experienced kindness like this before, considering what I did to your head."

Tom replied, "I just want to help Wiley out. He might be crazy, but he's still a great friend. So if you want something tangible to tell your boss, I'm going to need your cell phone turned off, any weapons that you might have in your possession, and your trust if you can indulge me?"

Holding his hand out in friendship, Juan embraced the rancher's hand, and Tom knew that just as long as he could keep Juan stoned, they would be fine to head out to Wiley's. So Juan and Tom made their way out to the back where Trigger was sleeping, and Juan refused to get on him, for fear of horse hair in his suit. Tom told Juan that he could take his car up to Wiley's, but he wouldn't make it to the house because of the booby traps. Juan shrugged his shoulders, agreed, and hopped on Trig. It's not very often that Tom had a passenger, so it meant Trigger may get a little frustrated with the extra weight, but anything at that point was better than getting impaled or blown up by Wiley's doing.

It was about three in the morning when they made their way up to Wiley's farm. Tom brought some extra beer for his new companion and meandered their way up to the entrance to Wiley's property. Telling Juan about the "no outsider" policy, he agreed to be bound by rope and blindfolded as a precaution because Tom knew that Wiley was not going to be a happy camper. At any rate, Tom secured Juan, and the two men made their way past the creek by Wiley's bridge and trotted up to the farm. Once the rancher arrived with Juan, it was mere seconds before Wiley stirred out of his bed (assault rifle in hand) and came outside to see Tom's newly tied-up friend sitting cautiously on the horse.

"You know, Tom, you're slowly getting on my shit list!" Wiley exclaimed. "Who in the hell is this, and why is he tied up and blindfolded?"

"This is one of your Southern associates where you purchased the tank from," Tom retorted. "I believe that he has a way outta this mess you're in with his boss, and I think we should listen to what he has to say," the rancher stated, not knowing that Juan had fallen asleep on Trigger.

"Tom," Wiley remarked. "You might have just broken one of our laws about outsiders, but if he's offering me a way out, I think we're gonna hafta hear this kid. With that being said, Tom, he's still a Mexi-mob member, and he'd better not backstab us with his bullshit!"

"Well, Wiley, if you put any Mexican mobster in a fancy suit out in a field of dope, you're going to see those brown eyes of his turn green," Tom added.

"You know, Tom, my eyes are already green," Wiley stupidly replied, not realizing that the rancher was referring to Juan. "Aren't yours green too, Tom?"

"Wiley, I meant that his eyes would turn the color of greed," Tom stated and left it at that.

So after a debate on where Juan would be sleeping that morning, Tom dismounted Juan off Trigger and laid him on the hammock outside the porch, still fully passed out. Wiley asked Tom why he brought Juan here, but the rancher reluctantly told him that he had no options and that Juan was looking to skim some cash on the side, off their operation. Little did Wiley know that Tom was just telling the crazy ole goat what he wanted to hear, but Juan still had every intention of taking Wiley back if the deal fell through. With the field of dope Wiley was getting ready to harvest, it was also an initiative to further keep ole Juan quiet and Wiley's tank paid. In agreement, Wiley led Tom to the kitchen for an early breakfast. They ate farm fresh eggs, toast, and bacon from a hog Wiley had slaughtered the other day. After their meal, feeling tired with a headache, Tom lay down on the couch and closed his weary eyes, wondering what kind of crap lied in wait for them that day.

With the passing of the dawn, Tom's diminished headache was woken by the sounds of cursing and broken glass. The rancher figured that Wiley and Juan were already in disagreement about his debt, but the swearing came from a woman's voice. Running out to the porch, the rancher witnessed Jennie yelling at Juan.

"You fucking bastard," Jennie shouted, pushing Juan who was still tied up. "Why did you run out on me?" Jennie angrily shouted.

She pulled the blind off his face and a shocked Juan said, "Jennie, it was my father and the family business! I wanted to be with you, but Father forced me away. I'm sorry."

And with that being said, Jennie stormed into the kitchen and grabbed a fresh bottle of shine, sobbing sadly at the table. With all the commotion, Wiley ran into the kitchen and held Jennie, drying the tears streaming down her face.

"How do you know this man, Jennie, and I'm guessing that Juan is LJ's dad?" Wiley asked. There was a long blank stare on Jennie's face. She turned toward her father and nodded her head. Now with all the emotion falling out of poor Jennie's heart, Wiley pulled out a knife in the kitchen and gave Tom the "I'm going to kill this prick now" look and ran out to the porch with the knife at his side. With the blade clenched tightly, Wiley drew a breath and raised the deadly blade into the air. Yet before the knife could pierce the flesh of the frightened man, a hand came out from nowhere, clinging on to Wiley's shirt. Terrified and crying, LJ begged him, "Grandpa you're not going to kill this man, are you?"

Wiley was suddenly taken off guard by his granddaughter's sudden advance, so the old man paused and smiled at her.

"Oh darling, I wasn't going to hurt Juan, silly," Wiley replied reluctantly. "I was just coming outside to free the man of his bonds."

Wiley wasted no time cutting the rope off Juan's wrists. It then occurred to Juan who the little girl was, and he embraced his daughter for the first time, holding her tight. Rejoiced over the fact that circumstances led Juan to his estranged girlfriend and child, Juan began to cry. With a quirky grin on his face, Wiley patted Tom on the back, and they disappeared into the kitchen, where it appeared that Jennie was now holding a sharp blade.

"He might be an asshole," Wiley stated, "but that little girl is in his arms right now, Jennie. I think you should hear him out."

"Why should I, Dad?" Jennie exclaimed. "I'm just supposed to forget the fact that he dumped me, when the asshole found out that I was pregnant!"

"Jennie, take a look out the window," Wiley told Jennie, and she peered out the glass looking at a happy girl and her father, bonding.

"He's lucky LJ came with me," Jennie happily sobbed and dropped the knife. "I may learn to forgive, but I will never forget what happened in Mexico!"

With the crisis averted, everybody came outside to the porch where Juan and LJ were sitting, and Jennie pulled up a chair. Juan whispered some Spanish tune in his little daughter's ear, and LJ was transfixed by the sweet melody. After Juan was done singing, LJ rose and disappeared into the kitchen to get something to drink for her father and herself. Jennie sat down next to her estranged lover and stated, "I don't give a fuck what you think is going to happen here, but I'm guessing that you're here to hurt my dad. Well, that's not gonna happen. In fact, if you wanna see LJ even five minutes from now, you need lie to your father and do whatever it takes to keep my dad alive. *Comprendhe*?"

Juan looked into her eyes and gently brushed his fingers against her face but was hesitant, and Jennie pulled away. "Jennie, this was meant to be," Juan replied. "If we never fall back in love, I understand, but I promise that I will spend the rest of my life making this up to you!" With that being said, Jennie smiled at Juan, and rose out of her chair to go inside the house.

Jennie had mentioned cooking breakfast, and Juan obliged by helping out. As Wiley and Tom sat under the porch wondering what the hell just happened, a thought occurred to Tom how Wiley could make finances right with Juan's father.

"You know, Wiley, we could give the weed to the Yellow Jackets, and they can figure out to get rid of the pot from there," Tom stated. "You easily have two million in change out in the field."

"It was stupid of me to purchase the tank, Tom," Wiley said. "I know that I may be a little crazy, it's just everything's going wrong with the world. It makes me think that I'm stupid if I'm not prepared."

Tom agreed with the poor guy. The rancher knew that things weren't right with the world, also sometimes life being the way it is, it can drive anybody crazy. Even someone who's already been diagnosed as a schizophrenic with bipolar tendencies. Sometimes we have to remember the good things about life, and not the people in suits not properly doing their job. So Tom felt it appropriate to reinforce this upon poor Wiley and told him that a two-million bill owed to

Mexican mafia for a tank tended to draw attention to an operation, yet Wiley had to make good on his word and pay the debt off.

Medical marijuana card or not, they had some major work to do and thought it was appropriate to have a talk with the Yellow Jackets. So Wiley and Tom took off and headed back to the bar, leaving the recently reunited family to their own devices. The boys showed up to the camp out where some bikers sat and drank coffee, hung over from the night before. Tom asked where Terror was, and his men said that their president was busy, which means in biker chat that he was getting some tail. So Wiley and Tom left ole Terror to his date and headed into the bar to Wiley's office. The boys sat down and had a drink and Wiley pulled some cash out of the safe for Tom.

"Jesus, Tom," Wiley exclaimed. "This is the fifth run of the season that you did for me. You've been running a lot! Here's your twenty grand, Tom." He handed the cowboy over the fat wad of bills.

"Thank you, Wiley," Tom replied and grabbed the cash.

"So how's business on the ranch?" Wiley asked.

"It's going okay," Tom added. "We're moving cattle to the winter grounds in the next couple of days so ill be helping out. Do you want to tag along?"

"No, Tom, I'm going to hang out here and keep the customers happy, but thanks for the offer," Wiley replied.

A couple of minutes later, there was a knock at the door. Terror came in with a huge smile on his face and sat down telling the guys about the conquests of the night before. Tom personally doesn't get the biker code when it comes to women because Terror's married, so to each his own. After having a meeting about the shipment, Wiley found out that Terror had a surprise for him when their van showed up to get the booze, and Wiley was excited. The Yellow Jackets have always been good to Wiley when dealing in arms so you could imagine the look on ole Wiley's face.

The van showed up a couple of hours later delayed, with a couple of prospects tired from the long drive. Tom and Wiley went to the back of the van, and when they opened the doors, Wiley's grin was priceless. In the back sat a Dillon Aero M-134 minigun and ten thousand rounds of ammo. You don't see Wiley cry very often, but Tom swears to this day that he saw a teardrop fall from Wiley's eye, in appreciation of the kindness shown by the MC. Impatiently, Wiley took the gun, and the rancher hauled out some ammo to an adjacent field where Wiley had some rusty cars. With the ammo loaded and the safety off, Wiley gave the biggest grin and pulled the trigger.

The minigun is an impressive weapon for those that don't know. The gun fires a 7.34 caliber NATO round from two thousand to four thousand bullets per minute. Let's just say that after a minute, Wiley was done, and the cars were truly holy. Wiley offered Tom a turn, but the rancher politely refused. Tom's very old-fashioned when it comes down to guns. In fact, he still has that German Luger holstered appropriately by his side currently.

Now by this point, more customers started rolling into the bar, and Tom decided to grab a bite to eat before the trek home. The cowboy was not exactly a cell phone guy, so the rancher figured that Maddy and the kids were wondering where the rancher was and had business to attend to at the ranch. On the other hand, Tom's walkie-talkie wasn't charged, and Maddy knew where to get ahold of the rancher this time of the day. So sitting at the bar, Rob brought Tom a BLT with coleslaw, and he started to eat when a gentleman in a business suit entered the bar. Honestly, all Tom could think was that Cavasos sent another thug to oversee his affairs. So the man sat next to Tom, ordered a soda, and grabbed a menu, sifting through it profusely like a food critic and asked, "What's good to eat around here?"

Tom humbly told the stranger that the broasted chicken was a delight, and the man took Tom's advice. Noticing his Caucasian appearance settled the rancher better, but tucked away under his jacket, Tom noticed a gun and a badge.

"Where ya from?" Tom asked while grabbing his knife and tucked it away by his leg, as to avoid a possible attack.

"I'm from Seattle and not here to startle anybody, but I'm with the United States Marshal Service doing some investigating around this area. My name is Elijah Evans," the marshal politely stated and reached out his hand for a shake.

Starting to feel the weight of his involvement in certain current crimes, the rancher replied, "Marshal service, eh? Who ya looking for?"

"Our field office in Laredo, Texas, informed me that a Mexican national with ties to the Cavasos cartel is in the area." He then pulled out a picture of ole Juan. “His father, Isidro, is the boss and sent his son up here to collect on a debt.”

“A debt for what?” Tom asked curiously while sipping his beer nice and slow.

“Oh some idiot bought a piece of military hardware from the Cavasos and never fully paid them, so there’s a Mexican enforcer running around Kittitas County looking for the guy,” the marshal stated.

“Do you know who the guy is?” Tom asked the marshal even more cautiously.

“No. The marshal service doesn’t have that information currently, but when we find Senor Cavasos, we’ll find the buyer,” the marshal stated. “You’re sure a very curious individual,” Ellijah commented, now looking at Tom with a smirk.

The rancher then replied, “My friend’s the county sheriff, and I’m sure he would like to talk to you about mafia types and such.”

“Yes! I’ve arranged a meeting with Larry today at his office. And who did you say your name was?” Marshal Evans asked curiously.

“Tom Wyatt, sir.” The rancher calmly announced then reached out his hand to shake the marshal’s, only to find a confused look on the man’s face.

“Aren’t you a legend around these parts?” Evans graciously asked while a huge grin began to develop.

“Yeah. I’ve been known to raise a little Caine every once in a while,” the rancher stated, and with the introduction, Tom turned back to finish his meal, only with sweat starting to drop from his brow.

Then Wiley came over, but before he could say anything, Tom interrupted, “Hey, Wiley. This gentleman is a U.S. marshal who’s looking for this man.” The nervous rancher then passed the photo to Wiley who stared at the photo like a child in a puppy palace.

Wiley, playing it smart, acted dumb yet curiously informing Tom that Jennie and her boyfriend were on their way to the bar. All the rancher could do was finish his meal, say the appropriate goodbyes, and hop on Trigger hoping to find Jennie and Juan before the marshal did.

Riding harder than ever, Tom and Trigger kept to the main road. With Tom’s heart beating faster than Trigger’s, he spotted Jennie’s car racing down the road, so Tom brought Trigger to a sudden halt, hopped off the horse, and blocked Jennie's rapid advance. The two exited the car in a panic, so Tom approached a confused Jennie and met the rancher halfway. Tom then informed Jennie about the marshal who was eating his meal at the bar, looking for Juan.

"Jesus Christ, Tom!" Jennie yelled. "We were two miles from the bar. What the fuck is going on here?"

"Jennie, you need to get Juan back out to Wiley's and keep him hidden, or there's nothing else anyone can do. Even Larry can't know about Juan's whereabouts until I've filled him in," Tom stated. "Just tell Juan to stay out there and not leave for anything. I have to head home and prep things for the cattle drive coming up."

With that being said, Jennie agreed and hopped back into her car then peeled out, going back the direction from which the motorist came. Tom then grabbed a beer for Trigger and himself smiling like a robber that just avoided the cops, while proceeding down the road, like everything was normal.

When the two arrived back at the Windy River Ranch, everything was surprisingly quiet and peaceful. Maddy had to go to Ellensburg to meet with her pastor, and the kids went as well. So Tom made his way out to the office to check on things. There's always something going on at the ranch, even if it's not busy. From the workers toiling around, to cattle getting out of their pens, it's quite relaxing to be a part of something that Tom's grandpa helped build. In the staging area, there's some ranchers setting up vaccinations to get the cattle ready for the twenty-mile trek to the train in Ellensburg while a pissed off Rufalo, who lost his winnings at the poker game, glared at his boss as Tom simply tipped his hat, walking ever closer towards the rancher's fortress of solitude.

Tom decided to head to the desk and review some bills and prepare paychecks for the ranch hands, trying to do anything to look busy and ignore the fact that a marshal was poking his head around the rancher's other business. After the rancher finished up with the finances, he decided to kick up his spurs and watch some television. Tom wasn't much of a TV guy, but sometimes it's relaxing to watch a baseball game or watch a good movie. Turning it on, Tom started flipping it through the channels, noticing that the news was on, and was complacent with that—until the news anchor switched over to a press conference at the Kittitas County courthouse with Larry and the marshal standing right next to him. Can you imagine how this was going to go?

After watching the show Larry and the marshal put on, Tom realized that this wasn't going to end well for Juan and that they had to move the pot quickly. Harvest time or not, it was imperative to deal with Wiley's troubles in an urgent fashion, or the marshal would be looking for the rancher next. All of the sudden, the walkie-talkie that was charging crackled to life, in the form of Wiley freaking out. Tom told the frantic man to calm down and come over to the ranch, which Wiley followed suit. After half an hour of waiting, the roar of several Harleys screamed down the drive, right up to the office. Apparently, Wiley needed a ride, so Terror and the boys picked Wiley up in the front of his driveway. Then, just as the desperation of the situation with Juan hit Tom, a light bulb began to glow in the rancher's head. The Yellow Jackets can move the weed for Wiley, and Tom knew exactly what to say.

Wiley, Terror, and a few brothers of the MC came inside to talk, so Tom graciously passed around some beers and everybody grabbed a seat. Wiley immediately began complaining about Juan after seeing what they had witnessed on the television. Wiley started calling Larry a NARC and Tom reassured him that the sheriff had just as much of a stake in all of this too. Remember, the MC had just loaded up the shipment, and they were doing it while the marshal was eating his chicken and the lawman was quickly on Wiley's trail. To make matters worse, Jennie, LJ, and Juan just showed up. When Juan came into the office, let's just say that you could hear water from the kitchenette faucet drip and a fly buzz behind Tom's ear. Everybody began yelling and shouting at him, thus the situation turned uncivil in a hurry.

Tom, seeing no other option, shouted at the top of his lungs, "Everybody stop and quiet down!"

The room temporarily paused, and the rancher added, "You know, Wiley, if ya didn't purchase that damn Panzer from Juan's dad, we wouldn't be knee-deep in cow shit right now. I have a plan, but it must be put into effect right away." The rancher then looked at Terror and stated, "Wiley's got a shitload of marijuana growing in his backyard, and we need to move it fast."

"Fuck yeah, Wiley," Terror added and gave him a fist bump. "Tom, I'll tell you what, I gotta take that shit down to So Cal, but when I get there, the pot will sell quick. I'll need a week at least. We're gonna want a cut, of course."

"Wiley, Terror's our best option here to make that cash you need to pay off your damn tank, but we need to harvest the Mary Jane—pronto," Tom stated. "Do you have any objections?"

"Well, the buds are pretty big," Wiley remarked. "I guess we could harvest the crop. But who's gonna help?" And just like that, all of the bikers raised their hands, shouting, "I will!"

It's kind of funny how things can seem so desperate, and then they hit a high again. The only thing that could screw this up right now is if Larry and the marshal show up; and apparently Tom's high was short lived because glancing through his window, he saw no other than the two least people he wanted to see at that particular moment. Automatic panic set in with everyone, so Tom's quick mind sparked to life and he told the MC that they were here to pick up a butchered cow they had recently purchased. As for Juan, Tom redirected him out of the back door and instructed the Mexican to go mix in with the hired help. The rancher managed to pull out a receipt book and started writing when the two lawmen came in the door.

"Howdy, Larry and Marshal Evans!" Tom said while writing at a nice calm pace. "Gentlemen, here's your receipt, and thank you for buying a cow from us. I hope you have a great barbecue. Now if you boys don't mind, I have to chat with my old friend Larry and the marshal."

"Absolutely, Mr. Wyatt," Terror replied. "We're gonna take Wiley home and start preparing the cow." With that being said, Wiley and the MC departed.

Now the look on the marshal's face was priceless but concerning.

"That's the Yellow Jackets MC," Evans stated. I wonder what they're doing so far up north?"

"The main guy Terror has family in Yakima, and I guess they're having a family reunion," Tom reiterated while kicking his feet up on the desk.

"Those guys are pretty bad, Tom," the marshal said. "You shouldn't do business with people like that," he stated with a worried look on his face.

"I didn't know that," Tom replied. "They stopped at the Coyotes to wet their whistles and were referred by the owner, but thank you for the information. I'll keep that one handy."

Then the marshal asked, "If those bikers are on their motorcycles, how are they going to carry the cow?"

"They already loaded the cow up earlier this morning. Musta had a family member come in to haul it away," Tom said. "So what brings you two here on this fine day?"

"Well, Tom," Larry snorted. "The marshal met you at Wiley's, and we got to talking, and I thought I'd bring him out here to see the Windy River Ranch."

"Your timings perfect, prick," Tom snickered while tucking a bottle of moonshine farther under the desk with his foot.

Larry then smiled and the sheriff graciously flipped Tom off behind the marshal's back. The rancher offered to show Marshal Evans around but offered up some bullshit excuse about Maddy coming home any minute and that he had a million things to do. In agreement to view the ranch at another time, the rancher parted ways with a handshake and the two lawmen made their way to the sheriff's patrol car. Larry, in fact, glanced over Tom's direction, only to be met with another middle finger. With everybody gone, Tom once again kicked up his spurs, grabbed a cold one, and wondered what in the hell he was going to do with Juan.

After sitting in the office for a bit, Tom heard the telephone ring. It was Larry apologizing for the whole marshal incident, and the rancher naturally accepted it. Larry informed Tom that Wiley was coming back over to drink and discuss the upcoming harvest. Tom figured he'd better fire up the barbecue and cook up some pork ribs that Maddy left out. So the rancher took a drink of shine and grabbed a fresh beer then left the office. Walking to the porch, Tom saw Trigger outside grazing on the pasture and went over to see how his friend was doing. Trigger looked at Tom and came over wanting brushed, so the cowboy grabbed a horse comb out of the stall and combed his horse thoroughly.

As Tom brushed his trusty steed, Juan spotted the rancher and approached the cowboy laughing. Juan then put his hand on Trigger's mane and offered to brush the horse, so Tom obliged.

"Tom, Trigger is a mighty impressive horse," Juan exclaimed as he continued to brush the mustang.

"Thank you, Juan," the rancher replied. "I originally got the beast from an Indian chief. Trigger was just a foal barely waned off of his momma's tit and was very much by her side, at least till our eyes met. The foal took one look at me and came running over. Even the chief knew that we were bonded from that point on, so Trigger left with me that same day."

"It's not very often that something as special like that happens," Juan replied with a smile. "I just want to say Mister Wyatt that you're a lucky man to have the life you do. I'd like to think that I could help out on your ranch, when all of this crap blows over."

"Just like when you saw LJ for the first time. You knew that you were bonded with your daughter, like Trigger and myself," Tom stated. "Just as long as you're on my side, Juan, who am I to tear you away from LJ?"

Juan then smiled and hugged Tom, which was something he wasn't expecting, but the cowboy always had a big heart and was not one to brush people aside under such circumstances.

"So how did my daughter get her name?" Juan curiously asked and Tom snorted in laughter.

"Well, Juan, Lupita Jr. was named after my mother-in-law," Tom replied. "Lupita delivered LJ on the way to the hospital, as a matter of fact. Lupita actually used to be a nurse practitioner, so she was kinda like a nurse that told the doctors what to do, under certain diagnoses. So delivering LJ was just another walk in the park."

"What an amazing woman," Juan exclaimed. "I must thank her for this act of kindness. I just wished I could have been there to see the birth of my child." Then Juan slowly lowered his head.

Tom looked upon Juan and cracked a smile, then replied, "Wiley had a camcorder and filmed the birth, at least till he passed out from watching Jennie squeeze little LJ out of the woman's who-who."

Both men started to laugh, and Juan thought it best to watch the video a little later down the line. The heartfelt Southerner did feel like he needed to have a word of kindness with Lupita, so he shook Tom's hand and departed for the house, leaving Tom still smiling over that story. When Tom was done brushing Trigger, he headed to the porch to sit down and drink a cold beer that he grabbed out of a cooler nearby. After a few minutes of quiet, Tom's peace was suddenly shattered by a rumbling noise just north of the property line. Tom quickly sprang to his feet as the rancher witnessed the trees starting to shake back and forth, then a huge metallic object appeared as it became visible, leaving the brush of the forest.

Several other people began to take notice, like the ranchers who were toiling away on their daily tasks, as well as Tom's family inside the house. Everybody went outside and stood in awe as Wiley made his appearance in the German tank. Among other vehicles one could drive to a home—say a car or even an ATV—Wiley was the exception to the rule. The crazy ole coot apparently took an old cow trail that Tom used back in the day to grace everybody with his presence. Nearing the house, Wiley came to a stop and popped his head out of the top of the tank, as smoke billowed out of the inner compartment, while the engine winded down. Tom let out a laugh and walked over to the tank, realizing that the smoke wasn't from the diesel engine.

"Wiley, you sure know how to make an entrance!" Tom exclaimed as he brushed the smoke away with his hat.

"Yeah, you know how I roll, Tom," Wiley replied as he hopped off the tank ladder. "Sorry 'bout bringing the tank over. It's just with the marshal, among other things, I figured that it was a good day to keep this bad boy in the woods."

Tom then paused and put his hands on his face. Lowering his head, Tom tried not to laugh in front of the group and asked, "So, Wiley, Larry said that you were coming over for a drink?"

"Yeah, Tom," Wiley replied with a cheesy grin. "I found a fifty-year-old bottle of scotch out in the barn and wanted to share it with you."

Tom then smiled with a smirk and asked, "Did you say fifty years old?"

Wiley laughed and pulled out a joint. While lighting the marijuana cigarette, Wiley replied, "Yes, as matter of fact! So where should I park the tank?"

"Oh, Wiley. I dunno. How about back on the trail past the tree line?" Tom stated. "I'll have some of the boys gather brush to help camouflage the tank. Just get her parked, okay, Wiley?"

Wiley drew a huge grin and hopped back into the steel laden beast. With the engine fired up, the crazy ole coot turned the turret and made his way back into the tree line. Tom ordered some of the ranch hands to help Wiley cover up his over exaggerated SUV, so the men followed after the tank. After a half an hour, the ranch hands covered up the tank, and Tom found it fitting to reward their hard work with a one hundred dollar bill. Wiley also opened the bar to the men after they were done with work, as a token of his appreciation, as well as to keep them quiet. With the men happy and quiet, Wiley followed Tom into the kitchen with the fifty-year-old bottle of scotch, and Tom uncorked the bottle, pouring the well-aged liquid into two glasses. Tom gave an eager Wiley a glass, and the old boy took a sip and cringed at the taste. Tom then took a drink and loved the smooth hooch as he swished it around in his mouth, feeling the warm liquid penetrating his belly. Wiley then passed his over to Tom, not ready to indulge in another drink, so he graciously accepted the scotch and sipped the liquid, enjoying every taste.

"Damn, Tom, that crap isn't my cup of tea!" Wiley exclaimed as the crazy ole goat put his hands in his mouth to clean his tongue.

"Well, Wiley, scotch is an acquired taste not meant for everyone," Tom replied, laughing at Wiley and thinking to himself where his friend's hands had been before they were inserted into the ole boy's mouth.

"Yeah, Tom. I get that now!" Wiley exclaimed, then whipped out a joint. "You mind if we can go into your office so I can have a little more something with flavor?"

"Sure thing, Wiley," Tom replied while picking up the bottle of scotch.

The two men quickly made their way out to Tom's office. The remnants of the day were all but gone except for a brilliant fiery red sunset casting its faded rays behind the mountains of the Cascade range. The ranch hands had all but disappeared except for one worker who was cleaning the stable. There was little airflow from the wind, making the stable a hot and sticky mess, including the tired young man still toiling away. Tom approached the youngster and ordered, "Son, you're still working?"

"Yes, sir, mister. Wyatt," the ranch hand exclaimed. The young man then spotted Wiley and smiled with excitement. "Mister. Holloway, that's a mighty big tank you have over there!"

"Thank you, youngster," Wiley replied back as he put the joint in his mouth. "By the way, just call me Wiley. It makes me sound old."

The young ranch hand then lowered his head in respect to Wiley's wishes and exclaimed, "You gotta deal, Mr. Wiley!"

Tom and Wiley looked at each other and cracked a smile, and Tom stated, "You ever drink scotch?"

"More of a beer kinda cowboy," the rancher replied back. "But shoot, I'd love to have a drink, if that's all right with you?"

"Son, always remember when a man offers you a drink, it's customary to always say yes. Even with this bottle in my hand!"

The young rancher instantly lit up and all three men entered the cool air conditioned confines of the office. The boys pulled up a chair and Tom fished out a fresh glass for the young man, then poured the liquid into the young rancher's glass. The boy then took a more than hearty drink then turned his head and a spit take, not being able to fathom the taste that just hit him.

"Not much of a scotch drinker?" Tom asked, and the young rancher shook his head. "You do realize that that particular drinks itself, in a bar, goes for roughly fifty bucks or so?"

"I'm so sorry, Mr. Wyatt," the boy muttered. "I think I'll just sip the rest of this drink."

Tom laughed and pulled an ice-cold beer out of the fridge and passed it over to the young rancher. "Drink your scotch, but chase it with the beer," Tom exclaimed, and the boy did so in earnest. After a few more scotches, as well as beer, the young man started to relax the hard work of the day away, while Wiley sparked up his marijuana cigarette and blew smoke rings as the skunky smell floated in the room. The youngster, fascinated by the odor, reached out for the joint. Wiley smiled, passing it to the rancher. The young man then inhaled and yet again did another spit-take, coughing out the smoke.

"You think that scotch is expensive, Tom?" Wiley muttered. "Mine goes for about one hundred dollars nowadays in the pot shops (referring to the Washington State Law regarding the purchase of such things), and he just coughed up about five bucks' worth!"

"Well, boys, I'm sure you'll figure that out!" Tom exclaimed. The rancher then rose and stretched, then said, "I think it's about time to go hang out with the family."

Wiley and the young rancher wished Tom a good night and the cowboy left the office and walked over to the house. As the rancher entered, he heard the sounds of the boys laughing while Maddy was preparing dinner. He smiled, knowing that his sanctuary was filled with love.

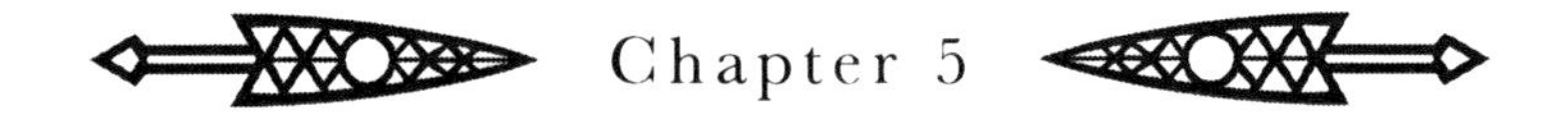

Chapter 5

Fields of Green

The night rolled on without a hitch. Maddy and the kids thought it would be great to have a family game night. So Tom's second oldest boy, Dixon, grabbed Operation. A little word of advice: Never play Operation when you have had a few beers and some fifty-year-old scotch. Let's just state for record that Tom only retrieved two pieces. After the game, Tom had the boys take a bath and brush their teeth, then hop into bed. How many of you ever want to get the youngsters into bed, so you can get your significant other in the sack? Well, men, let's just say Tom stayed patient so he could go to bed himself.

At the dawn of the next day, Willard the rooster started crowing his annoying "get the fuck up" song. Immediately rising, Tom loosened his arm from Maddy's rested head, kissed her on the cheek, and went into the bathroom to take a leak. Now, as one begins to age, they begin to realize how necessary it is to fully drain oneself. After waking up Maddy and getting her into the shower, the couple dried off, got dressed, and headed down to the kitchen to start breakfast before the boys got up. While they were down in the kitchen, Maddy had a worried look about her, and Tom smiled into her eyes. "You know that I can tell that something's not right," he asked while brushing her hair with his fingers.

"I know that information is being withheld from me about your current business with Wiley, but whatever that is, is it worth it?" Maddy curiously asked.

"I'm just helping an old friend out. One that might not be all there sometimes, but when he is, he has the biggest heart of gold," Tom replied.

"Jeez, Tom," Maddy interrupted. "That's so cheesy, but at the same time, the sweetest thing you ever said about a man!" she exclaimed, laughing while tears started to well up in her eyes. Holding her tight, Tom told Maddy about how Wiley acquired the tank. Maybe not the best move, but Maddy's look was priceless, and she made a reference about getting back to making breakfast with a blank stare on the woman's face.

The boys all stirred out of bed in almost synchronous fashion, rubbing their eyes while springing back to life with lightning precision. Dalton, Tom's youngest, came down first, smelling the fresh pancakes, and the intoxicating smell floating in the air. Then Dixon and Tommy ran down in a distant second with their toy pistols, hooting and a hollering like cowboys ending an Indian fight.

"Dad," Dixon said. "Tommy told me that there's a pirate's chest of gold buried on our land. Is that true?"

"Well, son," Tom replied while he set out the boys' plates. "It's just a myth I'm afraid, but we can pretend that the treasure is out there."

"But, Dad," Dalton said in his four-year-old baby voice. "And Wyet Erp left it here for us!" He was giggling as the young boy tried to spit Wyatt Earp out.

"That's true! Very true," the rancher replied. "It would be very fortunate for us, if you guys found that treasure for me," he said, trying not to hurt Dalton's feelings.

"But, Daddy," Dixon butted in. "How did the pirates bury it in our home?"

Please let me fill you, readers, in before I continue with the story. The legend of the gold began when Wyatt Earp landed in San Francisco. After the gunfight at the OK Corral, Wyatt was forced to move due to the murder charges following the incident. Wyatt went to Colorado first but found opportunities for vast wealth in California. Wyatt also dabbled in real estate to gambling joints and started to profit from their ventures. While taking a trip to the beach on a warm summer day with his wife, Wyatt decided to take a hike while the tide was low. As he was walking along down the quiet seashore, the lawman stumbled over something that almost landed the cowboy, flat on his face. Looking back, thinking it was a rock, Wyatt stared in amazement as the rock turned into an edge of an old rotted chest.

Curious, the lawman started to dig with his hands, and what ole Wyatt saw shining back through a seam in the old rotted wood put a smile on his face. Wyatt frantically dug up the chest, noticing that the tide was beginning to rise. To the lawman's excitement, the chest was full of old pieces of an unfamiliar coin that the lawman had never seen before. Picking every last piece of aged and rusted gold out of that chest, Wyatt placed the bullion far from the tide, temporarily hiding it till the cowboy could bring his horses that Josephine and the lawman were riding that day. When the two returned to the gold, a surprised Josephine and Wyatt retrieved the bounty and placed it in any pocket or sack available. After the couple left the beach and returned to their place in San Francisco, packed up all their belongings, sold off their investments, and heard about a land investment opportunity in Washington state. Heading north, the Earps eventually ended in the Teanaway Valley when Ellensburg began to boom around the early 1900s. Posing as gold miners, the two changed their names not to attract too much attention and eventually made friends with the locals. One would wonder why they would have to be secretive, but with that much in coin to protect, ole Wyatt decided to play the part of a homesteader and protector of the bullion.

In an undocumented incident that will live in Earp infamy, Wyatt was gambling in an Ellensburg establishment, drunk mind you, when he spilled the beans about the gold, and a group of Desperados caught wind of the incident who were in the bar that night. Not only did they beat and abduct Wyatt, but they also kidnapped Josephine and demanded that Wyatt reveal the location of the gold. Threatening Josephine's life, Wyatt folded and took the bandits to the gold. When they got to the cave that the gold was hidden in, another band of thieves surprised the Earps captors, apparently beating the abductors, and a gunfight ensued. The Earp captors were more the less taken out quickly by the other thieves that caught wind of the bullion, no thanks to a drunk Wyatt in that bar in Ellensburg. Wyatt thanked the group, but the men weren't there for his kindness; yet the thieves wanted the gold. After the thieves voiced their demands to take the gold, Wyatt pulled a stick of dynamite that was laying on the ground nearby and ignited the stick in the cave.

The only problem is that Wyatt booby trapped the cave so when it blew, it exploded and collapsed to a heap of rubble. With the angry mob breathing down his neck, threatening violence, Wyatt assured them that the gold was unretrievable, so with no other option, Wyatt sold off his assets to bribe the men. The lawman figured that if he could keep the bandits quiet, he could fetch the buried gold at a later time. Nonetheless, all were in agreement of the unfortunate circumstances, and the incident was published in the newspaper. The lawman praised the bandits for saving Wyatt and Josephine's life. Wyatt didn't want one mention about the gold to anybody, so the ex sheriff had kept the bandits at bay, and the secret of his gold safe. After all had settled down, Wyatt went back and unearthed some gold, which covered the bribe he had given the other bandits and had plenty left over to live his life out happily. The thing about the gold, that if it existed today, the remainder of the bullion would ring to a tune of billion dollars or more and Tom was positive that his cave had no gold contained within it.

Now assuring the kids that the gold was still out there, even though Tom thought it was a myth, rounded up some shovels, and sent the boys on their way to dig out in the forest. Now the rancher had been toiling with the notion of taking the boys out to the cave, but Tom still felt that connection between Gene and himself and knew that he would have to share his secret fortress of solitude. Yet looking at the excitement in his children's eyes, Tom felt that maybe the time had come to begin the boys journey, in their relentless efforts to nag their father for access to the cave. Tom and Maddy were in the kitchen after breakfast cleaning up, and the ranchers wife smiled at the man.

"I can tell by the look in your eye that you have a request," Tom asked as he put the dishes away.

"Why don't you go out with your boys and look for that mysterious treasure," Maddy asked with a huge smile.

"Treasure hunting is best left to children and dreamers," the rancher sarcastically replied winking at his wife.

"Do you really think it's a myth, Tom?" Maddy asked curiously.

"You know, Maddy," Tom replied. "Let's just say that if it wasn't a myth and the gold was on our land, I would have gone bust years ago trying to find it! Nonetheless, it's worth a look."

"And it will give our young explorers something to do as well," Maddy replied smiling with excitement.

"Do I get some lovin' tonight?" Tom asked as the rancher ran his fingers across Maddy's back.

Maddy turned toward her husband and ran her fingers up and down the front of his shirt and replied, "It depends on how much gold you find, honey."

With that being said, Larry crackled in over the CB, telling Tom that he was on his way to discuss the marshal problem. So the cowboy gave Maddy a kiss, wished his loving wife a great morning, and headed out to the office. After half an hour, Larry showed up looking as pissed off as ever. Tom offered him a chair, but he was restless and chose to stand and pace.

"Larry, what's wrong?" Tom asked, and the sheriff began complaining how the marshal is constantly by his side and that the only reason he wasn't out at the ranch was due to the fact that he made some bullshit excuse about taking the wife to the doctor's. It seemed that this lawman was unnerving Larry to the point that the two had to find a way to get rid of the marshal. Larry suggested giving up Juan, but they needed Juan to stall Isidro the best he could. Then Tom had a thought. What if the boys could prove to the marshal that Juan left Kittitas County?

"His initial credit card use tipped off the marshal service, so what if they start tracing Juan's activity heading back to Mexico?" the rancher suggested, and Larry cracked a grin. Tom advised Larry that the Yellow Jackets could take the credit card on their way back to California and a sense of relief overwhelmed the sheriff. In agreement, the men hopped in Larry's cruiser and headed out to Wiley's since the MC was out there harvesting the crop. Larry and Tom arrived at Wiley's about eleven in the morning, only to find most of the MC passed out from partying the night before. Terror and Wiley were on the porch bullshitting when the boys pulled up, so they rose to greet Larry and Tom.

"Jeez, Tom!" Terror said excitingly. "Wiley's one crazy son of a bitch! This asshole really knows how to blow up shit!" Seeing why Terror was so excited, Tom glanced out into Wiley's field still smoldering from the night before and noticed several craters.

"Blowing up skunks again, Wiley?" the rancher sarcastically asked as he opened a beer.

"Oh, Tom it was unreal," Wiley replied. "A whole family came out when the boys were harvesting and about damn near sprayed us! I grabbed some dynamite that was stored away and took care of the problem though!" Smiling, Wiley patted Terror on the back and led the boys out to the crop. When Larry and Tom arrived out in the field, the two men were speechless, due to the fact that the bikers did not party at all. They were tired from harvesting practically the whole crop. The only thing left was a line of marijuana about twenty feet long.

"Shit, Wiley, you guys really worked your asses off last night," Larry said, standing over the empty earth.

"You have no idea, brother," Wiley remarked and winced as he pulled out a joint.

When things seemed that they were at their best, a call came over the walkie-talkie. It was the marshal informing Larry that he was headed out to Wiley's to investigate an explosion, which a neighbor five miles away reported this morning. So besides killing skunks and harvesting pot, the group just found a new batch of trouble.

"Jesus, Larry! When is he gonna be here?" Wiley frantically exclaimed as he extinguished the joint.

"We have an hour or less. That asshole will be here soon,, Larry remarked with a certain amount of sustain on his brow.

In a frantic pace, Wiley woke up the sleepy bikers and told them what was about to happen regarding the marshal's upcoming arrival. Springing to life, the bikers rushed out to the field, pulling the plants and threw the marijuana into garbage bags. After tossing them into the van, the new issue was cleaning up the craters that Wiley left the night before. The men rushed out in the field with shovels and started filling in the holes, which were quite huge but managed to get the job done. With everything now completed, the bikers hopped on their bikes and coasted out of Wiley's with the van. In fact, Marshal Evans pulled into the driveway as the last biker disappeared around the corner.

Things seemed perfectly fine with the cleanup. The tank was already hidden in the forest under a camouflaged lean to, so Larry was relieved to hear that. All the questionable weapons and explosives that were inside the still room, had been taken to the panzer. The only problem left was a plant that was accidentally dropped in the melee of excitement, was now being eaten by Trigger. The rancher would have stopped him, but the marshal was now entering the front of the cabin so Tom let his trusty steed finish it off.

Marshal Evans exited his vehicle, stood up, and adjusting his tie wearing those wanna be FBI shades. The only thing off about this gentleman is the brand new Stetson that was propped on his head. You see, Tom personally doesn't get outsiders, or coasters as the boys calls them. They come over to the Teanaway to escape the big city; the only thing is, is that their only here to visit, and not here to try to blend in appearance wise. Now don't get the cowboy wrong. Tom loves the coasties because they come over here and buy the ranchers cattle. Plus Lue and Dad are coasters themselves; only they lived in Florida when Tom was young and now co-habitat in Bellevue, but still have their condo in Miami.

The marshal approached the three men, and the boys greeted the lawman. "So, fellas," Evans said. How y'all doin' today?"

"Doin' swell," Larry blurted out, trying not to crack up with laughter. Now Larry with his bullshit serious voice informed the marshal, "Well, Marshal Evans, I got the call when Laurie and myself were at the doctors. I know Wiley, so thought that this here lawman should head over to see what happened."

The marshal now focused his attention to Wiley and said, "What was y'all doin out here last night?"

Wiley then looked at the marshal and asked, "Tom. Is he high?"

Looking very concerned about Wiley's remark, Tom informed the crazy ole coot that the marshal gets drug tested.

"I'm pretty sure the marshal doesn't get high," Tom added. "You have to forgive Wiley, Marshal Evans. He hasn't been quiet right since the LSD test the army issued to him, while the poor fool was still in the army."

The marshal looked at Wiley with the sincerest gaze and then said, "Wiley, I'm truly sorry for what happened to you in the war, and I'd just like to say that I appreciate your sacrifice to our country!"

Wiley, not knowing what to say after the kind words of the marshal, looked at the rancher again and said, "Tom, I'm going to go poop now."

Almost doing a spit-take, Tom maintained his composure and wished Wiley a safe journey to the bathroom. The marshal shook his head, saying "poor man" over and over. So the boys took Evans out to the scene of the crime, which was a dead skunk family—or what was left of them. He saw the smelly rotting carnage and immediately backed off. Tom then proceeded to pull out a stick of dynamite, which was perfectly legal to own and informed the lawman that Wiley might not be right in the head but was an absolute genius. The rancher showed Evans the thirty sticks of the TNT that were used in the killing of the skunks, and the marshal dismissed the incident off entirely.

Marshal Evans looked at Larry and stated, "I'm not gonna charge him for lighting off some overgrown firecrackers," the marshal surprisingly stated with a smile. "I admit, fellas, I can't talk redneck worth a shit. But I can tell when a real crime is going on—and Wiley is a hero, plain and simple!" Marshal Evans then looked at Tom and asked, "You know, what's a federal marshal gotta do to ride a horse while I'm here. Tom, may I ride Trigger?"

Now looking at Trigger, the stoned horse was not keeping his balance very well, and this was not the normal alcohol-induced portion of Trigger. Tom told the marshal that his horse got a cactus stuck under his hoof and that it hurt like a son of a bitch. The marshal relented, but still walked toward Trigger who's eyes by that time, were blood shot red, and started to pet his side. As the marshal leaned in with more pressure, was about the point when Trigger fell down. Instantly in shock, Marshal Evans jumped back now more worried about the horse, than Wiley who returned with a trail of toilet paper that stuck to the bottom of his shoe. Larry reassured the man that horse shock only puts them asleep so their body can heal. Confused but satisfied, Marshal Evans shook his head in disbelief, then requested another time to ride Trig, and Tom agreed, but only when Trigger's hoof was fully healed.

With Evans happy, and not calling the ATF, the boys retired back to the vehicles while the marshal left in a cloud dust.

"Hey, Tom. Do you think I should blow the bridge when that dipshit drives over it?" Wiley asked.

"No, that's okay Wiley, but a drink would be really great right now," Tom exclaimed. Wiley then disappeared into the house and returned with a jar of shine and some beer.

"Geez, Tom. Trigger's fucking high, brother," Wiley spurted, and all Tom could do was reassure Wiley that Trigger would be okay. Wiley fetched a pail for Trigger's upcoming cottonmouth and filled it with beer, which Trig enjoyed thoroughly. With this crisis under control, Larry and Tom tied one off, basking in the warm late summer rays. As they were finishing off their drinks, a call came through on Larry's cell phone. It was Maddy on the other end, so the sheriff passed it over since Tom doesn't believe in such current technology. Maddy had rushed over to Ellensburg for a church luncheon and then went to the city library. Now back at home, Maddy wanted to meet Tom at the bar to share her news about whatever it is that she wanted to gossip about. So Larry and Tom hopped in his car, and left Trigger to nap off his high.

Arriving at Wil-E Coyotes, the men came in and the scene was dead. There were a few regulars having lunch, and Maddy was sitting at the bar already ordering. The two men sat down and ordered some drinks. As the boys sat, Tom noticed that Maddy had a very distinct smile on her face.

"Tom," Maddy said. "I did some digging about the old owners of the property, and they were the same couple that was involved in that kidnapping in the late 1800s. The old owner's last name was Stapp, in fact his name was Berry and the wife was named Josie. I looked online about the Earps, and his full name was Wyatt Berry Stapp Earp and her name was Josephine Earp. I also found the original deed to the land that Berry had sold—and guess what? It was to your great great-grandfather James Dilley Wyatt who bought it for the price of three thousand dollars. I guess he was a pretty good gambler because Wyatt Earp mentioned in the deed that it was sold as a poker debt."

"Shoot, Maddy. That musta been a poker bet because if the myth rings true, Wyatt or Berry was forced off his land and high-tailed it up to Alaska during the gold rush," Larry interjected.

"Maddy, it makes a lot of sense," Tom said keenly with a smile on his face. "The myth also said that it was buried in a cave that had collapsed, and the only cave on our property is Gene's old hideout. If there was any gold in the cave, I can reassure you that it's been long gone, for a long time."

"Maybe, sweetie, but why do you have to be so damn cynical?" Maddy asked, and with a more serious look on her face, the determined woman stated, "Don't you think it's about time to take me and the boys out to the hidden cave?"

"Well," Tom started. "If there's five billion dollars of Spanish bullion buried out there, I guess it's worth a look." So there they sat and ate their lunch, dreaming of the fortune that possibly awaited. After the meal, Larry took off on a call, and the couple left the bar in Maddy's brand-new GMC Yukon that Tom purchased for her a couple of months back, and this vehicle is mind boggling with all its computer monitors and climate controlled buttons. Tom personally liked it due to the cooler in the center console—and believe me when I say that Tom had some beers chilling inside the ice cold compartment.

After a short ride home, the two exited the Yukon only to find Tom's youngest boys fighting and Granny shooing them off with a broom. Maddy and Tom approached the children, and they were dressed up like a pirate and a cowboy. After straightening them out, Maddy told them that they were going to Dad's secret cave to look for the hidden treasure. With that being said, the boys said their apologies and went to find their shovels. Maddy thought that it would be appropriate to bring some cold water and a snack, while Tom brought his own, in the form of a longneck or six.

With all the treasure hunting supplies rounded up, the family was almost on their way, when Granny asked where they were off to, so Maddy informed Tildy about the treasure hunt. They offered to take her along, but at her old age, Tildy much rather preferred a glass of cold sweet tea, and some classic rock on her radio. So off they went to the hidden trail and is named appropriately because it doesn't look like a trail at first, due to the undergrowth and dense foliage blocking the entrance. Tom pulled some of the tree branches out of the way and held the rest while the family entered. Walking down the path felt much like being a child again. Remembering back to a time when Tom would walk with Gene and talk about life, or training. Now being in ole Two Boots shoes, Tom smiled as the boys rambled on about their lives.

The family slowly made their way down the trail, meandering through more brush blocking spots along the way. When they arrived to the top of the hill, the trail opened up to that beautiful micro valley with the waterfall and pond on the other side. Tom's wife just stood there in amazement and wondered why Tom had never brought her up here till today. Truth is, a gal the rancher liked back in his high school days, had an opportunity, but blew it when Tom found out that she was blowing everybody else in school, accept yours truly.

The Wyatts walked around the pond to the back of the waterfall and entered the cave. Grandpa built a door after that incident when Tom was young, so the rancher unlocked it and the family entered that untouched room where so many memories were made with Gramps and Tom.

TJ immediately makes a beeline for the knives, and Tom interrupted his forward pace by grabbing the boys shoulder telling his son to wait. Dalton saw the guns and bolted for the weapons, and again, the rancher slowed his pace, while Dixon was checking out all the old photos and newspaper clippings on the wall. Maddy viewed an old picture with Tom in the upswing motion of throwing a knife at a target when he was fifteen. Truth is, by that age, Tom was hitting targets some ten yards away, blindfolded; so the cowboy decided that it would be necessary to show such elite skills off to his family. Just to showcase his talents, Tom had the boys spin him around ten times. Dizzied, the rancher regained his bearings firmly, and threw the knife into the torso of the paper target. Let's just say that everybody's jaw dropped. It doesn't take much to turn Maddy on, but when Tom threw that knife so instinctually correct, her excitement was visibly not only in her smile, but also in her loins.

Dixon then brought his dad another photo, in fact one so old that it needed cleaned, which Tom then rubbed off with his handkerchief. The picture was that of a couple from the days when Washington State was still a territory. Curiously, Tom asked Maddy for a photo of his great great-granddad that was conveniently on her

Star Trek phone and compared the two. Surely enough, they were different men altogether. Maddy then proceeded to type on the phone until this look of disbelief overcame her shocked face.

"Tom, can I see the picture?"

The rancher obliged, passing it to her.

"This is uncanny, Tom," He passed the photo on the phone to the rancher. Tom's look was of total astonishment because the phone version and of his grandfather's matched almost alike.

"Geez Maddy," Tom replied. "Well, if Great Great-Granddad knew Barry Stamp, and this photo was indeed by that couple, they probably gave him a copy for a memento." Then like a flash, Maddy snatched it from the cowboys hands and opened the back only to find writing so old and worn, that it was currently non recognizable. Maddy informed Tom that she could take it to the University in Ellensburg. One of her church going friends is an expert in old writings as well as restorations.

Seeing this even more determined look in his wife's eye to find out more, took the photo and placed it in her handbag. The boys, seemed more interested about the weapons than the treasure hunt, and pressed Tom to teach them how to throw a knife. The rancher almost felt like a kid again with grandpa by his side teaching him the art of knife throwing, all over again, only now the rancher became the teacher. After their lesson, the Wyatts exited the cave and went back outside to picnic, to enjoy the unseasonably warm late summer day. All the rancher could think after sharing the cave, was that they really bonded as a family today, bringing a smile to the Cowboys face.

After lunch and swimming, everybody headed back to the house. The boys were exhausted, so Maddy laid Dalton down for a nap, and the two older kids sat by the TV and watched a movie. Tom suggested a nap for Maddy and himself, but she was already taking off to Eburg to go talk to her friend about the photo. Like a flash, Maddy hopped in the Yukon, honked, and took off down the driveway. Coming back inside, Tom entered the kitchen, and Granny was sitting at the table, drinking coffee, reading the current newspaper so the rancher sat down with his granny to chat.

"Well, how did the treasure hunt go, Tom?" Tildy asked while sipping her coffee.

"Granny, I'm sorry to say that we didn't hit the jackpot today," Tom said rather sarcastically. I did wanna pick your ear and ask what you know about the history of the land out here?"

"I know that your great great-grandad won it in a poker bet, just forgot the name of the gentleman he purchased it from," Granny said shrugging her shoulders.

"Does the name Barry Stamp ring a bell, Granny?" Tom asked.

"Yes, that's it," Tildy excitingly replied. "From what I hear, after your grandpa bought the land, the Stamps packed up and headed north."

With those words, the rancher's excitement peaked a bit, and it was funny because Maddy went and searched for information when all Tom had to do was ask his granny. It just wasn't a forethought to Tom that the gold could even be in the cave. Tom knew every inch of the cave, so if Wyatt lied about collapsing the cave, then why is it still there? The other problem, is Maddy will go to the press and spill the beans if there was even a fortune in that old cave. That's all fine and well, but if there's even the slightest chance that a billion of Spanish gold was present, then that part of the story should be left out. The last thing the rancher needed, was a bunch of treasure hunters trespassing on the Windy River Ranch, looking to fill their pockets with a treasure that isn't even there.

At any rate, it's still a story, and shouldn't draw too much attention, because as we know, Tom had other issues to deal with as of present. Satisfied with Granny's answer, Tom headed out to the office and seen that Jennie had arrived with LJ, for a visit. With Juan laying low on the ranch, Tom temporarily agreed to keep him on as a ranch hand. With an upcoming cattle drive on the line, the rancher needed some extra hands, and Juan was good with a horse.

The newly reunited family had stopped in for a late lunch, and Tom told them that they could eat out on the porch, so LJ could swim in the pool. While the girls took off to the porch, Juan pulled the rancher over to the side for a talk.

The newly integrated ranch hand informed Tom that his father was growing impatient with Senor Wiley for not being able to pay his tank debt. Juan decided to stall amidst his current situation, and up to this point, things have been well with his dad. However, if Isidro found out about his sons betrayal, the enraged cartel boss would send an army up here to erase anybody that knew him, and Wiley. I don't know about you, but a Mexican mafia war in the back roads of the Teanaway valley would bring the shine operation to an end. In agreement, Tom reassured Juan that their Cali associates had the situation under control. With that being said, Tom walked with Juan up to the porch, and Jenny was on the phone, with Wiley clamoring away about whatever the crazy bastard could think of. The woman had a look of shock as Wiley was crackling in her ear and then passed the phone over to Tom. It was evident in Wiley's voice, that the van that had the marijuana and shine, was just pulled over in Northern California. The way things are going, Tom was tempted to grab a shovel and head out to the cave, because Wiley's life expectancy just decreased dramatically.

Chapter 6

The Truth about Lightning

It was an early fall storm that had ascended to the Upper County bringing intense rain and violent lightning. Apparently, the rain wasn't enough to extinguish the lightning that sparked up an outcropping of trees only a few miles away from the ranch. It sent the whole crew into an immediate panic on that balmy ninety degree day in late September. The creek that runs throughout the Windy River Ranch had a couple of water pumps out near the area where the fire started, so Tom ordered the men to grab a sufficient amount of fire hose to quell this oncoming threat. The rancher left the office with great speed and whistled for Trigger, which happened to be scared of the thunder and lightning.

"Jesus Christ, Trigger!" Tom shouted, and then thought of the only thing he could grab to antagonize the scared beast. So Tom fetched Trigger a longneck out of the fridge. Trigger immediately saw the brown bottle wagging in the air, and made a fast determined run toward the rancher. Tom gave him the bottle and ran in for a few more. Hopping on Trigger, the two took off in hast, running like the beast has never ran in his life, and before Tom knew it, the two had arrived at the blaze in within minutes, beating the ranch hands. Tom immediately hopped off Trigger and ran to the irrigation hose sitting on a bank nearby the stream. The rancher pulled the pump hose off the bank with all of his might and slammed the hose on the ground. The rancher quickly turned the pump on and with a huge amount of water now saturating the forest, Tom spotted the smoke and flames gnarling his direction, so he proceeded to grab a shovel left by a ranch hand.

Running to the direction of the approaching fire, Tom shoveled what dirt he could find and threw the soil directly on some flames nearby feeling the oncoming heat grow by the second. Desperately, Tom radioed Larry, who was on his way, but EMS wouldn't arrive for at least twenty minutes, due to the rural location. The rancher told Larry to get bent and Wiley cut in with his walkie-talkie informing the two that he would be on site within five minutes. Tom shook his head with sentiment for poor Wiley, who's was coming to help, and continued throw dirt on the fire till it started spreading to the trees. Seeing that Tom was in danger, the rancher ran back to Trigger and walked him down to the creek to make a hasty retreat. That was all fine and well, but then the thought occurred to the rancher that the fence ten yards past the stream would make it even harder to cross.

With no other option, the two made their way quickly to the fence. Tom frantically searched for some wire cutters in his satchel, which unfortunately, the rancher did not have. When all hope seemed lost, Wiley cracked over the CB and said, " Hey buddy! I see you and Trigger over by the fence!" I'm the distance, the rancher heard a sound of hovering. Then the thought occurred to Tom that the particular noise that was approaching him even louder than the chaos of the fire; was Wiley, in a helicopter retrofitted with a huge water catch, dangling a good ten yards underneath the chopper.

"Tom, you're gonna get wet with one thousand gallons of water!" Wiley shouted over the radio seamlessly.

With that being said, Wiley released the catch submerging Tom and Trigger with a thousand gallons of water shattering the surface, knocking the duo directly to the ground. Rising up and a little shaken, but back on their feet, Trigger and Tom were relieved that the flames above had ceased.

"Tom. I'm headed to get some more H2O, good buddy," Wiley commanded over the air and disappeared to the pond nearby. Thanking Wiley, Tom and Trigger took off to the next hotspot to begin extinguishing the growing fire.

Now it's not the boom of the thunder, or the downpour of rain that scared Tom and his horse, but it was the clap and crash of the lightning over their heads. When Tom was a young boy, He got tangled up in a lightning storm, and was only seconds by the front door. It still didn't matter, because before he could enter his home, a lightning bolt crashed only feet in front of the young boy. Some people say when it hits that close, if it doesn't electrocute a person at that distance, that you'll only see the glow before unconsciousness sets in. Tom remembered that thoroughly, and had not forgotten about that incident, so the man who made that statement was truly mistaken, and Tom thought that the son of a bitch could kiss his royal rancher ass.

Just when Tom and Trigger thought they were done in for, the rain increased, and the lightning weaned. The sound of the ranch hands in their trucks rushing Tom's way, was a good sign that the crisis was getting under control, and Wiley's constant water drops slowly started to divert the fire from the ranch.

"Hey, Tom," Wiley cracked. "I have to refuel." And then Larry chimed in stating that there was a refueling station at the fire department, which was about ten miles away, for Wiley. Retreating to refuel, Wiley departed and by then, the men had the hoses hooked up, attacking the fire with lightning precision. Mere minutes passed by before Larry and the Upper County sheriffs arrived at the scene. Hopping out of their cruisers, the sheriff and his deputies immediately started helping anyway they could, grabbing shovels that the workers brought.

With the whole mob in order, the fire was starting to wane. The firefighters eventually showed up and began adding more water to the waning fire. Wiley returned with another load of water, and Larry looked on with his men in amazement as Wiley released the catch onto an outcropping of trees that had just started to burn. With that dropping, the major part of that fire had diminished. All that was left, was the ground fire, and keeping the violent flames away from the trees.

Returning with the last load of water, Wiley released the liquid onto the ground floor, knocking over some of the volunteers by accident, yet extinguished the fire, completely. With a smile on his face, Wiley retreated back to his farm, and the men relaxed.

Shouting with excitement, Larry said, "Jesus Tom! What the hell is Wiley doing in a helicopter?"

Just as amazed, all Tom could say was "Who cares. That old boy pulled through pretty damn well!"

With the men patting each other on the back, they knew that the fire was under control. All that was left was tiny smoldering piles of brush that the firefighters were currently dousing out. With a high moral, and a new adrenalized excitement, Tom congratulated everyone at the scene and called Maddy on the walkie-talkie to give her the good news. In response she told Tom that the barbecue was getting fired up because they were having a meal for all the volunteers. With the fire extinguished, Tom tipped his Stetson to the first responders, hopped on Trigger and headed back to the house.

The two arrived at the ranch and seen that Dallas had returned from Seattle with Lue. They might be from Florida, but Lue is a shopper, and there's no Macy's out here in the Upper County. Plus Seattle is a bay town like Miami, and there's just something more exciting than living on a city by the water. Plus Tom loved to fish for salmon, and their best to catch in the saltwater of the Puget Sound. Tom walked up to the couple and helped carry in shopping bags which Lue loved and bought Tom a very decent Stetson hat, which the rancher figured they didn't sell in the big city. Dallas questioned Tom about the fire and the rancher filled his father in about Wiley's helicopter, which got a very good laugh out of the ole boy.

After helping Dad and Lupita out, Tom started preparing the steak that would be feeding the hungry crew coming in soon. As Tom threw the juicy meat on the barbecue, Wiley and his helicopter touched down in the pasture by the porch. The crazy ole coot hopped out with a huge smile on his face and the ranch hands soon followed, patting Wiley on the back for his contribution. Maddy was preparing the sides for the meal, and Tom went inside, grabbing drinks for the thirsty crew. When the sides were close to being done, the rancher threw on more steak and cooked the meat to each of the men's liking. With all the food ready, the men grabbed their plates and dished up. The rancher had to admit that this was the least he could do, and it showed Tom the loyalty that his ranch hands and friends displayed under the uncertain circumstances of the surprise fire.

After the barbecue, the men had taken off accept for Wiley and Larry. They pitched in a hand and helped clean up after the meal. The boys then went out to the office and had some drinks while Maddy visited with the family so Tom could discuss business. Before Tom could get a word in edgewise, Larry asked, "Wiley, I didn't know you could fly a helicopter! This isn't one of those mafia problems that were gonna have to address in the near future, right?"

Wiley shrugged his shoulders smiling, and replied, "No, Larry, I've had this baby hidden for a while now. I bought it at an auction and just recently fixed it up."

"Well, you think ya woulda bought that damn tank at the same auction," Larry sarcastically stated.

"But, Larry," Wiley replied. "They didn't have a tank up for auction." Wiley retreated a bit while a tear fell down his face.

Seeing that Larry wasn't going to let this go, Tom added, "Boys. We will fix this! Wiley, you're crazy, we admit, and Larry, you're being a prick. I suggest everybody drop the whining and drink some shine."

Setting the bottle on the table, Larry grabbed it and took a swig, then Wiley went outside to light a joint. While the ole boy was outside doing his thing, Trigger happened to pick up the scent of what Wiley was smoking and wandered his way and the mustang nestled his head into Wiley's arm acting as sweet as can be. Wiley then asked Trigger if he wanted a beer, but then noticed why the horse was so friendly. After a few minutes had elapsed, Larry and Tom came outside only to find the two laughing and neighing, while Wiley blew smoke into Trigger's nose.

"I think you better add stoner to Trigger's resume," Larry blurted out while Wiley was trying to explain the holistic treatment that marijuana provided. At any rate, Tom grabbed Trigger by the reigns and led the poor boy back to his stall. When the rancher came back, Larry took off for home and Wiley was sitting by the office crying. Like any good friend, Tom comforted him as the tears streamed down his face.

"Wiley, don't you think it's time to start taking your meds," Tom asked.

"I want to Tom," Wiley replied. "When I do, the lasers go away though, and I know there not around, but I just can't comprehend them hitting me when I'm better. Man, what can I say, pot just mellows me out!"

Seeing that it was a lost argument, Tom agreed with Wiley and popped open a beer while the old man sat and puffed on his joint.

As the evening crept in, Tom built a fire and everybody gathered around it. The boys made s'mores, and after some minor whining, the boys felt sorry for Tom's friend, so Wiley ate a couple too. Feeling the weight of the day finally hit Tom, the rancher finished his beer, kicked up his boots, and closed his eyes. Dreaming, Tom was taken back to when he was a boy, playing cowboys and Indians outside. While he was running, Tom felt the heat of the sun pierce his body, hearing adults talking and laughing in the background.

Then all of the sudden, their tone changed from one of a happy and celebratory tone, to one of anger, then screaming. Tom realized they were yelling at the young boy to run, and looking over his shoulder, seen lightning of an evangelical scale crashing to the Earth behind him. Frightened and terrified, Tom ran as fast as he could. Then the lightning fell in front of the scared boy knocking him too his feet, and waking an adult sleeping Tom up, out of a cold sweat.

Tom awoke to the scene of an empty campfire. The rancher walked up to the porch and Wiley was sitting on the swing playing the guitar, so Tom pulled up a chair and let Wiley finish his song.

"Tom, can I ask you a question," Wiley stated. "If Juan is now a part of our family, then do I have a rich mafia boss for a family member?"

The thing about Wiley is that he never knew his dad. In fact, he grew up with his aunt and uncle. Personally, they never really showed Wiley the love and affection of a caring family. They felt Wiley more of a burden, than anything, so when he enlisted in the army, Wiley made it a point to never saw them again. Explaining to the old boy the dynamics of his real dad, Wiley accepted the fact, and kept playing his guitar. After Wiley finished the tune by the glowing fire, the rancher wished his friend goodnight, then Tom walked into the house and cuddled up with an already sleepy Maddy.

The day of the cattle drive had finally arrived. Tom gave the men four days off before the drive because they would be gone on that trek from the Teanaway, herding cattle to the cow train in Ellensburg. Nowadays, most ranchers take the cattle that are ready for market and throw them on a semi, then on to their next destination. Tom's grandpa was different however. It was considered a tradition to herd cattle to the downtown depot where the cow train awaited. This time of the year, all of the college kids are not quite in school yet and the town is relevantly quiet, so the cattle drive always happens the week before those students inflate Ellensburg's population.

The day started off peacefully with breakfast, then the boys played, and Tom watched the news. The rancher visited with Maddy and Wiley, who decided to ride with the ranch hands to Ellensburg.

After the visit, Wiley and Tom went out to the stable and fetched Trigger, who knew that there was a cattle drive by all of the activity, as well as the growing number of additional horses needed to make the drive. Well fed, Trigger was ready to go, so Tom put the saddle on him then went to get Betsy. After Tom hitched the horse trailer up to Trigger's old lady, the rancher told Juan that he was the trailer guy and, in earnest, hopped on Betsy. The ranch hands loaded up all their gear. From tents to endless coolers of food and alcohol, everybody was ready to begin the drive. The men already had the cattle contained within a tight perimeter of horses, so Tom said his good-byes and headed down the road, with the kids walking beside the group down to the edge of the property.

The morning drive was cool, but the sun started to warm the valley, and the men successfully left the ranch, positioning the cattle to start driving down cow road number 1. Cow roads are old trails that ranchers use to herd cattle and the trees also provided a natural fencing, help to keep the dumb beasts from wandering too much. Feeling thirsty, Tom grabbed a beer for Trigger and himself, quenching their morning thirst. Wiley indicated that he had to stop and take a piss, so Tom motioned Juan to pull Betsy over to the side of the road. Wiley in return, hopped out, took his shorts and undies off and proceeded to pee. He might have received some strange looks from the men, but he's crazy, and Tom as well as the men, shook their heads and looked away from the hairy ass staring back at them. Hopping back into the trailer, Juan and Wiley were soon back, falling into formation behind Tom and the group.

The morning had passed and the heat from the afternoon started to set in. There was a creek and a grassy area nearby, so the men took a break letting the cattle graze, also quench their thirsts by the Teanaway River.

"Damn, Tom, it's fucking hot out here," Wiley remarked as he wiped sweat off of his brow.

"Shoot, Wiley," the rancher replied. "Why don't ya stop whining and go cool off in the river?"

"Tom, you know I don't do water, unless you want one of those beers I brought," Wiley asked. Smiling, Tom refused and told Wiley to drink a couple, not realizing that Juan had drank a few himself and was already cooling off in the stream. Wiley looked intrigued and stripped down to his nakedness and jumped in splashing around like a drunk hippy, making the crew laugh, yet again, turning their heads to look at the more beautiful scenery surrounding them.

"Wiley, looks like you got a new swim buddy," Tom implied and Wiley kept acting like a jackass as always, but looked at Tom and smirked that cheesy grin.

After the break, the ranch hands rounded up the cattle and the group made their way down the trail. The weather was surprisingly hot for such a late day in the year; in fact the sun sets before seven, so the men had to haul ass to the camp. Down the road, Trigger was acting sluggish so Tom slowed down and cracked open a cold one for his thirsty steed. Trigger quickly drank the ice cold beer, and with a renewed sense of vigor, sprang to life, easily catching up with Betsy, neighing happily, while rubbing their necks together.

"Whoa, Betsy!" Juan exclaimed. "Geez, Tom, these two are going to need a little time together tonight, don't you think?"

"I agree, Juan, but for now, we need to keep pushing to camp which is still a couple of hours away," Tom replied. "In the meantime, why not have a beer?"

"Can I have one of Wiley's beers?" Juan asked, so Tom motioned Wiley to give him one, but Wiley was fast asleep after his swim.

"You want one? Go and get it," Tom replied. So Juan released the reigns and hopped into the back, digging into the cooler and grabbed a beer. Juan asked one of the workers, while he was in the back of the trailer if they wanted one also, which the men were ready for a round, so Juan obliged and passed more beer around. Just as long as the ranch hands can keep the cattle in line, Tom could care less how much beer the men drink and welcomed the men to indulge, relax, and enjoy the drive into Ellensburg. This might be a cattle drive, but the men and Tom have done it so many times, that this is more of a drinking and enjoying life kind of cattle drive.

Along the road, the men were starting to feel the effects of the booze and pot among all things, so they started talking boisterously, as well as burst out into song. In fact, one ranch hand had pulled out a guitar singing traditional songs which the men loved, but Tom wanted something else. The rancher suggested "More than Words" from the band Extreme, and the guitar playing Spanish drunk immediately began playing the song. His singing was almost spot on, besides the accent in the southerners voice. When the other five men began singing, it made Tom laugh due to said mariachi version of the song; yet the rendition was beautiful to say the least. Not for the fact that they knew the song, but due to Tom's liking of music from this particular time period.

After the song, Tom tossed more beers out to the men, as Wiley woke up from his nap, which was interesting because Juan and the rancher had to haul the ole boy out of the trailer when they arrived at camp. When Wiley sleeps, he tends to sleep harder than a rock, the crazy coot just weighs a lot more.

"Tom, I dreamed I was in that Extreme video," Wiley stated as he hummed the tune.

"Oh, Wiley, it wasn't all a dream," Tom replied. "Sometimes you just have to hear a good song, even when you're asleep!"

Looking confused, Wiley just shook his head and started digging around in one of the coolers for food. Tom pulled out some beef jerky that Maddy had personally made. One thing that Tom will never do is pay ten bucks for half a pound on dried cow flesh, when there's an endless stream of cattle in his freezer. A little further down the road, the moonshine running rancher heard a stereo and women laughing down the river. Tom looked across the road to the Teanaway River only to find six very beautiful women in bikinis enjoying the upper eighty degree day, floating the river. Wiley sat there like a kid in a candy store and all Tom could think was that they could easily be Wiley's grand kids. Wiley by no means is a pervert, he just appreciates the female body, hence the stripper poles in the bar.

"I'll betcha I can get in that inner tube with those women," Wiley said, and was received with laughter from the ranch hands and Tom.

"Wiley, I don't think you could get Chlamydia if you floated the river with those women right now, dipshit," Tom responded.

"Hey, ladies," Wiley shouted at the girls as they smiled and waved back.

"Hey, I'm the owner of Wil-E Coyotes, and these pricks don't think I can float the river with you pretty angels!"

Hearing what Wiley just said, the women blushed and motioned for Wiley to join them, laughing and taunting him with every bounce of the inner tube. Tom told Wiley that he could float with the girls down to the camp and that the rest of the group would join him in a few hours. So Wiley grabbed some of his specialty beers and disappeared into a sea of titties and ass. The man's fear of water goes away in a situation that involves either his best friends splashing around, as in their original debacle with the bull snake, or beautiful bikini-laden women floating in an inner tube. Sometimes, one begs to differ that Wiley isn't crazy at all. In fact, some have speculated that it's all a rouse to score the prettiest tail in the county.

Anyhow, Juan and the rancher rejoined formation and pushed the cattle hard to the evening camp. When they arrived, the ranchers were greeted by Wiley and the women who came by to drop him off. By that time, Wiley and the girls were stoned and drunk from alcohol, among the huge joint that the group was smoking upon Tom's arrival. In fact, Wiley found a way to sandwich himself between the women and when Tom showed up, witnessed the group hugging in an inappropriate fashion. Due to their lapse in sobriety, Wiley invited them over for dinner to soak up the alcohol racing through their system, and the girls accepted the crazy bastard's invitation. After the crew secured the cattle, Tom pitched his tent and fired up the barbecue. Wiley was already getting bored and decided to bring some C-4, just in case the group had any problems with skunks, which Tom proceeded to talk down his crazy friend by holding on to said explosives.

Finally, dinner was ready, and the men ate very well with a fine selection of steak and barbecued chicken. After drinking a couple jars of shine and having several rounds of beer, most of the men were already tired and sleeping away in their tents. Juan drank more moonshine and was highly drunk by the time Wiley came back to the fire with another huge joint, offering the ranch hand a puff, which Juan accepted. The joint was passed around by the two with Tom refusing, already being relaxed by the alcohol coursing through his bloodstream.

At about ten o'clock, the boys heard a noise in the sound of a truck approaching their way. Wiley anticipating the women from earlier, rolled up a fresh joint and sat with a happy grin on his face. With the lights turned off, the occupants exited the vehicle in the form of Jennie and LJ. Surprised Juan hopped up to greet them only to trip on a rock falling flat on his face. Tom and Wiley laughed hysterically at Juan's sudden trip while Jennie rushed to him, picking up the intoxicated Mexican, only to smell the alcohol with the pot emanating from his body.

"Jesus, Tom," Jennie said. "You think he's never been on a cattle drive before?"

"I'm starting to wonder myself," Tom replied and let out a big laugh. Jennie then helped Juan to his tent laying him down with LJ. After Jennie lay Juan down, she came back over to the fire, grabbing a jar of shine, and took a long, deep swig. Wiley passed the joint to Jennie, who eagerly took a couple of puffs while sitting back and drank more shine.

"Is everything okay, baby girl?" Wiley asked as his daughter passed the jay back his direction.

"Dad, my rent money was stolen out of my rig today," Jennie told Wiley and Tom while she lowered her head in shame.

"Well, who the hell would steal it from ya, dear?" Wiley inquired.

"I went to Ellensburg today to apply for a good job, and when I returned to the car, it was gone," Jennie replied. "I even locked my vehicle up, so I'm frustrated and don't understand how I could have been robbed?"

"Jennie, I have ya covered," Wiley smiled back and passed her the rent money. Jennie was so relieved that she hugged her dad and grabbed a beer. Apparently the boys weren't the only ones partying that night because Jennie was drinking more than even ole Tom, which impressed the rancher.

Around midnight, another car pulled into camp, and it was Larry who was accompanied by a deputy sheriff. The men exited the patrol car and came up to the fire, wanting a drink. Tom greeted the two and passed the jar of shine over to the men, who finishing off that particular jar. Opening another, Wiley took a swig and passed it around to Tom and the two tired sheriffs, who started to lighten up, relaxing their pains away with every sip.

"You know, Tom," Larry stated, "Babysitting that marshal is really starting to get on my goddamn nerves!"

"It must suck when you have to change his diaper, feed and burp the asshole too," Tom exclaimed.

"Yeah, I wished that was the case," Larry smirked. "I've taken the bastard on every dirt road and back alley in the Upper County, and I still can't get rid of the son of a bitch. Ever since the Yellow Jackets got busted in Cali with Juan's credit cards, Marshal Evans is more convinced than ever that Juan is still hiding up here. I just don't know what to do," Larry stated while shaking his head.

"I don't think there's anything we could do outside inviting the asshole to help drive cattle," Tom replied. "At any rate, I think we should drop it for now and smoke a joint," Tom said, smiling at Larry.

"Shut the fuck up, Tom," Larry replied and grabbed the jar of shine taking a deep swig. With the night getting colder and the group more inebriated, Tom decided to go to sleep. The rancher said his good nights and crept into his tent, worn out from the long day of riding his horse. Before the rancher closed his eyes, Tom heard yet another vehicle pull up. The tired rancher shook his head and laughed hearing Wiley shout out to the campground that the women from earlier had shown up!

In the light of a brisk cold morning, Tom slumbered out of his tent, and went to restore the dying fire. After the hungover cowboy set the fire ablaze, he grabbed a pot started some coffee. Looking at Wiley still sleeping in his chair with a cute blonde cuddled up next to him, knew his old friend must have had an interesting night. As a matter of fact, the deputy was cuddled up with female number two, so where was Larry, Tom wondered. Apparently he was safe with girl number three in his cruiser. In fact, Larry is a devoted husband so he slept in the front seat and the young vixen in the back, which would make Larry's wife proud.

Tom returned to the fire and pulled the coffee pot off, pouring a cup of black java. After filling some more coffee for the crew, Larry pulled Tom over to the side to ask about the drive through Ellensburg that day. The two discussed the arrival time into town and agreed on a route, then Larry and the deputy returned to the station to wash up, also change their campfire drenched clothing. Wiley said good-bye to the girls and the group broke camp, leaving that cool early September morning. If the ranchers and Wiley were going to be in Ellensburg by noon, they had to beat feet to make roll call by one o'clock. If the ranchers missed roll call, Tom would have to pay the reserve stall guy an extra days penalty pay to feed the cattle, and wanted to avoid it at all costs.

Arriving on the outskirts of Ellensburg, there was a train blowing through in the distance. The ranch hands moved the cattle to a field of grass off the side of the road, and the oncoming sound of the train startled the creatures. In fact, the noise was loud enough to make several bolt making the dumb cows run directly toward the train. Swigging the rest of his beer, Tom threw it down to the ground shattering the bottle into tiny fragments, and sprang into action. With Trigger breathing hard, they rushed past the men all trying to desperately reach the runaway cattle.

Running ahead near the tracks, Tom turned his trusty steed toward the oncoming cattle and began running onward toward them, when all the sudden, Tom startled the first cow stopping the dumb beast frozen in its tracks. Trigger bolted for the second cow and diverted it off its path, but a yearling that broke away from its mom was approaching the tracks quicker than ever. Grabbing his rope, Tom swung it with all the ranchers might and lassoed the young cow to the ground, only feet before the tracks and train passed the rancher. Breathing a sigh of relief, Tom secured the rope to the saddle and walked the escaped convicts back to the rest of the prisoners now all contained within the ranch hands perimeter.

The ranch hands quickly scurried the cattle back on the road and crossed into city limits. Before the group knew it, the men only had one mile left, however, this was busy traveled road that was busy with traffic. Tom radioed ahead to Larry who was awaiting the ranchers call and told Tom to proceed slowly. When the sheriff saw the approaching drive, he pulled into the lead, emergency lights flashing and began escorting the ranchers. Larry safely approached the drive to the stalls and pulled to the side of the road. When Trigger and Tom strolled on by, the idiotic horse lifted up his leg near Larry's window, but was immediately thwarted the a beer Tom had placed in his mouth. Trigger happily neighed and spit the bottle out, shattering it near Larry's patrol car. The rancher simply laughed and raised his beer to Larry taking a huge swig, and so did all of the men too as they walked on by. Then Wiley came by in the trailer, raised a buzz beer and saluted Larry too whilst blowing smoke rings from a fresh marijuana cigarette.

Arriving at the stalls, the men unloaded all of the cattle into the reserve area, where the cows were greeted by water and hay. The broker was hanging on the fence so Tom hopped off Trigger and greeted him by offering the businessman a beer. The broker gladly accepted the beer and the two men bullshitted about life, the cattle, and the drive to the stalls. After a few moments of Tom and the broker disappearing into the office, the rancher soon returned with a fat satchel of cash.

Tom hopped back on Trigger and trotted over to Larry who was eating a doughnut in his cruiser. "Well, what's the game plan?," the cowboy asked while pulling out a cold brew.

"Why don't you round the crew up and head over to the campgrounds where you can unload all your crap, then I'll meet you at the Last Chance saloon," Larry replied.

"Sounds good to me," Tom said and quickly rounded up the men who were eagerly awaiting their cash, and some much needed relaxation.

"I'm gonna take you through the college, so keep the beers low, Larry stated, but Tom had no intentions of heeding Larry's last statement.

The ranchers began their trek to the campgrounds which was only a couple miles away. Larry radioed ahead and had two cruisers parked at Main Street and University Way, which was incredibly busy that day with an influx of returning students. Tom had Wiley set down a smartphone that one of his dates accidentally left behind and passed some beers to the men. Tom and the ranch hands trotted down University way like war legends returning home to a hero's welcome. Only their welcome involved a bunch of irritated drivers cussing and honking their horns, and a sweet looking thing standing up on the seat in a friend's jeep, while revealing her precious bosom to the men as they passed by. Wiley then went back to the phone and began typing after taking a picture and sending it to his bikini date.

"Tom, these smartphones are really cool," Wiley remarked while he continued to tinker around with the phone.

"Why's that, Wiley?" Tom replied, turning the ranchers head to look at Wiley.

"Well, I received this thing called a text from one of Holli's girly friends and they're gonna come and hang out with us at the campground tonight," Wiley stated as he continued to type away.

"You didn't know about texting," Tom asked lightly without trying to hurt Wiley's feelings and intellect.

"Naw, not really, Tom," Wiley replied. "This Holly girl is something else. She told me about some roommates she had to kick out and just a bunch of drama." Tom then motioned Wiley for the phone but then changed his mind because at least, Wiley was engaged and talking to someone.

The men finally arrived at the campgrounds, which was still busy with fire fighters tents from extinguishing burns around the region this year. The men dismounted their horses, unloaded all of the tents, and set up camp. The tired men were all sitting around talking, so Tom grabbed a jar of shine and passed it around to the thirsty group. Larry came over and took a couple pulls and then took off home to change only to return later with the sheriff's wife to have some drinks at the Last Chance. Wiley's not very social when it comes to other people's bar establishments so the ole boy opted to stay behind at the campground and wait for his dates.

With that being said, the men and Tom walked over to the Last Chance. Entering the establishment was like a smaller version of Wiley's, but the food and local company was refreshing. In fact, Tom spotted some old friends that he hadn't seen in a while, so the rancher bullshitted and bought them a round. With all of the crew in the bar, except Wiley, it swelled to capacity, so the owner opened the outdoor area which made more room for the bar patrons to drink and enjoy the early evening. The tab was on Tom, so the rancher let his men order whatever they wanted for helping out on the cattle drive. With things at full steam, Tom sat at the bar watching the television and played pull tabs.

About an hour later, Larry and his wife Laurie show up. The couple were decked out in full country garb looking like they just left the rodeo, which the Kittitas County Rodeo is said to be one of the biggest events on the Professional Bull Riding circuit, and is held every year during Memorial weekend. Larry put some change in the jukebox and began dancing in the already crowded room. While they were dancing, the bartender came and asked the pull tab playing cowboy whose horse was outside. Seeing that it was Trigger, Tom ordered a couple beers and went outside to give his old friend a drink.

Astonished by the ranchers beer drinking horse, the bartender asked if Trigger wanted anymore, so Tom ordered a gallon of Budweiser in a bucket. With that, the bartender filled it and directed Trigger under a shady tree to drink his fill. The evening went on without a hitch. Tom and the men closed the bar down at one in the morning. After the last drink, Tom grabbed Trigger and the men left remaining, all followed suit.

Entering the campground, Tom heard a ruckus playing out in Wiley's tent. The rancher approached his tent and shouted out Wiley's name. The crazy old coot popped his head out smiling, and so did the three chicks in a bikini from the river the other day. Tom just let that be and made his way to the tent. Closing his eyes, Tom remembered falling asleep to the men shouting at Wiley to keep the hooting and hollering down to a more non sexual level. The only thing being that the ranchers were jealous of Wiley's dates, so the fool kept on making noise in the late night silence of an Ellensburg night.

Chapter 7

Never Ride a Horse Backward

After the cattle drive and drinking at the Last Chance, the men returned home to a cold and rainy Friday afternoon. The group was beat tired and eagerly waiting to drop their horses off to go spend time with their loved ones. Tom's children came out of the house and greeted the crew giving the men high fives as they rolled by. The group then proceeded to the stable and began putting the horses away to rest and eat. After Tom stabled Trigger, he called the men into the office for a surprise. With everybody inside, the rancher informed the men that the bonuses weren't as good as they were last year. In fact, the bonuses were doubled. The news was received well from the crew, with a happiness and a jubilation that was unexpected. With a thousand dollars in each pocket, the men departed and the only ones left behind in the office were Juan and Wiley.

"Tom, that was a nice thing to do," Wiley said and Juan agreed smiling at each other over Tom's kindness. Tom then took one thousand dollars and threw it over in Juan's lap.

"Juan, you worked your ass off and I'm not taking no for an answer," the rancher told Juan and the Spaniard gladly accepted the bonus money.

Juan took the money, shook Tom's hand, and walked out of the office still in shock that the rancher would do such a kind thing. The only thing that Juan left out, was that when he went outside to call his dad, the outcome did not end so well. Isidro screamed and cussed at Juan during the conversation which Juan followed up with a, "Go fuck yourself," then hung up the phone. Back in the office, Wiley was starting to talk about the government and lasers, so Tom figured it was time to send his crazy friend home. The rancher phoned Jenny and couldn't get a hold of her, so Tom gave Wiley the remote and a blanket to sleep off his trip on the cozy couch in the office.

On his way out of the office, Tom decided to go sit down on the porch, and crack open a beer. Maddy was getting lunch ready and the boys were playing out front, so the rancher sat in his chair and drank up. After about Tom's eighth beer, Larry showed up looking rather happy. The cowboy popped another longneck open for Larry and the sheriff sat down asking about the trip back home. Relaying uneventful information to Larry can be a double edged knife and Larry tends to ramble about useless gossip, so Tom kept the story short. That's probably why Larry makes an effective sheriff, because the man's always been an efficient detective. From trivial citizen complaints to even horrible crimes, Larry has always had a knack for getting down to the truth.

Larry did relay some information about druggies from the lower county raiding farms and businesses for copper wire. I guess it's pretty profitable for acquiring the drugs they need, but if people came on Tom's property to make a quick profit, they'd best settle for a body bag, and a long dirt nap. After finding about all the other matters that Larry handles on a daily basis, Tom was glad that they weren't on anybody's radar. In fact, the marshal was called back to Seattle, so the matter with Juan was dropped, for now.

Lunchtime was quickly approaching, so Maddy set the patio table. The boys came running over and sat down being loud, like normal, chewing their food down fast so they could, so the boys could get back to playing. After lunch, Larry and Tom helped clean up and the rancher told Larry about Wiley needing a ride home. Larry agreed to take Wiley home, so he went out to the office and woke Wiley up, leading the tired hippie to the patrol car, which he was not thrilled about at first, until Larry told him that it was a ride home. Wiley and Larry then took off, leaving the driveway in a cloud of dust.

About one mile away from Wiley's driveway, the two men spotted a couple of cars parked near Wiley's entrance, but figured that they were hikers or late season Morel mushroom hunters. The two entered the driveway and kept an eye out not spotting anything out of the ordinary and arrived to the cabin relieved that nobody was around. Larry turned the car off and both exited the cruiser. When they walked inside, Wiley thanked Larry for the ride, which Larry not expecting a compliment from Wiley, accepted it with a smile. Wiley offered Larry a jar of moonshine, so Larry accepted the ole boys invite and the boys made their way to Wiley's study to sit and drink.

"Here ya go, Larry," Wiley said passing over the jar of shine. "I hear you're still short on cash for your daughter's heart operation?"

"Yeah, Wiley, it's been tough," Larry replied. "I'm still thirty thousand dollars short, and I need ten thousand bucks to get her into the hospital," Larry stated, informing Wiley in a somber tone.

"Here ya go, Larry," and before he could get a word out, Wiley tossed him ten grand from the last shine haul.

"Wiley, I can't accept this," Larry said and passed the cash back to Wiley.

"But were friends and even though I show a certain amount of disgust for your job," Wiley replied, "You're family to me, Larry."

With a tear starting to fall down his cheek, Larry accepted the cash and gave ole Wiley a hug. Just then Wiley spotted something on his TV monitor that gave him great concern. Three questionable looking people were coming up to the bridge which automatically raised the alarm in both the men. Then one figure waved on what appeared to be a black SUV, crossing the creek bridge.

Wiley and Larry sprang into action grabbing two assault rifles from the den and ran for safety in the tree line to spy on their guests. The SUV pulled into the driveway and four people exited the vehicle armed with assault rifles similar to the boy's weapons.

"Jeez, Wiley," Larry whispered. "Looks like you have company!"

"I think we should create a diversion and get them to drive that piece of shit over the bridge," Wiley replied.

"Let's get to the other side of the creek," Larry said and the two made their way cautiously in the brush, stepping slowly as not to attract anybody waiting on the other side. When the men arrived at the creek, there were two men guarding the bridge with guns.

"Check this out, Larry," Wiley said and pulled a wireless igniter out of his pocket.

Back at the house, the men went through the cabin finding nothing and exited through the kitchen out to the pasture, toward the hidden German panzer. Wiley pulled out a special Bluetooth monitor and noticed where the men were headed.

"When I blow this charge, be prepared to shoot these fucking scumbags," Wiley exclaimed.

"Wiley, let's just take em by surprise for now and keep em alive so I can do my damn job," Larry replied. Wiley looked at Larry, cracked a smile and pressed down on the trigger, igniting a couple small charges behind the guards, startling the men. Even though the charge was a small one, the sound was extremely loud and almost stripped Larry of his hearing. By now, Wiley had raised his gun and the two men saw him. They were about to fire, but Larry regained his focus and drew on the two thugs.

"Throw your weapons down now or the rest of my men will carve you assholes up," Wiley stated. The two thugs, more confused than ever, laid down their weapons and Wiley grabbed some zip ties from Larry, leading his prisoners to a nearby tree. Warning the thugs that they'd be shot if they moved, rejoined Larry standing on the other side of the bridge, waiting for the other men to come strolling over in their pretty SUV.

At the pasture, the men that walked toward the charge, were blown off their feet. Two of the men rose to their toes and were deafened by the explosion. The other two however, did not rise to their feet as fast. The two thugs went over to their fallen brothers and saw that they were dead and no longer fully attached to their former bodies. Pissed off beyond belief, the remaining thugs hopped back into their car and peeled out of the driveway in a cloud of dust.

Wiley looked at his monitor seeing the vehicle approaching fast, so the ole boy told Larry to hide by the prisoners. Larry rushed over to the oncoming SUV while Wiley held his gun up and fired the weapon a few times, stopping the poachers dead in their tracks. One of the men carefully exited the vehicle with his hands in the air.

"You must be, Wiley," the thug asked.

"Yes, I am! Is there any reason you and your friends are encroaching on my private land," Wiley asked aiming his rifle at the pricks head.

"We don't want anybody hurt," the thug exclaimed. "We just want the money that you owe our boss, Senor Wiley!"

"Hey, Larry," Wiley asked in a sarcastic tone. "Is it okay if I can borrow two million dollars temporarily so these assholes can get off of my land?"

Larry felt around in his pockets while keeping his weapon trained on the poachers and replied, "Shoot Wiley, I seem to be a little short right now and I don't think these boys are readily leaving your land, so I say we shoot them!"

"Your asshole boss isn't getting his cash right now, so get your car off my property, or Larry and myself is gonna shoot you pricks," Wiley stated more intently than ever, with his finger on the trigger. Just as Wiley finished his words, weapons fire started screamed by the boys forcing them to take cover in the side of the road. Larry scrambled to his feet and fired back, redirecting the fire toward the sheriff, accidentally hitting both tied up thugs, wounding them mortally. The hired hands than began firing and directed the two in the SUV to cross the bridge. Now in a panic, the driver hit the gas and screeched his tires beginning to cross, but was unaware that Wiley just pressed the trigger.

The explosion knocked Larry off of his feet deafening him even more than the first explosion. Disorientated, the sheriff rose back to his feet, only to find a piece of the bridge had impaled the tree next to him, and the bridge was suddenly replaced by a huge fireball where the crossing used to be. Getting up quickly, Wiley rushed over to Larry to see if his friend was ok. With only cuts and bruises from the ejected shrapnel, Larry looked at Wiley asking what the hell just happened amidst all of the confusion. Wiley just smirked and told Larry that he was going to have to call it in, but the sheriff's patrol car was on the other side of the bridge, in the driveway.

"Jesus, Wiley," Larry exclaimed while looking at the bloody scene. "There's body parts everywhere!"

"I guess next time I'll only use three blocks of C-4," Wiley remarked, smiling like a child.

Larry shook his head agreeing with Wiley about the bloodbath that had just occurred, so the boys made their way across the stream amidst the blood and wreckage strewn on Wiley's property. When Wiley and Larry arrived to the cruiser, the sheriff picked up his CB only to find out that the wires had been cut.

Equally disturbing was the fact that there were two pissed off mafia thugs with automatic machine guns still in pursuit. Little did the guys know, that Jennie and Juan were headed out to Wiley's. When the couple pulled up, Juan immediately hopped out of the car and ordered Jennie to call the police. The Spaniard cautiously approached the side of the patrol car where Wiley and Larry were hiding and sat down with the boys. Larry briefly described what had just transpired, and then, after hearing about the boys plight, an idea had hit Juan.

"I have a plan, *senors*," Juan exclaimed! "Larry, lower your gun. And, Wiley, please give me yours." The two men looked at Juan with the strangest look and almost burst out laughing. "You two need to trust me," Juan stated. "If this is going to work, I need your guns right now! I'm going to act like I'm taking you hostage, but believe me, I won't let the cartel associates hurt you, I promise."

Larry then looked at Wiley and said, "Well, our options are kinda limited at the moment."

"Yeah, brother, I get what Juan's doing so let's give it a shot," Wiley replied. "Hey, we're gonna be on the fucking news no matter what, so we might as well go out with a bang!"

Larry and Wiley decided to indulge in Juan's plan so they acted like they were just captured and kneeled out in the wide open field with Juan holding his rifle at the boys' backs. Minutes later, a voice rang out in Spanish to Juan and he replied back in earnest, so the two remaining thugs came out in the open to greet Juan and his prisoners.

"I found these two ducking behind their car," Juan arrogantly stated. "Arazio and Humberto, you two look like you've just been through hell?"

"These *putos* just killed six of my men, Juan," Arazio yelled in anger. "Let me shoot these two *pendejos* so we can go home?"

"No, Arazio! My father gave me this job to finish," Juan replied. "Now lower your weapons and get out of my shooting path, you idiots. So we can get out of this shithole county!"

When Larry and Wiley were beginning to feel the effects of an untimely demise, Juan opened fire on the two unsuspecting thugs, dropping them like buried corpses. Minutes later, a battalion of sheriffs as well as WSP patrol cars flooded the scene. By the time law enforcement had arrived, everybody was hugging, and happy that Jennie had placed a call to 911. Larry then approached Juan and shook his hand congratulating the man for not letting ole Larry die that particular day.

Back at the ranch, Larry had just phoned the house, so Tom picked up and put it on speaker phone. Larry explained everything that had just happened, and Maddy was sitting there listening in with the rancher giving Tom the "get the fuck outta here speech," so the rancher tipped his hat and obliged.

When Tom arrived at Wiley's driveway, the rancher finished his beer and grabbed another one. A state patrol officer told Tom that he needed to stop drinking or the rancher would get a DUI, so Tom told officer (stick up his ass) to piss off, and radioed Larry. Tom then handed the radio over to the stater, and the trooper then passed it back, waving Tom in. When the surprised cowboy crossed the creek, he was impressed by the sight of the SUV. There was blood still discoloring the stream, making it unnerving to cross, but Tom treaded lightly as officers processed the scene. When the rancher got up to the cabin, Wiley and Larry were on the porch being interviewed by some investigators. Tom then grabbed yet another beer and sat in an adjacent chair next to Larry. During the initial interview, Wiley would make hand gestures Tom's general direction indicating an explosion. After their statement, it was just the three friends sitting on the porch staring at the site where the first explosion left a bloody crater about fifty yards away.

"The moonshine's safely hidden in the forest, right?" Tom asked Wiley.

"Yep, and the copper wire robbers couldn't get into the barn, so the investigators are steering clear of it," Wiley remarked, winking at the shocked rancher. Larry cracked a smile, the ranchers direction too, and Tom just left it at that. The investigation was ongoing and Wiley wasn't going anywhere, so the rancher decided to hang out with the two and listen to the officers at the crime scene asking questions about the explosives involved that had turned a Cadillac

SUV into a pancake. Wiley fully cooperated giving the investigators the weapons used and recorded disk drives in the house which was technically okay, due to the fact that Wiley only has cameras filming on certain areas in his property, and not usually the illegal areas.

After an hour, one of the lead investigators for the State Patrol approached Larry and talked about the shooting. The Trooper glanced over at Wiley smiling, telling the crazy old coot that he wasn't going to be arrested, in fact, praised Wiley for fortifying his property. The investigators looked in the charred remains of the SUV discovering trace amounts of drugs, more guns, and the remnants of a rocket propelled grenade. More questions were to follow, but for now, the investigators gave the shaken group the okay to leave. Larry had to stay behind and get a ride back to the station, so Wiley and Tom hopped on Trigger and took off for the ranch.

Heading down the road, Wiley was antsy and wanted a beer, and Tom did also, so Wiley fished a couple out of the satchel. Little did Tom know that Wiley somehow put a couple of his buzz beers in the same satchel from the cattle drive, and mindlessly gave the rancher one, not knowing what was going to happen next. Let's just say that the trot to Tom's driveway was fucking slow and there were six more buzz beers awaiting their thirsty mouths.

When Tom and Wiley finally managed to get up to the ranch, Maddy, Lue, Granny, and Dallas were sitting on the porch visiting, when the whole group erupted into hysterical laughter. Little did Tom know, but Wiley had somehow managed to turn around on Trigger, riding behind Tom faced the opposite direction. Maddy took a picture on her phone as Tom rode by, tipping his hat and wondered why Wiley kept asking about riding in a reversed direction.

So the two rode Trigger into the stable. Wiley hopped off the ass end, and Tom off the torso. Trigger wanted to kick his hindquarters in retaliation of Wiley's fat ass sitting on the poor horses rear end, but Tom refrained his steed with a beer; to add to that, Trigger was reluctant to go into his stall at first. However, hearing Betsy's neighing in the adjoining stall, the rancher could understand Trigger's indiscretion, so Tom walked his horse out and redirected him to the mare. Now, Wiley, giving Tom more of his buzz beers when the rancher had already been drinking, was one thing, but the disorientation of being high and drunk was too much for his legs to bear. Plopping right beside Maddy, Tom gave her a long slow kiss which received praise by Lue, Dallas, and Wiley who was telling everyone to never ride on a horse backward.

Everybody was curious about what had transpired at Wiley's but the ole boy was reluctant to tell anyone what really happened, so Wiley stuck with the copper wire thief story. Wiley, being an ex military man, had seen his fair share of strife and sacrifice, not only in the service, but also in life. Even though he managed to survive this long has always been a blessing, yet Wiley has dealt with depression and suicidal tendencies for many years now. Tom has always recognized that fact, that's why the rancher felt like it was his responsibility to get Wiley through this life, and being a friend of Dallas, also encouraged Tom to step into that friend roll, when his dad couldn't.

It was almost dinner time when the two ole boys arrived home and Lue was preparing fajitas in the kitchen. Tom came in for a glass of water and she was busily rolling tortillas and heating the fajita mix, so Tom pulled up a chair sitting while watching Lupita make culinary magic. The smell of the food flowing through the air was seductive, and being stoned only intensified the heavenly scent to the point that the rancher had his hands slapped a couple of time for trying to sample dinner.

"That Wiley is an interesting character don't you think," Lue asked.

"Lue, he's a little off kilter most of the time. So I guess Wiley rides the way he feels," Tom added.

"It's so good to see them together," Lue referring to Wiley and Dallas. "You know, if it wasn't for Wiley, you would have never ended up with your grandma and grandpa." That's something that was news to Tom. In fact, this was the first time hearing Lue's revelation, so the rancher was a bit taken back.

"So just how does Wiley come into play," Tom asked intently, knowing Lupita let her statement slip out.

"You have to remember that Wiley drank heavily with your dad at the time, and he always felt sorry for you sitting around at the bar," Lupita said.

"Well, Lue, not much has changed," Tom jokingly replied.

"Just know, Tom, that you're loved from all these people in your life and hanging around a bar all day long doesn't help things," Lue stated while putting her hand on his shoulder.

"It's okay," the rancher replied. "I'm just helping Wiley out until he gets better, and I'm drinking at Wiley's bar so be it for me not to take away my business, correct?" Lupita laughed and shook her head then replied, "Yeah, I guess you have a point Tom!"

After their talk, Lue told Tom that dinner was ready and handed him a plate telling how proud she was of the rancher for being such a good friend to Wiley. So Tom dished up and had Lue prepare another plate for Wiley. Lue shouted to everyone that dinner was ready and the group moved in accept for Granny and Wiley. The rancher brought out the food, handing them over to the two, but grandma had refused. Lately, Tildy's been more tired than normal, but the doctors say that she's as healthy as a seventy year old marathon runner.

At any rate, Tom helped Tildy to the walker she had nearby and escorted Granny to her room. When they entered Tildy's room, the rancher helped her to bed and she looked at Tom smiling more than normal.

"Tom, you're looking more like your grandfather with every passing day," Tildy said and reached over to her night stand pulling out her lucky coin. "Grandpa wanted you to have this when the time was right," and tossed it too her grandson.

"I can't accept this," Tom replied but Tildy refused to take back the shiny gold coin."

You know Granny," Tom said. "I went over to the tomb and visited Two Boots not too long ago. It was weird because there was an eagle perched on top of the tomb. It's fascinating how things can ironically intertwine like the eagle on this coin."

"Well, your grandpa always had a personal connection with eagles Tommy," Tildy replied. "I guess that connection goes beyond the grave."

"Well, you're maybe right, Granny, but I figure that there's more to the story that we quite don't understand yet," Tom replied.

"Then again, the answer just might be staring you in the face," Tildy stated. "Someday all the pieces will fall together and this coin should be the good luck that you needed all along." Accepting the coin, Tom wished her a good night and went back out to the porch. The rancher went to sit down and eat his meal, savoring every tasty morsel that hit Tom's palate while listening to everyone visit. Wiley ate his meal and then made eye holes in the tortilla applying it to his head, making Tom's boys do much the same.

After dinner the gals were washing dishes and laughing. Tom was on the porch listening to Wiley and Dallas reminisce about their days fighting in the rice fields of Vietnam, up until Wiley was transferred to his testing facility. Tom understood why the two were such good buddies in the war. From epic battles to raising hell in the brothels of Vietnam, the two men talked about everything they encountered along the way, and the friends they lost, as well.

Just like the coin Granny gave the rancher, it seemed like the pieces were starting to come together, so Tom pulled it out and began to inspect the coin. Its age was very old and worn, like Wiley, and you could still see the faded image of an eagle within it. Just like the coin, Tom could see all the happiness and sorrow in his life, yet those moments seemed frayed and worn like the eagle in the golden coin. Yet, these gifts the rancher has received is just another validation that Wiley was just as important, like Tildy's worn out coin.

"After their chat, Dallas said his goodnight and went to bed with Lue, leaving Wiley and Tom to enjoy the cool evening. Puzzled, Wiley looked over at the rancher staring in that childish posture.

"Everything okay, Tom?" Wiley asked.

Tom began questioning Wiley about his childhood with Dallas and the circumstances that led Tom to his grandparents, and in a rare moment of reflection, Wiley told Tom about his involvement. Feeling like grandpa was right there talking to his grandson, Tom gave his friend a hug, then told Wiley that he was fortunate that the ole boy got him out of the bar and to his grandparents. Feeling sleepy, Wiley decided to head for the office to get some shut eye and as for the rancher, cracked open a beer while enjoying the warmth of the waning fire.

The next morning Tom awoke to the sound of Larry crackling over the CB. The rancher answered only to find out that Larry was on his way out to pick up Wiley. Tom headed out to the office only to find both Trigger and Wiley gone. The rancher figured that Wiley headed to the bar to escape the law enforcement processing the crime scene at his property, so being curious about his disappearance, Tom grabbed Betsy and saddled her up, letting the mare take a good drink of water. Apparently, a mares behavior is the polar opposite of a colts, and being treated like a princess, gave Betsy the confidence to stroll over to the Coyotes with speed and ease.

Tom and Betsy departed the ranch and headed to the bar. Betsy seemed a little sluggish than normal and the rancher chocked it up to her date with Trigger, doing to a mare, what a male horse shouldn't the previous night. When the two arrived at the bar, Tom spotted Trigger in the back and left Betsy right by his side, while entering through the back door. The bar was empty except for Rob, Jennie, and a customer eating lunch, so Tom pulled up a chair, then ordered a beer.

"Ya sure you don't wanna buzz beer," Jennie asked jokingly referring to last night, but Tom reassured her that he was just fine. The rancher then asked if Wiley was in the office but Jennie told Tom he was out in the camper taking a nap. So Tom grabbed his beer and headed out to the RV park, only to find Wiley busy with the three women he met from the cattle drive. Figuring that the lucky bastard had returned the woman's cell phone, and hearing "Oh daddy," several times from the ladies, Tom headed back inside to wait for Larry. After a short time of swigging down some more longnecks, Larry showed up to the bar looking more distraught than ever.

"Tom, we found out who tried to attack us," Larry exclaimed. They are affiliated with a Mexican gang in Seattle known as the the Dementes, who's a known enforcer gang for the Cavasos cartel."

Like a smartass starting to get a buzz from the alcohol, Tom replied, "Well, we could always go to Seattle, wear some gang colors, and infiltrate their network. Hell, maybe we could pay them off with all of those firearms in your evidence room, Larry."

"That would be great if we could take part in such nonsense, Tom," Larry added, "But the investigators want to know why the Dementes were digging around Wiley's property."

"We could always wait until more come, shoot 'em, and ask them why they're so goddamn stupid before they succumb to their gunshot wounds," Tom added sarcastically while smiling at Larry.

"Don't be a smartass, Tom," Larry replied. "If the investigators get wind of the operation, the three of us are screwed! Hell, Tom, I wouldn't put it past whoever is targeting us, to get anyone else that has done business with Wiley."

"I get it Larry, but how do we make this tank problem disappear," Tom added.

"Tom, unless Wiley's dead, they're never going to stop," Larry replied. Then an idea hit Tom like a boxer in the ring.

"What if we kill Wiley then?" the rancher proposed winking at Larry.

"I'd prefer the real thing!" Larry exclaimed, "But I guess that'll have to do!"

Agreeing on a plan, Tom would go talk to Juan, because for this to work, he'd have to show his father proof of Wiley's fake death. Larry thought that it was borderline crazy, but it was the last option that they had to resolve Wiley's debt, while keeping the operation going. After the massacre at Wiley's farm house, the old coots death, would be even more ammo for Juan to deliver to his father. By this time, Wiley had conducted business in his camper and returned to the bar with the fine women that graced his camper. Larry and Tom pulled Wiley aside telling the old coot about the plan, but Wiley was confused at first, yet nonetheless relented.

In the meantime, Larry had to take Wiley back to the station to be interviewed about the attack at his ranch. Tom reassured Wiley that he wasn't going to be arrested and that a shower would help the smell of sex that emanated from his body. Wiley was his normal skittish self at first, until further convincing from his dates, whom were dancing on the pole, decided to help the undecided fool bathe, only with them as his escort. After an hour, Wiley came out refreshed and hugged Jennie who shook her head at her promiscuous father, who had a grin as big as a summer sunrise. She then hugged her father and the two men, hopped into the patrol car and disappeared down the road.

Since there wasn't much going on at the bar, Tom decided to take Trigger and Betsy home to talk to Juan about the plan. Riding down the road, the rancher wondered if Wiley was even crazy at all. He hates water then likes it. He can fly a helicopter one minute, then the next, he's a smelly ladies man. At any rate, Wiley is a funny, and misunderstood man that has the rancher constantly thinking about the mayhem Wiley will get into next.

When the horses and Tom arrived home, the rancher stalled both beasts and went into the office. Grabbing a beer out of the fridge, Tom kicked his feet up on the desk and turned on the news. If one could imagine, the main story tonight was of Larry and Wiley, and a gut wrenching pain overtook Tom's stomach. As he listened about the details of the story, the main emphasis centered around the sheriff and his lifelong friend, defending Wiley's property from armed copper wire thieves. The news is going to have a hay day when they find out that those copper robbers are from Mexico, so Tom pulled some Pepto-Bismol out of the desk and took a long drink.

However, at the moment, the rancher was satisfied with the story, so Tom turned off the TV and headed inside before Trigger's neighing became too much too bear. On his way to the house, Tom spotted Juan and pulled him aside to chat about the plan with Wiley. Juan was very skeptical at first and told the cowboy that taking some pictures wouldn't be necessary because his father wouldn't believe any fake death pics that Juan could send, unless Isidro had hard, physical proof of Wiley's untimely passing. Tom reassured Juan that if this plan worked, Larry could make the Mexican a new identity to continue to be with Jennie and Lue Jr. Juan was grinning from ear to ear at this point, so Tom knew that they had to produce those photos, and possibly some other kind of physical evidence real soon.

After their chat, Tom offered the distraught Spaniard a beer, so Juan followed the ranch boss to the kitchen. Tom then grabbed a couple cold ones out of the fridge and passed Juan a beer. The day was starting to come to an end and the women were in the kitchen preparing dinner. With the smell of good food flowing through the air, Tom exited to the living room with Juan to watch some football on TV. It was way cooler that evening than previous days of past, so Tom decided to grab some wood outside and make a fire. The main fireplace is centered directly in the middle of the living room and isn't the traditional mantle piece that one would perceive in a traditional cabin, but the chimney heats the house very well due to the fireplaces design; specifically altered to maintain heat at a much greater rate than a normal stove.

Grandpa always had a flare for the dramatic with his creations and the house was no different. The fireplace itself is a circular monstrosity made entirely out of river rock spanning thirty feet to the top of the ceiling. With river rock incorporated into the fireplace, the stove was a great place to gather on those cold winter nights. In fact, the seating was designed to heat up to a cozy warmer temperature when sat upon. Putting some crumpled up newspaper and kindling into the stove, Tom started the fire right up with a match, then sealed the deal with some apple wood he scored from a dead apple tree the ranch hands cut down last spring.

After getting the fire going, the rancher sat down in his recliner and popped open another beer turning on the game. Juan was excited at first to watch the game until he found out that it wasn't soccer that the two were watching. When the game started, Larry and Wiley showed up to watch as well. The rest of the evening was relaxing. Not only due to the homemade meal, but the fact that the rancher's team won by a touchdown in overtime.

After the game, Jennie came over to pick up Juan and Larry headed home as well, leaving Tom with a stressed out Wiley, who the rancher informed the ole coot that the two were on the news today concerning the copper wire theft.

"Gee, Tom, I didn't think I was going to be famous for blowing up some mafia thugs," Wiley exclaimed while he shrugged his shoulders.

"Well, Wiley, the public thinks that their copper wire thieves," Tom added, but Wiley looked confused as ever.

"You're telling me Tom that they came all the way from Mexico to steal copper," Wiley asked.

"No, Wiley," Tom interrupted. "They came to steal actual steel in the size of a World War Two tank!"

"But how are they gonna get it back over the border?" Wiley asked.

"I don't know, Wiley—unless they scrap it down and carry it on mules, I guess you're stuck with it," the rancher jokingly butted in.

"So you're not going to really kill me, right?" Wiley asked while backing away from Tom a bit.

"No, Wiley," Tom replied. "Just stop buying shit from the Mexican mob okay?"

"I promise that I won't," Wiley laughingly exclaimed. "But I hear the Taliban has some surface to air missiles for sale, and I also hear that their having a fifty percent off sale!"

"I don't think that'll be necessary," the rancher replied scratching his head, wondering if his crazy friend was serious.

After their conversation, Wiley and Tom went out to the office for a night cap. When they started to drink, Jennie called over the CB telling the boys that Wiley forgot something at the bar. About twenty minutes later, she showed up to drop off Juan and the three ladies that he left at the bar earlier. They stumbled out of Jennie's car drunk and ran to Wiley concerned about his current affairs with law enforcement. Tom pulled out the hide a bed for all four and told them not to be as loud as Trigger and Betsy.

The next morning Tom awoke to Maddy pushing him around telling Tom that Larry was calling for him urgently on the CB. Tom stirred out of bed and grabbed the portable CB from Maddy hearing Larry's voice crackle over the airwaves.

"Jesus, Tom," Larry said. "It's about time you got up! The marshal's back and wants to talk to Wiley immediately. Can you swing him by the station?"

"Sure, Larry," Tom replied and rushed out to the office to find all four people still sleeping. The rancher woke up Wiley and told the girls that breakfast was ready. Informing Wiley about the marshal's return, he reluctantly got dressed, then Tom got both Trigger and Betsy out of the stall. With both horses quickly saddled up, Tom popped open a beer and they hit the road to the sheriff's station. When the two men arrived, the station looked busier than normal with several black government looking vehicles, in the parking lot.

Tom and Wiley dismounted their horses and hitched them to a post near the entrance, walked into the building, which was busy with activity. Larry's receptionist waved the guys through to the office and when the boys entered, there was Larry, the marshal, and another fellow in a black suit.

"This is a fucking setup," Wiley screamed, only to find the marshal explaining Wiley's mood to the other gentleman.

"Wiley, it's okay," Larry said and offered the boys a seat. The marshal introduced the other fellow as FBI special agent Rick Tanner whom was smiling, yet still postured like a rock, when a defiant Wiley calmed down.

"Gentlemen, thank you for coming into the sheriff's office today," Agent Tanner said. "I'm gonna cut to the chase and say that the men who attacked you are associates of the Cavasos Cartel in Tijuana as well as the Los Banditos in Seattle.

"Tom, they are copper thieves from Mexico," Wiley said with a smirk looking at the postured FBI agent, only to lower his head.

"If I may interrupt," the agent continued. "There not up here in Kittitas County for copper. Quite frankly, they're here collecting on a debt." He directed the boys to a TV monitor ahead. The agent showed footage of a tank that was originally scheduled to go to a war museum in Canada, but was secretly diverted to the Upper County.

"Wiley I know that you've had your share of struggles during war and peace from what the marshal said," Agent Tanner stated. "We found the tank hours ago on your property, Wiley." With those words, Wiley's heart sank and the ole boy broke down, beginning to tear up, fearing an upcoming arrest.

"Wiley, the FBI has agreed not to press charges, or for that matter, arrest you," Marshal Evans stated. "Furthermore, since you're good friends with Sheriff Baxter, we've agreed to keep you detained under the sheriffs good faith and would like to ask you on behalf of the United States for your help."

Looking confused at first, Wiley then smiled and hugged Marshal Evans who had the best of intentions. Wiley put his hand on the marshal's shoulder, smiled, and agreed that he would love to reenlist. Agent Tanner then said man might end up losing his tank in the end, but that ole Wiley has a heart of a true hero. Larry then filled the marshal and Agent Tanner in on the plan to send photos of Wiley's death to Juan's father in Tijuana. The agent then interrupted and told the boys to hold off on the photo. In fact, Tanner was banking on pissing off Senor Cavasos enough for the mafia kingpin to pay the boys a visit on the near future. The rest of the day, the men were briefed on any future plans to tackle Isidro Cavasos, and his criminal syndicate, living the high life near the United States border in Mexico.

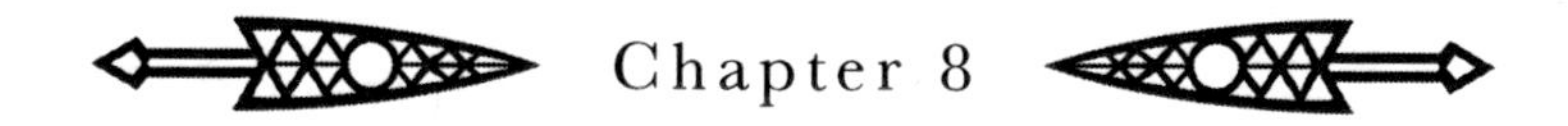

Chapter 8

The October Coin Storm

Have you ever heard the saying, "October is a transitional month"? It's the time of year where the days get shorter, the cold starts to set in, and winter's claws dig in a little deeper, with each passing day. It's a month of change and not for the better. In fact, Tom wondered why it hadn't snowed yet, which was a first for the Upper County because the region is usually covered with the white stuff by late September. Even a dusting would have sufficed, yet this was the first fall in years, that the snow has been tardy. With all of the stuff going on with Wiley's issues, Tom also wondered why they haven't been arrested yet, but like the weather, future prosecution could fall tardy as well which was fine by the rancher because the boys' current situation to help the government officials, staved off any handcuffs.

So it was two weeks ago, when Wiley and Tom met with Marshal Dipshit, and Agent Stick Up His Ass. Don't get me wrong, the plan is still in place to lure Senor Cavasos up to Kittitas County, but it's the fact that Tom volunteered to babysit Wiley. It hasn't been all bad, but when Tom's oldest son came up to the rancher and asked if uncle Wiley smoked marijuana, Tom knew that they had to give the crazy ole coot a designated smoke area. It was decided that Wiley would smoke in the break room, or out in the forest. Tom just didn't realize at that time that he was smoking with the ranch hands; but who is the ranch boss to tell them what to do, just as long as their relaxed, and enjoying their work.

Also, Wiley used to be a master ranch hand. He may have those crazy moments where he starts chasing butterflies that aren't there, but the man can still rope a cow quickly. It was mid afternoon when Dallas came rolling in with Lupita and his timing couldn't have been better. They usually don't stay so late in the year, but the hurricane season down south has wreaked havoc on Florida, forcing the two to stay in Washington State. The couple spent the day shopping in Yakima with Maddy and the boys who were tired and ready for bed upon their return. Maddy managed to pick Wiley and Tom up some barbecue wings from the Buzz Inn, which went good with the beer they were drinking that cold evening.

When everybody was relaxing from the long day, Tildy was sitting in her chair when she started to grab her chest. Panicking, Tom rushed over to his grandma and realized that she was in the midst of a heart attack. The rancher immediately picked her up and rushed her out to Maddy's car, then sped away to the hospital in Cle Elum. When they arrived, Larry was waiting, and the guys took Tildy out of the car into the emergency room. When the nurses rushed her off, Tom collapsed in a chair nearby and began to cry. A teary-eyed Maddy comforted him with Larry right by the ranchers side, assuring Tom that they got her help in time.

After an endless hour, the doctor came out to tell the group what happened, and he confirmed that it was indeed a heart attack—also that Granny had congestive heart failure. To those that don't know what that is, it means that she didn't have long to live. Grandma always prided herself with going to the doctor all through her life, but Tom guessed these things catch up to a person sooner or later, whether in good health or not. The doctor then informed the group that she was stable for now, and that the group could visit.

When Tom entered the room, it brought back terrible memories back when Gene was there battling his cancer, and all the rancher could currently do was try to be strong, and hold his granny's hand as she slept. After a short time, the nurse came in and told everybody that Tildy was on pain medicine, so when she woke up, she would be a little loopy which was fine, just as long as she woke up period. After a couple of hours, Maddy and Larry were getting hungry so they went to grab a bite to eat, leaving Tom behind to keep watch over his granny.

Minutes later, Grandma woke up, confused where she was and what happened. "Eugene, is that you," Tildy asked in a foggy drug induced state, referring to Gene.

"No, Granny. It's me, Tom," the rancher said fighting back the tears welling up in the sad ranchers eyes.

"Oh, Tom, thank god it's you! I wasn't ready to go with Eugene yet," Tildy said, starting to regain her focus. After explaining to his grandma what happened, Tildy cried but arrogantly shook it off in true Wyatt fashion.

"Tom, do you still have that coin?" Tildy quietly asked and the rancher told her that it was in his pocket. Tildy smiled at Tom holding his hand, and asked about the rest of the coins, which confused Tom at first, chocking it up to the pain medicine running through her veins.

"Eugene, you need to stop digging in that cave," she firmly stated. "We have plenty dear. Let Tom dig up the rest," and then the ranchers Grandma fell asleep leaving the confused cowboy wondering if he could try whatever it is the doctors was giving her.

About ten minutes later, Maddy and Larry showed up with some fast food for Tom. The rancher was not much for soda, so Larry poured some beer in a soft drink cup which Tom appreciated. Tom then told Larry and Maddy about Tildy waking up for a few minutes, but her disorientation made it hard to get a word in edgewise, not wanting to mention anything about the coins that the rancher refused to believe was in his cave. Since Maddy had a long day, Tom told her to head home and that he would get a ride with Larry, then Lue and Dallas showed up. Crying, Lupita brought in some flowers that she bought from the grocery store and Dallas stood right by his mom holding her hand fighting back the tears. Tom told the two about Granny's prognosis and they slumped down to sit, realizing that she wasn't going to make it very much longer.

Dallas, isn't the type that deals with death very well. After his wife's passing all those years ago, spiraled the man into a drunken depression that winded young Tom with the grandparents, and when Gene was in the hospital, Dallas chose to not even come in. So just the fact that Tom's father showed up today, made the rancher proud.

"It's very hard looking at such a strong woman laying there so frail," Dallas said and his son agreed, giving the rancher's dad a hug.

"Dad, I wouldn't put it past her to get up in the morning and start bitching about the service," Tom replied while cracking a somber smile.

After a couple of hours of visiting, Maddy and Tom decided to head for home because the rancher was positive that Wiley had gotten antsy, and Tom realized that his friend wanted information on Tildy. When the two arrived back at the ranch, Tom noticed that Wiley had started a fire out back, and that he was visibly naked, dancing around like an Indian at a pow-wow circle. Maddy contained her laughter, turned her head, and went inside to check on the boys. Curious and thanking god the kids were asleep, Tom approached Wiley who was burning safely and smoking a joint while traipsing around the fire.

"Isn't it kinda cold for your snake-bitten nuts to be out in this weather?" Tom asked and Wiley smiled.

"Tom, I'm doing an ancient Indian healing dance to help Tildy in her time of need," Wiley explained, while sitting Indian style.

"You know, Wiley, I don't remember them smoking weed and dancing naked while performing the ceremony," Tom stated. Wiley just laughed and continued dancing around the fire like a fool. The rancher decided to let Wiley be and came inside to get a beer, when he spotted Maddy sitting on a barstool at the kitchen table, pouring a glass of wine. Tom approached his distraught wife and asked," I have to admit that I can tell when you're stressed, and a beautiful woman shouldn't have to drink alone."

"I know, it's just the thing at Wiley's and now this," Maddy replied. "I'm starting to wonder if you're gonna be next, Tom, and you know what they say about bad things. That they all come in threes."

Tom pulled up a chair next to his loving wife and held her hand, then said, "If bad things come in threes, then I think after the next bad thing whatever that may be, will give us a little fortune," and then the rancher pulled out the coin. Flipping it, the rancher told Maddy what Tildy said today about the coin and that brought a smile to her teary eyes.

"You're the one that wants a treasure hunt, so let me excuse myself for a moment to go dig around Tildy room," Tom asked while he hugged his saddened wife.

"Thomas Eugene Wyatt, you will do no such thing," Maddy then exclaimed. "You can wait till Granny gets back and ask for her permission to do so!"

Tom agreed with his wife who finished her drink and disappeared to the bedroom leaving Tom to collect his thoughts. After the rancher finished his drink, he came back out to the porch where Wiley was getting dressed and offered the his crazy friend a beer, which the old coot gladly accepted.

"Well, Tildy should be okay for now, Tom," Wiley blurted out, smirking in confidence over his healing ceremony.

"I hope so Wiley," Tom said while flipping the coin Granny gave him.

"That's a shiny coin Tom! Where did you get it," Wiley asked. The rancher told Wiley that Tildy gave it to him for good luck and passed it over to his crazy friend to inspect. Wiley commented that it was old and heavy, so he bit down on it finding out if coin was real gold, which it was.

"Gee, Tom. You should take it into Jerry at the jewelry shop," Wiley exclaimed. "It might be a valuable one!"

"No, Wiley," Tom replied. This coin is priceless too me," and put it back into his pocket. Tom then wished Wiley a good night and went into the house to watch TV. Sitting back in his recliner, started to flip the coin and began to dose off as Wiley prepared a peanut and jelly sandwich in the kitchen.

The next morning Tom awoke to Maddy nudging him in the shoulder. Dallas had called Maddy telling the two to come down to the hospital. Fearing the worse, Tom sprang out of bed and took off with Maddy. When they arrived at the hospital, Maddy and Tom rushed up to Tildy's room. When the couple entered, Tildy was sitting upright, eating and bitching about the IV line in her arm. Smiling, Tom went over and gave his granny a hug, and Tildy looked over at Dallas, who had been by his mother's side all night, and told the group, "Now that's a good boy right there, Dallie," referring to her son. He also goes by Dallas because that's where Grandpa supposedly knocked up Tildy after a bar fight where some dipshit cowboy made a pass at Gene's ole lady.

"Get me the hell out of this death trap and get me home to my rocking chair where I can listen to my Lynyrd Skynyrd," Grandma joyously shouted. Everybody, even the nurse, erupted into laughter.

Maddy looked at her husband and exclaimed, "Tom, I hope I'm as feisty as Tildy when I'm her age!" All the rancher could think was "oh shit," so Tom looked her into those pretty blues and agreed.

The doctor, hearing the laughter, walked into the room smiling and made the proper introductions then said, "So I talked with Tildy this morning, and I think she's healthy enough to go home today!" Everybody was in shock at first, but the doctor informed the group that she still had congestive heart failure, but with proper medication, he could prolong her life. "I know that exercise is hard for a lady at your age," the doctor said. "Yet your muscle tone looks good. I just want to make sure that you get plenty of rest and relax."

"Goddamitt, Timmy," Granny interrupted (referring to the doctor). "Can I get up out of this bed and get the hell out of here, or are you gonna bore us to death all day with your bullshit?"

"Tildy, the doctor replied, "You're not the only one here that likes Seventies rock and roll," smiling while he filled out Granny's chart. Everybody began laughing again and rejoiced over Granny's comeback.

It was only a mere hour before the nurse was carting Granny down to the car, in a wheelchair, with Tom's precious grandmother telling the poor nurse to, Let her steer the damn death cart. Within minutes, they had Tildy loaded up in the car, and as Maddy peeled out of the parking lot, the old lady flipped off the hospital. Tom never realized how old people could hate hospitals, or death hotels as Granny calls them, but with everything Tildy's going through, he could understand why the woman felt the way she did. When they arrived home, Larry, with his wife Laurie, and Wiley were waiting for Granny, who was feistier than normal. Tildy then popped out of the car and with help, walked up the steps into the house, refusing to be carted around in a wheelchair. Once Tom got Tildy inside, the rancher sat her down in a rocking chair, and turned on some classic rock, while Tildy sat there sipping a fresh glass of sweet tea.

Lue and Dallas joined Tildy to talk, so Tom went into the kitchen where Maddy was preparing lunch, and the rancher grabbed some food, and helped his wife.

"So I might have been tight lipped about something Granny told me at the hospital the other night," Tom said. "Apparently Tildy thought she was talking to Gene and told me to let Tom dig up the rest of the coins," laying the gold coin on the table.

"It's such a beautiful coin and she's had it for a long time," Maddy said picking it up, feeling the weight of the heavy coin in her hand.

"I just thought that it was the pain medicine, but now I have to admit, my curiosity has peaked," Tom told Maddy. "Hang on to the coin and do some research for me honey," and gave Maddy a warm hug.

"I'll ask the professor at the college if he knows anyone that can identify it," Maddy responded. With the coin in hand, she took a picture of it and emailed it to the professor. With lunch now prepared, everybody sat down to eat. Tom made a plate for Tildy, but she was napping, so the cowboy put her food in the refrigerator.

After their lunch, Tom decided to shoot some beer cans. Wiley set up several in a line, on a old downed log, on the edge of the pasture about thirty yards away. When the cans were ready, Wiley moved out of the way and Tom pulled out the Luger as fast as he could unholster it, and opened fire. Instantly, the cans fell over without a forethought, and everyone looked in amazement as the smoke rose above the barrel.

Then Larry took a stab at the cans, pulling his gun out like an old man aiming slowly, but he knocked over every can with ease. Then Wiley's turn came up. Larry loaned Wiley his 9mm pistol and after looking down the loaded barrel with the gun pressed firmly in his eye, Wiley figured out that it was loaded, aimed for a can, and fired. Wiley missed the can by feet and the bullet fired out into the tree line. The next thing Tom remembered was a shrieking sound followed by a skunk coming out into the pasture, only to die. It was obvious by Wiley's expert marksmanship, that he clearly had won the skunk portion of the can shooting competition.

After the can shoot, Larry received a call from the marshal that he was coming out to the ranch to talk to Wiley with Agent Tanner. Larry, Wiley, and Tom went out to the office to await the two government agents. Stressed out, Wiley went to the break room to light a joint, while Larry and the rancher went back to the office to sip some moonshine. About twenty minutes later both men showed up and entered the office. Tom called Wiley up on the intercom and the crazy fool came running in smelling like marijuana smoke which Marshal Evans laughed off entirely.

"Wiley, Agent Tanner found you're still for making moonshine," Marshal Evans said. "You're not mass producing moonshine are you? Also, remember, were willing to turn the other cheek and not inform the ATF if you're truthful."

"I think I wanna puppy," Wiley blurted out but sensing the agents smell of Wiley's bullshit stated, "Or maybe since I'm helping you guys out, you can let my Yellow Jacket friends go?" The agent agreed and Wiley continued, "You see, fellas. People have been making corn liquor all over the Upper County since your great grandparents have been in cloth diapers. Shit, I know a guy in the Columbia Basin, out in the wide open desert, producing moonshine. Now down in Cali, it's too risky with overpopulation and law enforcement agencies constantly looking for marijuana, and meth producers. Now, if you go down South, you can purchase it, but transportation costs are too much of a logistical nightmare to bring it to the thirsty mouths of the western United States. So my friends in Cali come to the Upper County and buy moonshine from me. I save them a shitload of money by producing them a lot of booze while making a buttload of cash in return if you follow my drift!"

It's not very often that one hears Wiley spill the beans about anything, so it's just a matter of a few words when he narcs on ole Larry and Tom.

"Now besides the shine, I haven't done shit and my innocent friends here that have no involvement in my operation can testify to my current honesty, so I want my biker friends off the hook or the two of you can go fuck yourselves," Wiley exclaimed while slamming his hands down on the table. "Oh, and I want my goddamn equipment left alone 'cause I'm gonna get my liquor license to sell it here in my state, and I still want a goddamn puppy!"

"Wiley, we released the Yellow Jackets on all charges this morning," Agent Tanner replied. "It seems that the weed they were originally arrested on was going down to San Diego and being distributed by a Cavasos associate, so the agency made sure that the Yellow Jackets help the agency in busting any cartel members operating here in the U.S. Also, because you're cooperating, we're not going to care what your illegal activities consist of because we don't want to raise Cavasos suspicions, so he can come to us!"

"But what about Juan?" Wiley asked, lowering his head. Both agents now looked confused and then the marshal looked at Wiley and smiled.

"You're hiding Juan, aren't you?" the marshal asked. Wiley didn't quite know how to respond so he sat there and started rocking back and forth.

Tom, I'm gonna pick my nose now," Wiley said and inserted his pinky into his nose, eating the boogers as they were dislodged from his schnauzer.

Everybody sat back in amazement as Wiley got his crazy on. From the nose picking, to lasers hitting him, it was hard to tell if he was faking, or just plain crazy. Anyhow, Agent Tanner and the marshal gave Wiley the all clear to commence his operation which was surprising at first, but made perfect sense. The Yellow Jackets would deliver the weed to their Cavasos contact telling said person that the pot came from Wiley, which would bring more trouble in their sleepy little valley, which was fine with Tom because the FEDS we're still unaware of Larry and the ranchers involvement.

After the meeting, Wiley and Tom decided to blow off some steam at the bar. When they arrived, the place was packed with regulars and late season tourists enjoying the last of the seasonably warm weather. Jennie and Rob were busy as could be slinging drinks and cooking food, so Wiley hopped behind the bar and helped out, while Tom pulled out a jar of shine and dumped it into a shot glass, as to look inconspicuous. Maddy went home to hang out with Lue, Dallas, and Tildy, so the rancher expected Larry to come strolling in about five-thirty in the afternoon to give Tom a ride home.

After a couple more drinks, Tom was wondering why people were staring at him (Like they never seen a drunk rancher before). Suddenly, cop lights flashed outside the window and Tom figured it was Larry wanting to show off for the tourists. Larry burst in through the door looking panicked and rushed over to Wiley and Tom.

"Wiley, somebody just burned down your cabin! We gotta go now, fellas," Larry commanded as Tom sprang out of his chair.

"What? My house," Wiley asked almost in denial about Larry's statement. Looking pale with disbelief, Tom rushed Wiley out the door to Larry's awaiting cruiser.

When the boys arrived at Wiley's, the cabin was totally destroyed. The men were all standing side by side in absolute disbelief, not knowing what to say or do, accept to watch the firefighters extinguish the last remaining bits of Wiley's house. Wiley dropped to his knees and immediately began to cry. Tom came over to him, put his hand on Wiley's shoulder, and said, "I think this is intentional Wiley. We're gonna find these guys and burn down their fucking homes!"

Wiley then rose, looked Tom in the eye and replied, "I'm gonna find whoever is responsible for this, bury their body's in the ground, up to their heads, and see if my tank can drive over that goddamn speed bump!"

"Yeah, this isn't right," Larry replied. "The only people up here is law enforcement. This property has sealed off like a drum since the bridge incident and there are people here 24/7. I think I'm gonna find the entry-exit log book and see who was around at the time."

With that, Larry went to find who was currently in possession of the log book. It was chaos at first with all the firefighters buzzing around but then the men found no either than Agent Tanner talking to some WSP officers.

"Agent Tanner. Nice day for a BBQ! You mind telling us what the hell happened here," Tom asked while standing dumb founded over the extinguished blaze.

"Hey, Tom, just 'cause your granpappy was a sheriff doesn't give you the right to strut like he did," Agent Tanner replied. "At the same time, I understand what you all, even you Wiley, must be going through and I'd like to offer you my apologies."

"Do you have any suspects," Larry asked.

"Not yet," Tanner replied and looked into Wiley's eyes. "Wiley, who did you have stay with you? We found a body burned up beyond recognition with no ID. All I know right now is that the victim was a Hispanic male, in his early thirties."

Wiley froze only knowing of one person which was Juan but bit his lip trying not to over speculate. Larry shook his head from side to side and then asked the agent if any law enforcement officers were nearby at the time of the incident, and Tanner replied with a stern no. Larry then requested the logbooks, and the agent told the sheriff that he had already requested them. When asked about the means of the fire, Agent Tanner pointed to an RPG laying outside the house with investigators surrounding it, taking photos.

"We're gonna have to find out who originally processed the weapon and find out why it's still here," Larry remarked.

"I agree," Tanner replied. "The only problem is that due to the first attack, we can't rule out the cartels involvement."

When the agent said that, all Tom could think was bullshit! That gun was in law enforcements possession. The rancher motioned to Larry who was now shaking his head in agreement to what Tom was thinking and pulled the cowboy aside.

"So if I find this asshole first, I guess Wiley gets to take his tank on a stroll," Larry stated.

"We'll Larry, quite frankly, I think ole Tanner has a hand in all of this," Tom replied. "It just seems weird that one minute it's in the hands of investigators, then the next, it's outside Wiley's porch. Just like grandpa always said, "If it smells like shit, looks like shit, and tastes like shit," then Larry interrupted, "Then it's just shit!"

The boys urgently rounded Wiley up and thanked the agent for the info, then made their way back to the car. Once inside, Larry radioed his receptionist and asked her if she could look up Agent Tanner's credentials, just for shits and giggles.

"We'll fellas," Larry said. "Guess were gonna have to head over to Tom's and have a few. In agreement, they departed for the ranch, with lights and horns blaring, speeding like normal away from the new crime scene. When they arrived at the ranch, all was peaceful. Tom hopped out of the car and Maddy was waiting on the front porch with a worried look on her face which was only confirmed due to Laurie calling Maddy after hearing the news from Larry. She came up to Wiley and gave him a hug, consoling Wiley, as tears streamed down his cheeks.

In light of all that happened at Wiley's cabin, the boys decided to go out to the shop and get Wiley drunk. When the men walked inside, Wiley called Jennie to see if she had heard from Juan and his daughter responded with a no. Wiley told her what happened and Jennie broke down in the midst of the busy bar but did not tell her about the body, because the identity still had yet to be determined.

In the office the boys passed around some moonshine and cracked open more beer which Wiley began to drink uncontrollably. After an hour in engaging in the act, Larry got a call from Marshal Evans who had the badly burned body taken to the coroner for analysis. The marshal said that since there are no records of DNA or fingerprints on file for most illegal Mexican nationals, that he could only assume that it was Juan.

Finding out the news, Larry took an inebriated Wiley back to the bar to tell Jennie and when they arrived, it couldn't have been at a worse time. Larry escorted Wiley into the bar about the time Agent Tanner showed up with two other FBI agents. Just as Wiley told Jennie the horrible news, Agent Tanner approached Wiley from behind with handcuffs and detained the poor ole boy amidst heated cursing from Larry.

"Wiley Holloway, you're under arrest for the murder of known cartel associate, Juan Cavasos," the prick told Wiley as he slapped on the cuffs. A sad and very angry Jennie knew that her father had no part in the murder and proceeded to slap the agent on the face.

"Ma'am, it's my understanding that you harbored the fugitive," the agent said. "Would you like to be arrested too?"

"You're full of shit, you fucking prick," Jennie shouted in fury. "My father is an innocent man and wouldn't harm anybody unless you tried too first asshole!" With Agent Tanner getting enraged by the second, Larry rushed Jennie out of the bar while she struggled and cried in the sheriff's arms.

"Jennie, the agents full of it and you we know it darling. Hell, Tom and I think the bastard's up to no good. We just don't know to what extent yet," Larry said comforting a distressed Jennie.

The agents brought out Wiley and placed him in their government vehicle. "How's those log books coming along asshole," Larry exclaimed.

"Still waiting on them, Sheriff Baxter," the tight lipped agent replied as he helped a shaky Wiley into the SUV.

"By the way, government regulations state that you have to book Wiley in at the station before you can transport him any further, prick," Larry stated while still comforting Jennie.

"I don't think so, Sheriff Baxter," Tanner replied. "Remember, there's still the Lower County and I do believe the County Seat is located there, so we will take care of Mr. Holloway and you can keep doing the important work that you do up here, sheriff!"

"Yeah...Well, fuck you, you piece of shit," Larry exclaimed and the SUV soon pulled away from the bar with one helpless mother and a determined sheriff flipping Tanner off as he sped away.

When the agent left, a call came in from Larry's receptionist, and she informed the sheriff that Agent Tanner was placed on leave by the FBI in recent months on suspicion for accepting bribes from some shady figures, especially the Cavasos cartel. Angered, Larry told Jennie to close down the bar and that he was going to go get her father.

Back at the ranch, Larry crackled over the radio informing Tom as to what just happened and that Agent Asshole and his cronies would be driving by the ranchers place at anytime. Pissed off over the news, Tom then rushed over to the stable, saddled up Trigger and bolted to the road intersecting the Wyatt's driveway where ole Tommy would distract them. Minutes later, a black SUV approached out of the distance, so like any concerned friend, Trigger and Tom planted themselves out in the middle of the road, playing the normal drunk guy on the inebriated horse. Tanner saw the cowboy blocking the road ahead so he ordered the driver to stop and exited the vehicle, while cautiously approaching the drunk rancher.

"Mr. Wyatt, you mind explaining why are you in the middle of the road," the dumb prick asked.

"Oh I'm just trying to find my driveway," Tom mumbled in a drunken stupor. By then the other two agents popped out of the rig and approached the rancher.

"Tom, we don't want any trouble here," Agent Tanner said. "We just want through." That was about the point where Tom gently kicked Trigger in the side, motioning the mustang to lay down.

"Shit agent Tanner, Tom replied. "I don't want any trouble either but this dipshit of a horse is as drunk as I am and I can't get the fucker to move anywhere!" Seeing that Trigger or Tom weren't going anywhere, the other agents started to reach for their weapons forcing Tom to draw his Luger, shooting the two cocksuckers where they stood. When the agents dropped, Tanner reached for his piece, but was already staring down the barrel of Tom's Luger, cocked and ready to put Agent Tanner out of his misery.

"You drunk bastard," the agent exclaimed. "I don't think you're stupid enough to shoot a government agent!"

"Well, since I shot the other hooligans, what makes you think I won't shoot you, you fake prick," Tom responded while pushing the Luger firmly to Tanners head. "Lower your piece to the ground nice and slow and get on the ground, or I'm gonna tell Marshal Evans that you gave me no other choice asshole!"

Sensing that the crooked agent just fell into a trap, slowly lowered his weapon and dropped to the ground. After ordering the deuce bag to place his hands behind his back, Tom took a piece of cow rope old and fastened them on tightly to the agents wrists. After finding the key, Tom got Wiley out of the SUV and uncuffed the frightened man while the agent yelled and screamed at the boys, threatening to release hellfire upon the Upper County if he wasn't released. A couple of minutes later, Larry and Jennie showed up smiling at the jackass that the rancher just took custody of and the sheriff ran up to Tanner, kicking the clown forcefully in the man's side.

"Lemme guess, drunk horse in the middle of the road trick," Larry asked?

"Gets em every time, but I do have to admit that Trigger and I are very drunk," Tom replied swallowing the last drop of beer out of the bottle.

"You assholes will answer for your crimes to the U.S. government," Agent Tanner said but was immediately met by laughter.

"Don't you mean Isidro Cavasos," the rancher retorted? Tanner then got tight lipped and quit talking knowing that he had just been made.

"Apparently, my receptionist does a pretty good background check on all government employees," Larry stated. "So Wiley, do you feel like firing up the tank this evening"? With stars in his eyes, Wiley smiled at Larry and kicked Agent Tanner in his side.

"I'm gonna love driving the tank over this piece of shit," Wiley exclaimed as the crazy old fool took another shot at Tanners torso.

With the agent in Larry's cruiser, Tom shooed Trigger back to the ranch and all four made our their back to Wiley's cabin. When the group arrived, all was quiet accept for a handful of Larry's deputy's watching the property. When they saw the agent in handcuffs,

Larry explained what happened and had them leave Wiley's to the current crime scene in front of Tom's driveway.

Now alone, Larry escorted Tanner out to the field with the rest of us and grabbed a shovel out by Wiley's barn. Larry then uncuffed the bastard and ordered Tanner to start digging. Reluctant at first, the agent paused and complained that the boys were going to bury him alive, and he wasn't too far off kilter, so a few more blows to his torso with the shovel enamored the shady agent to dig further. After an hour of digging, the hole was ready and Larry ordered Tanner in after securing the agents wrists again with cuffs. Once Larry had recovered the earth around the agent, all that could be seen was his head popping out like a dad that just got buried at the beach by his children, only this agent wasn't moving at all.

Tanner started cussing and threatening the boys again, and up until the point where he saw the huge panzer knocking down trees where Wiley had hidden it, started to get worried.

"You know, now's a good time to tell us who you're working for, or were gonna let Wiley keep driving," Larry said, but the agent was now pale faced and tight lipped. Larry gave Wiley the order to drive and he did without a flinch, inching ever so close to the agent's head.

"See ya around, dipshit," Larry stated, and as the tank came only feet away, then Agent Tanner relented, spilling the beans about his association to Cavasos and killing Juan.

"Senor Cavasos paid me to eliminate Juan and to fly Wiley out of the country," Tanner exclaimed. "Please don't kill me! I'm just trying to give my family a better life, and this was my only way to make it happen!"

"It doesn't take much to make this corrupt asshole talk," Tom stated while laughing. The rancher then squatted down looking Tanner in the eye and stated, "You see, Agent Tanner, you might be a great father and a devoted husband, but you're bankrolling your family with blood money. Now I have certain friends that are in a similar position such as yourself, but I was always told that if it smells like shit Agent Tanner, it's just shit period!"

Tanner then drew quiet, as did Larry almost feeling for the agent due to those similar circumstances, yet with the information that Agent Tanner relayed to the boys, it was relevant to make a big move that would lure the cartel boss here. Since Tanner was corrupt, for now the men had to assume that Marshal Evans was just as corrupt so it was decided to keep their current affairs tight lipped for the time being.

"I don't know about you guys, but I'm getting tired," Tom exclaimed and the boys were in agreement, so they started walking away.

"What about me," Tanner shouted. "You can't leave me in this hole all night you fucking assholes!"

"It's okay Tanner. Well come back tomorrow and check on you then," Larry replied. With that being said, the boys headed off to Larry's patrol car while a pissed off corrupt FBI agent lay in a hole he dug all by himself listening to coyotes yelp in the far distance.

Back in the car, the men made their way to the ranch. Everybody was tired about the events that had transpired during the day. Tom asked Larry if they were going to leave the agent unattended, but Larry decided to call one of his deputy's to dig the bastard out. When the men arrived at the ranch, there were several deputy's and WSP investigators at the scene. Larry hopped out of his cruiser and answered some quick questions before taking Wiley and the tired rancher home.

At the front of the house, Jennie and LJ had already arrived and Maddy held the two, both crying over Juan's sudden passing. Everybody was so distraught with grief, that it took every last bit of cowboy in Tom, to be strong, and fight back the tears. Wiley approached Jennie and held his crying daughter telling the broken hearted woman that they caught the killer, and that Wiley almost got to run over the agent's head with the Panzer. Somberly chuckling at first, Dallas came up to Wiley and hugged him telling the grief stricken man that he wished that he could have been there to witness the speed bump.

Lue came around and handed out beer to the guys and the tired rancher. She might not be a drinker, nor approve of such drunken behavior, but she knew when a guy needed a beer. They immediately cracked the longnecks open and saluted Juan also to Larry's for his quick thinking in apprehending the killer so quickly.

"What about the Yellow Jackets and that weed their going to sell to that Cavasos' associate in Cali," Tom asked Larry.

"Shit, Tom, I hope the Jackets rob that bastard," Larry exclaimed.

"Wouldn't robbing the poor guy piss off his Isidro?" Tom sarcastically asked.

"I think I'd better call Terror," Larry said and disappeared out on to the lawn calling their California brothers. After a few minutes of watching Larry laugh and slap his knee at one point, returned with good news.

"Terror said that the deals supposed to go down tomorrow. I told him what happened and Terror said that he'll return the favor," Larry stated while smiling.

"Don't suppose things are gonna slow down around here anytime soon," Tom retorted while grabbing another beer.

"You still got that napalm torch Wiley gave ya," Larry asked, and the rancher said yes. "That's okay cause were gonna need it!"

The rest of the night was somber and Larry decided to stay out at the Windy River Ranch to keep an eye on things. Everybody quickly grew tired and withdrew to their beds for some much needed rest. For the rest of the night, Larry did not sleep a wink. In fact, spent the rest of the night pondering what kind of trouble that was coming to hit the Upper County like the Hurricanes so far away.

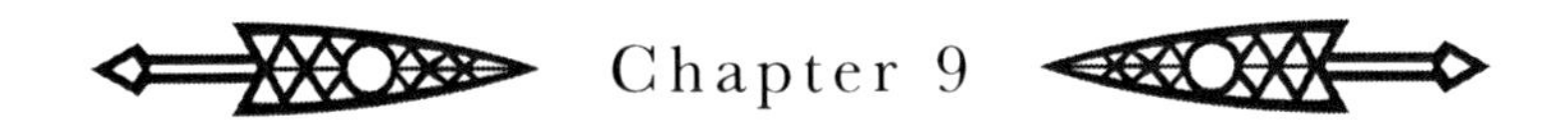

Chapter 9

FBI Agents Don't Fall from Heaven

The night of the tank incident was restless. Maddy and Tom had to burn off some steam when everyone went to bed, so the couple really never slept last night, even though the rancher was exhausted. After what seemed a catnap that night, Tom awoke to Maddy holding a cup of coffee informing the rancher that Larry just arrived and had some more news. Tom sprang up out of his bed naked, accept for some spurs Maddy had the rancher wear last night, and slithered into his day old jeans. Chugging down a cup of coffee the best Tom could, put on a fresh shirt and crept into his boots which were still strewn all throughout the bedroom.

When Tom headed outside, Larry and the marshal were both present. In fact Wiley was giving the marshal a high five, grinning from ear to ear. The marshal then smiled and shook Tom's hand apologizing for coming over so early, but the rancher figured, that the lawman would come over anyways.

"Damn Tom! You guys have been busy," the marshal said joyously. "With the Jackets in our pocket, were gonna open a whole new can of whoop ass on that Mexican cocksucker sitting in his mansion down in Tijuana! I'm going to let the Yellow Jackets rob Isidro's connection in San Diego today. I just don't wanna tip the guy off."

"So they rob him, the Yellow Jackets bring you the cash and you move in," Larry asked nervously while sipping on a coffee that Maddy graciously poorer for the sheriff.

"No. Not until we have confirmation that the prick calls his boss," Marshal Evans replied.

"I'm not so sure my family and Jennie are safe. I need to know that they'll be safe while this shit goes down," Tom aggressively told the marshal while staring the lawman directly in the eyes.

"I totally agree Tom," the marshal replied. "Is there anywhere they can go temporarily until there is resolve in this matter?"

"I have church friends out in Badger Pocket that would gladly take us in," Maddy interrupted.

Tom looked Maddy deep into her eyes and could tell that she was hesitant. Hell, the woman can handle a firearm almost as good as her husband, but Tildy, in her current condition, and the boys don't need to be witness to the adult problems in the Upper County. In agreement, Maddy went inside to start packing bags and Larry had other news for the rancher.

"Tom, if you wanna be involved in this, I'm gonna have to temporarily deputize Wiley and you to make this all legal," Larry stated and cracked a smile at both men.

"Actually," Marshal Evans interrupted, "I was going to deputize you two temporarily but, the Upper County regulations are a little more relaxed in these matters, so both Larry and myself thought it appropriate to make you boys legal till this situation winds down."

Larry then proudly took two sheriff badges out of his pocket and deputized the boys. Wiley looked at Larry smiling and gave the sheriff a high five as Tom gently shook the lawman's hand.

"So, now that you guys are onboard, you tell me what the hell happened to Agent Tanner last night out at Wiley's," the marshal curiously asked.

"Well, Marshal Evans, let's just say for now that the asshole got buried in his work," Wiley sarcastically replied.

"I know! I showed up at Wiley's and a deputy had just dug the poor son of a bitch out," the marshal replied. "He's been quiet and has lawyered up for now, unfortunately but still, the whole ambush scene with you and Trigger in front of your driveway. That shits just priceless Tom! Anyhow, you guys mind telling me his involvement?"

Tom then explained what had transpired and that Tanner was in bed with Cavasos; also, that the agent killed Juan and burned his body in the fire. It was a gut wrenching fact that a government employee would go to such extremes to make some side cash, but if this drug deal goes as planned, it would give Marshal Evans all the evidence that the lawman needed to secure an interagency warrant for Senor Cavasos arrest. In the meantime, the newly deputized sheriffs, and Larry, went out to the crime scene in the front of Tom's driveway to see what the investigators had found.

When the men pulled up, Deputy Morrison greeted Larry and the marshal, looking at the new sheriff's with utter disbelief. Wiley and Tom flashed their new badges at the clown only to get a pale blank stare out of the officer. Morrison informed Larry that WSP investigators found fake passports and ID's and no hits on the AFIS system that the FBI uses to identify criminals. Tom ordered the deputy to route traffic away from the Windy River Ranch and Morrison refused at first, until Larry agreed forcing the deputy to steam away. Larry then informed Marshal Evans about what they found, so Evans agreed to call his Mexican contacts to locate the identities of the two dead agents. After their talk, the men returned to the house for some lunch and to see how Jennie was holding up.

When they got out of the car, Jennie was sitting curled up on the porch swing in a trance looking at nothing. Wiley came up to her and sat down putting his arm around the grief stricken woman, only to hear her cries concerning Juan's death. Little LJ was also traumatized by his passing as well. It wasn't the fact of knowing her father for a short time, but it was due to how much Juan loved his daughter, and wouldn't be deterred from that love. Even in the midst of all the sadness, Tom's boys were there to play and keep the little girls mind off of Juan's passing. Suddenly, as sinister as the thought entered the ranchers head, Tom figured that if Tanner didn't want to name names, then maybe using the agents family against him would force the man to talk. The rancher told Larry to place some calls and to get the family here as soon as possible, so Larry phoned his receptionist to reach out to the agents family.

While Larry was working on finding out the information that Tom requested, Maddy had approached her husband about taking Tildy out to lunch at the bar to help take their minds off of all the current drama playing out in the Upper County. With everything presently calm, Tom agreed, so they rounded up Tildy and made their way to Wil-E Coyotes. When the group arrived at the bar, it was surprisingly dead, accept for the daily patrons that come in that time of day. In fact, Rob was the only one working and he thanked the Lord that it was mellow with all the current problems going on in their neck of the woods. The line cook noticed the shiny badge pinned on the ranchers shirt and thought Tom was bullshitting him at first, but the newly deputized lawman explained what happened, and Rob was simply awestruck over what took place the previous night.

Maddy and Tom seated Tildy and ordered their meal while the old lady kept looking at the badge pinned on Tom's shirt. "Ole Two Boots would have been proud of you grandson," she blurted and then requested some Skynyrd on the jukebox, which Tom laughed, then rose to bring up the selection on the music machine.

"It's weird seeing you with a badge Tom," Maddy said. "I mean, you had several chances with Larry and turned him down every time. So how does it feel on you?"

"I kind feel like an asshole Maddy," Tom sarcastically responded making Tildy laugh, almost spilling her sweet tea all over the table.

"That's exactly what your granddad told me when he wore the damn thing," Tildy said slapping her hand on her knee, and apparently the rancher should have contained his jokes because her heart started to race as she became short of breath. Maddy responded quickly by reaching in Granny's purse for a blood pressure pill and gave it to Tildy, calming the ole gal down within minutes.

Reassuring the two that the move to Maddy's friends was only temporary, the three ate lunch and Tildy reminisced about the past. Gene, back in the 1950s, ran for sheriff and was a damn fine one for ten years, until an on the job injury forced the lawman into early retirement. In fact, ole Sheriff Walters ended up taking Gene's spot—of course, up until the rancher removed Walters of that title. Anyhow, when Tom originally went home with his grandparents as a boy, the rancher remembered Gene even helping out Sheriff Walters on some serious cases, yet Two Boots could only handle so much and respectfully quit, deciding to concentrated on the ranch. Tom believed the cave was always an outlet for Gene to take out his aggressions on paper targets and what have you during those years running around with Sheriff Walters. From being a soldier to a sheriff, Gene was always a strong man, so wearing that badge made Tom feel like he was still around, which made rancher strangely proud.

During their meal, Maddy received a call from Larry on her cell, so Tom got up out of his seat to answer the call. Larry's receptionist had contacted Agent Tanner's family in Seattle and were on their way. Tom had a feeling that things were going to get worse upon their arrival, so the cowboy hung up and finished his meal, pondering what the next step should be. After they ate, Maddy rushed Tom down to the station where Agent Tanner was being detained. When the rancher walked in, several officers were in utter shock upon seeing the badge pinned on Tom's shirt. Larry and Wiley arrived minutes later and again, more shock as Wiley came in wearing his badge that was pinned to the man's baseball cap. All three men went into the viewing area adjacent to the interrogation room and watched the corrupt prick sit through the double glassed mirror. Larry's receptionist came into the room and gave the sheriff photos and addresses of the agents extended family members, just in case things went south with Tanners wife.

"So what were you planning on doing with the corrupt FBI again Tom," Larry asked, and Tom kicked his feet up on the desk, smiling at the sheriff.

"Oh, just threaten his family members lives in exchange for information," Tom replied.

"I don't think that's very legal," Larry snickered but Tom assured the sheriff that everything would be okay, and Tom would not harm any of Tanners family. With the photos and information, Tom entered the room while the tired agent looked up, only to lower his head again.

"Agent Tanner, you're looking horribly exhausted," Tom stated. "Do you need anything, like a soda or cyanide?"

"Nice badge," Tanner replied! "Why don't you go fuck yourself, asshole. And I want my goddamn lawyer now!"

"Fair enough," Tom responded. "Oh by the way, is your wife named Shiela?" He held the photo of the woman in front of Ricks tired eyes.

"If you think you're gonna get me to talk by threatening my family, you might as well try another tactic," Tanner stated and shied his head away from the photo.

"I suppose you're right, Mr. Tanner," Tom replied, "But the marshal informed me that he's going to seize all of your property until this mess is sorted out! Your home, cars...hell, even your pets are up for grabs unless you wanna tell me and the other people in the room what's really going on. Come on Rick! With a possible seizure of your property, you do realize that Sheila and the kids will have to move out. Do you really wanna mess up their lives even more because you don't wanna talk to us?"

Lowering his head again, Tom figured that the agent didn't want to throw his family under the bus, so the rancher slowly rose and began to walk out.

"Wait Tom," Tanner demanded. "I don't think you realize what kind of monster Cavasos is. He's the type of predator who preys on the strong and uses their weaknesses against them. My family is my weakness," and the corrupt agent lowered his head in shame. The marshal then entered the room reassuring Tanner that if he gave up Cavasos, then his family would be safely protected, and that Evans would halt the seizure. The agent with no other viable option, gave up contacts and information that would have taken the marshal service years to gain; even recorded conversations between Cavasos, ordering Juan's murder, which was encrypted on Tanners phone.

After the interview the door opened again, only it was a very sick looking Shiela who appeared frail and depleted, like she was in the later stages of cancer. Crying, she approached Tanner and slapped his face.

"Why didn't you tell me about Isidro," she asked, and Rick just sat there with his hands buried in his head. "He was so nice to the kids and us when we vacationed in Mexico! I just can't believe that this man is a devil, and you're doing the assholes bidding!"

"He promised to give you the best treatment that money could afford if I helped him," Tanner replied to his grief stricken wife. "For the longest time, the treatment was working dear and I never thought that things would end up this way," Tanner reiterated, but Rick could see in his wife's eyes that all love and trust had disappeared. Not knowing what to say, she turned her back and walked out of the room almost passing out, but Larry captured her fall, escorting Sheila to a chair nearby.

"I understand why you did it and why you had to," Tom told the shocked agent. "The only difference between you and I, is that I accepted the illness of my loved one and knew that only so much could've been done. In fact, my grandfather always told me growing up that he would never trade his grandson for all the money in the world. I always thought at a younger age that it was just something that our family members said to give us the confidence to do the same when we grew up, so we could do much less the same for our own. Tom then sat back down next to Rick and put the deputy's hand on the ex-agents shoulder.

"It's funny how the pages turn in life," the agent exclaimed. "So you're telling me that if your wife was sick and you could help her, even if it meant committing a crime to save her life, that you would stick to your moral high ground, just to watch her die, Tom?"

"I'd do whatever I could to help any of my family members or friends. If it came down to killing another human being to save my loved one, I'd consider it. I'm not gonna lie. Yet, the only difference between you and myself, is that I have a conscience. Also, I'm wearing a badge now and questioning an ex-federal officer why he's in bed with the Cavasos. So if making your life a living hell ensures that my family wakes up in the morning, then I will do anything that I can to ensure that security!"

"It sounds to me like you'd go to any extreme to save your loved ones," Tanner stated. "So why not kill me and get that off your conscience?"

"Because if I was out making deals and killing people, my loved ones would never forgive me and torturing my very soul to the grave. If you knew my grandfather, you'd understand," Tom replied then stood up, tipped his Stetson to the beleaguered agent and walked out of the room to leave Tanner alone with his guilt.

In the other room, everybody just sat emotionless wondering why this monster would put his sick wife in this situation. While she sat down with a blank stare on her face, the marshal pulled up a chair and held the poor woman's hand. Telling her that the government would help take care of her needs, Sheila broke down and started crying uncontrollably. So like any good patron, Wiley asked her to go outside with him to get some fresh air, which Sheila smiled and gladly accepted. As for the marshal and Larry; they decided to go into the sheriff's office for a drink.

"You know, you two make a really good team," Marshal Evans stated as he took a shot of whiskey that Larry had stashed away behind his desk. "So why didn't you ever deputy up for Larry, Tom?"

"Oh, for personal reasons, plus everybody in the Upper County knows that I'm way better at the job then Larry," Tom blurted out while taking a shot, and Larry did a lazy spit take, but did not phase the rancher in any way.

"You mean that you're better at drinking, asshole," Larry replied.

"Gentlemen, whatever the case may be, you only witness good partners once in a blue moon," Marshal Evans retorted. "Hell, I wished that I had a partner who could hold a candle to you boys."

All of the sudden, The marshal's phone rang and it was Terror informing him that his men had just pulled up to the pickup zone. Marshal Evans put Terror on speakerphone and Tom's biker friend put his phone secretly in a back pocket so the men could hear what was about to ensue. After the introductions, the conversation began mildly as the van with the dope backed up to Cavasos associates vehicle. While the men were loading the product, Terror asked, "So how's Juan been lately?"

Surprised, the thug smiled and answered, "Oh, I hear he's in a much happier place *vato*! How does that old saying go? When the game is over, the king and pawn go back into the same box."

Terror looked at the gangster and said, "Well fuck yeah, brother! Well anyhow, Wiley from the Teanaway sends his regards *puto*!" With that being said, the rest of the Yellow Jackets that had arrived earlier at the scene, raised up out of the hidden earth, loaded with automatic weapons that would make an infantry commander jealous. "Tell your men to lower their weapons, or my men will unload their ammo on yours!"

With no other option, the thug blasted Terror for the bike gangs betrayal giving the order for his cartel brethren to lay down their weapons. After Terror's men secured the scene, the president fetched his phone out of the back pocket and informed the group listening in, that all was clear. As so it was secure; up until one of the enforcers men tossed a grenade into the mix. The explosion was so clear and loud through the phone speaker, that it knocked the boys back in their seats, while listening to the melee in California. Then the boys heard sporadic gunfire and screaming. When all seemed lost, Terror picked the phone back up trembling. With his shaky voice told the guys that the moron thug, panicked, and the grenade misfired, but only on the Cavasos thugs.

Besides some cuts, Terror was surrounded by dead gangsters, three million in mafia cash, and a shit load of weed. Relieved, the marshal ran his hands through the lawman's hair and took another shot of whiskey.

"I'm starting to love the Upper County gentlemen," Marshal Evans exclaimed as Tom poured the lawman another snort.

"So what now," Tom asked, and Evans said that it was crucial that the Jackets pull any information off of the dead body's if necessary. At the same time, the marshal prayed that the cell phones seized by the Jackets could supply the evidence the lawman so desperately needed.

Excited, Eljah insisted that the boys head to Wil-E Coyotes to grab a beer, and the group all agreed. Who is Tom to refuse a drink from a fellow lawman, be them state or federal.

As the guys prepared to leave the building, Tom smelled an all too familiar scent flowing from a stump of pine trees in the distance, and began to follow the smell. Then the rancher heard some laughter emanating from the same location. When Tom jockeyed into position, only to see the source of his curiosity. That being no other than Wiley and Sheila smoking a joint that the crazy coot ironically brought into the sheriff's station. Tom tipped his Stetson hat and smiled at the two whom seem happily in content.

"Wiley, were heading over to your bar to drink," Tom stated. "Would you like to bring your new friend to blow off some steam?" Wiley shook his head, and Sheila's smile increased tenfold.

"Tom, I apologize for how I acted in there," Sheila said. "I just lost it and I'm still in shock about all of this. All the time, I thought he was cheating on me, but now I'll bet he wished he would have!"

"Sheila, my grandpa passed away from cancer and it's been a decade since Gene's been gone. All I remember about his struggle, is that he refused to let the cancer win, and his determination to beat that disease, prolonged his life substantially," Tom reassured Sheila while smiling at the torn woman. "He told me that you have to fight for the things you want in life, and sometimes those things aren't just things, but family."

Touched by Tom's sentiment, Sheila gladly accepted the invitation to hang out with the boys at Wiley's. As Tom helped Sheila into the car, she smiled at the rancher and said, "You're a good man Tom and you know what they say about good men. Is that they surround themselves around people just like themselves."

Trying hard not to shed a tear, Tom looked Sheila in the eyes and told her that she passed the bullshit test. Laughing, everybody hopped in the car and tore down the road to the bar.

When the group arrived at Wiley's, it was surprisingly dead, yet again. Wiley told Rob to hire a temporary bartender until Jennie was fit to return to work, so the new bar back seated the men and thanked Wiley for the job opportunity. Wiley then commenced to light up a joint with a perplexed marshal looking at him. Since it was Wiley's bar, technically it's his rules, legal or otherwise, and it's 2013, so now people can possess it in the State: However the Clean Air Act forbade just nonsense in public establishments but that did not deter the crazy fool one bit. After Wiley took a puff he passed the joint over to the lawman who was reluctant at first, but nonetheless, ended up taking a puff or two in celebration for the Yellow Jackets raid. It was pretty evident that the night was going to be a long one and Tom cherished moments like these. It's all about the people in your life and the connections you make that gives the man a reason to carry on, and the group seated with Tom that evening were all the friends that a rancher could be thankful to have in his life.

Up to today, Tom had no idea that he would be wearing a deputies badge, and that goes without saying, ole Wiley. Also, for that matter, meeting a woman scorned by heartache and illness was a tough burden to bear. Yet, to see the happiness in her eyes as if she had no cancer, was pleasing to Tom, as for the rest of the group. Moments like these are fleeting, and these memories to the rancher, need to be cherished and remembered.

As the night rolled on, for once, Tom made the choice to cut back on the drinking. The rancher worked on a glass of sweet tea which was unlike the man, but with all the tragedy, Tom knew that he had to be focused and determined to apprehend Cavasos, should the asshole make an appearance in the Upper county. The marshal and Larry had gone to the bar to watch the football game that Rob had recorded earlier on the DVR. All of the sudden, Maddy came in through the door with a confused, yet excited look about her, and pulled up a chair.

"Tom, the coin expert called me back and should be here in a couple of minutes with some important news about your coin," Maddy stated happily as she gave her husband an inviting hug.

"Are you sure the man's coming to bullshit about Tildy's coin, or is he just thirsty," Tom responded sarcastically as Maddy punched the rancher in the shoulder.

"Shut up Tom," Maddy shouted as Tom rubbed the area where his wife hit him. "He's a member of my church so I'm pretty sure the man doesn't drink. Tom, this is serious, so when the man shows up, please do me a favor a stow away the bullshit, okay?"

"How much is it worth," Tom inquisitively inquired as he put his arm around Maddy's back.

Maddy was hesitant but laughed as her fellow churchgoer came in and sat down with the rest of the group. "Evening everybody," Mr. Tate exclaimed sitting down and smiled. "Do you mind if we talk in private, Maddy and Tom?"

"It's okay, Mr. Tate," the rancher replied. These are my fellow churchgoers, and I trust them with my private matters."

"May I see the coin, Tom?" Mr. Tate asked, and Tom flipped it over in his direction. The numismatist took the coin and inspected it thoroughly, then smiled, almost shedding a tear, but nonetheless in shock. "Tom, this is by far the holy grail of coins! You see, the only other known coins that are exactly the same, are tucked away in a vault somewhere in Spain. There is suspected to be over ten billion dollars in this magnificent bullion being stored by the Spanish government. This particular coin, since it is in great shape for a coin of its time, is worth at least one million dollars!"

Everybody sat almost motionless at first, as if total surprise itself was not enough. Then the group erupted with excitement over this find while Maddy's fellow churchgoer ordered a round of whiskey for the group, himself included as well. Then Tom told the story of Wyatt Earp, and the legend of the Spanish gold. The rancher informed Mr. Tate that Gene had supposedly acquired it from his father, and he passed it on too Tildy, even though Tom never knew she had the gold piece. All Tom needed to know, was that Gene got that coin from somewhere. Either Wyatt paid the ranchers great great-grandpappy for the land and the gold was passed down, or his grandpa went to dig it up. This was the point where Maddy and the rancher decided to part ways and head for home, to speak to Tildy.

When they arrived, all was quiet. Dallas and Lue were up watching TV while Granny was sitting in her chair sleeping. Tom gently woke her up and moved Tildy to the wheelchair the hospital provided, then wheeled his grandma off to her room. The rancher laid down in her bed and temporarily exited the room so Maddy could dress the ole lady for a good night's rest.

"Tildy, that coin you gave Tom. Who did Gene originally get it from?" Maddy asked as she put Tildy's night gown on.

"He got it from his dad who got it from his dad, so on and so forth. I suppose the original owner was a gentleman by the name of Stapp, who once owned the property, which was in turn sold to Dally Wyatt."

Maddy immediately got excited, but as not to arouse ole Tildy who was past the point of sleep asked, "Do you by chance, have anymore of these gold coins?"

"Just like I told Tom, all you hafta do is find it," Tildy exclaimed and smiled. "But in the meantime, there's a wooden box in the chest at the end of my bed. I haven't been able to move that goddamn box in ages. Now, I'm gonna close my eyes and get some rest, darling," Tildy stated and gently closed her tired eyes.

Maddy proceeded to the chest and pulled out the box, struggling a bit, so Tom helped out grabbing the good fifty pound box. The couple took it into the kitchen setting the heavy chest on the counter and opened the contents inside. What the two witnessed, was beyond disbelief. The box was plum full of the coins, dirty yet still shimmering and both their eyes lit up.

"There's gotta be at least five hundred coins in the box, Maddy," Tom stated, and she readily agreed. Dad and Lue both rose in the excitement and rushed over to see what the ruckus was all about. The rancher gave both Lue and dad a handful of coins and told them that they were multimillionaires, as a joke of course. They were excited yet confused until Maddy and Tom told them what had been found out. It seemed for once, that things were going in a good direction for the month of October. To realize that they could easy sell these coins, possibly back to Spain, sent shivers down ole Tom's spine, and a new sense of hope and accomplishment overcame him.

"I guess there's only one thing left to do," Tom stated. "Let's call Spain and see if they want their money back!"

The rest of the night was a blur. Mr. Tate came over after hearing the news and fell to his knees when the scientist saw the bullion. Larry was in utter disbelief when he arrived and Tom told the sheriff that Gene must have funded the ranch for years with this fortune. Wiley and his new found friend Sheila were overcome with happiness when they looked into the chest and Tom reassured them that the money was indeed real. Whoever said that there is a millionaire born every minute, doesn't know the Wyatt's very well. In the same token however, the Wyatt's needs are taken care of for the rest of their lives. Now the big question that remained in ole Tom's mind was how do they sell this newfound fortune.

Being that it was late, everybody parted for the night accept for Sheila and Wiley, whom were temporarily homeless. Sheila had a hotel room lined up, but she was tired and Tom's hospitality ensured the gal that warm bed and a good breakfast in the morning would ease her mind. Thanking Maddy and Tom, Sheila wished everybody a good night as Wiley brought her bags out of the Yukon. Everybody retired for the night accept for Wiley and the rancher so, they stayed in the kitchen and made a late night snack. As Wiley ate however, he looked peculiar and upset.

"I can't believe that poor gal has to be involved in all of this," Wiley stated. "You know, we can call Thunder Bear and have a healing ceremony."

"I think Sheila would like that," Tom replied. "I love the ole medicine man and would like to see my friend again."

"I'll call him up tomorrow Tom," Wiley answered. "So how are we gonna say good-bye to Juan?"

"Well, how else do we," the rancher sarcastically blurted and Wiley proceeded to grin ear to ear.

"I'll ask Jennie in the morning," Wiley replied.

The next morning rolled around and Tom awoke to a happy Maddy rising to gold coins sticking to her skin, as well as the ranchers too. A word of advice to anyone who finds a lost treasure: Only have bedtime relations with your significant other with a crap load of cash to roll in, not coins. After the two prepared themselves for the day, the happy couple went down stairs only to find Lupita feeding the boys breakfast and Sheila grabbing food from the country buffet that Tom's step mom woke up early to prepare. Tom then went to wake Wiley, only to find that he wasn't there. "I guess I forgot to check Sheila's room," Tom pondered while smiling.

At any rate, the rancher walked a very naked Wiley to the bathroom to shower and pulled out some fresh clothes for the ole coot since his belongings were currently burnt. When breakfast was done, Larry showed up with news about the other men accompanying Agent Tanner the other day and the news was unnerving. Larry informed Wiley and Tom that the marshal's contacts came through and identified the men as a group known as Dos Demente. These men are the worst of the worst that works with cartels to extort money among other things.

The Dementes actually started training with British commandos and U.S. Special Forces in secret warfare. When these men completed their training, they took the weapons they were supplied with and vanished, only to form a group committed to torture, extortion, and kidnapping. Becoming as powerful than the Cartels, the Dementes agreed to help these syndicates run guns, money, and drugs to fuel their financial goals. So when Larry told Tom the news, the rancher knew that this was going to have a less than lackluster conclusion, figuring that ole Isidro was using them as mercenaries to find Wiley.

With the house still in mourning over the loss of Juan, Wiley approached Tom and asked if they could bring Sheila to the reservation for a healing ceremony. She was a little reluctant to go at first, but Wiley in his old hippy ways convinced her to go. Wiley told her how beautiful she was, so Sheila smiled and held him by the hand, giving the old coot a warm hug, agreeing to the healing. By that time, Maddy had all of the children's things packed for the temporary move and started to pack Granny's belongings. However, when Maddy told Tildy about the trip, the old lady flat out refused.

"I'm not gonna be intimidated by a bunch of youngsters with guns," Tildy reiterated. "Hell, leave me a piece and I'll shoot every last son of a bitch that comes through the God damned door!"

"Granny, these men mean business and I don't want anybody to get hurt," Tom stated and Tildy shrugged her shoulders while blowing the ranchers statement off entirely.

"Tom, your grandfather taught me how to handle a gun," Tildy replied. "Dammit, I might be a couple years shy of one hundred, but I'll be buggered if I'm not a better shot than you!"

Needless to say, the two left the conversation at that, and Tildy retired to her chair listening to some rock and roll. Honestly, Tom would have offered Tildy a pistol, but the ole gal still has Gene's Saturday night special tucked away, and if things got hairy enough, they could move the feisty woman, if need be.

With Tildy under Dallas and Lue's care until Tom returned home the rest of the family was well away to safety while the ranchers group had departed to the Yakama nation. Before the group passed by Ellensburg, Wiley needed to make a pit stop, so they stopped at a fast food joint. After twenty minutes had passed, the gals were starting to wonder if Wiley was okay, so Tom went inside to check. Upon a cool glance of the customers, the rancher spotted Wiley grubbing on some food in a booth, so Tom went to sit by him. Before the rancher sat down, there was a group of kids gnawing away on their kiddie meals, and one little boy said, "Hey, guys. Now that's a cowboy!"

Smiling at the children, Tom looked at the youngsters and flashed his badge, only to get the "cool" response from the kids. When the rancher sat down by Wiley, Tom told the little runts that Wiley had one to and he confidently flashed his at the awestruck children.

"But your friend looks like a hippie," one other kid exclaimed, only to be met with Wiley's cheeseburger being flung into said kids face. That was about the point where the two men decided to make their departure, with the poor child crying in the background to his mom and dad, who scowled at Wiley as the boys left.

"Wiley," Tom asked. "I think that we need to work on your filter."

Wiley replied, "Brother, that little kiddo made fun of me and that's just plain disrespectful!"

The rancher laughed at his crazy friend and replied, "Wiley, that kid was round about five years old, so I don't think the child knows any better."

"And the little fucker got a cheeseburger to the face for it," Wiley exclaimed.

The deputies left the restaurant entering the car and made no mention of this to the occupants, yet Tom found it hilarious, so the rancher pressed only to have Wiley mutter, "But the freaky little dude called me a hippy!"

With that being said, the group took off and Wiley told the ladies that he was constipated at the restaurant; trying to cover up the fact that he chose to eat than poop. With Wiley's little white lie being believed by the women, all was cool as could be, up until Sheila pointed out the catsup stains on his mouth, fingers, and shirt. Then Wiley had an idea.

"Hey, let's take the canyon road to Yakicrack (short for Yakima)." It was a good idea because it was a sunny Friday morning and the roads were fair. With a surprisingly warm temperature of eighty degrees, which was abnormal for that time of the year, the group sped down the two lane highway. The windy road was a joy for Jennie to drive as the Yakima River flowed right by their side. Then Tom spotted something floating in the river.

You see, one yearly summer tradition is to float the river, where one gets a group of several others, tying their perspective floatation device together. Essentially, floating the river loaded down with every beverage that the cooler(s) can hold. Anyhow, the eight very attractive college looking women in string bikinis automatically caught the attention of the male occupants in the vehicles. Tom didn't realize at the time how he missed being with Maddy all the time. With everything going on, it wasn't fair to be separated by his wife and children. As the women passed by, Tom remembered back to a time when they floated down the river, and Tom smiled as he pictured Maddy's string bikini overlaying her silky body, smiling, on a hot summer day of the past. No offense to the women on the river, but they can't hold a candle too Maddy.

Anyhow, after several groups of floaters, and plenty of beautiful women floated by, the group passed the Sundown ranch ending the canyon road. Hopping back on I-82, it was a matter of twenty minutes before they arrived at the reservation and to the home of Chief Thunder Bear.

When the group pulled up to Thunder Bears home, the chief was rocking in his porch swing playing with his granddaughter, smiling. Everybody exited the car and approached the chief as he shooed the youngster along. Now standing, the chief shook everybody's hand and invited the parched travelers to sit under the shade of the porch.

"Can I just say that it's unnaturally hot for this time of the year," the chief commented and then looked at Wiley. "Wiley, I believe the deal was a healing conducted by the tribe for twelve bottles of moonshine?"

"The jars are in the trunk," Wiley replied and got up to go fetch the booze which surprised Tom because quite frankly, the rancher had no idea that his friend brought extra supplies.

"Tom, beers in the fridge," Thunder Bear stated and Tom hopped up to fetch a cold longneck. "Hey, Running Drunk," the chief stated, "How was the trip over?" The Indian name Running Drunk was given to Tom which is the joke of the Tribe. Long story.

"Tom, can you grab my iPhone off the kitchen table?" Thunder Bear asked.

"Sure thing, chief," Tom replied and moseyed on to the kitchen. The truth about chief is that he rarely drinks anymore, yet due to the fact that he is co owner of a successful casino in Downtown Yakima, and gets a lot of free perks, one including free booze. Hell, one time Tom brought Trigger along and the perks got the best of the two. To add insult to injury, Trigger decided to mount the chief's prize mare, so Tom's horse was never invited back.

Trigger aside, relations couldn't be better with the tribe, and Wiley's moonshine sealed the deal securing a healing ceremony for Sheila. After Wiley carted in the corn liquor, and one case of buzz beer, the group began to reminisce about the past.

"Sheila, I feel a strong, unbreakable soul inside you," the chief stated, and tears started to well up in the sick woman's eyes.

"It is true what they say about the eyes," Thunder Bear asked. "If they are windows to the soul, then you have beautifully resilient eyes!"

Touched by the chief's kind sentiment, Sheila hugged the old fart and Thunder Bear pinched her rump. Shocked, Sheila asked if her ass was as strong as her soul, and the chief replied, "Well, I dunno, but nonetheless, you my dear, have a pretty ass!." Thunder bear exclaimed and shooed Sheila back to her chair. "The truth is, Sheila, that you're perfect the way you are and the demons that you'll face tonight will witness your fury, hopefully going back to where they came from." Touched, Sheila sat there and smiled while the boys continued to converse about life on that beautiful October day in the Yakima Valley.

Chapter 10

Rattlesnakes, Beer Cans, and Peyote—Oh My

A lot of questions are raised when it comes to our own mortality and the life that sustains every human's soul. There eventually will come a day when we have to face death and accept it before our souls pass on to the great spirits that lie in the stars. The healing ceremony, is actually based on the premise, that the person who's receiving the healing, actually dies during the ceremony. As their soul moves out of their body, they ascend to the spirits to ask them to heal their body. When the persons soul returns, they are said to be healed and protected from the demons therein.

After a time of drinking and talking about the boys current problems, Thunder Bears son came by to pick up his daughter. She was delighted to see her dad who just got off work. Tom had not seen the kid in a while so they shook hands, then Thunder Bears son sat down telling the group about the operations of his business, which is making cigarettes. White Swan, which is a part of the Yakama Nation, makes a good smoke named King Mountain cigarettes, appropriately named for Mount Adams in the south. Theo Burning Tree is actually a name Tom gave the boy when he was a young teenager because Tom caught the kid smoking pot with a group of his friends, so the trade for his witness to Burning Trees discretion, meant that Tom got to pick the name.

Theo quickly came and went promising to be at the healing ceremony that evening, which made his Yaqui, or father, very happy.

As the day progressed, the chief let his prize horses out of the stall and they prepared the stallions for the ride to the ancient grounds. The ceremony was to take place on sacred land that hasn't been touched by the gas powered vehicles that roam around nowadays. The grounds are also said to be the first camp of the Yakama Nation. Even till this day, Tom still goes there to and find arrowheads or some other kind of artifacts. Yet at the chief's request, cannot remove the trinkets, for any reason, ever, yet the rancher likes to screw with ole Thunder Bear at times by moving those artifacts around. After Wiley and Tom saddled up the horses, the rancher helped the chief up on his horse, who requested a satchel so Tom could load it down with beer. Smiling, the chief one-upped the rancher and directed him to a barn, where there was a device similar like a satchel, only a cooler that fits on the horse's rump. With the beverages loaded down in the satchel, the group began the trek to the grounds. Sheila was a little slow at first to ride, but she picked it up quickly and was soon racing her horse on short sprints as not to tire the beast out.

The first stop before the grounds, was an oasis where an ancient spring still flows pure water out of the depths of the ground. The group got off their horses to let them drink and Tom passed around cold bottles of long necks to the thirsty group. While the horses drank the rancher walked over to a group of trees to find a bathroom, and froze in his tracks. A rattlesnake apparently had positioned itself directly into Tom's path and was curled up shaking its tail violently. As Tom cautiously backed up the viper hissed even more making the ranchers adrenaline rise. Continuing to back up further, the pissed little fella struck out and as he did, the chief came out of nowhere and grabbed him by the neck, killing the rattler instantly. Thunder Bear then proceeded to look at Tom and asked if the rancher wanted lunch, which sounded really good as Tom's heartbeat began to diminish. They decided to take the healthy looking meal back to the campground and Tom asked if they should build a campfire, but the chief had a small propane stove tucked away under his satchel, which Tom was quick to grab.

Thunder Bear then took out some olive oil and a pan then began heating up the plate. As the oil started to boil, the chief skinned the viper and fillet it into tiny fine strips. When the liquid was as hot as could be, he took the meat and began cooking up the snake, which Sheila was reluctant to eat at first. Yet, after a beer and a joint that Wiley and Sheila smoked, the hungry woman enjoyed the smell emanating from the pan. When the snake was ready, Thunder Bear placed the cooked snake into a plate and everybody began to sample the amazing meat.

"It tastes exactly like chicken breast," Sheila exclaimed as she dipped into Wiley's helping.

Sheila ate one more piece but the chief told her not to eat too much. Due to the traditions of the ceremony, fasting was originally required, yet after many years, exceptions were made to the rule, so the gal obeyed. After the group's meal, the boys helped Thunder Bear clean up, and they were steadily back on their way to the ancient grounds.

After a few more hours, the group arrived to a scene of Indian elders and their kin beginning to ready the fire for the rapidly approaching ceremony. The grounds were very primitive, yet well kept, with a huge fire pit built out of the stone from the canyon walls nearby. There's not a lot of vegetation or trees, reflecting an almost desert-like scene, with the Yakima River, running only yards away from the groups feet. The band of travelers dismounted their horses and all the appropriate introductions were made for tonight's guest. Sheila was well received by the elders with hugs and handshakes making her feel like she was instantly one of the tribe. The chief then went over to the other elders and started to prepare the medicine for tonight's ceremony, which is derived from an ancient root long believed to promote a clean soul and a healthy body. In the meantime while things were being prepared, Wiley and Sheila disappeared to go smoke a joint and when they returned, the two were acting funnier than normal. Earlier upon the groups arrival, Wiley made a cup tea for Sheila who was feeling tired. He reassured Sheila that it would make her feel much better. Wiley also indulged in a cup and after a short time began to laugh constantly. Then the hallucinations set in making the two appear as if they were listening to Jimi Hendrix play the "Star Spangled Banner" at Woodstock.

"Wiley, you mind telling me what's in the tea?" Tom inquired.

"Just some green tea and peyote," Wiley replied and proceeded to take a sip. Now Tom wouldn't put it past ole Wiley to up the ante by spiking Sheila's healing ceremony. However, when she started to hallucinate, she was totally calm, and happy, all at the same time.

The moment had arrived for the healing, and the group made their way to the fire, as all the elders were sitting in a circle smoking the traditional peace pipe. Passing it around, the chief motioned for Sheila to join him and when she came down to sit, Thunder Bear wrapped a deer skin shoal over her shoulders. The chief then said some words in the native Yakama language and blew some smoke from the peace pipe in her face, chanting with the elders all in harmonious rhythm. After a few moments, Thunder Bear laid her down by the fire, grabbing an eagles feather, and chanted some words while sweeping Sheila's body from head to toe. The sound of the drums and other chanting voices started to crescendo, making Sheila's heart beat faster than ever, and that was the last thing she remembered before the lady passed out.

The next thing Sheila encountered were visions of the past and these black wisps of souls she knew whom had passed a long time ago. Then she felt and heard the voices of the ceremony, then realized that she was no longer laying on the ground, but floating over the group, ascending higher by every beat of the drum. As she climbed, black souls were trying to grab her, but they could not reach her now, and a sense of tranquility and peace overcame Sheila's body. Sheila then realized that she was no longer floating, now standing in front of a misty stream, hearing the voices of what sounded like children playing in the background. Sheila turned their direction and then saw an Indian woman standing by a tree, smiling back at her, holding a feather. As the woman reached out to give Sheila the feather, she woke up in a cold sweat.

It was now daylight and Sheila awoke, rising up only to find that no one was around. Still by the fire pit, Sheila turned her head to see if she could hear anybody, and spotted a feather that looked similar to the one the Indian woman gave the sick woman, in her vision. She picked up the soft feather and stood, wondering where all the people disappeared too. All of the sudden, Wiley grabbed her by the shoulder and frightened her to death, but Sheila's scare was soon replaced by a smile.

"What happened to me," Sheila asked and Wiley simply looked at her smiling.

"Well, your healing ceremony went very well," Wiley replied. "But when the chief found out that you were on peyote, he had me escort you on a spirit walk."

Thinking that it was the next day, Sheila asked for a phone so she could call her kids and Wiley informed her that Tom had called two days ago. Confused at first, Sheila then realized that she had been outside for two days with Wiley. Sheila freaked out at first, but Wiley quickly calmed her down and told her that peyote can have a more than timely effect, affecting the very flow of time itself. When she asked where everybody was, Wiley told Sheila that everybody was at the chief's place waiting for their return. Feeling her tummy grumble louder than ever, the gal gestured to Wiley about her hunger, so they hopped on their horses and departed for Thunder Bears place.

On the way back, Wiley had rolled a joint and passed it back and forth while Sheila laughed boisterously, as Wiley told her stories of the past adventures involving Tom and Larry. When they were almost to the chief's house, Sheila told Wiley about her healing experience. Mixed with the peyote, it was serene at times and then intense, like a freight train ready to hit a stalled car in the middle of the track. Sensing Sheila's confusion, Wiley reassured her that these traditions that the tribe carries, is for pure resolve and that she should think of how the experience coincides with her own life. At least for once in her existence, Sheila felt like there was a hope that she never really felt before.

The one thing about Sheila is that Agent Tanner swept the woman off her feet at the ripe ole age of eighteen. She never had to work. In fact, Sheila never graduated from high school. She spent twenty years raising their children and kept a beautiful home tucked away in the suburbs of Seattle. Sheila knew that Rick's job was a demanding one and even when she was diagnosed with breast cancer, the poor woman still felt brushed aside. Rick was by her side at first, going to doctors appointments and taking care of the kids, but when he started having dealings with the Cavasos, Rick had to prioritize so the agent could keep a steady stream of cash in the doctors pockets.

Finding out that her husband was corrupt was crippling at first, but she knew that Rick loved her; just loved her a little too late.

When the two arrived back at the chief's, the porch looked like it had been violated by a lost fraternity with a couple kegs, cases of beer, and some passed out strippers. The place wreaked of booze and stale cigarettes entwined with day old pizza. Wiley hopped off of his horse and approached Tom, who was sleeping in a hammock, with his hat covering his eyes, snoring away. Wiley proceeded to give ole Tom a gentle nudge to his bottom with a boot, waking Tom fast out of a peaceful dream that the rancher was having. That in turn awoke the rest of the group with the chief startling back to life, peace pipe still wedged in his mouth.

Sheila witnessing this like it was the first time in her life, started to bust up laughing, and at times, rolled hysterically on the ground. When she sprang back up, the chief stared at Sheila and looked confused at first, only to take another puff off of his pipe.

"Sheila, you're not the only one who had a healing around here," Chief Thunder Bear stated, referring to the party. He then greeted Sheila with a hug. "You look amazing! The color has returned to your face and you look so much better!"

Little did Sheila know, that before the ceremony, Wiley had secretly laced the drinking water with a peyote extract and that everybody at the ceremony had drank from it. The night when Sheila ascended, apparently the group was right up there with her, so they played and prayed for a day straight after that. Sheila had asked the chief if he had some food to fill her hungry belly. Obliging, he showed Sheila to the kitchen where Theo had brought some leftovers from a seafood buffet, so Thunder Bear fixed a plate for Wiley and herself sitting at the kitchen table, engorging themselves.

While they ate, Larry showed up with the marshal. The two got out of the car and the marshal pulled off his sunglasses looking in total shock at the scene set before him. Larry came over by Tom and sat down asking for a beer, which the chief directed Larry to the fridge on the porch directly behind him. When Larry opened the door, a stream of empty beer cans and bottles streamed out like a glassy aluminum water fall.

"There's only one beer left," Larry exclaimed. "Tom do you drink every place dry that you run into?"

"No, Larry," the chief replied. "That was the medicine for our healing ceremony!"

The marshal approached Thunder Bear and introduced himself shaking the chief's hand. Thunder Bear thanked him for coming over and then asked Marshal Evans if he could look and see if some deadbeat renters destroying his property down the road, had some warrants. Being that this was a reservation issue, the federal government had no jurisdiction, unless their invited by the tribe. Marshal Evans paused and scratched his head looking confused.

"I'm normally only looking for the suspects that have federal charges," Evans stated. "But I can go over there and pay them a visit with permission from the tribe of course," and winked at the chief.

"What happens at the res, stays at the res," the chief replied, laughing. "Just do me a favor and bring the pricks back to me in one piece so I can have a chat with them!"

"I suspect we could go take a look," the marshal replied, staring at Tom and Wiley. "Do we require an escort from the tribal police?"

The chief then pointed to one of the elders passed out on the deck. "You can see that he's a little busy at this moment, so I will inform my officer if anything pops up," the chief exclaimed then winked at the marshal.

"Tom and Wiley, let's go do some field training," the marshal stated and the boys looked at each other as Larry sat there drinking a beer, while shooing them away.

With the marshal and chief in agreement, Tom and Wiley shuffled to their feet and followed the marshal, to the car. Thunder Bear then looked at the sheriff sitting there drinking his beer and asked Larry if he was going to follow. Larry responded by asking the chief if he had any more seafood from the buffet, in which Thunder Bear laughed and directed the sheriff to the kitchen. After a couple of minutes, Marshal Evans and the boys arrived at the trailer. The men looked on in disgust at the property, seeing that the trailer and the land had appeared poorly maintained, so the lawmen exited the vehicle. There was garbage and animal feces spread throughout the yard, so the three made their way cautiously to the front door. Marshal Evans knocked only to get no answer, then banged on the door loudly. A few moments later, the door opened with a very young Spanish girl answering with a smile on her face.

"Ma'am, are you residing in this trailer," Marshal Evans asked as he looked at the filth inside the residence.

"No, I just came by to say hi to the guys and now I gotta go" the young lady stated, while grabbing her car keys.

"Ma'am, I'm with the U.S. Marshal Service," Evans stated. "Do you mind if we come in and talk to the tenants?"

The gal called out for one of the people inside but the men heard the sound of a body piling out of a window at the end of the trailer. Apparently the tenant wasn't up for a chat that day, so the marshal drew his gun and directed Wiley to follow his lead. Sensing that things didn't seem quite right, Tom bolted to the other side of the trailer, with the deputies gun drawn and shouted out to the man running away from the house.

"Stop right now or ill shoot, you dumb ass," Tom exclaimed, but the man just kept on running. Chasing the tenant at a fast pace, Tom overtook him within seconds tackling the idiot to the ground, and the quick thinking rancher jammed his knee on the tenants neck, securing the runner to the earth. "You do realize that it looks bad when you run from the law, right Tom asked as the tenant continued to struggle.

"I'm on the reservation asshole," the tenant blurted out while Tom slapped cuffs on his wrists. "You can't do this! It's illegal!"

"I'm here on behalf of Chief Thunder Bear," Tom said. "And the chief wants to have a chat with you! Now get your ass up and let's go."

Tom escorted the man back to Wiley and the marshal who were waiting by the car. Placing the tenant in the back seat, Tom had a pissed off look to himself. "Thanks a bunch for helping out fellas," Tom exclaimed and the two men laughed.

"Gee Tom, looks like you had it under control," Marshal Evans replied. "Wiley and I had to check the property anyhow for anything illegal."

Wiley then added, "And that *chica* was muy caliente! We couldn't let her go without proper questioning."

"But you let her go anyhow Wiley," Tom exclaimed as the adrenaline started to wane in the deputies bloodstream.

"We let the girl go and there was no one else in the trailer," the marshal stated. "Let's get the hell out of this shithole and get this guy over to the chief, boys."

The men quickly headed back to Thunder Bears and when they arrived, some more of the tribe elders had showed up to drink at the chief's house. Marshal Evans removed the tenant out of the car, uncuffed him and walked the detainee over to a very angry, yet calm Thunder Bear.

"I see you have delivered this piece of shit to me intact," the chief exclaimed as he passed the boys over a beer.

"Tom apprehended him just fine while Wiley and myself stood back and watched," the marshal replied with a smile on his face. Marshal Evans then took the nervous tenants ID and ran it, only to find no federal warrants, but a ton of statewide drug charges.

"Looks like you got a real winner here, chief," the marshal stated and ordered the tenant to his knees directly in front of Thunder Bear. "Looks like your tribal policeman is still sleeping?"

"It would appear that way, marshal, and there's no need to cuff the man any further," the chief exclaimed, only to get a dog collar attached to a chain out from under the porch. Shoving it in the tenants face, the chief said, "Here you put this on. Until you get me my rent money you are no better than a dog, so you will be treated like one!"

"Please, Chief Thunder Bear. I will get you the money right now. Have mercy on me and please let me go!" the renter begged as the marshal laughed and attached the collar to the man's neck.

"I'll let you go when you have four months of overdue rent in my pocket," the chief exclaimed. "Now why don't you disappear under the porch dog, and eat the scraps underneath!" The renter was reluctant at first, but the gun that Thunder Bear started to reach for, convinced the man otherwise, so the tenant scrambled quickly under the safety of the porch.

"Dogs don't sit like humans," Thunder bear stated as he peeked under the porch at the tenant. "If you're gonna sit on the ground, then you must sit like a dog!"

With the whole group now laughing, the tenant reluctantly sat down on his hind quarters and the chief told the group to that the tenant appeared hungry and thirsty. Disappearing into the house, the chief came back out with a couple dog bowls filled with water and food, then placed it in front of the disgraced renter. "You'll eat like a dog too, until you get me my money, doggy," and looked on in anticipation as the renter looked at the dog food. Now usually when a federal law enforcement official witnesses behavior like this, they are supposed to report it. Yet after witnessing the conditions of the renter's trailer, Marshal Evans sat back and cracked open a beer, laughing at the chief's new pet.

When the renter could not stand anymore embarrassment, he asked for a phone to call for the late rent money. The chief obliged and passed a cell phone to the tenant informing the man that he had to bark like a doggy while talking to his cash source. Practically everybody's eyes lit up as the human canine spoke to his contact while barking. After their conversation, there was not a dry eye in the house that could contain all of the laughter spewing from the chief's new pet's mouth. When the renter was done, he passed back the phone informing Thunder Bear that the money would be there shortly, and if he could take the collar off. Let me just say that to all of you fellow readers, that the chief did not budge and was resolute in his demands, forcing the poor man to remain under the porch. It might have been an embarrassing moment for the renter, but for Thunder Bear, it was another example of how the chief keeps order on his ancestors land. The thing that always struck Tom's fancy about the chief is that Thunder Bear states to be strong, is too be Indian and to be weak, is to be laughed at by an Indians strength.

After a time, the renter's mom showed up and got out of her car. She apologized to Thunder Bear in her sons lack of due diligence in paying his bills on time. Thunder Bear accepted the moms apology and commanded the renter to take off the collar and approach his mother. When the man stood in front of the chief, Thunder Bear said in a formidable tone, "Your mother is a good, honorable woman, and this is how you chose to honor her? The first thing you will do when you get back home is clean that disgusting filth of a property back to its former pristine condition. When you are done there, you will go back to your mother's house and do whatever chores she requires you to do because that's how sons honor their mothers!" Thunder Bear then did something unexpected and gave the money back to the renter's mom. She refused to take it, but the chief figured that after the costs for eviction and cleaning, that forgiving the debt would save him an even higher cost in the future.

With a smile on her face, the renter's mother hugged Thunder Bear thanking him for the sentiment and the chief gave the woman some buffet cards that his son had dropped off. The mom then took off and the son did as well, who immediately started cleaning the outside of the filthy property. When all seemed to settle down for the group, Larry got a call on his cell phone and walked off listening to the caller on the other end. After shaking his head up and down continuously. the sheriff put his phone down and said, "Hey, fellas, it's time to go back to Tom's. Tildy just shot two men trying to get into the property!"

"Jesus Larry, is she okay?" Tom asked not apparently knowing his own grandmother that well.

"She's fine, Tom, but the dead men lying in your house are a different story," Larry replied.

"I hope everything is okay with your grandma, Tom," Thunder Bear replied. "I'd like to thank you for bringing Sheila over here, and if you need any help with your troubles, please let me know." The men then shook hands with the chief and expediently made their way back to the Windy River Ranch.

When the boys arrived, the scene was chaotic—like normal—for a Teanaway crime scene. Tom ran inside the house to find Tildy sitting in her rocking chair sipping on her sweet tea, and hugged his grandma. Little did the boys know, but while they were at the reservation, three armed assailants decided to pay Tom a visit, but when the thugs pulled up, Tildy knew that something wasn't right. She could see that the men were armed, even though there guns were tucked away beneath their suits. Doing the only thing she knew how, Tildy took her gun and hid it behind the door and then cracked it open slightly.

With the gun at the ready Tildy said, "Howdy fellas! How y'all doin today?"

"Very well, ma'am, and thank you," the main thug replied. "Ma'am, were with the FBI and looking for Tom Wyatt or Wiley Holloway. Have they been around?"

Now Tildy was on full alert because the Hispanic accent in the man's voice was dually suspect answered, "Those two went to the store to get me some more sweet tea. Is there anything else I can help you with cause I'm listening to my Skynard and don't wanna miss what happens next boys."

"Ma'am, can we come in and have a look around?" the thug asked a little more aggressively.

"Depends, FBI agent. Do you have a warrant?" Tildy replied.

"We don't need a warrant, ma'am," the thug replied, and as Tildy shut the door, the prick stuck his foot in the doorway jarring the door. With every excuse an old lady would need, pointed her 38mm directly at his foot blowing a sizeable hole in it. The men drew their guns, and Tildy fell to the floor narrowly escaping the bullets flying inside the house. The door swung open and Tildy got a clean shot of another gangster who made the mistake of being in her line of fire. With one badly injured and one dead, Tildy quickly hid behind a desk to avoid being seen or shot by the third assailant.

After a few more shots were fired by the non-injured gangster, silence filled the room. Tildy had run out of ammo and was quietly curled up beneath the desk when the gangster called out.

"I'm guessing you're out of ammo," the thug shouted. "Look, old lady, we're just here for Wiley and Tom, so I suggest you give up, lay your gun down, and I promise I won't kill you!"

Looking around, the prick started to inspect the living room and noticed a huge desk in the corner. Within seconds, he was on top of her with the gun pointed at Tildy's head. "Well, old lady, you had a good life—and now, it's time for you to die!"

The shot was loud and instantaneous, only when Tildy opened her eyes, she noticed the gangster lying dead on the ground. She then realized that the shot didn't come from his gun, but from her son's pistol.

"Mom, are you all right?" Dallas shouted out, running over to his mother.

"I'm fine, son, but there's still one more outside," Tildy replied.

"No, Mom, you got the asshole," Dallas said. "You musta shot an artery 'cause he's deader than a coffin nail!"

Dallas went to his mom and gently helped her from under the desk. They both hugged each other and Dallas noticed the Skynard song playing in the background. "They call me the breeze," he commented. "Good song to have a gunfight to mom!"

"I suppose you're right, son," Tildy responded. "Now call the cops and pour me a fresh cup of tea!"

After Tom and the boys heard the story, they were in utter disbelief over what happened. Larry was briefed by his deputies over the incident while Tom sat with Tildy and Dallas.

"Granny, did the assholes say what they were doing there," Tom asked.

"Son, they wanted you and Wiley," Tildy replied. "They flashed their FBI credentials but I knew they were fake. You know Tom, if you wanna play with your friends, you best do it somewhere else from now on!"

Laughing, Tom agreed and hugged his dad not really knowing how to express his gratitude for being there at the wrong time. "Heck Tom, I was out feeding the horses and heard the gunshots," Dallas said. "I ran into your office and grabbed a shotgun, then when I got to the house, saw the thug standing over Mom and pulled the Trigger. I had no idea that she shot the other two idiots!"

"Dad, she's tough as nails and I'm besides myself that she took those men on," Tom replied.

When things seemed to be settling down, Granny had a sharp pain to her chest and felt weak. Tom and Dallas helped Tildy outside to an awaiting ambulance and told the EMT about her condition, so they whisked her away to the hospital in Ellensburg. After filling Larry in, the sheriff gave Tom his cell phone and called Maddy to tell her what just happened. Maddy was panicked but told Tom that they'd meet at the hospital so the boys hopped into Larry's cruiser and headed to Ellensburg.

When the boys arrived at the hospital, they were greeted by Maddy and Lupita, whom were forced to temporarily move into the home of one of Maddy's friends, due to the current troubles back on the Teanaway. Maddy drew close to Tom giving the rancher a hug and kiss, then turned to Wiley who was very quiet, and hugged the man as well. After embraces were given they all sat down and Lue brought the exhausted men coffee to drink. Not realizing that Larry and Tom were drinking moonshine out of a flask, the men continued to sneak some shots right into their coffee, drinking the corn liquor in earnest. The group was anxious and restless as the seconds seemed to pass like hours, flowing maniacally into a countless, impatient stall. After a long wait, the doctor finally came out and walked slowly with a look of concern about his face. The doctor approached Dallas and Tom, shaking their hands with a sadly half grin.

"Hello, everyone, I'm Dr. Mathis and we should get down to the heart of the matter. Tildy is a very resilient woman, for a person of her age. She did however have another minor heart attack and I fear that without proper treatment, that she might just stay in the hospital indefinitely."

Maddy started to cry with Dallas, who in turn realized that Tildy was to remain at the hospital. The doctor had mentioned heart surgery, but in Tildy's present condition, her age and heart problem would certainly kill her. Doctor Mathis did say that Tildy would have to undergo blood thinning treatments and that could potentially kill her as well, which was unsettling for the group. All the same, it was the best chance to decrease her chances of a stroke or another heart attack, so Dallas gave the doctor the okay to begin treatment. The doctor also uttered politely that she was sleeping, but otherwise ready for visitors.

The group entered the room where Tildy was resting. It was your typical depressing hospital room with all of the flashing lights and blinking knobs, as well as the touch screen do-hickeys, and plasma TV thing-a-me-bobbers. Dallas gave his mom a kiss on the forehead and pulled up a chair, sitting down as if a huge weight had been lifted from the man's shoulders.

"When you guys are ready to go, it's ok," Dallas mumbled. "I'll stay with mom. I don't want you all to have to wait around here." Touched, Maddy gave Dallas a hug and replied, "Dallas were all family in this room, so we will sit in shifts for as long as it takes."

"Maddy, Tom couldn't have picked a better woman to call wife, and me a daughter," Dallas responded and hugged Maddy tight. "And plus, you got a nice rack!" That's the thing about Dallas. Even though the chips were down for Tildy, the man still made the group exercise a much needed laugh. Dallas agreed to take the first shift which would last the rest of the night. Larry being tired himself offered Wiley to come home with him, but the old bat declined to go and continued to sit. As for Maddy, Lue and Tom, they agreed to go and get some rest at the wife's friends for the remainder of the night.

The three departed and Larry decided to sit with Wiley for a minute before the sheriff took off. "Wiley, you don't have to stay here my friend," Larry blurted out. "Why don't you come home with me and get some rest?"

"It's not that I don't appreciate your generosity, Larry, I really do," Wiley replied. "It's just that Gene and Tildy were there for me growing up, and I feel like I'm losing my mom."

"They were and still are a big part of my life too," Larry stated. He then rose and patted Wiley on the shoulder and wished the sad man a good night. As Larry left, he reassured Wiley that things were going to be okay and exited through the mechanical sliding glass door.

In Tildy's room, a tired Dallas remained at guard holding his moms hand. As Dallas sat, he reminisced about the past and all of the memories. Good or bad, they were all a reflection of his life and he was proud that he could sit by his mother's side sober, and not the drunken wreck that he used to be. All of the sudden, he felt his moms hand grab his tighter and she awoke.

"Dalley, is that you, son?" Tildy asked as she struggled to look around in the room.

"Yes, Mother, I'm right here by your side, and I'm not letting go," Dallas responded as a tear streamed down his face.

"Son, that's one thing I've finally learned about living in this life," Tildy stated. "That sooner or later you have to let go, and it's okay to let go, son."

"Mom, I will when the time comes," Dallas continued. "But tonight, let's not focus on such deathly thoughts. Let's get some sleep, so I can listen to you tell Tom who the better shot is with a pistol, in the morning." With that being said, Dallas lowered his head to the side or Tildy's bed. Tildy then took her hand and ran it through Dallas's aging hair comforting the man into a solace of sleep, as she sat their smiling at the man who saved her life.

Chapter 11

When the Fit Hits the Shan

The next morning, Tom awoke suddenly out of a cold sleep, springing to life. With all of the things going on with his granny, Tom wasn't getting much rest at all, nowadays. No longer being able to handle it anymore, the rancher decided to put the notion of buried treasure on his property, to rest. Tom didn't even bother to shower or eat, but threw his clothes on as fast as the man could, and sprang out the front door. Grabbing a shovel with a light, the rancher ran out of the front door and made his way out to the cave in the dark of that cold early morning.

When the rancher arrived, he unlocked the door and entered the cave. After hanging up the light, Tom fired up a propane heater and approached the weapons table picking up a throwing knife. Tom took dead aim, throwing the blade at a target and nailed it with deadly precision. The rancher then commenced to throw the remaining knives hitting the exact same region as the first knife, only the last blade missed its mark and ricocheted off of a picture frame, sending the old frame falling to the ground. Tom then dropped to his knees and started to cry, and could only think about Tildy, as well as the problems he was facing in the Upper County. In a rare fit of rage, Tom picked up an old axe and violently stabbed the old wooden rafters over head. The rancher dropped the rickety axe to the ground, and fell to his knees again, when all of the sudden, something hit the rancher in the back of the head. When Tom looked down at the ground where the object fell, his somber tone turned to a happy smile.

Tom immediately picked up the shiny object which turned out to be a coin that was an exact match to his. Suddenly, two coins fell, and then a cascading amount of gold spilled to the floor. Standing in disbelief, Tom grabbed the axe and tore open a larger hole into the roof (just enough to peek the ranchers head through), to see what lay in wait on the other side. Grabbing a head mounted flash light, Tom placed it over his head and raised a ladder into the wooden planks above. What Tom witnessed next, left the rancher utterly speechless. The whole roof was packed full of burlap sacks filled with coin, as well as the one that he had put a hole into.

"The legend of the gold is true," Tom thought to himself, and his sorrow was placed with a happiness and excitement that the overwhelmed rancher had never experienced before ever in his life.

Realizing the value that each coin was a million dollars or more, began to collect the bounty that lay on the ground and threw it into a satchel that he had close by. After all of the gold was picked up, Tom knew that his fortune just made him the richest man in the Upper County, as well as the State of Washington, and the rancher knew, that he had to protect the gold until it could be moved to a more secure location.

"There's really only one person for that kind of challenge," Tom thought to himself, with that particular person being ole Wiley Holloway.

Tom grabbed the satchel but before he departed, the rancher went over to the broken picture frame and picked it up, looking at the photo that Tildy had taken of both Tom and Gene, in a hot summers day roping cattle. As he began to pick up the frame, an old rolled up letter fell out. Curious, Tom picked up the letter and opened the preserved document. Tom's eyes automatically lit up when the rancher saw the writing on the other side, that read like this:

To whomever may find this,

Hell, why not just get to the point? Tom, if you're reading this here letter, I just want to say that that life is full of choices, and some of the choices that I have made in the past have been questionable, if not scrutinized. Son, what I can tell you about the choices that I never regretted—includes your Granny, Dally, the ranch, the cattle, you, and the shitload of gold bullion coin sitting directly above your head in burlap sacks! Yeah, dipshit, that's right. How do you think I kept us Wyatts flourishing all of these years?

Now I know that you just recently began our secret training, and I just want you to know, that I'm going to be a hard ass at times, but know this. Tom, I love ya just like Dally, and my one wish for you when you grow up is to grow up strong. Always love your family, respect your friends, and stay away from Willard Holloway's boys. That Wiley can be a jackass at times, but I still treat him like one of my own.

Tom, now with this newfound fortune, I hope you spend it right, and for the love of God, I really hope you're not in some bar, unmarried, looking for a piece of tail! Remember, son, always do right by others and they will return the favor tenfold, like I have done on this day by writing you this here letter. Tom, send Tildy a kiss my way, and I love you, son.

Always keeping you in my thoughts, Gene.

Tom looked up at the rafters and laughed like he just lost his sanity, but laughed nonetheless, at the coincidental timing of the letter, then realized that life is about choices, as well as good timing. Feeling like the rancher had been transported in the past, Tom started to cry, wiping the tears off on his tanned leather coat. Tom then picked up the broken picture frame and rehung the old photo, and stood back remembering that moment when the two stood side by side, laughing at Tildy who was telling the boys that she could rope a cow faster. Smiling, Tom flashed a smile at the old photo and then grew a whopper of a grin, when he looked at the satchel.

With the letter safely tucked away in his pocket, and the gold laden satchel on the ranchers shoulder, Tom left the cave, securing the door on his way out. The ranchers excited stride left him standing in the front of his office within in a matter of moments. Tom then opened the door only to find Wiley laying on the ground, curled up on the ground. Concerned, Tom approached Wiley and gave him a gentle nudge on the shoulder. Opening his eyes, Wiley looked at Tom and said, "Hey Tom, I'm a kitty! Wanna pet me?"

Now before ole Tom said anything, we have to remember that Wiley is the man for trusted security.

"Wiley, get your feline ass off of the floor and take a look at this!" Tom then opened the satchel exposing the shiny gold coins.

"Tom, that's beautiful, "Wiley stated almost dazed by the shiny coins. "Where'd ya find all of this?"

"Wiley, this is just the start of it, "Tom replied. "Grab your jacket and follow me!"

With that being said, the two men made their way to the cave. When they arrived, Tom had Wiley take a peek above the rafters, and the crazy fools expression was priceless.

"Holy Jesus jumpin' bald-headed Christ, Tom, "Wiley exclaimed. "That's a whole lotta gold brother!"

"Wiley, I think we need to secure this cave, "Tom stated. "Do you have any good ideas as to how?"

"Well, is there any way I can get ahold of the C-4 that the sheriffs took from me, Tom?" Wiley asked.

"I'll give Larry a call and have him bring your explosive," Tom replied. Just don't blow up the cave Wiley. There's kinda a lot at stake here.

"Fair enough brother! Okay, so I'm going to need at least ten bricks of charge, I'm also gonna need some detonator switches, surveillance cameras, and a blue tooth monitor," Wiley continued. "We also need to have a power source and there's no electrical cables nearby, so we need to use a generator for now until we can get some solar panels or another energy source put into place."

"I think I can help ya with all that stuff," Tom graciously replied. "But with everything going on with Tildy, let's keep this between us and the family for now, ok?"

Wiley concluded by saying, "Tom, were fucking rich dude! But brother, I will protect all of this wealth if I can borrow some cash to rebuild my home?"

"Wiley, I'll build you whatever the hell you want, free of charge, just as long as you can help protect the gold."

"Tom, I think I'm gonna take you up on that offer," Wiley exclaimed as he jumped up and down for joy. Then the happy clown hugged Tom who smiled at Wiley and wondered how the hell the crazy fool ended up in the ranchers locked office.

With a plan in place, the boys headed back to the ranch, and when they entered the house, Maddy was already wide awake preparing breakfast. The two soiled men sat down at the bar and Maddy poured them a cup of hot black steamy java after she just recently returned from her friend's house in Badger Pocket, just a couple of nights ago. Larry actually let Tom and Wiley come back sooner putting a couple deputy's in place to keep the ranch secure.

"Boys, you up doing ranch stuff early this morning or what," Maddy asked and Wiley began to smile, sniffing the sizzling bacon floating in the air. Tom then placed the satchel on the kitchen counter and opened the bag. Maddy looked at the contents therein and her eyes lit up like diamonds, reflecting off of the shiny gold coins staring back into her face. She then froze, almost in a state of shock, only until a smile formed on her beautiful face which looked right back at Tom.

"You found it, Maddy frantically exclaimed in amazement. "You found the gold Tom! I can't believe this! I am trying to contain my excitement but I don't know what to say! How much is in the bag and is that all of it?"

Tom smiled at his wife and responded, "Oh round about two hundred and fifty million dollars, or more, and there has to be at least twenty more bags just like this back at the cave."

That was about the time when Maddy dropped the spatula she was holding, and fainted to the floor. Tom immediately rose to his feet and rushed over to the rancher's unconscious wife, holding her gently. Wiley suggested that they raise her feet to avoid shock, so the ole boy grabbed some pillows and a warm blanket to comfort Maddy while she was temporarily napping. While Tom was waiting on Wiley, Lupita heard the commotion in the kitchen and came rushing in to see what happened. She automatically seen the satchel with its shiny bounty and peeked over to Tom who was still comforting Maddy.

"Tom please tell me that that's not the gold, or I am dreaming," Lupita asked, smiling at the rancher.

"Lue, this is the gold, and you're wide awake," Tom replied smiling at Lupita who was motionless.

That was about the point when Lupita fainted to the ground. With a smile on his face, Tom yelled out, "Wiley, get more pillows and a blanket for Lupita too please!"

After getting the women cozy, Tom had finished up breakfast, and that was about the time when the boys came barreling down the stairs to the kitchen. For now, Tom had moved the satchel into a cabinet above the fridge because nobody really uses them for anything, and had Wiley zip his lip about the gold to the kids. After breakfast, Tom rushed the two oldest boys to the school bus, and kept the youngest behind. By then, Lupita and Maddy had regained consciousness and sat there like two giddy school girls awaiting a major all inclusive shopping trip to downtown Seattle. With everything going on however, that trip would be postponed till Tom could exchange his coins in properly.

After Tom fixed the ladies a plate, told Maddy to get on the phone with the Spanish Embassy in Seattle, and then left with Wiley to go get the supplies they needed to secure the cave. The first stop they traveled too was the sheriff's office and Larry was temporarily on a call, so the boys headed to the evidence locker and grabbed the C-4 with all the other gadgets Wiley would need to booby trap the cave. While they were in the room, Wiley's nose started to go a flurry with excitement. When he turned his head in the direction of the smell, he noticed about twenty pounds of marijuana, within an arm's length of his reach.

"Wiley, I hope you're not thinking what I'm thinking," Tom stated, and Wiley just stood back and smiled.

"Tom, don't you need to use the bathroom or something?" Wiley asked and Tom informed him of their current troubles, so

Wiley played pet and loaded up the gear. Yet, when Tom had his back turned, Wiley may or may have not grabbed a couple of baggies and tucked them under his shirt. After a couple of trips back to the evidence room, the boys were almost out the door when an all too familiar voice stopped them dead in their tracks.

"Wiley, could you not part with some of your belongings?" Larry asked and shook hands with the two men.

"Larry, I found the gold," Tom replied. "I think you better come with us because you not gonna believe how much!"

Larry's gazing accusatory stare, turned from a boss getting ready to lay into one of his temporary deputy's that smelled like ganja, into a look of utter disbelief and excitement. "Tom, please tell me that you're not full of shit right now 'cause I really need some good news," Larry exclaimed as his smile increased further.

"Larry, if I was yanking your chain, don't ya think I'd be by Tildy's side at the hospital?"

"All right, fellas," Larry replied. "Let's go have a look see and have a drink because if this is truly happening right now, then, boys, I think that we mighta just changed the game." Larry smiled like a giddy child at the fair with bag of cotton candy as he made his way to the patrol car.

When the boys arrived at the ranch, Tom and Wiley began to unload all of the gear. Larry hopped out of his car with a jar of moonshine and took a refreshing gulp. Tom had to find a way to haul out the gear so the rancher headed for the stall and went to grab Trigger. Only when Tom arrived at the stall, his trusty steed was nowhere to be found, until the rancher heard the unnatural sound of horses mating in the distance. Tom figured that he'd better have a drink of shine from Larry's jar so Trigger and Betsy could finish their business before proceeding to the cave.

In the meantime, Tom pulled the cart out and ordered the guys to start loading up.

"Where's Trigger Tom," Larry asked looking around while listening to the horses neighing ceaselessly.

"Him and Betsy are a little busy," Tom replied. "Let's give 'em, say about until their mating song ceases and we'll be on our way!"

Round about half of an hour later, Trigger was finally done and successfully hooked up to the trailer, then the two meandered their way through the trail. Tom proceeded to drink moonshine, passing the jar to Larry and Wiley, who rode in the back of the trailer with the gear. To keep electricity flowing through the cave, Tom also loaded two decently sized diesel generators in the trailer which had to move slowly, as not to accidentally set off the C-4 by some misguided bounce of a generator, and knowing the boy's luck, they best travel slow. When the men arrived at the cave, Larry hopped out of the trailer and bitched about Wiley wanting him to pet the crazy fool like a damn cat, yet by that point, Wiley was way too stoned to realize how crazy he was acting. And who's to say what the old fart should and should not do, after watching his cabin smolder in the cold night.

Tom unlocked the door and turned the camp light on, then returned Larry's flashlight, while the boys entered the cave. Tom directed Larry up the ladder and he slowly climbed peeking his head with the flashlight through the hole. Larry suddenly popped his head back out and looked at the two men, grinning from ear to ear. He then proceeded down the ladder and almost collapsed to the ground, but Tom caught the elated lawman's fall. The sheriff then just sat their getting emotional, until Wiley got real close starting to purr. Larry pushed Wiley out of the way jokingly and sprang back up to his feet, looking Tom in the eye.

"That old SOB had it here all along Tom," Larry exclaimed! "I can't even fucking process what's going on right now and I've been drinking. Tom, thank you, brother, for including me in all of this—and you're one rich rancher right now!"

Tom then embraced Larry's shoulder and replied, "A wise man once told me that were all friends of equal wealth, fortune or not, but this one's just as much yours as mine, Larry!"

"Tom, I told you that," Wiley remarked with Larry and Tom smiling back.

"Larry, earn your keep and help us secure the cave," Tom asked, and Larry began happily offloading the generators with Wiley. After the boys hooked up the power, Tom pulled out a jigsaw and cut a bigger hole in the roof, pushing the heavy bags of booty to make the hole wider. When the hole was shored up by beams, Larry offered to climb up and take a look around. Feeling no resentment, Wiley and

Tom agreed, and Larry made his way up to the cavicular hole and started to get really excited.

"Tom, holy shit! There must be like at least twenty bags up here just at a glance," Larry exclaimed, as happy as a clam could be.

That was about the point where Larry and a good portion of the gold came crashing to the ground. Panicked, Tom and Wiley circled Larry, picking him up who was covered with some the golden coins that hit the ground.

"Gee, Larry, you realize you have about twenty million in loose change lying on you," Tom stated and Larry rose to his feet smiling in utter joy.

"You need to get a huge ass safe for all of this, Tom," Larry exclaimed, and Tom dropped to his knees, laughing.

"We should head back to the ranch and grab some more beer," Tom stated, and the men followed suit. When they got back to the house, Lue had taken off to the hospital and Maddy was sitting in the kitchen having a snack while talking on the phone, so Tom have her a hug. When she hung up, there was a new and refreshed look to Maddy. Tom's wife had just gotten off the phone with a representative of the Spanish Embassy and the news couldn't have been more promising.

"So I just got off the phone with the friendly gentleman at the Spanish embassy in Seattle and he would like to see the gold Tom," Maddy stated. "The man said if its verified as the real thing, the Spanish government would pay us out to have it back!"

Now, skeptical Tom would like nothing more than too keep the gold and not have any new people coming out on his land, but then again, it was worth a shot, so the rancher agreed. Until the delegate showed up, the boys had a lot more work to do to secure the multibillion dollar cave, so the men grabbed more supplies and headed back out. In the meantime, Maddy, rounded up some of Tildy's belongings and went back to the hospital.

When Maddy arrived, there were some church friends that heard the news bringing food and drink to the Wyatts in their time of need. Maddy thanked all of them and decided to sit in the lobby to wait for a call from the Spanish delegate. As she sat typing on her phone, a gentleman in a sharp dressed business suit, sat right beside

Maddy. The man asked for the time which Maddy obliged, and then the person asked why she was there.

Maddy smiled at the friendly man and said, "My husband's grandmother is here and she's not doing so good."

"I'm sorry that she is here, ma'am, and apologize for I have not given you my name," the gentleman replied. "My name is Jaime and it is a pleasure to meet you," and shook Maddy's hand.

As the two greeted each other, Maddy felt through Jaime's friendly exterior, and had a premonition that something wasn't right. "May I ask where you're from?" Maddy stated.

"I'm from Mexico, ma'am, and I'm here waiting on a friend of mine that got hurt earlier today," Jaime replied as he sat with his head down.

"That's too bad," Maddy stated. "Is he going to be ok?"

"Oh the doctors are patching him up right now," Jaime stated. "I didn't catch your name, *senorita*?"

"I'm sorry, Jaime. My name is Maddy Wyatt, and may I apologize to you because as much as I would love to talk to you Jaime, I must excuse myself and go back to Tildy's room. It has been an absolute joy talking to you Jaime", Maddy replied graciously, then got up and started to walk back to Tildy's room.

Now the thing that Maddy didn't know is that Jaime and the other gentleman getting patched up were the two that started Wiley's house on fire. As Tom's wife began to walk away, Jaime sprung up out of his chair and started to casually follow her. As she walked, Maddy had a strange feeling that something wasn't right and began to pick up her pace. While glancing over her shoulder, Maddy seen him closely approaching, until an officer walked right by which she knew, and began to chat, as not to raise Jaime's intentions. Seeing her now talking to a sheriff, Jaime walked by and smiled, then continued to walk on with a worried Maddy glaring back.

"Officer Davis, can you raise Larry on the CB," Maddy asked. "It's important!"

"Sure thing, Maddy," the officer replied back. "Is everything ok?"

"I don't know yet, Steve," Maddy stated. "Tom's with Larry, and I need them here now!"

With that being said, the officer called Larry and wasn't getting through. Maddy figured the boys were in the cave working, so she asked if the deputy could escort her, which he did without a wince.

Back at the cave, the boys had set the C-4 charges, the surveillance cameras, and fortified the door. With all of the work almost complete, the men sat down for a beer and Wiley started cleaning up the left over mess from all of the supplies they just installed. Tom decided to grab the portable monitor that was used for the cameras and began to tinker with it.

"Tom, careful with that dude!" Wiley exclaimed, "The monitor is in sync with the C-4, and if you hit the wrong button, Maddy will be digging us outta here!"

"Sorry, Wiley," Tom said apologetically and passed the monitor back over to Wiley. The crazy coot then showed Tom how everything communicated with the monitor then pulled out a little trigger-lookin' do hickey and gave it to the rancher.

"Whatever you do Tom, do not ever, ever, ever, press this trigger unless you have no other option," Wiley stated. "When the fit hits the shan, this little badass will ultimately protect the gold and its range is up to five hundred feet, so you're safely away from the blast zone!"

"Gee, Wiley, hopefully we won't have to use any of this at all, but thank you at any rate," Tom replied and placed the trigger in his jacket. "Now that we have the cave secured, how do we secure the perimeter?"

"Well, Tom, I will work on that," Wiley replied. "But you two should head in to see Tildy because I don't need any one around until the perimeter is secured."

"Fair enough, Wiley," Tom retorted. "Larry, let's head into town and go see Tildy," Larry agreed, and the boys left for the hospital, leaving Wiley and Trigger to their devices.

Back at the hospital, a nervous Maddy was calming down over that feeling she had about Jaime. The day was already stressful enough, but Tildy had awakened and was sitting up, bitching about being back at the doctors.

"Maddy, did you bring my belongings, dear?" Tildy asked.

"Yes, Granny," Maddy replied. "I took that peace maker that you like and placed it under your pillow!" Elated, Tildy smiled and turned on her radio listening to the classic rock station out of Wenatchee. After a couple of minutes had elapsed, the doctor came in with good news of downgrading Tildy from critical condition, to stable. This pleased Dallas who was terrified over his mothers plight, and Maddy was overjoyed also. After the doctor exited Tom and the boys weren't too far behind. Little did they know that they were being watched by Jaime who was on his cell phone talking to Isidro.

"How far away are you boss," Jaime asked.

"We will be there in three days," Isidro replied. "I want that fool Wiley wrapped in a box with a fucking bow on his head! For that matter, wrap up Tom and Larry too! I want to make sure we set an example to any other business deals that have gone awry."

"No problem, Father! You don't worry about anything. Ill tail those pricks until you tell me otherwise," Jaime replied. Isidro agreed and Jaime hung up the cell phone. For now, Jaime knew where his targets were, so he decided to go back to his cabin rental. One would think that criminals would conduct business in a hotel room but ole Jaime knew better than that. With all of the unknown variables, the thug preferred the peaceful country calm, where a person could scream and no one could hear them. When Jaime arrived, he brought in some fast food he had ordered in Cle Elum and placed the meal on the dining room table. Jaime then took the meal and walked into the bedroom where a rather strung out female was laying in his bed.

Jaime then took the food and set it by the table right beside her. He then took his clothes off and laid down next to the girl.

"You should eat something," Jaime said, and the thug unwrapped the burger, passing it over her way.

"I don't want it! I'm not hungry, I just wanna go home," the terrified woman shouted and refused to touch her food.

"You're not going anywhere, bitch," Jaime replied. Then he proceeded to pull out some heroin from the inner lining of his jacket. The thug then took a small amount and began heating it on a spoon. When the drug had liquefied, he fixed the concoction into a syringe, and shot it into his arm. After mere minutes, Jaime relaxed and started to zone out.

"Want some of this?" Jaime asked and passed the syringe her way. The woman reluctantly took the needle and injected the rest into her arm.

"Better than a fucking burger, right?" Jaime stated, as he lay there feeling the effects of the heroin course through his bloodstream.

"Yes, Jaime, it is," the girl replied, as she lay back, relaxing from the drug.

"If you want more, you know what you have to do," Jaime replied, and the female shimmied her undies off.

"Hold on a second," Jaime asked kindly and hopped out of the bed, then went into the adjoining bathroom. With the burger in one hand and his prick in the other, Jaime peed in the toilet and tossed the burger into the bathtub nearby.

"You can have that, asshole," Jaime stated and walked out of the bathroom listening to the muffled screams of another victim imprisoned within his cabin. The thug then proceeded back to bed and hopped on top of the female. Commencing to sexually abuse the woman, Jaime finished up and laid next to her falling fast asleep. The drug induced woman quietly got up then went into the bathroom and approached the bathtub. She then told the figure laying down in the tub to keep quiet and removed the gag from the unfortunate individuals mouth. She then took the burger and placed it next to his mouth so he could eat and gobbled up the meal quickly.

Quietly, the prisoner said, "You have to get out of here and go get help immediately!"

"But he has what I need, and I can't live without it," she stated with her head down, trying not to cry.

"What's your name?" the gentleman asked kindly.

"My name's Casey," she replied with a smile on her face.

"That's a very pretty name," the man replied, smiling also. "Casey, if you get me outta here, I'll get you whatever you need!" Casey was reluctant at first but agreed and carefully went to get the man some of Jaime's clothes to cover his naked body. Casey then took a knife and freed the male prisoner of his bindings.

"Thank you, dear, for helping me out," the man said and then proceeded to get dressed. Fully clothed, he then peeked out the door only to find Jaime sleeping but noticed a pair of cuffs still tied to the bed. The man approached cautiously after grabbing the gun Jaime left on the nightstand. Before Jaime could come back to reality in his drug-induced stupor, the man had already cuffed the cartel thug to the bed, staring down the barrel of his 38mm pistol that the prisoner took as the thug slept.

"It's kinda funny how things change, don't you think?" the man stated, pointing the gun even closer to Jamie's temple.

"If you think you're going to get very far, you're badly mistaken, brother," Jaime implied, but the victim just stood there and smiled back. "You might as well kill me now!"

"Oh, Jaime, I have no intentions of doing so, and don't call me brother," the man replied and then commenced to pistol whip Jaime back into an unconscious slumber. The man then went through Jaime's personal belongings and found the heroine. He then tossed it to the female and they quickly left out the front door. The man then took Jaime's car keys and hopped into the thugs car with the scared young woman. When the two were safe and in town, the man dropped off the woman, gave her the drugs, and sped away as she stood outside, feeling the wind brush her face.

Back at the hospital, Tom was sitting by Maddy and Tildy visiting, when Larry came inside with Laurie to drop off some flowers and visit. While Maddy and Laurie chatted with Tildy, Larry and Tom took a little walk outside.

"Tom, I just got a call from Wiley and he has a surprise," Larry stated, while smiling.

"Oh shit! What is it now Larry," Tom asked, and as the words flowed out of his mouth, a car honking its horn pulled up to the boys. It was no other than Wiley and Juan!

"Holy shit," Tom yelled in disbelief, and Juan got out of the vehicle giving the rancher a hug. "Jesus Juan! Where the hell have you been?"

"Oh just hanging out with my brother Jaime, handcuffed and gagged to his bedpost," Juan stated.

"Do you know his current location," Larry asked with concern.

"Yeah Larry, and I think we should apprehend him quickly because when Jaime gets called to do jobs, things don't turn out well for his targets," Juan replied with urgency.

Larry then answered in reply, "You know Juan, there's always room for another deputy sheriff," then deputized Juan on the spot.

Even though Juan wasn't a U.S. Citizen, the sheriff still found a great use for him and figured that he could sort the whole mess out later.

"Larry I don't know what to say," Juan gasped in utter astonishment as the sheriff handed him a badge.

"Well, then, let's hop in the car and go fuck us up a bad guy," Larry replied with a smile. The boys quickly sped away to Jaime's, arming their guns and laughing about what they were going to do with a drug addict that's handcuffed to the bed. At the hospital, Maddy just got off the phone with Tom explaining what happened to Juan, and what the boys were going to do. Maddy told her husband about meeting a man named Jaime and gave the rancher a brief description which Tom then told Juan. The missing Spaniard confirmed the description and Larry radioed a couple deputy's to go protect the Wyatt's at the hospital. Relieved, Maddy hung up and told Dallas and Lue what was going on. About ten minutes later, Officer Morrison showed up and greeted the group who was on edge, but relieved that protection was there.

"How's Tildy doing," Morrison asked as he shook Maddy's hand.

"She's doing just fine," Maddy replied. "Jimmy, when Jaime talked to me, the man mentioned he had a friend here being patched up. Is there any way you could see if he's still in the hospital?"

"Sure thing, Maddy," the deputy replied. "I have another officer coming up here in a few minutes and then I'll go see if the gentleman's still around."

After a couple moments, the extra deputy arrived at Tildy's hospital room, and Morrison went to the nurses' desk to ask about the patients currently staying at the hospital. It was a busy night, so Morrison inquired specifically about patients that have been either abused, or in a fight. The nurse typed away, and informed the deputy that a gentleman by the name of Diego Leija was seen for a puncture wound by a fallen tree branch, also the patient had bruising in several areas. The nurse gave Morrison the room number and the deputy was well on his way, slowly pulling out his service revolver as he approached the room.

Cautiously, Morrison peeked quickly around the corner and raised his pistol to the bed that was covered with a privacy screen. The deputy grabbed the curtain and slowly pulled it back, only to find an empty bed. The officer then opened the bathroom door only to see another empty room. Deputy Morrison then left the room urgently in a quick step back to Tildy's. Back at Tildy's room, Maddy sat their holding an empty cup of coffee still little freaked out over the events of earlier.

"I have to get another cup of coffee and use the bathroom," Maddy stated and rose to Dallas who placed a coffee order as well. The officer accompanied Maddy down the hall to the coffee machine and started pouring a cup of java. With Maddy's current stress level, she drank her coffee same as Tom's, which was black and piping hot. After a quick trip to the bathroom, Maddy and the deputy returned to Tildy's room.

Just as they entered, a knife and hand came out of nowhere grabbing the deputy by the neck, slitting the poor man's throat. The assailant then shoved Maddy through the door and dragged the officers lifeless body inside, closing the door. Inside the room, the thug now had his pistol out in plain sight, scaring the women and pissing off Dallas.

"Everybody needs to keep it down or this pretty things next," Diego exclaimed as he pulled the blade closer to Maddy's neck.

Diego then took Maddy and threw her at the base of Tildy's bed stirring the old lady out of her slumber.

"What the hell is going on and who's the cock sucker with the sissy blade," Tildy asked unaware of the situation.

Don't you disrespect me that way you old bag of bones," Diego exclaimed as he directed the blade at the old lady and Tildy just sat there with that old pissed off concern look she maintains so well.

"Listen here, boy," Tildy replied. "You wanna talk about respect, then don't disrespect your elders, you piece of shit! Hell, you can't even hold a knife the right way with those sausage shaped fingers!" Diego just laughed and started to walk toward Tildy with the deadly blade. Just as he was ready to strike, Maddy grabbed a lamp nearby and swung it as hard as she could, knocking Diego to his feet. As he regained focus and rose to the man's feet, a bullet came screaming by, delivering a shot to the head that dropped Diego back down to his knees.

"That might not be how you handle a knife, but that's how ya handle a goddamn gun," Tildy exclaimed, as smoke poured out of the barrel.

After the shot rung throughout the hospital, Deputy Morrison was on alert entering the room, gun drawn and pointing at the Wyatt clan. Morrison then lowered his piece and asked Tildy to do the same, which the ole gal did without a forethought.

"What in the fuck just happened?" the deputy exclaimed as the adrenaline coursed through his veins.

"I'm getting a great show tonight in this death hotel," Tildy replied.

Morrison gave a huge sigh of relief and radioed for more units to come to the scene quickly as officers were at the scene within minutes. The officers ran into a building that was being rapidly evacuated after the gunshot was heard. Deputy Morrison and then looked at the dead Mafia thug laying on the ground and looked at the bullet hole in the gangsters head, and sighed. As more officers entered the room, the look was much the same upon the deputy's faces, and Tildy just sat there smiling at the deceased fool.

The boys had just arrived at Jaime's hideout. With the fading light of day slipping slowly away, the men got out of Larry's cruiser quickly and drew their guns, not knowing what to expect. When they approached the house, Larry bumped Tom out of the way and took the lead.

Whispering in a calm tone, Larry said, "Were gonna go in real quietly and clear the house room by room if we have to, so we all need to stick together! Especially you Wiley. I don't want you running the fuck off after lasers, ok?"

"Yeah Larry I'm cool," Wiley replied. "Shit dude, it's just like being in the fucking jungle, like back in my Nam days anyhow. Ill cover who's in front of me."

Larry then had Tom take a pebble and toss it into the window nearby that was open. That was about the point when a naked uncuffed Jaime, opened fire on the men with his

AK-47, sending a cascading volley of bullets toward the boys. They immediately bailed off the front porch and took cover as the bullets traced all around them. Larry radioed ahead for backup, but wasn't getting a reception, so he ordered the men to fall back into the tree line. Tom opened fire at the house and the men raced off as he kept firing. With Larry and the boys now reloading their weapons, Jaime opened another barrage of hot lead screaming in all directions.

When Jaime was out of ammo and in the process of reloading a fresh clip, Tom ran at a fast pace toward the tree line, making it just micro seconds before more bullets came racing his way.

Juan then yelled out, "Jaime! Come out and give yourself up, brother! I'm here with the sheriff, and you got nowhere to go!"

Hearing his brother's voice in the distance, Jaime replied, "No, *hermano*, I'm afraid that I'm not going fucking anywhere! I can do this all night, Juan." Jaime let out and evil laugh and opened with another salvo sending the boys into more cover as the bullets continued to scream past them. Larry tried calling 911 on his cell phone, but Juan must have had a cell phone jammer because the sheriff's phone wasn't working.

"Whoever gets to my cruiser first will find some flash grenades that the great State of Washington hooked me up with," Larry stated. "They're in the trunk and also a couple of shotguns. I say that if Juan's asshole brother doesn't wanna come out, we're gonna have ta flush him out!" After another salvo of Jamie's gun, all the men opened fire, running at full speed to the patrol car now only feet away. Larry grabbed the shot guns and flash grenades, passing out the weapons evenly. When Jaime had to reload, the men sprang into action with only mere seconds until the thug opened fire again. Tom grabbed a shotgun and began firing into the window with Juan, while Larry and Wiley tossed two flash grenades into the cabin. After the explosion, Larry then kicked open the door and laid down further cover fire. The sheriff took a quick peek inside and could already see that Jaime was wounded, laying down in absolute pain.

Larry quickly approached Jaime and kicked away the machine gun, then slapped some cuffs on Jaime's hands. Bleeding from the stomach, Wiley found some paper towels and quickly applied pressure to the wound only to find more blood coming out. "Larry this guy is screwed," Wiley said and Larry shook his head with Juan and Tom standing over the dying man.

"I never thought that it was going to end like this," Jaime exclaimed while the wound grew more grievous by the second.

"Life never ends the way we want to when we work for a monster like father," Juan replied. "At least you can die knowing that there is at least someone here who cares for you; even though you showed me nothing but brutality and evil growing up."

"It is all a part of father's plan, Juan,," Jaime replied as he started to cough up blood. "Did you think your life was going to be all ribbon and bows?"

"No, Jaime, you're right about our lives, but now I have a new life away from father, and I don't have to do his bidding anymore!" Coughing up a little more blood, Jaime drew in a deep breath and grew a little more distant. His eyes started to fix and dilate but could still here Juan's voice as his consciousness slowly crept away. "It's too bad things had to end up like this for you hermano," and Juan kissed his brother on the forehead as poor ole Jaime passed away.

Little did the boys know that Jaime had called his father during the gunfight and put his cell on speaker phone. Juan spotted the phone and picked it up, only to find silence on the other end.

"Dad, I know it's you," Juan said, only to find the sound of men talking in a panic on the other end.

"Juan, are you okay, son?" Isidro asked in a somber tone.

"Yes, Dad, in fact doing a lot better than my brother who has quit the family business," Juan said in reply.

"Is Wiley and Tom with you?" Isidro asked.

"Yes, Father, and I think it's time that you cut your losses," Juan replied.

"You know I can't do that, son," Isidro continued in a more aggressive tone. "In fact, I won't consider Wiley's debt paid in full unless I have his head sitting on my desk!"

"Well, then, Father, I guess you're going to be disappointed because I have no intention of letting that happen," Juan exclaimed.

With that being said, Isidro retorted in a harsh violent voice, "I guess I'm going to have to pay you boys and my granddaughter a visit." He then hung up the phone.

All of the sudden, Larry's radio crackled back to life with word of the incident at the hospital. The boys were relieved that everything was okay as Larry called for backup at the cabin, and the county corner to clean up the mess that the boys just made. With the news, Tom, Wiley, and Juan hopped in Larry's cruiser and headed to the hospital because Larry had to stay behind and secure the scene.

When the boys arrived at the hospital, the scene was chaotic with several police cars and ambulances transporting patients away from the current crime scene. Tom was greeted by Officer Morrison who had a somber look, and they were swept away to Tildy's room with several other deputy's looking sad, also concerned. When the boys arrived, Tom knew why the deputy's were so quiet, and by the tears in Maddy's face, automatically realized what had happened. Tom gave Maddy a hug along with Dallas and Lupita, looking at his granny who had just passed away moments ago with her pistol still on the old lady's chest.

Tildy's Twelve Gun Salute

A couple of days had passed since Tildy's death and the shootout that had occurred inside at Jamie's. The morning was cold and dreary as the last of the deciduous leaves had fallen, only to be replaced by a foot of fresh snow from a northerly storm system. The ranch hands were busy plowing out the Windy River Ranch as Tom and Maddy sat, eating an early breakfast cooked by Lupita. The tone was a somber one, but nonetheless highlighted by Tom and Maddy's boys playing outside in the new fallen snow. Ever since Tildy's death, everyone had been relatively quiet; even Wiley's normal giddiness was replaced by a constant cycle of smoking pot and sleeping to mask his grief over a woman that he considered a mom. After breakfast, Tom was visiting with Dallas when Maddy got a call. After a few minutes of talking, she hung up and began to smile.

"Tom, that was Ferdinand Antivero from the Spanish consulate in Seattle," Maddy exclaimed in joy. "He's close by and wants to take a look at the coins!"

"Well, looks like we have a visitor everybody," Tom replied, and went to fetch Wiley. The crazy ole coot was holed up in one of the guest rooms, so Tom knocked on the door and went inside only to find Wiley naked. With what looked like a piece of jerky still hanging from his mouth, Tom nudged Wiley out of his slumber and threw a blanket over the ole boys body.

"Jesus Tom! Can't you tell when a depressed man just wants to be alone," Wiley asked while the piece of jerky fell onto the bed.

"I know with everything going on that things are tough," Tom stated. "But in the advent of Granny's demise, our fortunes have increased further with a visit from the Spanish embassy. They're coming over now, so throw on some clothes and let's make our fortune complete!"

Tom then patted Wiley on the shoulder and smiled while the sad man picked the jerky back up gnawing on it mildly. After Wiley decided to bathe and dress, he came out to the kitchen sitting by Maddy smiling. Maddy patted him on the shoulder and kissed the man's cheek.

"Wiley, were all going through a tough time here and I understand if you grieve better alone, but you know that we're all here for you darling," Maddy stated and Wiley's cheesy grin began to return.

"I know, Maddy," Wiley replied. "It's just that Two Boots and Tildy were like parents to me. It's been rough all the way around and I'm sorry if I haven't been here like I should." Wiley then smiled hugging Maddy and pinched her ass. "Damn Maddy, the things we could do if ya dumped Tom," and Maddy laughed hysterically. All Tom could do is smile and shook his head giving Wiley his off banter praise.

After a short while, a knock came at the door, so Maddy sprang up to answer. "Hello Maddy," the gentleman said and extended his hand out for a shake. "I'm Ferdinand from the Spanish consulate and I am pleased to be at your front door, yet I'm a little cold." Maddy smiled, graciously leading their guest in, and all the appropriate introductions were made as Ferdinand warmed himself by the fireplace. "I didn't realize there would be snow on the ground so soon," Ferdinand exclaimed.

Tom then extended his hand. "Ferdinand, I'm Maddy's husband Tom Wyatt. Thank you for coming to our home!" The rancher then pulled out the shiny coin Tildy gave him, and the embassy assistant held it in his utter astonishment.

"This is the Eagle Grande coin," Ferdinand explained. "There are only a few of these left in the world that's not in the country vault, and this coin is essentially priceless! I will pass it along but this one coin can make you a very rich man Mr. Wyatt!"

"Uh, how much did Maddy tell you about our situation with this here coin," Tom asked.

"I was informed by my secretary that you had a rare coin that needed to be verified," Ferdinand replied. "I just didn't realize that you had the real thing here. We always get calls about rare Spanish artifacts, but this is a true diamond in the rough," and gave the coin back to Tom.

"Gee uh, Ferdinand, I think you better take a trip with Wiley and me out to my cave," Tom stated leaving an almost blank stare on the assistants face. Since Ferdinand wasn't equipped for the weather, Maddy rounded up a snow suit, boots, and a warm winter jacket, which ole Ferdinand slipped on.

"You know Tom, I've heard about you before. Aren't you a legend around here," Ferdinand asked, and Tom patted the consulate curator on the shoulder, then smiled like he'd heard that before from no one in particular.

"Ferdinand, let's head out to the cave, but there's one more thing that I have to grab." Tom went into the kitchen and picked up a full jar of moonshine. With drink in hand, Tom, Wiley, and the curator headed out to the cave. The walking was very tough and slow going at first, due to the immense amount of snow that had dumped all over the ranch. Tom took a sip of moonshine and offered Ferdinand a drink, but the assistant graciously declined, due to the fact that he rarely drank, except on auspicious and celebratory occasions. To make the journey slower, Wiley had placed several booby traps along the way and was constantly looking at trees or any still uncovered markers, as to avoid being blown up. All of that aside, the men eventually made their way to the entrance of the cave and Wiley turned on the generator after dumping more gas into its thirsty engine. Tom opened the door and escorted Ferdinand inside the cave which was still warm from the last time the boys were inside it. By then, all of the bags of gold had been removed from the upper rafters and placed on the wooden table that had at once held all of the weapons. Tom then took one of the bags dumping the gold out on the table, and Ferdinand about fell over in disbelief. After realizing that there were at least twenty bags of bullion, the assistant dropped to his knees in shock.

"Mr. Wyatt, I think I'll take that drink now," and Tom passed the jar over to Ferdinand. Still kneeling on the ground confused yet excited, the curator sipped off the jar and cringed, passing it back to Tom who stood back, trying to contain his laughter.

"Do you realize what you have here Mr. Wyatt," Ferdinand asked and Tom shrugged his shoulders. "Let's just say when the Spanish government cuts you a check for this missing fortune, you will be quite possibly, one of the richest men in the world!"

"At any rate Ferdinand, I'm not one for material wealth," Tom replied. "I just wanna give it back and go from there."

Ferdinand then began pouring over every bag of gold smiling with each bag that he inspected. After the assistant was done, Ferdinand pulled out his cell phone and called whomever he answered to in Spanish, yet Tom could tell that it went very well by the arm flailing, also jumping, that the curator partook in. Wiley in his friendly demeanor, pulled out a fresh joint and offering Ferdinand a puff, but the Spaniard refused because of his job, so Wiley puffed away while Tom and the curator drank.

"That was my boss on the phone," Ferdinand continued. "He's the main ambassador in our Seattle embassy and couldn't quite believe what he heard, so we will be expecting a visit from him tomorrow."

"I don't wanna really draw a whole lot of attention to what we have here," Tom asked nicely as not to rock the Spaniards boat, and Ferdinand laughed.

"It's okay," the happy assistant replied. "My boss will bring a security detail to help you protect this treasure until it can be safely transported away. We're not about to blow the lid on this until we have everything in place."

"Do you mind if I have a word with your boss?" Tom then asked.

"Well, yeah, Mr. Wyatt," Ferdinand said with a smile on his face. Ferdinand then phoned his boss with the satellite phone and told the ambassador that Tom wanted to introduce himself. The assistant shook his head in a positive way and gave the rancher the phone.

"Mr. Wyatt, might I say that this is a genuine, rare honor to meet the current owner of our lost fortune," the ambassador exclaimed. "My name is Bernado Cortez. I am the acting ambassador for the

Spanish consulate in Seattle. I would just like to say that I am overjoyed from the news of Ferdinand, and that I am actually on the phone with the prime minister of Spain as we speak!"

"Oh, sir, I apologize for interrupting your phone call to the man," Tom kindly stated.

"No worries, *vaquero*," the ambassador replied. "Actually, the prime minister has been listening on us too in a conference call. I couldn't just hang up on my boss," the ambassador replied as Tom heard another voice chuckling in the background.

"Mr. Wyatt. My name is Gustavo Lucero and I am the current prime minister of Spain. "I would like to extend a hand of friendship and gratitude for finding the lost treasure of Hernan Cortes."

"Well, gee…uh…I'm honored," Tom replied, not quite knowing what to say. "Who exactly is that?"

"Mr. Wyatt, he was the famous Spanish conquistador known as Cortes," Bernardo stated. Cortes was trying to find a route to India after he conquered the Aztecs, and during a horrible storm, the ship loaded with the bullion sank off the coast of what is present day San Francisco. Cortes still had gold, but the bullion they harvested into coins was believed to be lost, until now that is!"

"As the prime minister, I will need a total of all the gold so we can cut Mr. Wyatt a check," Gustavo asked, and the men were all in agreement with Tom, smiling away.

"By the way, Mr. Prime Minister, you can call me Tom," the rancher stated.

"You know, I believe I've heard of you, Tom," the prime minister stated. "Aren't you a legend around your area?"

"I hear that a lot," Tom jokingly replied. "Yeah, I guess I am. Just never really lived up to the hype in my own mind!"

"Well, after we get our fortune back, your legendary status will be a worldwide phenomenon," Gustavo excitingly replied. "It was a pleasure to hear from you Tom and I will be in touch. I want to wish you and your family the best in the upcoming holiday season and good day to you sir!" With that, the Prime Minister finished his call and Tom passed back the phone to Ferdinand, who talked briefly with the ambassador.

"Gee Tom, how did it go," Wiley asked.

"Wiley, I think after all of this blows over, were going to spend a little time in a warmer climate healing our cold bodies," Tom replied. Excited, Wiley agreed and the men made their way back to the house. When they went inside, Dallas was playing with the grand kids and Maddy started preparing lunch. Tom offered Ferdinand a beer which the gentleman accepted, graciously drinking the longneck down fast, then grabbed the jar of moonshine.

During lunch, Tom filled in the assistant about all of the problems that the boys had encountered, and Ferdinand was taken back in shock. From the difficulties with the cartel, to Tildy's passing, the curator was in absolute emotional disarray and wanted to help out anyway he could. With a security detail coming to protect the treasure and Larry's constant deputy presence, Tom felt like he for once, could sit back and grieve for Tildy. In fact, with a funeral in the next couple of days, Ferdinand told Tom and Maddy that the Spanish government would help out with any funeral expenses, as a friendly way of expressing their gratitude for finding the lost treasure. With that being said, Tom felt like it was time to take everybody to the Coyotes for some drinks and celebration.

So after lunch, everybody piled in Maddy's Yukon while Dallas and Lupita stayed behind to watch the boys. As they were driving to the bar, Wiley started complaining about cramping and feeling the urge to go to the bathroom, but Tom just laughed it off.

"Tom you should try these breath mints that I got from your medicine cabinet in the bathroom," Wiley stated.

What's the name of those breath mints ole buddy," Tom asked while he sipped on his moonshine.

Wiley then looked at the box and replied, "Ex-Lax chewables, Tom." Everybody began laughing at poor Wiley, whom can hook up an IV line, but apparently struggled with reading. Wiley passed the box over to Tom, who noticed that every last laxative had been eaten.

"Maddy, you're going to want to get us to the bar real quick," Tom exclaimed while ole Wiley ripped a stinky fart in the car that was reminiscent of a shart. If any of you readers are unfamiliar with that word, just ask someone close by and I'm sure they will fill you in!

In a matter of minutes, the group entered the parking lot at the bar and exited the vehicle quite rapidly, to escape the smells that were exiting Wiley's crevice region. As they entered the bar, Tom noticed

Larry who had been nursing a longneck at the end of the bar, so the rancher pulled up a chair.

"Having an interesting day Larry," Tom asked, as he ordered drinks for the thirsty group.

"Yeah, I have, but I hear that it isn't half as interesting as yours," Larry replied and saluted Tom finishing the rest of the sheriff's beer. "It's ok, I'm not butt hurt. Maddy called Laurie after your meeting with the prime minister of Spain, asshole!"

"Yeah, he was a great guy with only nothing but good news Larry," Tom replied.

"So when is the gold going bye-bye," Larry butted in and Tom filled the sheriff out only on what he knew, which satisfied Larry immensely. "You know, Tom, I have a surprise for ya, and they'll come walking through the door pretty soon."

"Well, Larry, whoever they are, I hope they're thirsty," Tom replied as he swigged down his full beer. The rancher then ordered another beer for Larry and himself and looked back at the group, all of whom were there except for Wiley, who was currently emptying the bathroom of any present visitors.

After a time, when the group was relaxed, while enjoying the early evening. Then the door opened and no other than Thunder Bear and some members of the tribe came into the bar then the chief approached Tom with a long sad look on his face. Tom smiled and rose to shake Thunder Bear's hand, only to be met with a hug.

"I heard about Tildy and I just wanna say that I'm truly sorry for your loss, Tom," the chief stated, with a tear falling out of his eye.

"TB, it's okay," Tom then replied. "What can I say? She went out with a bang!"

Thunder Bear then took a step back and laughed saying, "I can only imagine Tom! I also heard what really happened, and jeez What kinda bullshit has Wiley gotten you into?"

"Well, it's just not me, Thunder Bear," Tom replied. It's Larry and half the Upper County nowadays."

"Speaking of Wiley, where is that piece of shit?" Thunder Bear asked.

"Oh, he ate a little something that made him get the shits," Tom stated while cracking a smile.

"Well, I guess I'm gonna have to piss outside for the time being, Tom," the chief jokingly replied.

The chief then laughed out boisterously and Tom opened a tab, ordering a round for everybody in the bar. As the night progressed, Wiley eventually came out of the bathroom and had a seat with the group which had increased with the presence of Thunder Bear and his tribal delegation.

"Hey, Wiley," Thunder Bear exclaimed. "Heard ya been having a shitty day?"

"Ha-ha, very funny," Wiley replied and gave the chief a hug. "The funny thing is those laxatives cleaned out my system and now I wanna eat. Dinner's on me everybody!"

When Wiley shouted his announced, everyone gave out a big cheer and the celebration had begun. Not only was it a dedication for Tildy, but it was also for the gold, which few people knew about at that particular time. After an hour of eating and drinking, several more cars showed up and two very sharp dressed men came into the bar only to be greeted by the drunken mob. The men were very closed off, and took a seat at the end of the bar, talking to Jennie, who was busy serving drinks to the Wyatt Party. While the men questioned Jennie, Larry and Wiley had to use the bathroom, but since they were all full, the boys decided to piss outside at the RV park. When they walked out the door, Larry looked at the three cars that had showed up with their lights still on, and more men waiting in those vehicles.

Larry gave a friendly nod to the men and whispered, "Wiley, I think we got a problem here. We need to get to your trailer and grab some guns if you catch my drift, pronto!" Wiley agreed and they disappeared around the corner while the men hopped out of their vehicles; now only carrying AK-47s. In the bar, Tom noticed the men talking to Jennie and casually strolled up to the bar in a drunken stupor, then ordered a beer, pulling up a barstool near the men.

"Howdy, gents!" Tom exclaimed. "So what brings you to Wil-E Coyotes this cold, November evening?"

"Oh we're here just checking out the scenery," one of the men said with a cheesy smirk. "And what's your name, *vaquero*?"

"Tom Wyatt," the rancher replied, only to see the tone change from a friendly one to a more serious leer. Before Tom could blurt out another word, one of the men pulled a pistol, but the quick thinking rancher pulled his knife, stabbing the man's hand to the bar. As the other thug pulled his gun, was met with a hatchet thrown to the back by Thunder Bear.

"Get these women into the cooler right now," Tom urgently exclaimed, and the lady's were rushed into the open refrigerator, just as bullets started to fly into the bar from the outside. The men hit the ground hard and Rob returned fire with his AK-47, mortally wounding one of the shooters outside.

All the men were behind the bar in the kitchen taking fire from all sides from the gangsters outside, and Juan shot two more thugs that had come a little too close to the window that the Spaniard was firing through. A couple of minutes later, the firing had stopped and a voice yelled into the bar.

"Lower your guns right now," the thug exclaimed! "We have the entire building surrounded and will take it by force if necessary!"

"I guess you boys wanna have a chat," Tom shouted out to the thugs outside and the voice agreed. "Keep your guns close and be ready for hell to break out," Tom told his friends.

So this Mexican mafia prick enters the bar, assault rifle in hand, but not ready to fire yet; only to negotiate. Maddy was shaking in borderline shock but Tom held her in his arms and reassured her that he was going to kill the scumbags, then shut the cooler door. The thug positioned his gun nozzle down, strutting into the bar like he was General Grant sticking one to General Lee. Tom ordered Rob and the rest of the men to lower their weapons, which they did in earnest as the gangster looked at the group. The arrogant asshole slowly lowered his weapon and placed it on the table in front of him, then took a seat near the rancher. Truthfully, all Tom could think about at the time is why he keeps getting into these situations. As a matter of fact, why Larry is never around when a person needs him.

"Look, *vato*," the thug said in a low non threatening tone. "Just give up, Senor Wiley, so I can go back to Mexico! I tire of these games and my boss has grown impatient with Senor Wiley!"

"You're not going to let us walk out of here regardless, asshole, even if I cough him up," Tom replied. "I think what you should do is go back to your boss, and tell him, that he can go fuck himself," Tom reiterated in the same calm tone.

" Are you the Tom Wyatt that's a legend around here," the thug asked as Tom cracked a brief smile, shaking his head.

"The one and only," the rancher replied while spitting on the floor. The gangster then reached his hand out to shake, but all Tom could think about was cutting it off.

"I must admit," the thug continued, "I'd be less than willing to cooperate if I was in your position, so I brought someone here that can hopefully talk some sense into you." With that being said, another man walked through the door which made Juan cringe in anger.

"Ah Juan! My long lost, lying, backstabbing son," the man exclaimed! "I'll bet you wish that you were in Mexico now fucking some cheap whores and partying! Do you agree?"

"No, Father," Juan replied. "That was a former version of a man that you corrupted to do your dirty work, so why don't you go back home and kiss my ass!"

"No, son, I don't think I will be doing such things until you've handed Wiley over," Isidro exclaimed.

"Mr. Cavasos," Tom interrupted. "What if I have a better proposition for you?" The determined rancher then flicked the gold coin over to Isidro, who inspected it thoroughly. "That coin is a one million dollar piece, and I have more pieces like that one there."

Isidro inspected it and noticed the eagle on the coin, then looked at Tom and smiled. "You know Mr. Wyatt, I am a curator of artifacts, therefore I am familiar with this coin and there were only nine coins in antiquity, accept for the rest safely guarded in Spain. So now, all of the sudden, you have the other eight of those coins? Either you're full of shit, or you stumbled into a lost fortune which could make you even more wealthier than me," Cavasos stated.

"I'll give you five million in coin for your troubles," Tom replied. "I have no intention of turning Wiley over too you or anyone else, for that matter. So we can either work out a deal, or we can keep shooting each other until this situation is resolved!"

"I think you have more gold, Senor Wyatt! I also think that every man has a price, and my price is the rest of the bullion for your lives," Isidro stated. "Don't make me look like a fool in front of my men! I want the rest of the gold now," raising his voice in a violent fervor.

"Well, then, asshole, I guess it's just you, me and the hiding spot," Tom stated then looked the evil cartel boss squarely in the eye.

"You know, Senor Wyatt, I like your style, but it will be me and a group of my fellow associates," the thug replied laughing while patting ole Tom on the shoulder.

"No deal unless you let these people go," the rancher stated but Isidro informed Tom that no one was going to leave until the gangster had viewed the gold for himself.

With that being said, Tom left with the prick, while ten of Cavasos associates stayed behind to watch the rest of their prisoners. Little did Tom know, that Larry and Wiley were out in the tree line watching the events unfold. Quite frankly, if the ranchers hopes rested in those two, then Tom might as well shoot himself. The rancher also prayed that Larry didn't call the whole law enforcement community to the bar right now because that would be a death sentence for the hostages in the bar, including Maddy. As much as it pained poor Tom, the rancher with five of Isidro's men exited the bar and made their way to his vehicle, driving rapidly to the ranch. As they drove, Tom looked the men up and down, trying to get their personal descriptions as to identify them, after the rancher killed the scumbags.

"Larry, I gotta get over to my trailer," Wiley said urgently as he started to fidget nervously.

"Don't tell me you gotta aircraft carrier stashed out there," Larry replied in a sarcastic, sheriff that wanted to kill Mexican cartel member tone.

"Nope Larry, just my minigun," Wiley stated with a cheesy smile on his face.

Larry flashed a grin back Wiley's direction, shook his head, and both men made their way cautiously to the RV park. When the boys arrived, the two were stalled by the three mafia thugs right outside the camper adjoining Wiley's, making sure no unexpected surprises came their way.

"We're gonna have to creep up on em with our knives, stick em from behind, and put a bullet in their heads for hell of it," Wiley stated with a more fervent tone.

"Be realistic idiot," Larry replied. "Wiley, if we shoot these three deuce bags, the sound will attract the rest of the dick heads, and that'll jeopardize the hostages in the bar."

Unfortunately while Larry was talking, he didn't realize that Wiley had snuck up behind the first one and slit his throat. The other two hearing the ruckus, rushed over to the other side of the trailer. One thug was greeted with a knife thrown to his jugular, and before the other knuckle head could fire a round, received a knife, thrown by Larry, to the chest; immediately dropping him like a big tail buck. Wiley entered the trailer quickly and grabbed the minigun rounding up as much ammo that the two men could carry. The boys cautiously, made their way back to the bar and hid with gun at the ready behind a tall bush covered in snow.

"Larry, can I shoot my gun now?" Wiley asked in a childish tone.

"Look Wiley, if we take them out now, that will endanger Tom and I'm almost positive that we need both sides to be in communication. We can't do anything until Tom calls us," Larry stated. "Once we know that the prick has the gold, you can open fire!"

Wiley now had one huge grin his face, and a finger on the trigger, cocked and ready to inflict massive casualties when the time was right.

Walking the mafia associates back to the cave was unnerving for the rancher. Constantly jabbing Tom in the back if the rancher fell out of step was enough for any cowboy to pull his knife out and carve them up, but with Maddy and the rest of the people at the bar, Tom just couldn't chance it.

About halfway, the rancher remembered the booby traps that had been put in place by Wiley, so the anxious cowboy began to inspect the land and found a trip wire buried under a snowy log. Acting like he slipped, Tom fell down to the ground hard and as one of the thugs began to pick the rancher up, Tom tripped the wire. The poor gangster that leaned over never saw the two hundred pound log swing through the air, crushing the thug on contact. With Isidro's men temporarily stunned, Tom and Juan made a break for it. Running as fast as they could, the men bolted with every last adrenalized breath they had and arrived at the cave within moments. Locking themselves in, Tom then loaded up on weapons and ammo and radioed to Larry, only to get silence on the other end.

When Isidro regained his focused, he ordered his men to follow Tom to the cave. The remaining gangsters were hot on Tom's trail, following the fresh snow tracks. Seconds later, another associate of Isidro's perished as the man tripped a mine, knocking Cavasos flat on his back. Now in a visible rage, the mob boss arose with a distinct ringing in his ear from the blast and cursed Tom's name, while running quickly, following the fresh tracks of snow that the boys has just laid down. Within minutes, Isidro was at the entrance and peered into the cameras while banging on the door, talking on his cell phone.

"There's something I think you should see, Senor Wyatt," Cavasos exclaimed looking up at the camera and flung the cell phone under the door to the other side. Tom picked it up only to find Maddy with a gun to her head, panicking for her life.

"Let us in right now or your wife is dead, asshole," Isidro yelled in a violent tone. With no other option, Tom unlocked the door and was met with the butt end of Isidro's pistol, stinging him in the face. Isidro ordered both men to the ground. The mob boss looked at the rancher and said, "Senor Wyatt. You're a very honorable man, and I thank you for sacrificing this fortune to save your friends." Truthfully, Tom thought he was a lying piece of shit while the asshole was talking on his phone to the associates at the bar.

"So here's the gold, now let the hostages go," the rancher firmly told the mob boss.

"We do have a deal," Cavosos responded. "You want me to set them free? Then so be it"! He called back his associate and told the thugs at the bar in Spanish to kill the group. It's a good thing Tom understood Spanish. I am sure Tom would thank Lue and his ranch hands, but at the moment, that could wait.

Just as he gave the order, Tom felt around in his pocket and pulled the C-4 trigger priming the five charges, which reverberated throughout the cave.

"I think we should step out into the breezeway and have a chat," Tom stated with a smirk on his face. "Tell your men to stand down," the rancher forcefully stated holding the trigger, while Isidro and his remaining cronies trained their guns on both Juan and Tom. "Go ahead and shoot us," Tom continued. "You shoot Juan, I pull the trigger, and if you shoot me, it'll go off, so let's see just how good of a shot you are!"

"Lower your guns," Cavasos commanded, so Juan and the cowboy rose up and walked out to the breezeway cautiously. "You're not going to blow up all of this gold, *senor*. How can anybody be so dumb," Isidro asked laughing in a sinister tone, as Tom played with the trigger.

Walking back even slower, the boys reached the edge right by the waterfall. "You're right," Tom told Isidro, now seeing the cartel boss starting to fidget from all of the adrenaline coursing through his body. "I'm not going to blow the gold up. I'm gonna blow you assholes up with it!"

With those words, Tom looked at Juan smiling, pressing down on the button and jumped off of the waterfall into the pond below. Rising to the surface, the boys regained their breath, witnessing the fire above, while feeling the ground shake and dodging debris, while the cave collapsed. Swimming fast for the shore, the boys got out of the freezing water, breathing harder and faster than never before. Realizing that the walkie-talkie was in Tom's pocket and now soaked, ran as fast as the rancher could to the house to get a fresh one to call Larry.

"They're just standing around, Larry," Wiley said. "I just want to kill these assholes and get everybody out of there!"

"Wiley, just sit tight," Larry replied." Watching one of the thugs on the phone, Larry saw the thug shake his head and put the phone back in his jacket. The thug then raised his arms and all ten gangsters raised their weapons to the ready. In Spanish, the leader ordered, "Ready. Aim…"

Then Wiley yelled out, "Fire!" Distracting the mafioso in his general direction. Wiley then squeezed the trigger and the rounds flew out in hundreds of waves, ejecting hot stinging daggers of depleted Uranium bullets, easily cutting through all of the gangsters. When the last one fell, Larry and Wiley walked out into the parking lot and approached the entrance looking at the dismembered and bloody bodies, lay in the cool November night. All of the sudden, the last thug stepped outside with Maddy, holding a gun pointed to her head.

"Put your guns down now, *putos*," the gangster ordered, but Wiley and Larry weren't budging. The thug starting to shake and flinch with nervousness, threatening to kill Maddy, so Larry and Wiley both set their guns down and raised their hands.

"If you shoot her, were just gonna put a bullet in your head, asshole," Larry urged.

Pointing the gun directly at Larry, the thug smiled and started to pull the trigger, when a shot coursed through the tree line, hitting the gangster right between the eyes. Plopping the thug to the ground dead, the person who shot the gangster came out of the woods. It was Dallas, and he smiled, running over to his daughter-in-law, giving her a hug. Maddy immediately ran to Larry, crying, as the sheriff held her tight. The carnage was unbearable with blood and body parts strung throughout the whole parking lot. Then the thought occurred to Larry that Tom was now in immediate danger.

Trying the CB, Larry radioed Tom, but to no avail. Little did he know that Tom was still running to the house, while the mafia driver was sitting outside his car armed, waiting for the next person to come walking out. Finally, Tom left the trail and entered the kitchen grabbing a CB, calling Larry as the cold from the ranchers wet clothes sent shivers down his spine.

"Larry, are you there, over," Tom asked, and Larry answered telling the rancher what just happened at the bar. Reassured and pissed at the same time, Tom grabbed his pistol off the desk, then left through the kitchen. Walking slowly and checking every square inch, the two men proceeded to the side of the house where Juan had a perfect view of the driver, who was outside smoking a cigarette.

Cleverly, Tom picked up a rock and threw it hitting the back of the car, shattering the back window. Distracted and on alert, the thug unloaded his clip, shooting in any direction he thought relevant. With his last bullet exhausted, the gangster loaded a new clip, and the rancher appeared with his pistol pointed at the gangsters head.

"Put the gun down asshole," Tom urgently ordered the man and the thug nervously kept reloading even faster. Seeing no other option, Tom fired his gun, only to hear click after click, and realized that there were no bullets in it.

Laughing, the thug looked at Tom now with a fully loaded gun and said, "So much for being a legend, Mr. Wyatt! Time to go to sleep." The rancher drew quiet from the sudden shiver of deaths hand and closed his eyes expecting to be the next family member to occupy the Wyatt tomb.

Mere seconds had passed, when Tom heard a charging growl and then a terrified scream from the driver. The rancher opened his eyes only to find Chester the bear mauling the unsuspecting driver to an early grave. Tom then dropped to his knees and let go of the pistol, finally taking a deep breath while Chester ripped apart the gangster's now lifeless body spraying the rancher with the gangster's blood. It seemed like hours, but only minutes had passed by when every law enforcement official, came into the driveway, lights blaring, scaring Chester away. Juan came over and helped the rancher to his feet who was worn, shaken, and borderline in shock.

"Gee Tom, sorry but I ran out of bullets to, but it looks like it didn't even matter," Juan joked and cringed as the mutilated corpse lay only feet away.

"I wasn't expecting Chester to still be up this time of the year either," Tom replied. "Shit Juan, I'm sure glad Larry showed up finally. It always seems like he's never around any real action!"

Juan laughed and stated, "You know Larry's gonna be pissed when he finds out that you blew the gold up!"

"Well, Juan, if the story about Wyatt Earp with the gold is true, it wouldn't have been the first time either," Tom exclaimed.

y then, the officers had leapt out of their vehicles, guns drawn, combing the area where the thug was just killed. Larry then exited his vehicle with Maddy, and Jennie. Maddy immediately ran up to Tom who was wet and cold from the plunge into the pond, and hugged her husband. The officers covered both men in some emergency blankets and the boys began to laugh hysterically while Larry pulled out a bottle of shine, to warm their frozen bodies.

"Jesus Tom, what in the hell happened too that poor bastard over there?" Larry asked while looking at the former gangster.

"Oh, the son of a bitch got a face lift it appears," Tom replied. "Also, I may or may not have blown the gold up back in the cave."

"You've gotta be shitting me Tom," Larry exclaimed. "You ain't no goddamn Wyatt Earp, you know," Larry stated while laughing away.

"That's not the half of it," Tom added. "How many people can say that they have a dead cartel boss and billions of gold Spanish coins blown up on their land?"

"It would have been nice if you coulda kept the gold intact, at least," Larry said and Tom just bobbed his head, smirking with laughter.

Just as Larry turned to look at the scene, a bullet came flying out of nowhere, striking him near the heart. The sheriff hit the ground hard and Tom leaned down to catch his friend. It was Isidro who shot Larry, and the piece of shit was injured, but very much alive; at least till the rest of the deputy's put about twenty rounds into the man. Tom kneeled there holding Larry immediately applying pressure to his wound, as Larry began to drift off into unconsciousness. Tom frantically screamed for an ambulance in which an EMT who was on the scene within seconds, already began inspecting the sheriff's wound.

"Tom, I'm going to need you to keep applying pressure on the sheriff's wound while I get a stretcher," the EMT stated, then temporarily disappeared to grab the transportation device.

Larry regained consciousness temporarily and looked Tom in the eyes while blood poured slowly out of his heart and said, "Jesus Tom. I can't afford to take time off of work right now. With Evelyn's heart condition and all. I gotta get this fixed!"

"Yeah, Larry I know," Tom replied trying to keep pressure on the wound. "Let's get you fixed up first so we can get Evey healthy. Plus I'm getting tired of loaning you money!"

Larry laughed but the pain was unbearable and began passing out. The EMT returned quickly and secured Larry to the stretcher having Tom still apply pressure to the sheriff's most grievous wound. Within seconds, the paramedic secured Larry in the ambulance and a second EMT began to apply pressure as the back door shut. With Larry now being tended too, the paramedic turned on the lights and sirens, disappearing quickly away from the scene. Tom, who was in a state of shock, walked past Maddy and the group almost silent, slowly making his way to Isidro. When Tom was close, he pulled out his firearm and stood over the mob boss, as the bastard lay there shaking, but still very much alive. Officer Morrison joined Tom, seeing, that the ranchers pistol was drawn at Isidro, and stood next to the shaken up cowboy.

"It's funny that the last memory this prick will have, is a picture of the us two standing over him," Morrison stated as Tom looked at him. "I'm not going to take your pistol, so if you want to put this asshole out of his misery, go ahead."

Tom loaded a bullet into his Luger, then pointed the pistol at Isidro and placed the barrel of his gun directly on the boss's head. Isidro who was still shaking, looked up at Tom's eyes and said, "I'm a dead man anyway rancher. Just tell Juan that I wish I could have been a better father. You can do what you may now Tom. I'm ready."

Then Juan and Wiley stood next to Tom, as well as the officer, whom all were now looking down at Isidro. The mob boss caught a brief glimpse of Juan and reached his hand out, but it was met with a kick of Juan's boot.

"Gee Tom, he should have taken the money when it was originally offered, don't you think," Wiley commented, and Tom looked back at his friend with a smile.

"Yeah, Wiley, I suppose he should have," Tom replied, then looked at Juan with a somber tone and continued, "Why don't you put your dad out of his misery?" he said, passing the pistol over to Juan who then pointed it at Isidro, placing the barrel in the mob boss's mouth. Before he could pull the trigger, Juan relented and rose, returning Tom's firearm.

"No, Tom, I think not," Juan responded. "No, I think this piece of shit can just lie here and suffer," Juan then placed his hand on Tom's shoulder and said, "Let's get out of here and go check on Larry."

Tom looked Juan in the eyes and shook his head in agreement. "Yeah, I think it's about time we hit the trail," Tom replied and walked away from a dying mob boss who made nearly two months of the rancher's life a living hell.

As they walked away, Wiley brushed up against Tom and asked, "Why didn't you shoot him?"

"Well, Wiley, I thought about it. But I thought it more convenient for Juan to do, and you heard the man. So let his dad suffer." The two ole boys left it at that as Isidro lie there on the ground struggling to move his eyes any further. As he felt his breathing shallow, the once vicious gangster finally realized that he breathed his last breath as the once clear portrait of the men standing over him, subsided to a darker shadow of death smiling right back at the cartel boss. The shadowy figure then placed its unworldly hand over Isidros neck, as he thought of Juan and Jaime playing on the beach as children for the very last time.

Chapter 13

The Choices We Make

Out of all the things that could have gone wrong, Tom never imagined Larry would have taken a bullet the way the poor bastard did. Now I know that this far in the book, you might be wondering about the hilarity of it all, yet this most grievous calamity actually plays an important part in the further adventures of ole Tom Wyatt. Even though the shooting was intentional, everybody knew that ole Isidro was dead, yet the mob boss for his evil in the end, tried to make peace with his son.

The only problem being that he was just too bad of a man, and Juan would rather see his father suffer in his final moments for all the countless thousands of lives that he affected. From the drug addict trying to score their next fix, to mass killings on Isidro's home turf, lives meant nothing to him. It would seem that his greed consumed the man, enough to come and collect on a German Panzer tank, just to prove a point. Well, as Tom would say, "point taken."

Back at the scene, the ambulance whisked the wounded sheriff away and everybody was panicked amidst the carnage, as well as the violence that had just occurred. The deputy's that were present were busy taking witness statements and poor Tom was too enamored by all that just happened, so he disappeared around the corner and vomited heavily. When he regained his constitution, Officer Morrison approached the rancher and put his hand on Tom's shoulder.

"Jesus Tom, I can't imagine what you're going through right now so let's get your statement later," the deputy stated. "I know that I may have treated you unkindly in the past, and I feel bad for that."

"Gary, it's all right," Tom replied. "I was never a fan of yours that much anyhow, but you're a good officer, and all is forgiven." Tom then extended his hand out to shake the officers, and was met with a kind smile.

"Tom, let's get you out of here and go to the hospital," Morrison replied.

The two men hopped into the deputy's cruiser while Morrison bolted down the road, lights and sirens blaring. The deputy then pulled out a familiar bottle of moonshine and commenced to sip off of the bottle.

"I never had you pegged for a moonshine drinking cop," Tom stated and the deputy smiled.

"Well, when you have a slave driving boss like Larry, this helps to calm a person's nerves down," Morrison exclaimed.

Within minutes, the boys had arrived at the hospital and Tom ran over to the nurses desk to ask how Larry was doing. The nurse graciously informed the rancher that Larry was in critical condition and currently in surgery. Tom didn't say much else but nodded his head and sat down in an unoccupied seat in the waiting room. It was only moments before Maddy and Laurie had showed up and Larry's wife had an almost frozen look about her. It was one thing to be traumatized by the violence at the bar, but when you have your husband shot right in front of you; some would say that witnessing that particular crime, was an even more ambiguous burden to bear. Maddy helped Laurie to a seat and Tom pulled out a jar of moonshine passing it over to Laurie, who sipped the drink with a blank, cold stare on her face.

"Tom, where were you," Laurie asked and the rancher put his arm around her to comfort the pain of Laurie's day.

"Laurie, I was right there when it happened," Tom replied. "I really thought that I blew that son of a bitch up back at the cave." Laurie then sat silent, still in shock, and Maddy glanced over at Tom and began to cry.

"Laurie, your man's gonna be okay, darling," Maddy stated and gave Laurie a hug.

"Larry's a tough man, but he could be dying right now and I couldn't even help him if I tried," Laurie exclaimed.

Tom then rose and asked the women if they wanted any coffee, but Laurie was happy drinking the moonshine that the rancher provided her, so he went over to the table that had a coffee maker but noticed something peculiar. The machine itself was rather small and when the rancher placed his cup underneath it, nothing came out.

"Maddy, what the hell is a Keurig," Tom asked and she laughed only to get up to demonstrate how the machine worked. Taking an even smaller cup which resembled a mini packet of coffee creamer, Maddy dropped it into the brewer and pressed the button.

"It's not as hard as it looks," Maddy stated as the machine began to brew a fresh cup. "I've always wanted one of these. There so convenient and they brew really fast."

Impressed, Tom took his cup and sat back down, dropping a shot of moonshine into the warm coffee. Taking a sip of the dark liquid, Tom smiled and commented how that was the best cup of java that he had in a long time. Starting to feel tired, the rancher then tipped the brim of his Stetson over his eyes to catch some much needed shut eye.

When the rancher awoke hours later, the women had disappeared and Tom's neck had hurt from the way he slept. The cowboy got up and went to the nurses desk close by to ask about Larry, which the nurse told Tom that Larry was out of surgery in the critical care ward just down the hall. Smiling, Tom wished her a good day and made his way to Larry's room.

When Tom arrived, the rancher knocked on the door and entered. Maddy was close by talking on her cell phone and Laurie was sitting by Larry's side crying. The sheriff was hooked up to every wire and machine in his room sleeping from the gun wound to his torso, so Tom took a seat by Maddy, putting his arm around her while she chatted away.

"Larry's gonna be okay, Tom," Laurie stated, in which Tom smiled rubbing his face, trying to hold back the tears. "It's okay, cowboy. At least you came back from the cave in one piece and did your best to kill the bastard that wounded my husband."

"Are you sure he's gonna be alright, Laurie?" Tom asked again, holding Larry's arm.

Laurie replied, "Tom, he's a tough son of a bitch! The doctor said that there was some internal bleeding, so he'll be on blood thinners for a while. I guess he'll be done drinking for a bit."

Laughing, Tom hugged Laurie, about the time her husband began to stir. "Hands off my wife," Larry spoke in a low, hurt tone. Laurie smiled and kissed him on the forehead then Larry looked over the rancher's direction.

"Larry you look like shit," Tom told his hurt friend and the sheriff replied, "That's weird because I feel like I've been shot, but with all of this damn pain medication in me, I couldn't feel anything right now, even if I wanted too!"

Laurie asked if he was okay, and Larry replied in earnest. He then asked Laurie if Tom and him could have a quick talk in private. Laurie took no offense, and left the room with Maddy to go get a cup of coffee.

"Did you get that bastard and the gold?" Larry asked.

Tom humbly replied, "Yeah, and kinda. It was your men that finished the job Larry."

He looked Tom strangely in the eye and asked, "Like you shot the thug kinda, and you have the gold?"

"Kinda like the gangsters are dead and buried with the gold in the cave. Oh, and Wiley's booby traps took care of a couple of them, as well."

Looking at the rancher, Larry started to laugh but his wound sent a sharp pain resonating throughout his body.

"I guess ole Wyatt Earp would be rolling in his grave right now after blowing up the gold for a second time, eh Tom?"

"Well, Larry, I mighta left out something else," the rancher interrupted. "Before Granny past away, she told me that I'm Wyatt Earps great, great, great grandson."

Larry proceeded to change his happiness to a look of confusion. " Gee Tom," he said. "I never had you pegged for a gun tooting, entrepreneurial pimp/ lawman!" Smiling at each other, the sheriff then said, "Tom, I have a little favor to ask. I'm gonna be out awhile, and until I get back to normal, would you mind watching the office?

It's just that the men can get really rambunctious at times, and we're required by law to at least have a sheriff oversee them."

At first, Tom was taken back, and then the thought occurred to the rancher that Larry was too hurt to return in time for the upcoming election the following year. Tom paused, then looked Larry in the eye and told the injured sheriff to give him the badge; but only until he was healthy enough to return to work. The cowboy also told Larry that when they recovered the gold, the ole goat would be rewarded with a fifth of the fortune, which Tom thought ironic because they usually drink alcohol by the fifth; so why not share the five billion the same way. Larry looked at Tom almost in shock and started to tear up, but nonetheless, stiffened up, handing the rancher the badge.

"That's an expensive badge Tom," the injured lawman stated. "There's always a high price to pay when you wear this. Never forget it buddy!" The rancher then placed the badge on his shirt right about the time Laurie returned with her coffee.

"Did I miss something?" Laurie asked while staring at the badge attached to Tom's long-sleeved button-up polo. "Actually, Tom, it's a great fit on you!" Laurie stated, then looked at Larry smiling, and kissed her beloved husband on the lips.

"Tom, I wanna spend time with my beautiful wife, so why don't you go shakedown a doughnut stand or something," Larry asked, and Tom obliged, smiling. Leaving the room, all Tom could think about, was the election that he conceded to his friend, and how treating people fairly, sooner or later, comes back full circle.

Maddy was soon behind Laurie and returned only to see the shiny badge that Tom was sporting and punched the rancher in the shoulder. "So I step out for a minute and you're wearing Larry's badge! Tell me that this is some horrible joke," Maddy asked and Tom laughed.

"I wish it was sweety," Tom replied and held her close. "It's only temporary until Larry is healed and back on his feet."

"Thomas Eugene Wyatt, nothing you've done in this life has been temporary," Maddy replied and began to tear up, but remained strong. After a few minutes of Tom holding Maddy, she looked the newly appointed sheriff in the eye and said, "Okay, I'll accept this but only under one condition."

"Oh, what's that," Tom interrupted, smiling.

"If you get hurt, I will make it my mission in this life to kick your ass, rancher," Maddy exclaimed as she kissed Tom on the cheek.

Tom hugged Maddy giving her a much needed kiss and they both agreed that this would be best until Larry was well enough to resume his duties. On their way out of the hospital, Officer Morrison was there to greet Tom and all the rancher could think was, "Oh shit, here we go again!"

The officer looked at the badge and asked, "Did I miss something in the last hour, or is that the sheriffs badge pinned on your shirt?"

"Well, I guess I'm the new sheriff in town," Tom said with a grin on his face.

"It's about time you pulled your head out of your ass, Sheriff Wyatt," the deputy replied. The two men then shook hands as the officer stood there in total agreement with Larry's decision. "Well, Gary, where are we with the investigation," Tom asked.

"We have about every law enforcement agency imaginable at the bar and your cave. Tom, I've heard the story about what went down on your property all of those years ago, and it just seems so ironic and surreal too me. Were you trying to copy Wyatt Earp, or what?"

"I didn't blow the gold up deputy," Tom said. "I just buried it temporarily."

"Yeah, but still Tom that's pretty crazy," the officer added while scratching his head.

"Gary, nothing that I've done in this life has been anything but normal," Tom replied. "In fact, as my first act of sheriff, I'm promoting you to sergeant if that's okay?"

Morrison was stunned at first considering past issues with Tom, but then cracked a smile and shook the new sheriff's hand. "It'll be an honor to work with you Tom," Morrison exclaimed and the rancher smiled at his new sergeant.

"That's Sheriff Wyatt too you, asshole," Tom replied and both men laughed as Maddy stood back shaking her head.

Sergeant Morrison and the couple left the hospital and headed to the station where the media was waiting for a press statement about the events that unfolded in the Upper County. When they arrived, every news network in the state of Washington was present and the cameras were rolling as Tom exited the vehicle. It was chaotic at first with all of the reporters trying to get in a word in edgewise over the last, so Tom raised his voice, quieting down the crowd.

"Ladies and gentlemen, I'd like to thank you for coming here today under the circumstances," Tom stated. "First and foremost, Sheriff Baxter was injured in a shooting incident last night. The sheriff's currently in critical care but stable and is believed to make a full recovery. The assailants that attacked the bar were quickly taken out, but one injured thug managed to shoot the sheriff before the man was neutralized by the fine deputy sheriff's you see before us. For now, I will be acting sheriff of the Upper County until Larry is well enough to assume his position. I will take questions now but only one at a time please and let's not make them too complicated because I'm new to all of this," and the gallery or reporters began to laugh. One gal raised her hand and Tom waived her on to ask a question.

"Sheriff, it is common knowledge that the suspects shot and killed last night were associates of the Cavasos cartel in Mexico. Any truth to that rumor and if so, why are they in Kittitas county," the reporter asked.

"Well, uh, good question," Tom stated trying not to give too much information away, yet at the same time, had to be truthful. "They were here on account of my friend Wiley. The man is an ex military crazy ole coot that leased a tank from the cartel, and well, they came here to terminate the lease, but Sheriff Baxter was at the bar during the incident to help quell the threat."

The reporters then bursts out into a frenzy of questions concerning the tank, so the acting sheriff raised his voice, yet again, and the crowd drew silent.

"Let's try this a different way and let me point to the reporter to ask the next question if that's okay," Tom added. The rancher then pointed his finger at another reporter and gave the go ahead.

"Sheriff, there has also been several incidents up here this year involving similar violence. Is all of this tied together," the reporter asked.

"Yes, the cartel has tried several times to make contact with Mr. Holloway, but has been thwarted every time by the rapid response of the Upper County sheriffs, WSP, and other federal agencies," Tom replied. "I can't stress enough the rapid response of these institutions.

Without their bravery, valor, and patience in the matter, the violence would have erupted to a most unwholesome conclusion."

Just then a convoy of black GMC Yukons pulled up near the press conference. A gentleman in a sharply dressed black suit exited the SUV and walked over to Tom as the crowd looked on in awe, with his security detail taking the perimeter. The gentleman than approached Tom and shook his hand smiling. The man then took the microphone from Tom and said," Hello ladies and gentleman! My name is Bernardo Cortez and I am the acting ambassador representing the Spanish consulate in Seattle. Today is a most joyous day for the citizens of Spain for this amazing man that you see before you. I can't express enough gratitude, on behalf of the Spanish government and its citizens, for this kind hearted man, for finding our most valuable lost treasure." The crowd confused at first, erupted into a flurry of questions and Tom had whispered to Bernardo that the press had not been informed of the gold, as well as, the circumstances therein.

With a look of surprise on his face, Bernardo looked at Tom and said, "I feel a tad bit embarrassed right now like I just gave up the ghost!" Tom laughed and reassured the ambassador who was expected to be there today, that the cat was just let out of the bag. After Tom had quieted the gallery for the third time, he said, "Oh yeah. There's that too. I stumbled into a lost treasure of the Spanish government." Not knowing what to say next, Tom paused and then said, "The fortune was originally discovered by my great, great, great, grandfather, and I just recently discovered its hidden location on my property. The Spanish coins that were discovered are roughly five billion dollars in total and Ambassador Cortez has graced us with his presence to collect on the missing gold. I kinda wanted to save that surprise for later, but the cats out of the bag now," and the press erupted into a flurry of laughter. "All joking aside, I was present at the bar when the incident occurred, and I encouraged the main mob boss to go to my cave where it was hidden. The only thing that they didn't realize that the cave was booby trapped with explosives and well, and the remaining cartel associates are currently buried with the gold!"

The crowd more enamored than ever erupted yet again into a maze of questions and Bernardo looked at the acting sheriff in utter disbelief, hearing the events that had transpired, for the first time.

"Since the ambassador has graced the Upper County with his presence, I would like to hold another press conference for another time so we can sort these events out. For now, that will be all of the questions that I can answer, plus, I have to explain to the Ambassador why his gold is yet buried again," Tom exclaimed and entered the sheriff's station with Bernardo.

The men came in through the front door and the look of shock overcame every deputy hearing what had just happened. After a pause, one officer started to clap, and then the rest followed with cheering. Maddy was sitting on a bench nearby and ran to Tom, kissing and hugging the sheriff, astounded by what Tom just told the press. Tom then escorted Bernardo into Larry's office and shut the door. Tom sat down and told the ambassador about how Wyatt Earp had blown the gold up in a previous incident but only recovered enough what Wyatt could at that time, leaving the rest of the gold for future generations. Bernardo sat in awe almost in a hypnotic shock, speechless over what Tom had just told him. The sheriff then pulled out a jar of moonshine tucked away in Larry's desk and passed it over to the ambassador, which he embraced the jar graciously. After a couple drinks, Bernardo put the jar down and said, "So you're telling me that you're the grandson of one of the greatest lawmen of the old west?"

"It would appear that way Mr. Cortez," Tom replied. "Apparently, my ancestors and I have serious issues with blowing up Spanish bullion." He then took a sip of the moonshine that Bernardo just ingested and looked the Spaniard in the eye only to watch the ambassador take several more gulps of the corn liquor.

"I think that there is a pattern definitely starting to evolve Mr. Wyatt," Bernardo exclaimed while laughing.

"Well, let's just hope that one day soon, your gold is safely tucked away in some underground vault, and not under thousands of tons of debris," Tom added. "The good news is that the gold is secure and I'm going to buy some excavators to remove all of it from the collapsed cave. It'd be my pleasure if you came over to inspect the damage." Tom then took the coin that Tildy had given her grandson and flicked it over to Bernardo.

"That's definitely one of the coins," Bernardo exclaimed and held it in his hands, entranced by its shiny, yet faded beauty.

"My granny had it for the longest time, but my grandpa was the original owner," Tom stated and Bernardo sat there entranced. "I'd let ya keep that one, but it's been in the family a long time."

"Considering there's more, I think this coin can be overlooked," Bernardo said jokingly and flicked the coin back too Tom.

"You know, that the Spanish government will help out with any excavation that should be undertaken on your property. Mainly since we're dealing with artifacts, Tom, we need to hire a team of specialists to remove the bullion, so I don't think that bulldozers will be required. I'd rather help fund the sciences anyhow and feel it necessary to help those causes," the Ambassador stated and Tom felt thankful for Bernardo's cooperation. After a couple of drinks and planning for the removal of the coins, there was a knock at the door and Wiley stepped in as happy as a clam.

"Wiley, have a seat," Tom said, so the ole boy shook the ambassadors hand and pulled up a chair, smiling with that familiar smirk that Tom had been so accustomed too.

"Hey, Tom, I guess that C-4 really did the trick eh," the crazy ole coot exclaimed and Tom introduced Bernardo too Wiley, explaining how his friend rigged up the ranchers cave with the explosive. With a state of shock on the ambassador's face, he looked Wiley into the eye and exclaimed," So you're one of the gentlemen responsible for blowing up the gold."

"Oh, Mr. Ambassador, I'm not gentle with anything I do, and I like it to appear as securing the gold from thieves," Wiley jokingly stated. He then looked at Tom and asked where the break room was where he could smoke, but Tom was wise to Wiley's devices, suggesting otherwise. Bernardo then asked if it was possible to go look at the cave and see what could be done to begin the excavation immediately, which Tom heartily agreed to the ambassadors request. However, Tildy's upcoming funeral had to be addressed and the whole mess at the bar, as well as Tom's ranch needed to be resolved, so the sheriff agreed to take Bernardo with his men to the cave before anymore publicity was drawn.

To handle the current crisis of dodging the anxious press, Tom and Bernardo rounded up Maddy, departing through the rear entrance. As the group piled into their prospective vehicles, Wiley peeked his head around the corner of the building in the back of the station taking a quick puff off of a joint that he had snuck in, and hopped into the car. Then Maddy hit the gas, speeding away from the chaotic crowd of reporters, waiting to get the story of what really happened at the Windy River Ranch. On the way, everybody was in high spirits, with Tom, passing a jar of moonshine back to Bernado, who sipped the ignitable liquid while listening to Wiley talk about all of the adventures that the boys had been through recently.

"A snake bit you in the nutsack," the ambassador asked while trying to refrain from not losing his laughter.

"Oh brother. Bernardo, you have no idea what this man has put me through in the last few months," Wiley replied while smiling back at Tom, as the rancher winced back at his friend, letting the ole coot soak up the glory of the moment. "I buy a German Panzer and the whole Upper county gets flipped upside down!"

"Well, Senor Wiley, I must admit that we tend to make certain purchases in our lives that affect other people as well," Bernardo replied and pulled out his cell phone, flipping through his pictures. "Look at this," and the ambassador passed the phone over to the crazy coot.

Wiley gazed at the photo with amazement and asked, "Geez dude. Is that a Russian MIG fighter?"

"Yes, it is, Wiley and I enjoy flying it whenever I have free time," Bernardo replied. "My point being Wiley, is that I've purchased my toy legally and didn't have to deal with cartels and such. Who knows, maybe one day soon, I'll take you up in my toy."

Wiley was taken back with the ambassadors sentiment and lowered his head, unsure of how to react, then lifted his head and smiled.

"Bernie, would you like to check out the tank sometime," Wiley asked smiling, and the ambassador thanked him with a nod of his head.

After a short time, the group had arrived at the ranch and exited their vehicles. Bernardo breathed in the refreshing cold mountain air and exhaled, taking a look of the Stuart mountain range tucked away in the north, shaking his head in amazement over the Teanaways majestic beauty.

"I love being in the mountains," the ambassador stated. "There's just something about the trees and the fire burning from your chimney that takes me back to when I was a young boy. Tom, you should feel lucky by not having to deal with the fast paced ways of city life. To live out here is to say that you've truly lived!"

Tom smiled at Bernardo and offered a tour of the ranch which the ambassador and his entourage accepted. The undersheriff led the men around to the stable, glancing over his shoulder at Bernardo, who was enamored by all of the pictures of memories past and present hanging from the walls of the stable. After the tour, Tom led the entourage into the office, and asked Maddy if she could prepare a late lunch, which the sheriff's beautifully pleasant wife graciously offered, departing to the house. After a few drinks and laughs, Bernardo's curiosity had peaked, so Tom led the men outside to the cave. Along the way, Wiley slowed down the party, showing the men where to step, as to not get blown up by any booby traps he discovered along the way, which as a precaution, the sheriff dismantled as they made their way. Bernardo was quite impressed with Wiley's precision in laying these devices and was simply amazed as the trail opened up into the micro valley, witnessing the pile of heaping rubble still smoldering from the incident the night before.

When they arrived, there was still some investigators processing the scene and the entourage was shocked by all of the blood covering the entrance of the cave.

"Wow! There must have been quite a showdown here," Bernado exclaimed and Tom replied, "The booby traps got a few of the bastards as well, ambassador."

Looking at the cave, Bernardo picked around and saw an object shining under some debris. Digging in, the ambassador loosened the coin from the earth and smiled. "This is the place, the ambassador stated and placed the shiny piece of bullion in his pocket. "I'm getting hungry. I can imagine that Maddy has a meal prepared for us?"

"I can imagine she does," Tom replied, and walked away with the group back to the ranch house.

Upon their return, the reporters had begun piling into the ranch, and several deputies were securing the anxious mob, waiting to get a story. Tom offered to go inside to eat, but Bernardo feeling uneasy about the noise, felt it necessary to address the crowd, so they could eat in peace. The two men approached the group who were already shouting out questions which were also being drowned out by the other reporters asking about the incident.

Tom placed his hands down to his waist and said, "The ambassador and myself will now offer a statement and answer a couple of questions if you agree to exit the property when the conference is done. This area is still a crime scene, and I would appreciate the candor of your part, if you can respect my wishes." The crowd drew silent and Tom continued, "I just escorted the ambassador and his entourage back from the cave, and the ambassador was in shock that I blew up his bullion. Yet when a man has no other viable option, one has to make a choice. For now, the gold is safe. May I add that anybody trespassing on my land while this excavation is still undergoing will be prosecuted under the fullest extent of the law. Also, I just recently lost my grandmother, so our family is in a state of mourning and again, I wholeheartedly advise the public at large, that our wishes be respected. Just like my comments a little while at the station, not much has changed, but as more information comes to light, I will fully cooperate with you."

One reporter than blurted, "Mr. Wyatt, what are your future plans with your newfound fortune?"

"Well, a lot," Tom replied. "The main thing that I want to do first and foremost, is give Larry some cash to aid in his daughter Evelyn, who has a heart condition. Then who knows from there."

The group of reporters then paused and some hearts lightened hearing about Tom's generosity. There were other questions concerning the removal of the gold and Tom's grandma, which the rancher answered in earnest. Bernardo then put his hand on Tom's shoulder and told the rancher that he would finish with the questions so Tom could go grieve with his family. The rancher then smiled and departed into the solitude of his home. After a while, Bernardo answered all appropriate questions and the crowd dispersed into a peaceful scene of quiet and tranquil calm. When the ambassador was done, he entered from the chilly cold of the outdoors, and headed toward the fireplace to warm up. Tom approached the ambassador with a jar of moonshine, which the delegate accepted, and sat down to relax, while having a drink.

As Bernardo sat, he glanced over at Tom, who smiled raising his glass and looked at the mood of the room; which was quite surprising to the ambassador because after all of the loss, as well as the violence that transpired over the whole week, everybody was in great spirits.

Sitting there smiling, the ambassador was approached by Dallas and Lupita who offered their introductions, then came a knock at the door. Tom went over to answer and to his surprise, it was Terror and the Yellow Jackets, who drove up in a motor home after hearing about Tildy's passing.

"Jeez, Tom, you really have a hopping house today," Terror exclaimed. "We heard about Tildy and thought that we'd come up here and help you through your grief."

"Thank you, brother," Tom replied and hugged all the men, shaking their hands as they came strolling in.

"Well, how was the drive over Terror," Tom asked while passing some shine his direction.

Terror took a drink and replied, "It was quite nice actually. The weathers been so warm that we haven't ran into much snow. In fact, it took us about fifteen hours straight to get here!"

Tom sat back and laughed because most people that adhere to the rules of the road usually takes them about a day and a half of straight driving to Southern California. Tom then escorted Terror into den and sat down. Terror pulled up a chair, lighting up a cigarette while drinking more shine.

Tom then said, "Terror, I just wanted to apologize with all of the stuff that happened down in Cali. I had no idea the FBI was going to bring you boys into all of this, so I'm truly sorry."

Terror sat back and laughed with a huge grin on his face, then replied, "Brother, everything worked out ok. In fact, had Wiley not purchased that damn tank, I might be sitting in a damn cell waiting for my court date by now! It all worked out in the end though and I'm looking forward to doing more business with you guys and Larry. Where is that crotchety asshole at anyhow?"

"I guess nobody told you yet," Tom answered and Terror shook his head. Tom drew a breath and filled the biker in on what happened over the last few days, making Terror all most lose his emotions, but assured the man that Larry was doing well.

"So you had a shootout with the Cavasos cartel, blew up your cave with all that loot, and Isidro shot Larry. Sounds like you country folk have been dealing with some interesting shit lately," Terror replied laughing.

"Well, it's been a wild ride so far Terror," Tom responded. "For helping us out, I figured that you and your men deserve a cut out of the fortune when I get my check!"

Terror's eyes lit up like a pervert in a sex shop. Not knowing what to say, he shook the ranchers hand and gave him a hug. Then the biker asked Tom to follow him out to the RV for a surprise. So, Tom smiled and rose out of his chair, following Terror out to the RV. When the two arrived at the trailer, Tom noticed a couple of the bikers unloading a vehicle off of the back and Terror had him look around the corner. When Tom seen this car, he got real quiet and started to shed a tear.

"Check it out, brother," Terror exclaimed. "It's a 1965 Shelby Mustang GT 500, with all of the bells and whistles!"

"Terror, I can't accept this after all I put you through," Tom replied.

"Hey, Tom, after all the shit that you've been through in these last months, while helping us out, it's the least me and the boys can do," the biker replied. "Plus, I know you have a thing for mustangs with attitudes," referring to Trigger.

Terror then passed Tom the keys and both men hopped in. The rancher fired up the car and Terror said that he wanted to go for a drive, so Tom obliged by flooring the gas pedal, knocking them both back into their seats.

"For fuck sake, Tom, now that you're sheriff, don't you think this would make the perfect cop car to go busting all of those bad guys?" Terror asked.

Tom let out a huge laugh and replied, "Yeah, I think this will make a great fit for my new line of work! Speaking of sheriffs, you wanna go drop in on Larry and say hi?"

"Hell yeah, brother," Terror exclaimed, and Tom hit the gas speeding to the hospital.

The men arrived at the hospital a short time thereafter and screeched to a halt, with Tom smiling in excitement over his new toy. The two quickly made their way up too Larry's room and Tom amidst all of the Shelby excitement, forgot to knock and strolled into the room, only to find Larry sitting up erect, and Laurie was giving the naughty lawman (what we call up in these parts), a mouth hug. The two men did an about face, almost embarrassed, but at the same time, laughing their very hearts out. After Laurie adjusted her husband's bed gown, the boys turned back around and smiled at Larry, who appeared rather impaired from the medicine.

"Geez, Tom, just 'cause you're sheriff now still means you have to knock on doors," Larry stated and Tom hung his head low, sitting down, with a huge grin spread across the man's face.

"I brought you a peace offering," Tom said and pulled out a huge stack of cash and handed it to Laurie. "You get yourself and your daughter better you ole bastard—or else I'm gonna personally tell Laurie behind your back that she can spend your cut of the loot on whatever the hell she wants.

Larry looked at Tom and smiled, not knowing what to say. "That's one hell of a peace offering, Sheriff Wyatt," Larry exclaimed.

"Well, Larry, there's plenty more to go around, so I figured, why not just let you have it," Tom replied.

Laurie not knowing what to say, gave Tom a hug and kiss on the cheek, then Larry shouted in joy doing more of the same thing. Terror sat back and smiled not knowing what Tom had planned for their injured friend. After they had visited for a bit, Larry started to get tired and Laurie was looking a little worse for the wear, so Tom offered to give her a ride home. Laurie was apprehensive at first, but she needed to rest, and Tom wasn't going to hear the gal say no, so Larry kissed his wife good night. The three were soon on their way and Laurie noticed Tom's new ride commenting about how it was a good fit for the rancher.

When the boys arrived at Laurie's, the grandparents came out taking notice of the muscle car, and greeted the tired woman. The grandfather then approached the driver side, smiling at Tom as he put his arm on the window rest, and the rancher rolled down the window to shake the man's hand.

"Geez Tom, we heard about Spanish coins but didn't think you were buying such an impressive vehicle already, the older gentleman said smiling.

"Naw, Jim, this was a gift from my friend right here," pointing to Terror, who was pleasant, yet well mannered. "I must say that you and Ella haven't aged a bit."

"Well, thank you, Sheriff Wyatt," Ella replied smiling. "So Laurie called and told us that you gave Larry the cash to help our granddaughter get better? Tom, you're a really good man," she said and hugged the rancher, kissing Tom on the cheek. "So when's the funeral service for Tildy?"

"Well, with everything going on, we wanted to bury her this week, but we're going to conduct the service next Sunday," Tom replied while holding back a tear.

"Aw, Tom, everything's going to be okay," Ella reassured Tom and gave him another hug. "Well, I am freezing out here, so I'm going to go back inside. Let us know what time the services start and we will be there Tom." Ella then bid the boys farewell, and made her way back into the house, but Jim was reluctant and looked at Tom with a serious stare, realizing that the man's son was wounded, but ok.

"So I know you're sheriff for now, Tom, but I have a question," Jim asked shyly. "I'm a little low on liquid, and was wondering if you might have a little gas to fill up the ole tank?"Tom took the remaining jar of moonshine which was about three quarters of the way full and passed it over to Jim. "That one's been previously used so it's on the house Mr. Baxter," Tom stated while passing the jar over."Well, that's much appreciated, Tom, and just call me Jim," the old man said while taking a pull off of the jar. "You know Tom that I knew both Gene and Tildy very well, and I must say, if I didn't haul all of that corn liquor back in the Fifties, I'd a never met Ella. It's kinda funny how choices can affect a man so much. What do you think about it?""You know Jim, I'm starting to think the same thing," Tom replied smiling at Jim, as the old man enjoyed the moonshine. "Jim, Two Boots left me a letter," Tom stated then showed the old document to Jim, whom after reading the letter, laughed and cried all at the same time. Tom then explained how he found the letter and Jim just stood there and shook his head in bewilderment.

"Jim. If there's one thing that I do know about choices, is that friends are just as much as family, as Apple pie and tittie bars. I consider Larry to be like my older, in fact, much older brother, and you've been a good influence in my life, Mr. Baxter. Just know, that the choices that I've made, being good or bad, have turned out pretty damn well."

"Never had a doubt in my mind son," Jim exclaimed, smiling over the fact that his buzz was starting to kick in. "Anyhow young man, I am proud of the choices that you made and I know I can't replace ole Two boots by any means. But I have a shitload of stories that I'm sure you haven't heard yet."

Taken back with Jims kindness, Tom shook the man's hand, as well did a polite Terror, and as the old man walked away, he said, "Keep that letter everywhere you go from now on. Voices from the past echo truth even till this day, and I know that you might not be a religious man, but these signs define us of what we are, and who we'll become."

With that being said, Jim thanked the sheriff for the shine, while slowly meandering his way up the steps, into the Baxter home, and Tom with his temporary sidekick, hit the gas steaming away to the packed house of delegates at the Windy River Ranch.

Chapter 14

The Force Is Strong with This One

When Terror and the sheriff arrived at the ranch, there was an influx of vehicles that wasn't press related, yet Tom knew that the reservation had just showed up, to pay tribute to Tildy. There were several motor homes and fifth wheels with people smiling as Tom pulled into the driveway. The boys exited the Shelby and Chief Thunder Bear walked up to the boys, shaking hands, offering his sentiment for the ranchers loss. The chief then looked at the muscle car sitting in the garage, in shock, and drinking a pull of moonshine exclaimed, "I love the new ride Tom, but did Trigger take the good news well?"

"I haven't told him yet TB," Tom replied looking reluctant considering with everything else on his plate currently. "Trigger's been rolling with me for some time now, so I'd hate to keep my horse outta the loop."

"Geez Tom, all you need is some party lights and a battery pack on Trigger's rear. You can pull over people on bicycles or other horses I guess," Thunder Bear replied while scratching his chin in confusion.

"Chief, I always get the bad guy, and Trig has always been there ready to throw down," Tom stated. "I really don't know if my horse will be fit for the job when it comes to certain things like car chases."

"Yeah, but with all the beer drinking and carrying on with Betsy, I'm guessing he'd be good at shaking down teenagers having a bonfire or something," Thunder Bear replied, laughing. "Hey Tom, do you have any more of that corn liquor that I could quench my pallet with?"

"Sure, chief. Let's head out to my office for a pull real quick," the sheriff replied in earnest. So the three men headed out to the office in the midst of a winter storm that began to take shape, releasing light flakes that almost seemed to float in the air, suspended. Right before the men entered the shop, a pair of headlights parked by the guys, and a shadowy figure stepped out of a black sports car. Tom seen the badge and laughed as Marshal Evans approached the rancher, with a look of total shock upon his face.

"Tom, I heard about Tildy and I am so sorry you lost her," the marshal stated.

"Thank you, marshal," Tom replied. "Wanna head in with us for a drink?"

"Yeah I'd like that," Marshal Evans exclaimed. "I think you need to catch me up on all of the events that have unfolded over here."

As they made their way inside from the approaching storm, the office was cold, so Tom threw in some wood into the stove and lit a fire. Marshal Evans took a seat next to the chief, which they shook hands and briefly reminisced about the renter incident. Tom pulled out a fresh jar of moonshine and passed it over to Thunder Bear, who took a longer drink, than what was the norm for a light drinker, to warm his cold bones. The marshal then motioned for the jar which surprised the chief. Then Thunder Bear realized that he wasn't under the jurisdiction of the United States government, so the comical Indian just shrugged it off and passed the jar. Tom had set the fire ablaze and shut the door, opening the flue, to allow more air to suck into the fire, heating things up quicker. Just as Tom took a seat, Maddy came into the office, lighting up the cold, disparaging room.

"Hey, sweetie, Wiley claims that there's two kegs of beer out here to help quench our guests thirst," Maddy asked and Tom laughed. "He's actually out by Trigger's stable searching right now."

"Oh they're outside past the break room, sweety," Tom replied. "I'm going to brief the marshal here on things and then well all mosey inside sweety."

Maddy smiled and the marshal approached her for a quick hug, again expressing his thoughts, as well as prayers, for the family's loss. Maddy started to cry but assured Marshal Evans that she would be ok. Tom's wife soon departed, as Wiley followed her and talked the poor woman's ear off as they went to look for the legs of beer. Back in the office, Tom gave the marshal a detailed report concerning the gunfight at the bar, concerning Larry's attempted assassination. Marshal Evans was taken back with all that happened, but relented nonetheless, figuring that Tom and the crew had been through enough, leaving all other pertinent questions for a later time.

"I really can't believe that you blew up the gold Tom," Marshal Evans jokingly exclaimed. "What are the odds that a descendent of Wyatt Earp blows up the same Spanish gold? It's just mind boggling boys," Evans continued as he took a pull off of the jar.

"Yeah I know Marshal," Tom agreed. "I'll be hearing about this for some time now, I can imagine."

"So a marshal, cowboy, and Indian walk into a biker bar and order their drinks," the chief began. "The marshal orders a soda, because he's the sober driver. The cowboy orders a whiskey and beer because he gently wants to ease into the man's buzz. The Indian, on the other hand, orders a moonshine. The bartender/ biker informs the Indian that they do not serve such things in their establishment. Anyhow, the moral of the story is that your lawyer is a whore!" The room erupted with laughter, only Terror sported a look of confusion about him.

"Hey, my mom was a lawyer for years," the biker exclaimed, making the men crack up even more.

After the joke subsided, Tom commented that there was a case of shine out near Trigger's stall, so the men left the office and made their way to the awaiting stall; only when they arrived, Wiley had tapped one keg, pouring the golden liquid into a bucket. Trigger neighed at the boys and began drinking his fill, finishing the beer quickly.

"Hey Tom! I couldn't resist," Wiley stated. "Trigger's been feeling neglected lately ever since you got that other dang mustang!"

Trigger's ears perked up and the horse gave his owner a look of distain as Wiley poured more beer into the horses bucket.

"Wiley, he doesn't know about the car yet," Tom responded. "Well, at least till ya blurted it out!"

"Oh jeez," Wiley remarked. "Trigger, forget what I just said and enjoy your beer." The steed reluctantly lowered his head accepting the peace offering.

The men had another brief laugh, while Tom loaded the keg and moonshine onto a hand truck nearby. With the booze ready to ship, the men exited the stable and pushed the run flat wheels of the hand truck through the snow, which was beginning to drift. Within minutes, the boys had reached the porch which was filled with Spanish and Indian delegates, enjoying the outdoor fireplace, as well as the propane tower heaters keeping the covered porch warm. There was a flurry of activity, from the chief's tribe preparing drums for a pow wow. Also, Ambassador Cortez was helping Maddy and Lupita prepare an authentic Spanish meal, which Lupita was taken aback by the ambassador's cooking expertise.

Dallas was playing video games in the living room with the grandkids, and spotted Tom so he went into the kitchen, pulling up a seat by Lupita.

"Honey, do you need help with anything in here," Dallas asked and Lupita immediately put her husband to work, due to the fact that they were feeding thirty plus people that night. "Hey Tom, there's a little surprise for you on your desk in the bedroom."

Tom curiously shook his head and headed to his bedroom. When the rancher entered, there appeared to be a video camera on the desk, so Tom sat down and turned it on. The images that appeared were of his granny, and Tom broke down as he saw her sitting in that rocking chair.

"Dallas, turn off the radio for a minute," Tildy exclaimed. "I'd like to take a minute to talk to my grandson." Dallas then turned the radio off and retired behind the camera. Tildy sat there smiling and said, "Tom, I made a video for everyone that I care about, so I guess I'm up to you, now son. "I know in my old age that I've tightened up my emotions a bit, so what I'm about to tell you breaks my heart, yet I know you'll understand. For some time now, I've been sick, in fact, Dallas is the only one that knows what's going on. By now, you know that I have heart problems, but what you don't know about is my brain cancer."

Tom drew a breath and slumped into his seat as Tildy continued, "I figured if everybody knew, that it would eventually be me in the hospital on my death bed, and you know that I wasn't gonna go out like that. Tom, I love you. I love the family that you've raised and the help that you give to others. It took your grandpappy some time to come around on my way of thinking, but with you son, I seen that kindness at an early age. Tom, whatever you do in this life, continue to keep doing good works and helping people."

"I'm guessing by now that you're close to selling the gold, so always remember that it isn't necessarily money that brings us happiness, but what we can do with our own wealth to help those that need it the most. As for Wyatt Earp, we as a family, might not have retained that name for some time now, but you are a descendant of that name and should carry it with pride in anything you do. In fact, you should give Larry a break as sheriff. The man's been complaining about the job lately and needs to be there for his daughter, so if you wanna start with a good deed, help Larry."

Tom then cracked a smile over the irony of Tildy's statement.

"Tom, again I love you and expect nothing but the best from you as I watch from heaven. Whenever you feel down and wanna chat, just look up and start talking and I'll hear ya boy."

The recorder went blank and Tom sat at the desk shedding a tear over Tildy's last request. The rancher then looked up and said, "Granny, thank you for letting me know how ya feel, and I guess you and ole Gene must be having a laugh at this badge pinned on my shirt. I know that I won't get a response from you, but you can bet your ass that I'll still talk to you, Granny."

Just then, Maddy strolled in and wrapped her arms around her husband, embracing him for a few moments. Tom gazed into his wife's eyes and planted a big kiss on her awaiting lips.

"I watched mine a little earlier ago and it totally took me by surprise," Maddy exclaimed in shock. "She told me some things that should best be left between Tildy and I, but she did suggest that I supported you for running as sheriff."

Tom wrapped his arms around Maddy and laughed. The rancher then responded, "I guess Larry's complaining carries on, especially after watching Tildy from beyond the grave."

"Tildy loved him too and soaked in his bullshit like the rest of us," Maddy replied. "Besides the irony, you have to admit that Tildy hit that one on the head?"

"Yeah, I'd have to say that she nailed that one," Tom commented as he kissed Maddy again. "You know, that beds been pretty lonely lately. I think we should mess it up," and playfully tossed his wife on the bed, while messing it up properly.

Downstairs in the living room, the chief was warming his bones by the fire and heard a thumping noise emanate from the bedroom above. Laughing, he looked at Dallas who was sitting next to him and said, "That musta been a hell of a surprise, don't you think?"

Dallas shrugged his shoulders and replied, "Well, surprises tend to come in unexpected forms," and sat there with a smirk while drinking his coffee.

After some time had passed, dinner was finally ready and the masses swarmed to the huge dining room table that Two Boots made from an old log that had fallen, years ago. The table is so huge, that Gene had to build the dining room around the sixty plus person beast, which was a challenge because he had to build the foundation and put in a floor before Two Boots could frame the building. The dining room has always been the crown jewel of the Wyatt household when there's large gatherings, and tonight was no different. Some of the bikers and Indian elders had helped set the table, which took a fair amount of time, but within minutes, was packed to the brim. Everybody began to fill their plates topping off all of their drinks, as Bernardo and Lupita brought out three full cuts of Spanish seasoned prime rib. By this time, Tom and Maddy came down to join the group, only to be greeted by an inebriated Thunder Bear, moving his hips while plumping them in an inappropriate fashion, making Maddy blush. With everybody seated, Tom rose and raised his glass.

"I'd like to make a toast tonight," Tom stated and the group drew silent. "First and foremost, I really appreciate everybody gracing the Wyatt home under these circumstances. Tildy wanted her life to be a celebration, so thank you on my families behalf in our time or grief, for coming over. Second, I'd also like to thank Larry and the Kittitas County sheriffs for their hard work in the unfortunate circumstances that occurred up here -also- as of recent. Larry is expected to pull through his gunshot wound, so I'd like to pay my respects to that greater power that pushed the sheriff through. So, to Tildy and Larry, I salute you!"

"Tom raised his jar high in the air with the group and drank a mighty gulp. Gustavo then raised his glass and saluted Tom for giving back the Spanish government it's royal treasure, and everybody drank again.

Dinner commenced without a hitch. The group ate their fill and the rest of dinner included jokes, also Wiley mentioning a pow wow in Tildy's favor, afterward. After the meal, most of the group had disbursed, accept for a couple of Terrors prospects, who cleaned the table and helped the gals wash up all of the dishes. Outside on the patio, the Indian elders had all of the traditional drums in place and began playing their ceremonial instruments, to check their sound before the pow wow commenced. Inside, Tom helped the gals put leftovers away and inquired where Wiley had disappeared to, but Maddy shook her head in confusion. Curious, Tom broke away from the girls and went out to the patio only to find Wiley not in sight. Unfounded, the rancher left the patio and headed for the stable, when he heard a couple voices talking a short distance away. As Tom approached, it was no other than Wiley and Chief Thunder Bear smoking a joint around the corner of the stable.

"Tom, I think you need to take a puff," Thunder Bear stated, but the rancher politely declined.

"Naw, TB, Tom's a lawman now and shouldn't be indulging in this stuff," Wiley exclaimed while he inhaled the weed.

"Wiley, may I point out that you're still a very much deputized sheriff," Tom stated as Wiley suddenly hacked from his puff. "You know, Mary Jane might be legal now in the state of Washington, but as officers, I am afraid that the Upper County has a no tolerance rule against its use."

"Right, we have to keep up appearances," Wiley replied and loosened his badge from his hat. "Sheriff, if my time has been most valuable to your efforts, I would like to relinquish my post and hand this back to you."

Wiley graciously handed the badge back to the rancher and Thunder bear stated, "I think it's best for the whole county that Wiley be left to his devices!"

"I would have to agree with the chief," Tom replied and laughed as the two best friends shook hands.

"Wiley, I think we should go hit some drums and look like we're entertaining people," Thunder Bear suggested and the men agreed then made their way back to the patio.

Back at the patio, the whole group had piled onto the generous deck drinking from a fresh keg of beer that Wiley had tapped a short time ago. Little did they know, but Wiley had called Jennie at the bar, ordering his daughter to shut it down for the night and to refund the current customers their money. After Jennie cleared the bar, Rob and Juan loaded up all available kegs, loading them into the line cooks truck, then speeded over to the ranch. When they arrived, found it impossible to park in the driveway, so Rob navigated the maze of mobile homes and vehicles, driving the rig to the back of the house near the patio. The boys and the prospects quickly unloaded the alcohol right about the time Thunder Bear gave the okay for the pow-wow to commence.

As the drums began to beat, voices chanted in a long lost language. Their singing vivaciously echoed throughout the group, bringing back memories of Tom as a small boy, standing in amazement at his very first pow wow (that Gene had taken the young lad to), in a past time, so long ago. Tom thought the sound was sad and depressing, yet remembered that moment, and another unfortunate memory of the young ranchers past, which happened to be at his grandfathers funeral, as a matter of fact. As the drums played, a figure appeared out of the shadows in the form of Sheila and her children. The kids were mesmerized by all of the people and live music that penetrated the ranch. Sheila shoved her kids along to go and explore, and approached Tom with a smile.

"Sheila, you look great," Tom exclaimed, and reached out to give her a hug. "How ya doin?"

"Oh, Tom, I heard about Tildy passing away, and couldn't imagine what you're going through," Sheila replied. "I just felt like we had to get away and come to see your family."

"Sheila, thank you for coming over here," Tom stated and gave the woman another hug. "How's life been going since the whole Rick thing?"

"It's just not the same over in the suburbs since Ricks been gone," Sheila replied. The people in the neighborhood knows what's going on, and the kids are getting teased at school. I dunno, it's just a mess right now."

"Well, Sheila, you know that we don't pass judgment around here," Tom responded. "You're welcome to stay here as long as you need. Who knows, maybe it's time for a fresh change of scenery."

"I think you're right, rancher," Sheila exclaimed trying to contain her laughter. "I feel really good when I come here, and my parents live so far away. It just feels like home to me since I was last here."

"That's a fair enough statement," Tom inferred. "If you and the kids are hungry, Maddy can whip up something for you guys in the kitchen."

"You know Tom, I think we need a bite," Sheila replied and gathered the children to eat a much deserved meal.

"Hey before you go Sheila, that whatever you decide to do, Maddy and myself have made the decision to help your family by any means necessary," Tom stated. We thought it right, that you should have all of your debts paid, as well as a college fund in place for your kids." This part may have not been mentioned up till this point, but the two figured it was the right thing to do. Sheila broke down and began to cry. She quickly pulled it together and asked her kids if they wanted to live in the Upper County, only to get a cheer of excitement upon the children's faces as the youngsters watched Wiley dance like a fool.

"Tom, I'm so grateful that I don't quite know what to say," Sheila exclaimed. She then gave Tom another hug and the rancher smiled.

"Welcome home, Sheila," Tom replied and tipped his hat to the overwhelmed woman.

After a time, the pow wow had concluded, and the party was livelier than ever, as the guests enjoyed the beer and moonshine that the boys provided. The hour was getting late, so Maddy rushed the kids off to bed, as well as any other child with a bedtime, and uncorked a bottle of vintage wine, so the ladies could look like sophisticated drinkers. Well at least in the ranchers mind. Then again, one could appear a sophisticated drinker; at least till they start cussing like a sailor and falling off the particular chair they were no longer butt cheek hugging. At any rate, Tom spotted chief sitting in a chair nearby, so the rancher took a seat. Thunder Bear, by now, was well into three sheets of a particular wind, and looked up at Tom smiling.

"You know, Tom, Tildy was a smart woman and I have the notion that she was involved in this tonight," Thunder Bear exclaimed.

"I can see a definite pattern starting to evolve," Tom responded, thinking about the video he watched before dinner. "She knew that I was gonna be sheriff again and I didn't even see it coming until after she passed. She knew where the gold was, and figured out that I was going to restore honor to the Wyatt name in the process thereof."

"It's kinda like the movie Star Wars," the chief interrupted, and Tom started to laugh asking about the similarities. "Well, Luke Skywalker restored balance to the force when he killed the Emperor, so in a way, you've done the same, Sheriff Wyatt!"

"You also have to remember that the Ewoks aided the Rebels in shutting down the force field thing-a-ma-jiggy, that protected the Death Star," Tom replied. "It's because of their efforts that helped restore order and balance to the galaxy."

"So in a way, you helped restore balance to the Upper County," the chief stated and Tom laughed raising his longneck for a cheer. "I think we shall tell ole Larry our theory tomorrow, Tom!" Thunder Bear then rose and about stumbled back down, so Tom helped him back upright, as the chief muttered, "The force is strong with this one."

The rest of the night was a typical Wyatt party gone out of control. At one point, Wiley smoked so much, that he decided to get Trigger out of the stable and ride him back to the party naked. Everybody was laughing at Wiley and everything was fine till Sheila went outside. Wiley had been busy most of the night and didn't realize that she was there, so it was a surprise when Sheila hopped up on Tom's horse disappearing into the stable, as the crowd cheered them on. As the night started to wear down, most of the guests were either too drunk to get a word in edgewise, or passed out, except for Tom and Wiley.

"You know, Tom, I can't say it enough, but thank you for always being there for me," Wiley commented and Tom tipped his hat. "I know that this might sound weird but shouldn't we have Tildy's service this weekend?"

"It's not a weird question," Tom replied as he took a sip of his beer. "Hell Wiley, everybody's here or in the county nearby and the chief is technically a priest. I can't see a better way to send her off. I'll call the funeral home tomorrow and have them bring her here one last time before she joins Gene in the tomb."

Wiley smiled at Tom with that sarcastic smirk and said, "Fair enough Tom. If she was alive, she'd be bitching right now how much she didn't want to be there."

"Yes, she would, Wiley," Tom butted in. "I remember when we buried Grandpa driving to that death trap; all she wanted to do was give me the money and handle the coffin expenses. I kinda sorta gave in," Tom replied as Wiley did a spit take, laughing.

"Well, Tom, I think you're a helpful kinda guy," Wiley muttered while smiling even more.

"Wiley, thank you for the sentiment, but I think it's time for me to head into bed," Tom stated, and rose off of the couch making his way to the bedroom to rest his body.

The next morning started off with Tom's children bouncing on the bed, waking up the tired rancher. They told their dad that breakfast was ready and Tom rose out of bed, stretching his muscles for the upcoming day ahead. After the sheriff got dressed, he made his way down to the dining room that was still packed full of guests, so he sat down and started to eat. The meal was your traditional three eggs, bacon, potatoes and toast ordeal, yet before Tom could eat a morsel, a tap on his shoulder startled the hungry man.

"Good morning, Sheriff Wyatt," Marshal Evans said while holding his head in pain that the lawman incurred the night before. "You mind if we talk in private?"

"Sure thing, marshal," Tom replied and grabbed his plate departing out to the office. When the two reached the room, Tom threw in more firewood to re spark the flames he made the night before, and the two men took a seat.

"Tom, I just got off of the phone with the main office and it would appear that Isidro's cronies have been reaching out to the Dementes," the marshal stated. "You're going to have to put your officers on immediate alert because the threat seems credible."

"So you think their coming up here to take vengeance for Isidro's death," Tom replied as he paused from eating.

"Yeah it looks that way, sheriff," Elijah stated as he grabbed his head again.

"Here, marshal, take this," Tom said and passed the lawman a jar of moonshine. "We've decided to bury Tildy tomorrow at the tomb, so do you think this is a good idea?"

"I think just as long as you have the security in place, that we can manage the funeral, but you'll have to be on guard, Tom," Marshal Evans replied.

The two men sat there for a minute so Tom could sink the burden of his responsibilities into the sheriff's hurting soul. Tom then called Sergeant Morrison and informed the Officer about the situation and Morrison told the sheriff that he would brief the men immediately. After Tom hung up the phone, Thunder Bear walked in grabbing his head as well, so the marshal passed the shine over for the chief to drink.

"Geez, Tom, what a party was last night huh," the chief stated, then the sheriff informed Thunder Bear about the current crisis, which sunk the chief farther into his chair. "Ole Wiley informed me on your plans with Tildy. Do you still wanna proceed?"

"Yeah, chief, I think that would be best," Tom responded.

"The elders brought their weapons hoping to hunt on your property after the funeral, so you have the Yakama Nation at your disposal, Tom."

"Well, chief, I think your game is going to try to hunt all of us at this rate," Tom stated sinking into his chair.

"Running Drunk, we will help you out. All you need to do is grieve for Tildy," the chief stated and took another drink.

"I appreciate everything the elders and you have done for us," Tom replied and smiled as the chief took another drink of moonshine. "Also, I'm going to leave you and Sergeant Morrison in charge of security. At the funeral however, you and your men are relieved of duty!"

"Fair enough," Thunder Bear said and the two men shook hands.

"I think since these men are crossing federal borders, I can authorize the use of our marshal s as well Tom," Evans stated. "I'll get on the phone and call up some agents."

Enamored by all of the support, Tom thanked the men and they left the office. Tom told the guys that he was going on a ride, and pulled Trigger out of the stalls, who looked a little worse for wear from the night before. Tom threw a saddle on the horse and placed a bit in Trigger's mouth, then hopped on the steed, disappearing from the stable. After a short time of riding, the sheriff reached his destination. Tom hopped off of Trigger and stood before the tomb that Tildy would occupy the following day.

"The sheriff then took his hat off in respect for the dead and said, "Well, Grandpa, it looks like you're not going to be so lonely anymore." Tom then pulled out the coin that his grandma gave him a couple of months back and flicked it in his hands. "You know grandpa, you could have told me about this before you passed."

All of the sudden, a familiar sight appeared and perched on a tree nearby, looking at Tom.

"Hello old friend," the sheriff exclaimed and the eagle continued to look at Tom. Then the rancher heard another familiar tone, in the form of a man's voice.

"Roost," the voice shouted from the thick winters brush, then repeated himself again.

"Rooster Dowe," Tom exclaimed and the shadowy figure appeared out of the thicket, in his normal hermit-like, scruffily self, wearing a bear skin shoal.

"It's been a while since I've seen you around these parts," Rooster stated and the men shook hands.

Before the story continues, I feel a little explanation about ole Rooster Dowe. Years ago, when Tom was a young boy, Rooster decided to leave the confines of society to live a life of his own in the wilderness. With one thousand acres of his own, the man took off his clothes and shoes, fleeing into the forest to not be seen by us norms, as ole Rooster calls his fellow man. For thirty five years, the hermit has not only lived off of his land, but the Federal lands of the Wenatchee National Forest in the north, and the Wyatt land in the south. Now it's not like Rooster to just wander on to other people's land, but when the hermit first started his journey, accidentally trespassed on Wyatts land, and ran into Gene when the rancher was on a hunt.

Now Gene at first, thought Rooster a hippy lost in the woods, and offered the hermit a tour of his land, which Rooster followed happily while explaining to the rancher his circumstances. After hearing Roosters story, Gene thought the hermit to be crazy at first, nonetheless befriended Rooster, helping the man, if the hermit ever needed. As the years passed, their friendship strengthened: In fact, the two would barter goods in exchange for tracking game, which by that time, Rooster became an ace in discerning elk and deer movements, filling Gene's freezer. A couple of years before Gene passed, he took Tom out on a hunt and the young rancher finally met one of his grandpas best kept secrets. Rooster was a fountain of knowledge for young Tom, and the two men would disappear for days tracking elk movements, while deterring poachers that would come illegally encroach upon the mountain mans land. In fact, that's where Tom's education in the cunning ways of stealth, helped the rancher to hone his skills as a hunter; as well as to watch those whom illegally entered his property to hunt.

Ole Rooster learned over the years to become completely invisible to the outside world. The hermit quickly became not only a survivalist, but a natural list, dedicated to preserving his environment and those who dare come to threaten it. The story's of Roosters adventures might be too many words to currently put in this novel, but the wealth of information that Tom gained from the hermit, helped the rancher to become the man that he is today. In fact, the Star Wars parable that a drunk chief presented to Tom the other night talking about restoring balance to the force, is very much a theme to both men, that are currently standing at the Wyatt tomb.

"You know Tom, I still come by from time to time, just to say hi to ole Two Boots," Rooster stated and Tom smiled.

"Well, Rooster, I know that you didn't know Tildy very well, but she passed away not too long ago, and we're going to bury Granny here tomorrow," Tom muttered while holding his head down. "I just came by to get some peace of mind from ole Gene."

Rooster placed his hand on the sheriff's shoulder and said, "It wouldn't hurt if Gene could talk back as well. I'm sorry for your loss, Tom. You and I both know how it feels to lose someone that we truly loved. How did Gene best explain death?"

Tom scratched his head for a second, then laughed. "I believe that death is like a mistress with a loud mouth," Tom replied. "After the deed is done, she goes into town and tells everybody what she did, and who she did it with!"

Rooster cracked a smile and replied, "That sounds about what ole Gene would say!"

"I hope you can attend," Tom asked while looking back over at Rooster with a smile.

"You know, Tom, I've met Tildy in the past," Rooster exclaimed and Tom had a look of confusion about him. "I'm guessing Gene never told you the story?"

Tom continued to shake his head which made Roosters eyes light up. The hermit began by saying, "It was a late summer day and you were still very much a young boy. I guess Gene sealed a huge meat deal with a fast food franchise and celebrated a tad bit too much that night, forcing Tildy to go and hunt. Now being on an angus ranch, you think that there would be plenty of meat, but Tildy couldn't come to slaughter an animal living so close to her. So with shot gun in hand, Tildy left the ranch, determined to bag a deer big enough that she could haul back to ranch. With plenty of ammo, and a lunch she neatly packed, headed out to the tree line, disappearing out of site.

"About halfway, Tildy was getting hungry, so she found a warm spot along the river bank, and began preparing her meal. When all of the sudden, she heard a ruckus in some bushes nearby. Little did she know, that it was me, wondering why a female was poaching on Wyatt land.

Tildy raised her shot gun and yelled, "Who's there? I've got a piece and I'm not afraid to use it!"

I raised my hands and slowly appeared as to not frighten the woman any further. "Please don't shoot, ma'am. I'm friends with Gene and have permission to be here."

Tildy lowered her gun and looked me up and down, then replied, "Geez, sir, you look like shit!"

We both looked at each other and began to laugh. After all of the proper introductions, Tildy shared her meal and I agreed to help the woman bag her deer. We ended up eventually tracking a small herd about a mile from the ranch house and Tildy shot a beautiful five point buck. I always found the ole gal close to my heart and at the end of every summer, she would set a lunch out for me at that same river bend where we first met!"

Rooster began to shed a tear and Tom smiled as the hermit shared his story.

"I guess Two Boots is here talking to me anyhow," Tom exclaimed and Rooster heartily agreed.

"Tom, I'm tracking some elk just north of here and need to bag one for my freezer," Rooster said sarcastically because the man lives on no electricity. "You wanna go out for a bit, for old time's sake?"

The sheriff smiled at Rooster and replied, "I couldn't find any other way to honor my grandparent's memory. I might have a favor to ask of you!"

Intrigued, Rooster asked what the favor was and Tom told the hermit about the chief needing help to bag an elk. Rooster paused in thought at first, then agreed. So Tom and Rooster would herd the elk the chief's direction to shoot the beasts; also, the hermit would be rewarded with meat for helping. Tom then pulled out his walkie-talkie and reached Wiley, who was still in bed cuddling with Sheila, informing the cozy man about their plans. Wiley laughed and sprang out of bed, getting dressed within minutes. Surprised, Sheila asked what all of the ruckus was about, so Wiley filled her in, while a sense of excitement overcame the woman, because she had never been on a hunt before. With her curiosity peaked, Sheila quickly put in her clothes and followed Wiley out to Thunder Bears RV.

When the two arrived, Wiley knocked on the door, and Theo opened it smiling at the crazy ole coot.

"Hey, tell your dad that the hunt's on for today," Wiley stated and Theo Burning Tree called his father, who was at the stable checking out the horses.

"So Tom's going to herd some elk our way," Thunder Bear asked and Theo confirmed the hunt. "Tell the elders to grab bows and plenty of arrows."

Theo asked why they couldn't use firearms and the chief replied by wanting to hunt in honor of their ancestors. Theo agreed at the Chief's wishes and hung up the phone. Thunder Bear's son then thanked Wiley for the message from Tom, and Wiley smiled back respectfully.

"Hey, if you boys are going on a hunt, Sheila would like to go as well," Wiley asked and Theo was excited that the first time hunter would get to see their traditions. While the elders prepared, Wiley and Sheila went into Tom's office and grabbed three M-16 sub machine guns that Tom had retrofitted with silencers. The rancher called the weapons Lazy Hunting Guns due to their deadly accuracy and quiet discretion. The two quickly departed the office and met the elders who were by that time, all gathered at the meeting spot and the group laughed at the cheaters, which Wiley took in stride.

"Did you forget how to use a bow and arrow Wiley," the chief remarked, and Wiley smirked.

"Naw, chief. We're just here to clean up what your arrows can't get," Wiley replied, laughing.

"Fair enough," the chief stated and the group began their journey, with Tom directing traffic on the other side of the walkie-talkie.

"You know, Tom, I'm glad that we're doing this today," Rooster exclaimed. "I feel like it's the olden days again and glad to help out the elders!"

"I'm glad that I ran into you as well," Tom blurted as he unscrewed his jar of moonshine, taking a sip.

"You know, I don't normally, but wouldn't mind a good luck sip for the awaiting hunt," Rooster asked, so Tom passed the ole hermit his jar, which Rooster sipped earnestly at first, absorbing the warm liquid into his belly.

Just then, the two men heard something ruffling the forest floor nearby, so the boys disappeared off of the road, and hid in the thicket. What at first appeared as a sharply dressed man holding an automatic machine gun, turned into two men, then three. After fifteen men passed the boys by, they looked at each other in panic.

"I don't think they're poachers," Rooster exclaimed while whispering to Tom.

"I think the hunt just changed," Tom replied, then briefly filled in ole Rooster on his current problems. "I guess we're gonna have to herd these deuce bags up and strike!" Tom got on his walkie-talkie again and told Wiley about the oncoming threat heading their way.

In a panic, Wiley got on his radio and called dispatch, but didn't get a signal. He then asked one of the elders to call the police on their cell phones, yet again to get no signal. Wiley radioed Tom back and told the sheriff about their plight, and the rancher held his head low, knowing that it was going to be a long day.

Chapter 15

Trigger's Vengeance

Already a fair distance into the woods, Thunder Bear ordered one of his men, back to the Windy River Ranch, to raise the Deputies. The men were distraught at first, but all agreed that it was a great day to hunt and honor the ancestors that came before them, even if it meant hunting humans. Also, the chief ordered his men hidden out of sight, until Wiley heard word from Tom. The air was a fog, thick in tension, yet the men relented and disappeared into the brush, holding their bows at the ready. On the other side of the Indians, Tom and Rooster were plotting their next move. Both men slowly followed behind the group of thugs, stepping on the forest ground carefully, as not to disturb tree branches, or anything else that could give them away.

"Jeez, Rooster, I'm kinda lost on this one,," Tom replied while scratching his head.

"Yeah, that many men with bows and arrows a can prove to be problematic, for the most part," Rooster exclaimed as he held his bow at the ready. "You know Tom, if we can lure them into the canyon, so the chief and his men can be there to greet them."

What the hermit was talking about is a mini canyon not much taller than twenty feet, and it was only a hundred yards away. If Tom and ole Rooster could deflect the armed gangsters inside the canyon, then the chief could take care of the rest. Rooster agreed that Tom should take off south and start making a ruckus, which would attract the thugs attention, in theory. So Tom, grabbed his trusty thirty commando knife and disappeared before Rooster even knew that the sheriff was gone. Moving swiftly yet quietly, Tom proceeded South and halted, waiting for the gangsters noise as they traipsed through the woods, like a bear walking through a meat packing plant. When Tom arrived at the canyon, he dug around in his pocket and found a piece of C-4 as well as a detonator, and placed it near the entrance of the canyon. The only problem now was how did ole Tom get the men's attention?

Without a forethought, Tom pulled out his Luger and pointed it up into the air. The sheriff got on his radio and shouted, "Wiley, you boys better be close to the canyon, cause when they come through, the fits gonna hit the shan!" Tom then slammed down the radio hearing Wiley reply, "Five minutes brother," and then fired the Luger in the air automatically alerting the gangsters to Tom's gunshot.

Within seconds, the thugs were within striking distance of Tom, so he stayed hidden hoping that his gunfire was enough to attract the thugs into the canyon. The armed thugs began to search feverously for the shooter who fired the weapon, but the alerted men weren't having any luck.

Rooster, seeing his friend pinned down, swiftly climbed up to the canyon and started yelling, "Roost! Roost!" Now alerted more than ever, the gangsters fixed their weapons and ran into the canyon.

"What the hell was that," Thunder Bear replied as they jockeyed into position, and Wiley smiled.

"I'll be a son of a bitch," Wiley replied quietly. "That's Rooster Dowe, Tom's friend. If you see a scraggly bearded old man nearby, don't fire!"

The chief and elders shook their heads then raised bows, waiting to strike.

"Wiley, I don't know if I can shoot anybody," Sheila replied while shaking but Wiley held the frightened woman close.

"You'll know when the time's right, Sheila," Wiley exclaimed. "Just wait for the signal, and I'll be right by your side!"

At the entrance of the canyon, most of the thugs entered, surveying any nook and cranny for this mysterious noise maker. With the men at a safe distance, Tom peeked his head out of the brush and spotted two men searching the area near the explosive that the sheriff hid. Tom crackled in on the walkie-talkie, checking on Wiley and the elders, with Wiley reporting that the thugs were just beginning to pass them, on the canyon floor below. The sheriff then pulled out the detonator as the two thugs dug near the area of the hidden C-4. The explosion was instantaneous, ripping the two unknowing gangsters apart and scaring the other thugs that just witnessed the detonation. The chief and his elder shouted out their war cry, firing a volley of arrows into the unsuspecting gangsters, hitting several mortally.

As those men lay there covered in blood, the remaining six gangsters took cover behind trees, or whatever protection they could find. Realizing that they were facing a foe firing arrows, one gangster laid down covering fire hitting Thunder Bear in the arm. Wiley responded by firing back and then realized that within his pocket, was a fresh grenade. The crazy ole coot pulled out the grenade and yanked the pin. "Let's see them lay down fire now," Wiley shouted, and threw the explosive down to the awaiting gangsters. The explosion was violent, kicking up shards of debris and dust toward the group. That was when the firing had stopped, so Wiley cautiously approached the gangsters with his gun at the ready, only to find a charred mess of blood and separated human body parts.

"Wiley turned around and shouted, "I think we got em!" As Wiley smiled, a still conscious thug, pulled out his pistol, only to be met with a bullet to the head fired by Sheila.

"Holy shit," Wiley exclaimed. "Nice shot killer!"

Sheila ran out from her position and held Wiley, who was shaking from the sudden exchange of gunfire. The chief and his men also ran to Wiley's aid, checking for signs of life amidst the wounded thugs taking care of any doubt that they should ever walk erect again. After a couple of minutes, Tom appeared out of the distance, gun armed in his hand, and spotted the group. The sheriff passed several body's shot up with arrows or bullets and the scene, was gruesome to say the least.

"Damn, Tom, you're just about as efficient as Larry when it comes down to gunfights," Wiley shouted as Tom secured his weapon.

"Very funny, Wiley," Tom replied smiling. "The only difference being, is that I always find trouble. Larry's just a sissy when it comes to such entanglements!"

The chief then approached Tom holding his arm in pain. Wiley quickly diagnosed the wound and ripped off a part of his shirt, creating a makeshift tourniquet. A hurting Thunder Bear pulled out some moonshine that was in his back pack and began to drink.

"You know I love to hunt," the chief stated. "But when your game hunts you, I guess it makes things more exciting." Thunder Bear then laughed as hard as a wounded chief could but the bullet wound immediately took the wind out of the man's sails.

"You guys did a great job today, and I'm forever in your debt," Tom replied as he went to help Thunder Bear.

A couple minutes later, the group heard more noise and voices shouting, "Kittitas County sheriff's department! Is everybody okay, Sheriff Wyatt?"

Thinking of the only thing that Tom could, replied, "Yeah, we're just out here playing Cowboys and Indians!"

The group looked at Tom and paused at first, then erupted into laughter. The rest of the sheriff's office that was in the area (that is, Sergeant Morrison), who walked past the carnage and approached Tom.

"Geez, Tom, did you even give 'em a chance?" Morrison asked, and the sheriff cracked a smile.

"When you hunt, it's best to not surprise your prey," Tom replied and shook Morrison's hand.

"Are these the Demente punks that we were to be on the lookout for," the sergeant asked with a total look of disbelief on his face.

"That's a great question, sergeant," Tom answered while holding the chief upright. "Let's get the chief here some medical attention and let's regroup at the ranch office."

The men agreed and stayed on alert while heading back to the office. Before Tom left, he turned his head to the sound of, "Roost... Roost" echoing far off in the distance. Tom tipped his hat to Rooster and made it a mental note to remember to get the man his meat, one of these days. As the men walked back to camp, something was troubling Wiley. Tom looked back at his friend, with worry, and asked, "Wiley, what's on your mind?"

"Geez, Tom, shouldn't it be what's in your mind. Not what's on it," Wiley exclaimed and the sheriff laughed. "Naw Tom, something just doesn't make sense. If these guys are a bunch of ex Mexican military assassins, don't you think there would be more bodies piled up on the canyon floor?"

Tom paused and looked at Wiley with a determined gaze and said," Old friend, there's no doubt in my mind!"

The two men smiled and began walking with the rest of the hunting party, while a short distance away, footsteps walked silently on the forest floor. Monitoring the groups every step, the shadowy figures communicated back in forth with hand gestures until the hunting party was within steps of the stable. The two men paused and looked at each other, confused by all of the activity at the ranch. From the bikers, to the Indians the mysterious figures stared on, shaking their heads.

"Call the rest of the men," one thug demanded and the other man got on to a walkie-talkie, while in Spanish, communicating the orders that were just handed down.

"We're going to need more ammo and some rocket propelled grenades, yes," the other thug asked.

"Just get our men here," the thug replied. "Tell the men that we attack after dark!"

When the men arrived at the office, they were greeted by Terror and the Yellow Jackets, as well as an ambulance with several deputy's awaiting their bosses return. Tom walked the chief into the back of the ambulance and the paramedic began hooking up an IV while treating the wound. The medic asked questions about Thunder Bears pain level, which the chief looked at the young man and replied," Well, considering that I've been shot, I'm doing just fine. Tom pressed for the chief to go to the hospital and brief Larry on the incident, but the stubborn Elder was hesitant at first. After the sheriff reassured Thunder Bear that he would be released that evening, the chief gave Tom a hug as the pain medicine began coursing through his veins. With Thunder Bear secure, the paramedics closed the back door, and tore down the gravel driveway.

"Terror, I need you and your men in my office for a briefing," Tom asked as he rubbed his aching head.

"I'm right with you, brother," the biker president replied and went to collect his men.

"Morrison, go get Bernardo and his security detail," Tom demanded. "We're going to need their expertise in the matter." The sergeant rushed off right away to find the ambassador and his men while Tom and the rest of the group walked to the office. When they arrived, the rookie sheriff sat down behind his desk and pulled out a box of cigars, passing them around to the group.

"Tom, aren't we supposed to smoke cigars unless we're celebrating something," Wiley asked as he sniffed the stogie.

"Well, Wiley, with everything going on, I think we should get the celebration over with," Tom replied. "I can tell you that we need a perimeter, and I don't know if cameras are going to cut it this time."

"We need eyes on the ground, only hidden so they don't get picked off by these assholes," Wiley stated. "Communications should be done by cellular phone text only, with ringers off." Just then, the Yellow Jackets and Bernardo with his security detail, entered the office. Tom then told the group about the canyon incident and the oncoming threat that Wiley and the sheriff had a hunch about. Everybody showed immediate support but Tom knew that he didn't have enough firepower to quell the awaiting attack, so the sheriff ordered Morrison to round up as many weapons and available deputies that the sergeant could find. Terror also wholeheartedly agreed, immediately pulling some of his men, to hide out and form a perimeter on the cold November Day.

At the hospital, Thunder Bear arrived just as happy as a clam, yet ambiguous to the blood still dripping from his wound. The paramedics took the chief inside to the awaiting doctors. As Thunder Bear sat, a voice sounded out of the background shouting, "Thunder Bear! What are you doing here?" Startled, the chief turned his head to only find Larry's wife sitting down beside him.

"Hey, Laurie, not much," the chief replied. "Just having fun out at Tom's and got shot!"

"Holy shit, chief!" Laurie exclaimed. "Lemme go and get Larry. He's up and around and doing okay."

"Sounds good, Laurie," Thunder Bear replied, and the excited woman departed to find the injured lawman.

Within a matter of minutes, Laurie escorted her husband down to the chief who was sitting there with a huge smile on his face. Larry laughed and sat down with the fully medicated tribal elder and asked, “Tom’s not abusing his powers of office, right?”

“Naw Larry. It would appear that Isidro rose from the grave,” the chief stated while smiling away.

Confused, yet intrigued, Larry shook his head and then asked, “Is everybody okay?”

“Yeah, accept for me and the dead Mexican thugs laying out on Tom’s property,” Thunder Bear replied.

Larry patted the chief on his hurt shoulder by accident and got up, leaning on his cane, looking at Laurie. She could tell by the look in her husband’s eyes that he was ready to go and help. Laurie leaned into her husband and gave the lawman a gentle kiss. “Don’t say another word asshole,” Laurie stated as she smiled at Larry. “Go get those bad guys, but first, we gotta get you cleared to leave the hospital.” With that being said, the two temporarily left, while chief Thunder Bear laid down, smiling at all of the butterflies that mysteriously appeared in the busy ER.

Back at the ranch, Sergeant Morrison returned with a whole arsenal of weaponry that the lawman retrieved from the weapons locker inside the station. Tom came outside and ordered Morrison to distribute weapons and ammo out to the Yellow Jackets, then asked everybody to gather for a word. When the group assembled, Tom cleared his throat and said, “Well, everybody, I can imagine how you are all feeling right now in the wake of this last attack. Tildy musta wanted to be buried with a bang, just didn’t realize that we were sending her out this way.”

The group of men laughed and Tom continued, “Any man or woman that decides to raise arms to deflect this threat, I salute you. Yet at the same time, I worry about your own safety. So I offer you a choice, so fight for what you believe in. Whether it be a loved one or a piece of land, fight for whatever idea that is that keeps you grounded! Everybody here knows why I fight and it’s more than my idiot friend buying tanks from Cartels. Now what I fight for is larger than any asshole in a three piece suit. No offense to you, Marshal Evans!”

The lawman tipped his hat to Tom and the sheriff continued, “This is about family, friends, and doing anything in my power to keep them safe, while believing in those ideals. I don't wanna send anybody to an early grave, so I leave the choice up to you."

The whole group erupted into shouting and raised their weapons. With everyone's newly recharged positive moral, in Tom's back pocket, the sheriff ordered the group to take up positions to complete the perimeter. Bernardo had his men take post outside of the house, but as people started to take position, Tom had a revelation. Surely, a unit of trained mobsters would secretly pick these men off one by one, so the sheriff ordered the men to hide. After an hour of positioning the group, Tom entered in through the kitchen, and a distressed Maddy was sitting at the kitchen table drinking a glass of water. Tom put his arms around his wife and kissed her on the cheek as she stared at her water.

"I packed an overnight bag and Jane came by to pick the boys up," Maddy mumbled as she shed a tear. "I guess you're going to ask me to go to Jane's as well?"

Tom witnessed the helpless worry in Maddy's eyes and held her tight. After a couple of moments, the sheriff smiled at his distraught wife and said, "So, I hear you're good with a gun?"

Maddy's tone changed from one of worry and cracked a smile. "Yeah, I've been taught by the best, but I cannot remember the man's name who taught me," Maddy replied smiling at her husband.

Wiley and Sheila walked into the kitchen overhearing Tom's conversation, sitting down while opening a soda. "That's an easy answer," Wiley retorted while taking a sip. "I taught you killer!"

Tom and Maddy began to laugh hysterically and the sheriff patted Wiley on the back.

"Yeah, Tom, I have to admit, I've had a couple different teachers," Maddy exclaimed.

Tom then looked at Maddy in surprise and exclaimed, "I always had you pegged as a one trick pony!"

The two went to hug, just as bullets shattered the windows of the kitchen, forcing the group to take cover. As fast as the first barrage that shattered Tom and Maddy's moment, was met by a volley from the group outside. Tom asked Maddy if she was okay, and she was shaken but steadfast. The men took the women upstairs, rapidly running up into the master bedroom. When they ran in, Tom turned off the lights and placed the ladies by the fireplace to be protected from any bullet fire. The sheriff then looked through a window to deduce where the weapons fire was originating from, only to be forced back by a fresh stream of bullets now shattering the bedroom glass. After a minute of firing there was a pause, and then the bedroom phone ringed.

The group thought nothing of it first, until the phone rang again, forcing Tom to crawl to it cautiously. When the sheriff picked up the ringer, he answered hello, and a voice asked, "Is this Tom Wyatt?"

"I'm guessing you know we're in the bedroom," Tom asked while looking at the rest of the group.

"Mr. Wyatt, it's finally a pleasure to meet you, I just wish it could've been under certain circumstances," the voice replied with a sincere regret. "So as your men search for my men, I just want to let you know that my men are a lot smarter than that. The truth is, is that you have a quiet sizable force, and your men haven't been harmed yet, so I'd like to negotiate."

"Negotiate what?" Tom asked while scratching his head.

"We know that you tried to blow up Isidro in the cave only to have our employer shot by your Upper County sheriff," the thug exclaimed. "I want everybody responsible for this mess, Mr. Wyatt, including you. Just remember that if you refuse me, I will order my men into your property, and every last soul not responsible for my employers death, will die as well."

"Well, I appreciate the offer, asshole, but I think I'll take my chances here," Tom exclaimed as his temper started to boil.

"Mr. Wyatt, not only are you a legend in your county, but I know in my heart that you're an honest man, so I'm going to give you a choice, "the gangster said as friendly as could be. "I'll give you thirty minutes and then you'll leave me no other choice. Choose well Tom Wyatt," and the thug hung up leaving a dial tone.

Tom hung up the phone and looked at Wiley with immediate concern. "Send a text to the men and tell them to stay put," the sheriff exclaimed as a smile started to form on his face. "I have some of your C-4 left over from the cave, Wiley. Mind helping me out?"

"Wiley then looked right back at ole Tom and smirked. "I'm one step ahead of you brother," the crazy ole coot remarked. I may, or may not have laid some charges a fair distance away from the perimeter, but something still isn't right.

"Oh, what's that ole buddy," Tom asked as he crawled back to the pinned down group.

Wiley took his finger and felt around a hole burrowed by a bullet that hit a piece of the fireplace. "I'm no mathematician, but I know a fifty caliber hole when I see one.

Tom then inspected the hole and smiled at his smart friend. "They're hitting us from quite a-way's away," Tom said and Wiley's heart sank again.

"There's so many vantage points out here, Tom," ole Wiley replied. "This particular weapons range can be effective from a half mile, to a mile in circumference from the ranch. That's a lot of areas of opportunities to hide."

Tom looked at his watch in which the rancher set a timer, that had dwindled down to less than twenty six minutes. "Well, as ole Two Boots would say when we'd hunt for pheasant, "If they ain't gonna come out, then I guess we'll have to flush 'em out!" Tom stated with a smile.

The two men grinned at each other and Tom told the gals to stay put, to wait for the boy's return. Cautiously, Wiley and Tom exited through the back door of the kitchen just as two bullets came screaming past their heads, forcing the boys to duck for cover. Wiley told Tom that he saw muzzle flashes from two separate locations and the old goat just happened to catch one flash near an area the man had designated for explosives. After a minute of gunfire, all fell silent again and Wiley scratched his head on which detonator to press.

"Wiley, take a minute to tell our men out near the explosives, that you're about to set one off," Tom asked and Wiley followed suit.

After a few moments of checking charge, Wiley smiled yet again and shouted, "Ah ha," then pressed the trigger.

The explosion was fast and loud as it rumbled on the forest floor near the ranch. Wiley texted to see if the men were okay, and the whole group reported back as fine. The two men sat there and Bernardo crawled over to the boys to see what their next course of action should be, in which Tom informed the Ambassador to grab a gun. As some trees in the distance started to burn from the explosive, on that cold November night, the three men made their move and quietly disappeared into the forest.

As they walked quietly, Tom kept checking his watch that had dwindled down to less than ten minutes.

Then suddenly, the men came to a pause as they stumbled upon one man crouched down into the snow, with his sniper rifle ready to fire. Wiley quietly pulled out a gun but Tom motioned him not to arm the weapon; instead, Tom drew his thirty commando knife and silently crept up to the unsuspecting shooter, quickly slitting the thugs throat. Tom then motioned Wiley to take the gun and whispered, "Scan the area, and if they shoot, get a real hard look at the muzzle flash. In fact, before they start shooting, wait for my order to detonate more C-4." Wiley shook his head and took aim through the scope as the two men left for the area of the blast.

Tom and Bernardo, skillfully crept through the forest floor as they drew near to the explosion. When they arrived, the fiery scene left one shooter dead and another was still burning from the forceful blast. Just then two guns jabbed the men in the back. "Geez Tom, you scared the living piss out of me," Terror quietly stated and Tom was relieved that it wasn't the trespassers. "We saw the blast and broke perimeter to check it out." Before Tom could get a word in edgewise, a shot rang out of nowhere dropping Terrors fellow biker dead in his tracks, forcing the men to take cover.

"Two minutes left before they call me again," Tom quietly exclaimed. "This kinda sucks because I used the landline inside the house!"

"I'll text Maddy to have the asshole call my number," Terror replied while pulling out his cell phone. "What's the plan next boss?"

"Oh, we'll all find out in about thirty seconds," Tom replied as he carefully took the sniper rifle from the dead thug.

After the required time had passed, Tom had not heard anything yet and sat there ready to kill anything unfriendly. Just then, a call came in on Terrors phone, that registered as unblocked, so the sheriff took the cell and placed it up to his ears and answered.

The voice appeared to laugh at the sheriff and exclaimed, "Very good, sheriff, but you just don't seem to get the point! Look over to the north in the forest," so Tom turned his head and spotted a train that had just come to a halt with what appeared to be Wiley's tank on it. Then a message appeared on Terrors phone, so the sheriff opened it, and the image was Maddy with a gun to her head.

"You really give me no other choice, so I think that we're going to take your beautiful wife north with us," the thug fiercely stated.

Losing his cool for a brief second, Tom paused and then replied, "You're not going to get that far asshole, and if you hurt my wife, I'll bring a fury of hellfire that you've never experienced ever in your pathetic, fucking life!"

"You see, Mr. Wyatt, you still have to get past my shooters, and there are two left," the thug exclaimed. "I'm not entirely worried, however, if you make it past my men, you still have to catch the train Tom."

The prick then hung up the phone and Tom looked at Wiley cringing at the thought of what that man was doing to his wife.

"Fuck it Wiley, I can't let her go," Tom angrily exclaimed while looking at his friend who was safely hiding next to the lawman.

"Well, then, let's go get her," Wiley stated, then smiled with that trademark smirk.

Terror gave the boys the go ahead, rising up out of hiding to lay down covering fire while Tom and Wiley bolted. The sound of bullets whizzing past the boys was all they could feel and Wiley got a mark on both shooters, laying down hidden in the brush, as Tom took cover behind a tree. Wiley carefully timed the shots and by a pure stroke of luck, aimed the dead gangsters fifty caliber sniper rifle at his first target, then pulled the trigger. After pulling off a few more rounds, that shooter had all but exhausted his firing efforts and Wiley took aim at the second shooter, pulling his trigger a third time, only to hear complete silence after a few moments.

"He might just be playing dead," the ole boy yelled out to Tom. "Let's go finish this prick off!"

The two ran as fast as they could toward the second shooter while cautiously raising their pistols to strike. Wiley quickly spotted the area that he shot at, and both men lessened their pace to a pause. With Wiley's hands, he directed the sheriff to approach from behind, so both men quietly moved into position. Wiley was the first to spot the shooter whom had been hit by the crazy ole coots round, and was profusely bleeding from the chest. Wiley moved in slowly, ready to pull the trigger but the man laid there flailing from shock. Tom was in position and looked at the thug as he lay here bleeding not thinking the prick was no longer a threat, until the gangster pulled out a grenade, then pulled the pin.

"Grenade!" Tom shouted and both men took cover, only to feel a hot wave or sand, rocks, and body parts, flying by the two.

After mere moments of taking cover from the explosion, Tom rose to his feet, shaking and regained his bearings. The sheriff quickly gathered himself and ran over to Wiley, whom was also jolted by the blast. Tom rubbed his shoulder and Wiley quickly came to, wiping the debris off of his face. Just then in a far distance the train began to move and Tom knew that he had to get their fast, or Maddy would be lost, so both men checked each other for wounds. When no gunshot injuries were found, Tom knew next that he had to get Trigger's attention, so the sheriff whistled loudly and called for his horse. After a few minutes, Trigger arrived and came up to Tom, letting the rancher put his hands on the horses snout. Trigger then breathed hot steam out of his nostrils in the midst of the cold winter night, and fixed his gaze upon Tom's determined eyes.

Tom smiled into Trig's eyes and said calmly, "They got Maddy Trigger! We need to catch that train fast, but there's not a drop of beer around. I'll tell ya what buddy. I'll stop Betsy's birth control injections if you can get me on that train fast!"

Trigger changed his mood from one of being angry at the gangsters that took Maddy, to a determined horse that would stop at nothing to get Tom on that train. Tom then hopped on and Trigger who sucked the sheriff back in his saddle, as the steed bolted for the rapidly escaping train. As they sped, Trigger's hearing detected the vibrations of the train as it rumbled down the track, and picked up a speed that Tom has never felt on his horse before. The two hit the main road south out of the Teanaway and a deputy was parked on the side of the quiet road, gunning any speeders that might tempt fate during the officers lunch break. What seemed as a quiet meal for the deputy, quickly turned an alarm on the radar gun, as Tom and his horse screamed by at sixty five miles an hour.

"Holy shit," I do believe, left the deputy's lips and the officer peeled out determined to see who spoiled his lunch.

The officer reached the horse and its rider within seconds and knew automatically that it was Tom and Trigger. The deputy tried radioing Tom and dispatch, but to no avail. The officer then drove next to Tom while the sheriff looked at the officer and shouted to the top of his lungs, "The train!" as Tom pointed to the beast speeding away in the distance. The deputy obliged nodding his head and sped past the sheriff. Then Trigger refused to run down the road, ignoring Tom's commands, cutting down an old trail, that almost threw the cowboy off balance. As they drew close, the sheriff could hear the sound of the train as it stormed down the tracks. The path started to climb uphill forcing every muscle in Trigger's body to spark to life, racing up the steep incline. The hill quickly leveled out, and Trigger gunned it again, as Tom spotted the back of the train, now below their running path.

That particular path was the start of a short canyon and the sheriff's right side started to increase in elevation, limiting Tom's options to enter the train from its side. In the distance, the sheriff spotted the Deputies lights illuminating and assumed that his officer had radioed dispatch, yet Tom didn't assume anything and kept riding as fast as Trigger's legs could carry them. Ahead in the distance down the road, Tom looked again, and was alerted to a rock slide that blocked the trail. The sheriff tried to slow down Trigger, yet before they met the block in the road, Tom's crazy steed jumped and landed on one of the cars on the train, losing control. The two slid from one boxcar to another, and when all seemed lost, they came to an abrupt rest, in a soft cushiony material.

"Trigger, we hit sawdust ole boy," Tom exclaimed in joy and rose to his feet, arming his pistol. "You stay here and keep an eye on the place, and Betsy is all yours."

Tom's horse was tired yet alert and neighed for Tom to go get Maddy back. When the horse turned his head back to its normal position, Tom had already climbed over to the next boxcar and disappeared. On the other side, Tom found the Panzer that Wiley was supposed to be returning to the Canadians, only this train was a decoy, and heading to Canada to escape United States prosecution. I do have to admit that you have to hand it to the Dementes. Escape by speeding train is a great method because if you don't have a way to derail the beast, then you can keep going.

Down the road, Tom's deputy couldn't reach dispatch so the officer pulled out his cell phone and called 911. The only signal that the officer heard on the other end was a dial tone, which the deputy suspected that someone had a hand in shutting down dispatch communications completely, as to avoid the law. The officer then called another deputy who got word and immediately raised the other deputy's that were processing the scene at the Windy River Ranch. Sergeant Morrison was fielding statements from the press when another officer tapped him on the shoulder, immediately stopping the questioning and raced for his vehicle nearby. Within minutes, the sheriff's of the Upper County were in fast pursuit, and now, temporarily communicating by cell phone.

Back on the train, Tom mingled his way past Wiley's tank, when he spotted two guards on post in the back of the boxcar that was holding Maddy. At first, he drew his weapon and pointed it at the sentries, but figured that the blast would attract attention, so the sheriff pulled out two throwing knives, taking aim. Both men were standing there loaded with fully automatic weapons, and sharing a cigarette, so Tom waited for his moment to strike.

"Eurillo, you have to realize that the 49ers had no chance with Seattle at Century link field," the thug blurted.

"I also hear that the stadium is so loud, that scientists put seismic sensors in there, and Washington State University in Pullman, picked up the vibrations," the gangster replied. "Hey, lemme get a drag of that smoke, essay."

"Just as Eurillo past the cigarette, his joyous look was replaced with a blank, motionless stare, as the knife that penetrated his neck, which stuck into the aluminum side of the train.

Without a forethought, Tom threw his second knife, hitting the second thug in the hand holding the deadly assault rifle, again sticking deep into the trains siding. Before the gangster could raise the alert, Tom appeared out of the shadows and covered he man's mouth, right about the time that the other thug fell into the awaiting wheels of the train.

"How many men are in there and don't lie to me because I can stick you with these all night long," Tom stated as he pulled a fresh knife out of his back belt.

"Seven men!" Eurillo exclaimed as the pain of his new wound started to override the shock of the injury.

"Where's the woman your boss took?" Tom stated with a fierce tone while shoving the knife deeper into the siding.

"She's in there, I swear," Eurillo replied while shaking from the pain.

"Well, this is your stop," Tom said almost relaxed, and threw the injured man off of the train, to the cold waters of the Cle Elum River below.

The sheriff glanced through the back window with determined eyes, and spotted his loving wife sitting on a couch nearby crying, with three men holding weapons similar to the football fans who preoccupied the back. All of the sudden, a dark figure appeared in the doorway and glanced out of the same window that the sheriff was using as surveillance. Alerted but not concerned, the gangster walked toward the back door and glanced back, grabbing a cigarette out of the gangsters pack, then made his way outside. When the thug opened the door, he stepped outside and looked at the river below, which was looking even smaller due to the increase in elevation. The prick then lit his cigarette and took a deep puff, blowing smoke into the cold wintry night.

"Hey, asshole!" Tom shouted. "How about you drop that gun and the smoke as well?"

Taken by surprise, the thug slowly lowered his firearm and started to drop his cigarette until Tom requested to smoke on it. The two men stood there and the thug had an extreme look of worry on his face, as Tom puffed away on the cigarette.

"My granny before she passed away, God rest her soul, told me that I should help anybody no matter the circumstance, so I'm going to help you by giving you a choice," Tom stated as he took another puff. "Get off of the train, and do it now!"

The gangster then cracked a curious smile as Tom requested his weapons and cell phone, which the thug cooperated. After the exchange, the fellow gladly hopped off the train and safely fell into the river below as the change in elevation, made the jump a livable one. Tom then keenly scanned the area and noticed one thug going into another boxcar, leaving one gangster left in the room. Tom cautiously opened the door, and as the hired thug turned to look, Tom threw another blade into the poor man's frontal lobe, instantly dropping him to the ground. Maddy panicked, but then looked at Tom while the sheriff placed his finger over his mouth, quieting Maddy instantly. The sheriff took the knife and cut the duct tape binding Maddy's hands, directing her out of the boxcar to the cold night awaiting outside.

"Sweetie, no time to talk so you get to hide in the tank with me and wait for the Calvary," Tom shouted, so they sped to the top of the tank and Tom unscrewed the top hatch, disappearing with his scared wife into the armored vehicle.

"Tom," Maddy exclaimed. "They wanted to do bad things to me once they got out of the U.S.!" When I seen you, I knew things would work out baby."

"Well, unless they got a grenade launcher, then you and I can sit in here until help arrives," Tom replied while holding a still shaken Maddy, tightly.

Inside the boxcar, the four other thugs were discussing plans to enter the Canadian border, when one of the armed gangsters noticed that the other car that contained Maddy was now empty. Now very much alerted, the four men piled into the vacant boxcar, and armed their weapons as they cleared the car and carefully exited outside. Looking around, it was apparent that their hostage had bolted while Tom and Maddy viewed the thugs crossing over to the tank with their guns focused to shoot whatever slightly moves.

"Tom, what are we going to do?" Maddy asked in a panic, and Tom drew silent.

"I wish there was a shell in this damn tank that we could fire at these punks," Tom whispered. Then all of the sudden, the modified tanks computer system that Wiley installed came to life and said, "There is one round in the chamber available to use. Would you like to fire at a target Wiley?"

The computer's voice was so audible that the thugs heard the noise from the tank, and were only feet away from crossing over.

"Target the four thugs in front of us and open fire," Tom exclaimed. The computer accepted the order, firing the huge shell downward at the unsuspecting men, incinerating them as the shell blasted into the boxcar ahead. The force of the explosion was too great to keep the tank car on the tracks so the remaining cars that were separated from the caboose, started to derail. Tom ordered Maddy quickly out of the tank and the two dove into the icy river waters below, barely missing the boxcars as they slid past the couple into the river. Cold and disorientated, Tom spotted Trigger struggling in the waves, so the sheriff landed Maddy on a nearby beach, and swam with all of his might, reaching Trigger only to lead the tired horse out of the water.

Until Tom's backup reached them, the sheriff rapidly gathered some fire wood and started a fire. The tired cowboy continued to build the fire as to not only attract the deputies to their location, but to ensure his wife and Trigger would warm up in a hurry. Within moments, the deputy Tom originally saw, pulled up to the couple and hopped out of the car with temporary warming blankets.

"Sheriff, is everyone okay here?" the deputy asked as he wrapped his boss and Maddy up.

"We're okay, Deputy Jennings," Tom replied, huddling close to his wife. "Go and grab some more blankets for Trigger, if ya have some to spare."

"Yes, sir, right away," Deputy Jennings replied. "The other men should be here any minute boss," and with that, the officer ran to his car to get more blankets for the cold, tired steed.

"So do you think this is the end of the cartel harassment?" Maddy asked while she stood shaking next too Tom.

"Well, dear, if it's not, then we will just have to take things a day at a time," Tom replied while holding Maddy tight next to the warm fire.

The next morning was cold but sunny, and Tom opened his eyes while propping up out of a horrible nightmare. Maddy was peacefully asleep, and Tom smiled as she turned in slumber. The sheriff quietly rose from bed and hopped into the shower, warming his aching muscles. When Tom got out, he dried off and threw on a fresh pair of clothes and picked up his hat, dusting off the events of the night before. The rancher walked down the stairs and strolled by the hallway filled with those memories, both past and present while smiling at his grandparents in their earlier years. When Tom reached the kitchen, he opened the refrigerator door, only to pull out a beer then turned, to find Larry and the chief sitting on some barstools at the counter, also drinking a brew.

"Well, it's about time you got up," Larry stated while holding up his bottle in salute, so Tom clinked his bottle mutually.

"It's been really busy lately, Larry," Tom replied and gave the former sheriff a brief hug.

"It's going to be a busy day with Tildy's funeral as well," the chief exclaimed as he took a drink of beer.

"Guys, I don't know if I should continue with the funeral after all the bullshit from yesterday," Tom stated but Larry shook his head in disagreement.

"Tom, you got all of these people here, half the county, and my injured ass, (for cryin out loud) to come here today to pay our respects," Larry pointed out. "I think that it's time to turn the page Tom, because the other side might be well worth the read, and Tildy would expect no less from you."

The sheriff put his hands behind his head and smiled that Larry actually grew a pair, ordering the rancher around like that and continued to grin.

"All right, fair enough," Tom muttered and finished his last sip of beer. "I think I'm switching to coffee today, in light of funeral."

Larry and Thunder bear looked at each other and smiled, while doing much the same thing as Tom. It was still early in the morning and even though the sheriff hardly slept, still felt worn out, so he finished his coffee and went out to the stable to go watch TV in his office with the boys. Tom quickly lit a fire in the wood stove and then turned the television on. The early morning National news was airing and pictures of the train flashed on all boards, as a well-mannered woman, informing the nation about last night's incident. The men looked at each other in awe at first, until the lady mentioned Tom's fortune, still buried under the rubble. All Tom could do was wink at the men and kick his feet up on the desk, while the dusty Stetson hat dropped below his eyes, luring the sheriff back to a cold sleep.

A couple of hours later, Tom regained consciousness, only to find himself in an empty room, with the local news playing, which was no surprise to the battered sheriff at all what the talk of that day was about. Good ole Tom shook his head and took a deep breath, then exhaled slowly. All of the sudden, the phone rang, so the lawman picked it up and it was no other than the press. With Tildy's funeral today, he hung up the phone and called Sergeant Morrison, to get the rest of the men on perimeter control, to keep out the oncoming wave of reporters sure to invade yet another crime scene at the ranch. With that underway, Tom breathed a little easier, and rose to stretch his achy muscles.

As the sheriff left the office, Tom could hear something very peculiar emanating from Betsy's stall, so the rancher slowly approached her pen only to find Trigger, practicing on the mare, for when the day came that she went into heat. Tom shook his head trying to hold back the laughter, while slowly leaving Trigger and Betsy to nest. When Tom came outside, he was greeted by several people cheering the sheriff for his efforts, but all he could think about was Terror, and the man he lost last night, so Tom headed out to the Yellow Jackets RV. The sheriff was at Terrors doorstep within minutes and hugged a couple of bikers that were smoking outside the door, assuring them that everything was going to be alright, which brought a smile to the men's faces.

Tom entered slowly at first to see Terror sitting at a table drinking a beer, so Tom went over to the coffee maker and started to brew a fresh pot of coffee. With the lawman's back turned, he said," Damn Terror. I should have not put your men out there that position like that," and lowered his head. "I'm so sorry brother."

Terror rose and put his hand on the sheriff's shoulder in comfort and replied, "Come on Tom, this wasn't his first rodeo. The man knew what he was getting into and made the choice. You see Tom, that's why I like you so much. You might be as ugly as cow dung on a passed out hooker, but you give people the right to choose their own path. Hell bro, sometimes I don't even give my men a choice at all, yet we're all brothers and I'll ride with you till the end Tom; if that's what it takes!"

The sheriff then turned around and smiled at Terror. "You might be a little bit prettier than me, but I wholeheartedly agree with you, so why not be my deputy?"

The look on Terrors face was priceless at first because how many one percenters get asked a question like that? "It wouldn't hurt to change things around a bit, I suppose," Terror replied smiling away. "Man, I've been in the game for so long and I've never thought what it would be like to work on the other end of the stick!"

Tom smiled then poured a fresh cup of coffee and offered Terror a cup, which the biker accepted, then the two men sat back down, proceeding to talk. After the visit, Tom left the Yellow Jackets trailer and made his way back to the ranch house which was abuzz with life, in preparation of Tildy's funeral. Tom spotted Maddy, who had just helped Lupita and Jennie make breakfast, then sat down to his wife who was nursing a cup of coffee. Maddy drew close into Tom, and then the sheriff held his loving wife tight. After a couple of moments, Maddy's phone rang, so she answered it, when a huge smile came to her face. After a few minutes of hearing Maddy continuously say thank you, she passed the phone to Tom and said, "Honey, I think you're gonna wanna take this!"

Tom placed the phone to his ear and the voice said, "Hello Tom. This is President Carson. I just wanted to extend my deepest sympathy and gratitude on the behalf of the American people for the loss of your grandmother."

Tom was shocked at first not knowing what to say. Instead, the sheriff paused then replied, "Mr. President, thank you for your kind words. There's been a lot going on in the Upper County nowadays, so I wish that my tone was happier, but regardless, your sentiment means a lot."

"Yes, I hear there have been some problems over there," the President stated. "My cabinet wanted me to not say this, but I'm the President of the United States, so they can kiss my ass. The men that you eliminated have been giving the U.S. plenty of problems lately. In fact, you and your men managed to take out several top leaders in the Demente's hierarchy. For the United States, this is going to put a temporary halt to all drug and human trafficking. Now I know from my reports, that some of your volunteers might not be the most outstanding people legally, yet they helped deter a national security issue. Tom, when all of this blows over, I'd like to personally welcome you and those responsible for shutting down the Dementes, to the White House for a visit sometime."

Tom then smiled and looked at Larry and Thunder Bear, then replied, "Mr. President, it would be an honor to come over for a visit, and I will let you know."

"Thank you again, Tom," the president replied. "I'll have my aid give you a direct number to me personally if you ever want to talk, and I hope you vote for me in the upcoming election!"

"Well, Mr. President, I'm not much of a democrat, nor politically minded, but I'll keep that one in mind," the sheriff joked as to not give away the fact that Tom wasn't a fan.

The president laughed, catching Tom's drift, and wished the sheriff well, then hung up. Everybody that heard Tom talking, and immediately cheered for the sheriff, as their eyes lit up in joy.

"I think what we need to do now is get this funeral going and turn a bad page into a good one," Tom exclaimed as he looked over at Larry.

The afternoon came in a hurry and the group gathered at a church in town that had Tildy's coffin laying by the alter, surrounded by a countless number of flowers that parishioners left, as they paid their final respects. Tom and Maddy exited the car, joining up with Larry, who stood there with his cane, looking at the sheriff.

"You know, Tom, I always knew that we'd be here someday saying good-bye, just never knew it would be like this," Larry stated as Laurie walked over to him.

"It could be worse, Larry," Tom responded as he wrapped his arms around Maddy. "After all, Grandpa could be here right now up in the front pew drinking moonshine and bitching how the Seahawks lost another game!"

The group busted up with laughter because if you knew Gene, that even a funeral would deter his football addiction.

"At least Tildy got too see them win a super bowl," Larry exclaimed as they all smiled at Tom's original remark.

The church began to fill to capacity quickly and Tom knew that everyone wouldn't be able to see the funeral, so the sheriff allowed a news cameraman to video tape the event. The man quickly set up his equipment and began filming as the priest came out, standing up to the podium. After his holy speech, the priest asked if anyone wanted to talk on Tildy's behalf, so Tom slowly raised from his pew and approached the podium. Tom looked at all of the mourners and paused, fighting back the tears. Then the beloved grandson said, "I'd like to thank everyone who could attend Tildy's funeral today. My grandma was an amazing woman who during her life touched all. Even those who couldn't be here today, and those that have passed away well before her. Later in life, those that knew Tildy, could recall the feisty old lady sitting in her rocking chair, listening to rock and roll music, while drinking tea, but she was anything than a person who took to sitting down for a great deal of her life."

"I'd like to think that my own musical interests were spawned by my grandmother. Remembering my childhood when I first went to live with Gene and Tildy, she always had music on and rarely watched the TV. She always extended a hand in friendship and helped countless people whether it be financial, or just needing a person to listen too. To say the least, my grandma was always there to lend an ear. So, from rock and roll to friendship, Tildy will surely be missed, yet we come today to honor her memory and feisty spirit. At the funeral service today, we honor my grandma, in the story's that we pass along in the advent of her death. Grandma, I love you and I hope you're doing okay dealing with Gene's BS!"

The mourners laughed as Tom shed a tear, then took his seat, as they played "Free Bird" in Tildy's memory. The tears streamed down Maddy's face while Tom comforted his grieving wife and so did everybody for that matter. Even Joe Stamper, an old man who never shed a tear for anybody, let one fall for Tildy. After the main service, Tom and the boys took their pallbearer positions and lifted the coffin, slowly walking the casket out of the church while the song, "Amazing Grace" rang out through the air.

When they exited the church, the pallbearers placed Tildy's coffin in the back of Tom's horse trailer, as Trigger stood there with his head down, still feeling Granny's presence. When the coffin was secured, the Indian elders, dressed in their ceremonial garb, walked in front of Tom, as several sheriffs' cars drove ahead to start the funeral procession. The day was cold as the mourners followed the coffin to the tomb where Tildy would be laid to rest. The clouds above were heavily building with precipitation and the winds began to howl, as Tom felt the cold of winter hit his exposed face. As the procession drew nearer to the tomb, the winds picked up and the snow started to fall in the midst of the traveling mourners. Just to stay warm, Tom pulled a wrapped up blanket off of Trigger's back and covered himself to escape the oncoming weather.

Finally at the tomb, Tom climbed off Trigger and opened the doors to the tomb. The sheriff motioned for several of the boys to come inside, to reflect for a moment, so Larry, Wiley, and Thunder Bear entered the tomb as Tom fell to his knees crying. After a few minutes of consoling from the men, Tom rose to his feet, and noticed an old, dusty jar sitting by Gene's tomb. The sheriff picked up the jar and polished off the dust, only to find that the liquor within the jar still looked good to taste. Tom looked at the boys and laughed, remembering a time, when he got drunk and set the jar in the tomb years ago, for his grandfather to enjoy. The Maddy entered the tomb wondering why the boys were taking so long, up until she saw her grieving husband with the jar of corn liquor.

"Don't you boys think we should save the drink until after the funeral," Maddy exclaimed as she looked at Tom with a keen eye.

"I think we can save this one for another time," Tom replied as he started to put the jar into Maddy's purse.

"Wait one second," the chief exclaimed in a relaxing tone. "I'm the one who got shot here! Pass that over sweetie." Maddy laughed and gave Thunder Bear the jar. The chief then unscrewed the lid and took a pull.

"I call seconds," Larry replied and took the jar, sipping the aged moonshine.

Wiley then commenced to whip out a joint and the group focused on Wiley, and yelled the crazy coots ole name. "Wiley, don't even think about it," the group said in perfect sync as Wiley winced, putting the joint back in his pocket.

The men exited the tomb and gathered around Tildy's coffin. Terror was not far behind as were Marshal Evans and Ambassador Cortez. The men started to pick up the coffin, but Larry was finding it difficult to balance the cane with the box, when all of the sudden, a hand reached out to grab Larry's handle. It was no other than Tom's friend, Rooster Dowe. Tom turned back and tipped his back, smiling at Rooster. "Thank you Roost," Tom exclaimed, then the men picked up the coffin and disappeared into the tomb. They slid the coffin into place as Tom began to shut the door, then paused and pulled out the original coin that Granny gave him months back, placing it into the vault. "I love you grandma," Tom said with a smile, then shut the door.

The men stood back for a minute to pause and reflect. The boys then put their arms on the others and smiled. They then left the tomb, yet the sheriff kept it open, so the rest of the mourners could view the tomb. After the proper respects were paid, the sheriff then raised everybody's attention and the crowd drew silent.

"Well, here she is. Back safely with Gene after a couple of decades," Tom said as a tear fell down the sheriff's face. I'd like to thank everybody again, for coming here today and as for Tildy, she will dearly be missed."

After the procession had dwindled down to just a few family and friends, Tom locked up the tomb and went over to Rooster who was talking to Maddy; making Tom's wife laugh, with every word that came out of the old farts mouth.

"I've heard you mention this fine gentleman's name before, and I would like to say that's it been well worth the wait," Maddy stated while giving Rooster a hug. "So dinner on Sunday and I won't take no for a answer!"

"I promise that I will attend dinner Maddy, and thank you for your kindness," Rooster replied as he shook her hand.

"Breaking a few rules, are we?" Tom asked while he wrapped his arms around his loving wife.

"Yeah, I figured that it's time to stretch my wings a bit," the hermit replied as he sarcastically stretched his arms to reach for Maddy. Rooster then said his good-byes and disappeared back into the forest as his eagle leapt off of the tomb, and flew off into the twilight.

After the funeral, Thanksgiving had come and gone and Christmas was in full swing at the Windy River Ranch. Things started to mellow out after the press left the peaceful Teanaway valley. Maddy was busy decorating with Shiela and Lupita, with the Wyatts new Christmas budget, while Tom and Wiley sat at in the kitchen drinking coffee. Wiley went back over to the coffee cup for a refill, and noticed that there wasn't any creamer, so Tom tracked down his busy wife. When he found Maddy, he asked about more creamer and she replied, "It's in the cabinet above the refrigerator."

"Maddy, we never use those cabinets," Tom stated and happily returned to the kitchen. When he opened the door, noticed a satchel that was sitting up in the cabinet, and took it to the table.

"Did you find the creamer," Wiley asked with a smirk, and Tom replied, "Wiley, I've got something better. The sheriff unlatched the top of the heavy bag, and several hundred pieces of Spanish bullion fell to the table, as Tom dumped the gold laden satchel on the table.

"Wow Bernardo's gonna like this," Wiley exclaimed and Tom replied," Well, I guess Maddy's Christmas budget just got a little larger!"

In the midst of their joy, Tom realized that he had to go to the station that day to play boss, so he wished Wiley a great day and left the house, sliding into his newly retrofitted Shelby Mustang police cruiser, then fired up all seven hundred horses up. Just as he was getting ready to leave, Trigger slowly walked by and turned his head toward Tom, while lifting the horses leg in the air, only to urinate on the sheriff, as well as the car. Tom then looked at Trigger and casually stated, "All right Trigger I get it. You win!" After a shower and a fresh change of clothes, Tom and his trusty steed rode down the snowy driveway of the Windy River Ranch to the deputies awaiting their boss's return at the station.

After hearing this story, the two men looked at the old man in total disbelief of the tale that this rancher just weaved. The old man ordered another round for the young ranchers to let the story sink in. After a couple of minutes, Barry, the rancher sitting next to the old man, sat there and shook his head, still processing all that was just told to him; while Jasper looked all together confused. Barry turned his head to the old man and said, "I'm having a hard time taking this all in. Your story's pretty accurate. It's just that I don't understand how you know specific details."

The old man looked at Barry and laughed. "Son, I'm a product from that generation," the old man exclaimed. "I guess I'm a Tom fan!"

The men all started to laugh but Barry was still unsure about the legend of Tom Wyatt. "So if you're such a Tom fan," Barry muttered, "Then why did he disappear off of the face of the Earth so long ago?"

The old man smiled and scratched his head while nursing his bottle of beer, immersed in thought. After the old rancher paused, he turned to Barry and replied, "That's a very good question and I imagine it had to do with his wife."

"What happened to her," Barry asked while smiling at the old man.

The rancher then paused for a couple of seconds trying not to get choked up, then replied, "Son, life happened to her," then the old man set his empty longneck down on the bar. "Lupita, you mind closing my tab," the man asked the busy waitress at the end of the bar, and the young men proceeded to get antsy.

"Sir, there's so many questions I'd love to ask," Barry exclaimed as the rancher left a tip for the waitress.

"I've been coming here pretty regularly lately so I'll tell you what," the old man said as he put his hand on Barry's shoulder. "The next time you boys come in and I'm here, I'll tell ya whatever you need to know."

Smiling, the old man said his good-byes and the boys stepped outside to smoke a cigarette as the old man climbed into his vehicle. After he fired up the engine, the old man waived and peeled out of the dusty parking lot.

"Damn, Barry. That's a classic car if I ever saw one," Jasper exclaimed as he lit a cigarette. "What do you reckon that car is?"

Barry stood back and shook his head, as an idea hit him. "Jasper, that's a nineteen sixty-five Mustang Shelby GT 500, by the looks of it."

"Well, shoot, Barry. I wanna hear more from the old fart, at any rate," Jasper stated as he put his cigarette out. As the rancher disappeared out of site, Barry looked at his friend and smiled, saying, "Yeah Jasper, I think we'll be coming back tomorrow because I think that old man has peaked my curiosity."

The two men looked at each other and laughed, while enjoying the cool summer night outside the bar. After a couple of minutes, the boys headed back into the bar and shut the door, as the sound of an old Van Halen tune rang throughout the air.

About the Author

Jake Shelton was born into a working-class family of farmers and construction workers in the small town of Moses Lake, Washington near the fertile desert lands of Mae Valley. After graduating from Moses Lake High School in June of 1995, Jake pursued some college credits and worked as a screen printer and at several small jobs, until he accepted a loading position for United Parcel Service in the summer of 2001. Since then, Jake has worked his way up to being a delivery driver, which is a position that he has enjoyed since the spring of 2007. Jake is happily married and has four children. He currently resides in Ellensburg, Washington. *The Legend of the Drunken Rancher* is Jake's first novel and was inspired by the people and the glorious mountainous scenery of Upper Kittitas County.